MY KIND OF TOWN

MY KIND OF TOWN

A JOE BUONOMO MYSTERY

JOHN SANDROLINI

MYSTERIOUSPRESS.COM

OPEN ROAD

INTEGRATED MEDIA

NEW YORK

Cover design by Mauricio Díaz

978-1-5040-2570-6

Published in 2016 by MysteriousPress.com/Open Road Integrated Media, Inc.
180 Maiden Lane
New York, NY 10038
www.mysteriouspress.com
www.openroadmedia.com

For my uncles, Emil Sandrolini,
George Plumb, and Louie Esposito

Giants lived here once.

MY KIND OF TOWN

Hog butcher for the World,
Toolmaker, Stacker of Wheat,
Player with Railroads and the Nation's Freight Handler;
Stormy, husky, brawling,
City of the Big Shoulders

—*Carl Sandburg, "Chicago," 1914*

I

1

CHICAGO, 1943

We were throwing them back at the Vernon Park Tap, just Butch and me. There'd been some press earlier, along with the ubiquitous navy flack and a few overeager victory girls, but we'd managed to ditch them all along the way to my old Taylor Street neighborhood.

Now the two of us were lining up the shots in our sights, dedicating them to lost comrades and knocking them down, one after another. So far, I had three confirmed, Butch, two and a probable, but there was little doubt we were both headed for ace that night.

It felt good to be on the undercard with America's biggest war hero as his PR tour swung through the heartland. But it was better still to have some time to talk with someone who understood, someone who'd lived it, someone who knew the value of talking about anything other than *it*. Tonight we weren't navy poster boys pushing war bonds. We weren't even fighter pilots. We were just two guys on barstools letting go of a little stress the old-fashioned way. And we were doing it alone.

Or so I thought.

There'd been an older gent down the rail from us for a while, but he'd gone off to the phone booth and then drifted out. Other than the tender, we'd been the only guys in the bar the last half hour. Butch had been telling me about his father, a man well known in Chicago before his murder in 1939, and far better after.

About ten, a side of beef in a herringbone coat came through the door, shook off some weather, and threw his hat on the bar. He grabbed a seat two stools down and ordered a beer. He looked straight ahead. Mostly.

Butch and I kept up our conversation, but quieter. Twenty minutes passed.

Another man came in, sat at the far end of the bar. The big guy finished his beer then got up, put on his coat, and picked up his hat. He paused a moment, faced us.

"Excuse me," he asked, "but aren't you Butch O'Hare—da fighter pilot?"

Butch nudged my shoulder, gave me the "here we go again" wink.

"Yes, that's right. I am," he replied.

"Gee, imagine that . . . right here," the big guy said. "The guy who shot down all them Japs. Can I shake your hand, mister?"

Butch smiled, extended his arm. "Sure."

They shook. The big guy stood motionless, a toothy smile curling his purple lips.

Butch matched his grin awhile, then said, "Nice to meet you." He turned back toward me and began to speak again.

"I . . . I heard you talking about your father," our visitor interjected.

Butch glanced back, a wary look on his face. "Yes, but it's a private discussion with my friend here."

I took the opportunity to put some space between us. Spinning around on my stool, I held out a hand. "My name's Joe. I'm home on leave. How's about you just let us catch up quietly, please?"

He wasn't buying what I was selling, looking right past me toward Butch. "Yeah, yeah, I understand, Mr. O'Hare. But I knew him, see?"

"I'm sorry," Butch said. "I don't care to discuss my father with strangers. That isn't something we do back in St. Louis."

The big guy shrugged. "Okay . . . I was just hoping maybe you could tell me about him and Mister Capone—"

"Hey," I said, getting a little more Chicago about it, "he doesn't want to talk about it—okay? Let it go, huh?"

A fat guy in a wifebeater and a red-stained apron came out of the kitchen through the swinging doors, half a cigarette hanging out of the suet ball that passed for his face. He laid his big bare arms on the bar top, resting as close to the Formica as his Falstaffian gut allowed. I realized then that the tender had flown.

"Sure ya won't talk wit' me?" the big guy chirped.

"Hey—what is this?" Butch demanded.

"Just a friendly conversation, pal—about your old man."

I got up, stood between the bruiser and Butch. The front door opened again, a jolt of cold air swirling in as another heavy stepped through. He grinned. Then he locked the door.

The big guy leaned in, rested a hand upon the bar. I'd seen catcher's mitts smaller than that hand.

"Dis doesn't have to be difficult, fellas," he said, spreading his arms as if he were giving the benediction.

The guy at the door stepped forward, hand in his pocket. I cut a glance at Butch. He nodded almost imperceptibly.

Suddenly, I was grabbing a bottle from the bar top, slamming it down on the big guy's forehead. He staggered backward in a shower of glass and Blatz, spewing obscenities. He was still wiping his eyes when I put him down for the long count with my barstool. I flung it at the other guys on my follow-through then and turned to shove Butch toward the kitchen, but he was already halfway there, his right arm buried to the elbow in the cook's billowing apron.

We flew through the swinging doors, stutter-stepped around a waiter, and shot out the back way, rigatoni dishes crashing down behind us as we bolted into the alley. Butch broke out ahead, spun, looked back at me. "It's your neighborhood, Buonomo . . . which way?"

Half a block away, the clang of a streetcar bell rang like a clarion through the gauzy air.

"That way," I shouted, pointing through the sleet. "Head toward Racine. We'll jump that car!"

"Check!"

We tore down-alley, splashing through puddles, freezing water spraying up around our feet like shell bursts on the sea. Behind us, I could hear two of the hoods coming out of the restaurant, breaking into pursuit. The streetcar was just a few hundred feet away now, stopped dead on our side of the cross street.

"Come on, Joe," Butch shouted over his shoulder, his long, loping strides covering the last yards as the car began nudging forward.

"Right behind you, Butch. Get on!"

He leaped onto the running board, turned, extended a hand toward me.

I stole one last look over my shoulder. We had a good lead but not good enough. It was a split-second decision.

I took Butch's hand then used his momentum against him as he pulled me, shoving him through the folding doors onto the floor of the car. I hit the street a second later.

He staggered up, swinging on a strap and staring dumbstruck through the doors of the green-and-white trolley. He fought his way through them, started to jump off the rapidly accelerating car. I stabbed a finger toward him, bellowing, "You stay on that car, O'Hare! I can handle this!"

He looked on, hurt, confused, into the growing distance between us.

"Chicago's not losing any Medal of Honor winners on my watch," I yelled as the car rolled off across the intersection into the wintry night. "See you back at the Palmer House," I promised, not knowing that I would never see him again.

I turned toward the sound of charging feet, watched them close in, wondering if they might've been a little more careful about rushing headlong toward the men who just dropped two of their own. But those guys were never known for their grasp of the obvious.

The toughs came on fast, legs pumping hard across the wet pavement. I dug in, squaring myself up in the boxer's stance I'd learned in these streets, raising my fists before my face as the dark men converged on me, my lips parting in the faintest of grins as I leaned my first punch.

2

THE GREAT PLAINS, 1963

Tiny little squares of Nebraska crawled beneath me, the angled glass of the unheated cockpit window cool against my face, the O_2 mask dangling from my hand delivering jolts of clearheadedness on demand. I was seriously hating life that morning, two hours into a cross-country flight and three hours into an epic case of the Old Crow shakes. The 100 percent pure oxygen was helping, but I'd been having more than a little trouble following the specification recitation from the test pilot. Somewhere in there, I'd drifted off, to a place I knew but long long ago, an old friend by my side.

I felt a tap on my shoulder then, looked back with a start, caught a flash of the world's most famous blue eyes.

"Hey, paesan," he said.

I winched up half a smile through desiccated lips. "Hey."

He gestured with a hand. "What do you think of this little number, Joseph? Learjet makes 'em right down there in Bumfuck, Kansas, somewhere. They let me have this prototype all week for free just so I can see if I want one or not. Whatsay, Lindbergh?"

I rubbed my eyes. "Frank, you know I don't know shit about jets. Better call Lindy."

"Lindbergh shmindbergh," he replied. "A guy's a great pilot, he's a great pilot, and you're the greatest goddamn pilot in the whole world."

I grinned at him. "You know how you can tell when a Sicilian is lying to you, Frank?"

He smiled back, shook his head lightly. "C'mon. Stop it already."

Frank and I didn't hang around much anymore, not after the way it all went down in Baja back in '60. It wasn't anybody's fault, but things could never be the same after that.

So it came as no small surprise when that old bird Jilly Rizzo, Sinatra's new number one guy, rousted me that morning on *The Ragged Edge* and declared without fanfare, "Mr. Sinatra would like that you should accompany him to Chicago today."

Now, Frank Sinatra was not a man many people refused, not without gulaglike consequences at least. The boy singer and the bow ties were long gone. Loved by millions and feared by thousands, Frank was a full-blown titan of the entertainment world: rich, famous, charming, magnanimous, and volatile. Very volatile. Infamously imperious, and inflexible to a fault as well, he was also genetically incapable of accepting no for an answer from almost any other man on Earth.

There were three exceptions: Jack Kennedy, Chicago mob boss Sam Giancana, and me. That was the list—in its entirety. And considering that Jilly had broken in on what would have been round two of my B-girl bacchanal, I had every reason in the world to tell the "Chairman of the Board" to go pound sand down a rat hole, but I figured I should at least say it to his face given all that we'd been through together.

We barely had a chance to speak before departure. Frank had arrived, per usual, at the last minute by limo while I was going through preflight checks with the factory pilot. All I knew up till then was that Jilly had said Mister Sinatra needed me, which could've meant anything—including a pizza run—given Frank's neediness. But when I buttonholed Frank at the boarding steps to interrogate him about the details, I found the look in his eyes deeply troubling. And when he said that he *needed me* needed me, I was in. A bond's a bond.

Then we were off for "the town Billy Sunday couldn't shut down." And as far as Sundays went, this weekend's Bears–Packers showdown at Wrigley Field was shaping up as a battle for the ages—tickets to which, I decided on the spot, would be the compensation I'd be wringing from Sinatra for this impressment aboard ship.

I had the virgin mother of a headache, and some very serious reservations about some things that lay ahead, but I also had seventeen thousand four hundred reasons of my own for being out of California for a few days anyway. And Chicago really was one helluva town.

Besides, I hadn't been home in a very long time.

3

The Chicago sky was steel gray with streaks of rain. Not bad for mid-November, really, but a little sketch for Meigs Field, Chicago's pocket-size lakefront airport. The Lear pilot said he thought we had the numbers for a wet landing, but I knew his real precipitation concern was Lake Michigan, which bordered the field on three sides. I'd sat at bar tops longer than that runway—and seen too many friends go skidding into the Pacific off a carrier's slick deck to tempt fate when we had better alternatives nearby. Sinatra pitched a royal bitch about it, but he capitulated when I went back into the cabin and pointedly reminded him that I, not he, was the "greatest goddamned pilot in the whole world."

Truth was, we probably would've been okay at Meigs, but taking foolish chances wasn't something I got paid to do anymore. And since I'd already been shanghaied away from a beautiful brunette sunrise by Frank, I'd be damned if I was going to risk getting my feet wet just to save him thirty minutes on his drive time across town. There was something I needed to do at the other field anyway, someone I wanted to pay my respects to.

"Okay, kid," I said to the company pilot as we began our descent, "it's settled. Let's go take a crack at the world's busiest airport: Chicago O'Hare."

We touched down just after two. Five minutes later, the kid taxied into Reiger Aviation and shut her down. We'd radioed ahead to Meigs to alert Frank's limo service about the change, but they were still in transit. Frank and I killed time burning a smoke in the charter building while Jilly schlepped the bags down. Frank was edgy; he didn't like waiting.

"Lousy day," he opined.

"I dunno," I said, "rain's already stopped, and there's better weather coming in—what we had most of the way. It'll clear up by this evening."

"Good. 'Cuz I got a big night planned for us, and rain ain't a part of it."

I couldn't suppress a smirk. "I'm sure that you made that request with God himself, huh?"

"Frank Sinatra is big, pal, but he ain't *that* big. It still goes God, Kennedy, Sinatra, in that order," he said, stepping down the rankings with his hand. "But I gotta tell ya, the last two are neck and neck anymore."

We walked toward the front doors, Frank acknowledging various employees with a nod or a wink as they stared from a cautious distance, then handing a twenty to the starstruck kid who held the door open for us.

On the wall outside, I found the shining plaque dedicated to the airport's namesake, whom I'd come to call on. I turned and walked toward it, a lump forming in my throat as I neared. It was heartening to see his image again, frozen in bronze though it was.

"Who's that, the farmer whose land got took here?" Frank cracked as he crushed out a Camel under his heel on the sidewalk.

"Come and see," I said softly, beckoning him with a head nod.

He stepped over, put a hand on my shoulder, leaned into my back. Neither of us spoke as we scanned the memorial dedicated to the fallen ace.

I glanced up. Frank's face was frozen now, too. His eyes slid toward mine. "That was some man, Joseph," he said quietly.

"You bet he was. Did ya know the president came here to rededicate the airport to Butch a few months back?"

"*Butch?* You knew him then?"

Before I could respond, a fleet of black limos sailed up to the curb and dropped anchor. Several Guido types climbed out of the middle one, one of them entreating us with a sweep of his arm and a bow.

"Welcome back to Chicago, Mr. Sinatra. Our friend sends his compliments."

Frank held up a palm. "We're waiting for Jilly; he's getting the bags."

Two men almost tripped over themselves rushing from behind the car. "We'll get them, sir," one of them said as they flew past us.

I looked at the muscle, then back at Frank. "Really, Frank? This is your limo service? Outfit guys? I'll get a cab."

"Give it a rest, Joe. Sam Giancana's a friend of mine. Besides, I'm here to do 'ol Momo a favor."

"Like that favor he just did you by screwing you out of the Cal-Neva Lodge and your Nevada gaming license? Is it ever gonna sink in that these guys are playing you like a penny slot?"

He burned me with his eyes. "Mother, please."

I threw up my hands, sighing.

A silver-haired rake in a gray hat stepped forward, hand extended. His gold-link bracelet looked genuine, but the mile-wide smile was an obvious fraud. Between the fedora and the ivory exhibit glimmered a pair of disturbingly cold gray eyes that matched his charcoal suit perfectly. It was a fair bet that those orbs had presided over the closing of many others.

"Vincenzo Bo'palazzo," he announced in a husk of a voice. "*Un honore grandissimo*, Signor Sinatra."

Frank shook his hand. "*Grazie.* You're the guy they call Vinnie Bop, right? I love that."

I made a face, felt my stomach churning. I didn't think it was the Old Crow.

The mobster smiled, sharp teeth glistening in the murky sky. "Vinnie'll do," he said, a hint of malevolence coming through his South Side whisper.

Frank's eyes widened as he sized him up anew. "All right then. Guess you're moving up in the world then, Vinnie."

He shrugged his tailored shoulders. "Some guys move up"—he paused, flicked three fingers off his chin, watched them arc slowly toward the sidewalk—"other guys move down."

He smiled at his boys. The Sicilian chorus chipped in on cue with laughter.

I leaned in toward Frank, whispered, "Nice company you're keeping, Sinatra. I'm sure the Sons of Italy would be proud."

He let that slide as I walked off to find some better air.

A couple of the other boys filled in my space, offering Frank deference a cardinal would've envied. One of them lit another cigarette for him, the others kissed different sections of his ass by turns.

Frank tired of them pretty quickly, signaling impatiently for me to rescue him. I was in no mood to bail him out, but friendship obliged me. Walking over, I stepped between him and the reception committee.

"Yeah, pal?"

"What was that you were saying about a ceremony at this place a few months ago?"

"Jack Kennedy came here back in March or April or something—I read it in the *Press-Telegram*. They had a big ceremony, rededicated the field to Butch. His mother, Mayor Daley, they all came out. Music, speeches—the whole nine yards. What . . . didn't you get an invite?" I ribbed, knowing that Frank had been getting the cold shoulder from the president ever since the inauguration over his high-visibility high jinks with his mob playpals.

"Nah, I think I was making a movie with Dino or something. My loss, I guess."

One of the goons broke protocol, stuck his oversize proboscis where it didn't belong. "Dem Irish, always waving their asses in the air. Dose O'Hares weren't so clean—and neither's Kennedy."

Frank stiffened up. I beat him to it, brushing an arm across his chest, letting him know this one was mine.

"Butch O'Hare was a friend of mine," I said, spelling it out for him through clenched teeth. "And President Kennedy's a friend of Mr. Sinatra's."

The poor guy didn't read too well. He held his palms out, mining for laughs. "Whatsamatter, you guys part Irish or somet'in'? One of dose guys is a welsher, d'other was a sucker."

Eyes fell in the semicircle. One guy looked clean away. Vinnie's glower could've melted rocks.

"You know," I said, "during the war we weren't Italian or Irish—or Jewish, or Polish, or anything else. We were American. You would've known that if you'd been there."

"Sure, buddy, sure," he blathered on. "But old man O'Hare was *connected*. Da kid coulda taken it easy. Dumb mick got himself killed playin' hero and now dey go and name—"

I'd run out of letters to spot him. Seeing white, I lunged forward, pinning him hard against the side of the car, jerking his tie up tight against his chin. "Shut your ziti hole, guinea," I seethed. "Eddie O'Hare's lying on the bottom of the sea. Don't say another word—not in front of his memorial, not in front of me."

Frank had me from behind then, waving the others off. "It's all right, boys; back off," he ordered as he pried my hands off the stunned gunsel, counseling, "Ohh, ohh, easy there, Joey boy," in my ear as he backed me away. "I've got enough troubles with these guys right now."

Even in my highly charged state that one still registered.

Then Frank took charge of the situation as only he could. "That guy," he said, pointing to the lingual diarrhetic. "Get him outta here—*now!*"

His fingers popped like a bullwhip and the boys paid heed, hustling Johnny *Stugots* off in the last car toward what would surely be a very unpleasant meeting with his boss.

Life's hard. It's harder if you're stupid.

Six minutes, one cigarette, and a lot of blown smoke later, Frank convinced me to ride in the limo with him and Jilly down to the hotel. But I made him promise that Jilly would be the driver for the rest of the weekend while the Outfit boys kept their distance. I didn't like playing the wet blanket, but Frank had absolutely nothing to gain and literally millions to lose through his foolish and dangerous Mafia associations.

But I don't know why I bothered harping on him—an FBI interview, a Senate hearing, and two decades of bad press hadn't gotten through to him. Why the hell did I think another browbeating from a guy with my checkered record would?

4

Traffic wasn't too bad considering. I was dog-tired but kept my eyes on the road, marking the many new features that had sprouted up since I'd last made landfall in my hometown, like the slick black Northwest Freeway we were rolling down.

When we'd ridden long enough, I looked across the backseat at Frank and asked, "You mind telling me just what the hell I'm doing here now?"

He launched into a rambling spiel about ostensibly being in town to take trailer shots for his just-wrapped film, *Robin and the Seven Hoods*, some kind of a gangster musical set in Chicago. When he got to the part about me needing to be fitted for a tuxedo at the hotel, I cut him short.

"Frank?"

"Yeah?"

"Let me rephrase my question. You mind telling me just what the hell I'm doing here now?"

He exhaled heavily, then spit it out. "I'm singing at the Villa Venice tonight for a lot of important people. You'll need to be properly dressed."

"Villa Venice? *Momo's joint?* Get bent."

"You're a real ball-breaker today, you know that?" he shot back. "First you go mustang on Carpaccio's guy and now you're—"

"Who's Carpaccio?"

"He's one of the guys you'll meet tonight."

"The hell I will."

"Joe?"

I grunted. "*What?*"

"I'd like you to meet these guys."

"You said you needed my help. You didn't say I'd be rubbing elbows with the blackjack set. Don't you know by now that I am all finished—"

"Joe!" he blurted out, an unmistakable urgency in his voice.

I bit my tongue, drew a breath, offered a cautious, "Yeah?"

"I'd *like* for you to meet these guys. I'm doing an unannounced special show for them. Do you understand me?"

I made a sour face, rapped him on the arm harder than I intended to. "What gives with that, Frank? Why are you doing shows for those animals?"

"You're familiar with the concept of 'command performance,' are you not, Joseph?"

"Of course I am. But Sam Giancana ain't exactly the Sun King."

"God knows that. But let me be clear here: This is not something I can say no to."

I scoffed at him. "At this point in your life, you can't reach down there and grab your *coglioni* and tell ol' Momo to shove it?"

Frank chuckled bitterly, gazed up at the velvet headliner, slapped his hand on his thigh. Then he looked at me. "I'm going to tell you a little story, Joseph, and it's a story that does not leave this Lincoln. Do we understand each other?"

I nodded, reached for my Luckys. Frank stopped me with a wave, pulled out his cigarette case, flipped it open. He plucked out a Camel short, handed it to me. Then he hit it with a Cartier lighter, the little diamonds glinting in the plush dark back of the limo.

"Sam Giancana helped put Jack Kennedy in the White House," he declared flatly.

I arched my brows. "He was the one who wrote that little *K-E-double-N-E-D-Y* jingle? That was *so* clever!"

"Cut the shit," he said with a glare. "Look," he went on, "everybody knows that Daley delivered Illinois in the general."

"Yeah. So?"

"But do you know who delivered West Virginia when Jack was struggling in the primaries?"

"I'm thinking it wasn't Mother Jones."

"Uh, no."

"So . . . maybe . . . I don't know . . . the guy you're going to go warble for tonight?"

"Mm-hmmm," he hummed. "And why would he do that?"

"'Cuz he's an ardent believer in the platform of the Democratic Party?"

"Fat fucking chance."

"Okay then, because Bobby Kennedy told the mob he was going to go easy on them if they delivered the coal miners' vote?"

Frank sat up, assessing me with surprise. "Quick study, Buonomo."

"You should've met my professors."

We each took a drag on our smokes. I blew out some gray air, watched it slip through the top of the cracked-open window. "So what's the problem then?"

Frank exhaled a cloud through his nose. "Attorney General Kennedy not only isn't going easy on those guys, he's doubling down on them—hard, see? The FBI is tapping lines, tailing guys, rousting people, squeezing informants. Perhaps you've heard of a certain fella not too long for this Earth, name of Valachi?"

"Is said fellow making headlines all over America of late, telling Mafia tales out of school and the like?"

Frank pounded the seat back. "Damn right he is. And he and the FBI are making life very difficult for some very important people."

I knew Frank was getting to something serious, but I was enjoying egging him on. "So . . . Hoover's boys have finally acknowledged the pin-striped elephant in the room. I ask again, what's the problem here?"

"The problem is that Sam Giancana and the high-ups are pissed, that's what. Bobby flat out reneged on them."

I turned up my palms. "I can see how that might be socially awkward for you at the next inauguration, chum, but other than that, why would you care?"

"Because I was the go-between!" he shouted. "I made calls, I put people together, I vouched for both sides. And guess who's standing here now with his *bra'zhol* hanging out? Now do you get it?"

I sat back in the deep-cushioned seat, letting out a whistle as I reclined. "I'm afraid I'm starting to."

Frank stared at me, his head rocking back and forth, his face tight behind the curls of smoke emanating from his hand. I gazed back at him, at the cars zipping by around us. Jilly hit the horn at someone, laying on it hard.

"Christ, Jilly, lay off the New York shit, would ya?" Frank barked. "A ten-second blast'll do here."

"So," I asked, "are you telling me that Sam's holding you responsible?"

"Not quite, but he's upset. Very upset. So in answer to your question, that's why I'm doing these shows for him. He says I owe him."

I tilted my head, threw up my hands. "A couple free shows? You're getting off easy."

"You bet your ass I am."

"So . . . why am I not playing post office with Bunny Whooz-it again?"

Frank leaned right into me, placed his hand on my shoulder, squeezed hard. "Because maybe I got wind that something's up, that's why."

I looked over at him very intently, making sure I'd understood him. "What kind of thing? A *thing* thing?"

"I think so," he said uneasily.

"*You?* C'monnnn . . ."

"I don't really know, but Sam's been quieter than I've ever seen him. They say that's how it happens. One minute you're laughing with the boys, then—bang!"

"You are seriously overreacting here."

"I'm just playing it safe. There's been rumblings on the wire that somebody big is getting taken out. It was like this just before Anastasia got hit."

"You might want to stay out of barbershops for a while then."

He rolled his head, groaning in frustration. "Would ya please help me here, Joe? You're right, it's probably nothing, but I'd feel a lot better knowing you were around the next couple of days. A lot of the right people will take notice if they see you next to me again—think word isn't already out about you necktieing that guy back there?"

Our eyes met, long seconds ticking by in the smoke-filled space. Frank had a disquieting look on his face, one I hadn't seen in a long time.

I bit down on my lips, made a fist. "Last. Time. Ever," I growled, burying my hand into the seat cushion with each word.

"Of course," he replied, nodding earnestly.

"And no guns."

"I understand."

I jabbed a finger into the handkerchief sticking out of his pocket. "One more thing . . ."

He looked down at my finger, back up at me. "Name it."

"About that football game. You better put us in old man Wrigley's box tomorrow. I wanna know the plays before Halas does."

"It's done."

I put my hand behind his neck, leaned in until our foreheads nearly touched. "You sing for these fucks tonight, then we stay the hell away from them for the rest of the weekend, okay? Nothing, *nothing*, good ever comes from associating with them."

I could make out the hint of a smile on his tight mouth as he nodded, see the tension visibly fading from his face as he processed what I'd said.

"Jill," he called out, "where's that cocktail shaker? Let's have a splash back here. And step on it, would ya? Let's get this weekend started!"

Frank prattled on the rest of the ride, a completely different man, the weight of the world off his shoulders and onto mine. I settled back in my seat, listening vaguely as he talked about "this Italian songbird Miss Claudia," his escapades from last month's visit to Chicago, his next movie, et cetera. *Yak yak yak* it all went as the miles rolled by.

Something bright red flashed by outside. I looked out, gazing in bemusement at the enormous pair of neon lips puckering up on the roadside, catching Frank leering at them too when I turned back inside. I had no idea what the Magikist company did, but I knew exactly what that voluptuous mouth represented to the man sitting next to me: that the old frontier town was still as wide open and beckoning as she was the day they snookered her from the Indians.

Chicago truly was that most American of all cities, as "small *d*" democratic as they come. She didn't do blue blood. She didn't do social register. She didn't do Hollywood connections. Chicago did hunger. Chicago did brass. Chicago did balls. And she was still the girl who could be had by the guy with the biggest pair.

5

Doormen swarmed us at the Ambassador East. The manager came out to meet us in the lobby, handing us all keys to suites on the top floor along with a promise to do everything on heaven and earth to make our stay comfortable. Frank requested we all meet in the Pump Room downstairs at six in "proper evening attire."

There was an Argentine tailor waiting for me in my suite to make sure that happened. He'd brought two assistants with him, along with half of Marshall Field's showroom. I was riding pretty low in the saddle, but I consented to letting him get his work done. It was easier than arguing with Frank about it.

Señor Pepe fitted me up with two suits, a blazer, and a killer midnight tuxedo with an understated velvet lapel. He called over to his store for several pairs of shoes then went to work while I knocked off for a couple of hours. The suite was empty when I awoke except for the suits, blazer, four dress shirts, five ties, and three pairs of shoes. Everything fit great. Classic Sinatra.

One hot shower and one cold beer later and I was ready to take on Primo Carnera. I slipped into the tux, fired up a smoke, and checked my watch. It was time to meet the boys downstairs. I jumped the elevator and rode it down to the lobby, then hooked a right up the stairs, through the green-and-black doors and into the house restaurant.

The Pump Room was no ordinary hotel eatery. Frank had assured me of that, building it up pretty good on the ride downtown. The place didn't disappoint, what with the red-jacketed waiters whipping up Caesar salads tableside, brandishing orders of lobster thermidor in front of the many plush booths, and parading through the dining room with all manner of flaming things on skewers.

It was early, but the Gold Coast crowd was out in force and buzzing, all eyes on the crooner in front of the bar telling a story with his hands for Jilly and a clutch of supernumeraries. Despite Frank's intense efforts to keep a lid on his comings and goings, someone on the inside invariably gabbed and word got out that he would be at a particular town or place, guaranteeing a small riot. I think he liked the attention anyway.

"Good evening, Joseph," he said as I approached. "Manhattan?"

"Smashing."

Frank whispered to Jilly who then shouted out, "Johnny, couple more Manhattans for Frank and Mr. Joe Buonomo here."

Jilly had many gifts that made him a close friend of Frank's. Discretion wasn't one of them. It was okay, beneficial even, if the mob knew I was in town, but the general public was another matter altogether. The minute Jilly dropped my name aloud, he drew attention to me, attention I didn't particularly want, especially in that town. Frank hung out with all manner of movie stars, athletes, and celebrities who lived for the secondhand glitz he spattered on them, but I was none of the above and operated exclusively under the radar—as much as anyone can sharing a Manhattan with Frank Sinatra in the Pump Room.

But there had been a time when I was a somebody in Chicago, whether I had wanted to be or not. Sure enough, my name tumbled for someone.

A pasty little man smiled at me, said, "Say, are you any relation to the Buonomo of Second World War fame?"

I hesitated, but I knew I was boxed in. "I, uh, I served in the war, but I'm sure a lot of guys named Buono—"

Jilly kept on drowning me. "Yeah, dis is the guy, pal. Joe Bones. Shot down a couple hundred Japanese planes, decorated by Roosevelt. A great American."

I felt myself wince, saw Frank doing the same when I opened my eyes.

I murdered Jilly with a look for a few seconds then leaned over and muttered, "Twenty-nine, Jill. Twenty-nine. If you're going to throw me in the river, at least get your numbers straight."

I eye-fried him some more as Frank eased him away for a lecture. Turning to my questioner, I said, "It was far less than that, and I didn't meet the president. And it was all a long time ago. Sorry."

He made a pale, doughy smile. "Nothing to be sorry about at all. I'm Sy. Nice to meet you." A smallish hand emerged. His soft, cold mitt gave me the willies when we shook. "I knew your face was familiar. Don't tell me," he implored, wagging a finger up and down. "Wait . . . wait . . . I've got it! Battle of Midway, wasn't it?"

Someone handed me my drink. I threw half of it back in one swallow. "Yeah. That and a few others. You have a remarkable memory, buddy. That's better than twenty years ago."

He smiled in false modesty, his pink skin crinkling in fleshy folds around his eyes. "One has to in my line of work, Mr. Buonomo."

I girded myself for his answer. "Which is . . . ?"

"Oh, I write a society column for the *Tribune*, like Mr. Kupcinet does for the *Sun-Times*. Mr. Sinatra always makes for great press— and to have him here with a local war hero—well, that's just dandy. Might we get a photo?"

I finished my drink, saw my heart lying there at the bottom of the glass next to the cherry. "Damn," I said.

"Come again?"

"Sorry, uh . . . Sy, right?"

Nodding smartly, he said, "Yes, that's right," then proffered his business card.

I took it, read it aloud. "Sy Huser. Your eye on Society. *Chicago Tribune*, et cetera, et cetera, et cetera."

"The *H* is silent."

I refocused on him. "Come again?"

"It's pronounced Yoo-ser—no *H*," he said without even a wisp of irony. He made the soft, dimply twinkle again.

"Is *that* right?" I couldn't help but grin a little. "Sorry, Sy, no photos today. Mr. Sinatra's your story here anyhow."

I signaled to Frank, stepped back.

"But—"

"Please." I turned, waved a hand over my head. "Hey, Frank, come finish your story for the boys here, huh? They're on deadline."

A waiter came wending through the crowd with a plate of rumaki, another behind him with caviar and crackers. I took a sniff, then passed on both and excused myself.

I marched over to Jilly, gave him *the look*, jammed my empty glass into his chest. He fumbled with it, spilling whiskey on his suit coat. "Sorry, Joe, I didn't mean no harm."

"Neither did Frankenstein. I'm gonna grab a hot dog. See you guys out front in thirty."

"Okay, Joe." The sheepish grimace on his face was almost comical enough to make me laugh. But not quite.

Two men held doors for me as I stepped out of the Ambassador in my tux, heading south toward Skinny's Red Hots to get the bad taste out of my mouth and some real Chicago food into it.

I wasn't that pissed at Jilly even though he should've known better. The truth of it was it really wasn't that big of a deal—but it wasn't a good omen. My own family didn't even know I was in town, and publicity was one thing I never looked for.

I'd come home on a whim to help a good friend out then get back out of town before anyone knew I was there. Now there was no telling how many people this Huser character was going to blab to, with all the ensuing baggage that entailed. Revisiting old comments like "Whatever happened to Joe Buonomo? I heard he wasn't right after the war" ranked just below "Turn your head and cough" on my itinerary. Butting heads with the Outfit ranked even lower, but that box had already been checked, too.

Right about then, I started to get that feeling that it wasn't going to be all wine and roses for me that weekend after all.

6

The walk did me good. I went down Dearborn, burned a smoke on the way. Man, they had some houses up in that part of town, but everybody seemed to be hiding behind heavy curtains, and nobody—nobody—was hanging out on those big front porches. Granted it was November and fifty-four degrees, but front porches were made for hanging out on; that's what we all did back on Taylor Street.

That got me to thinking about my old neighborhood for the first time. I quickly concluded I wasn't ready for all that just yet and shunted the thought back to the crawl space of my brain. Better to limit my concerns to hot dogs and looking out for Frank than to delve into my old demons, I told myself. It wasn't one of my more courageous decisions.

Skinny's was right where I'd last seen it, hadn't changed hardly a bit. The price for a dog and fries had gone up to almost half a buck, but it was still a bargain. I gave the counterman a nod, said, "Dog with everything, no onions."

"Dat's not everything den," he replied, the Chicago thick over his native Mediterranean tongue.

I wrinkled my lip, turned up my palms. "Right you are, pal."

He looked down at me from his booth. His fortyish face was nice but a little tired, his black hair well streaked. "So ya want it or what?"

"Huh?"

"Da dog . . . Ya want it or what?"

"Yeah, I want it. I just ordered it, didn't I?" I said, tilting my head as I sized him up.

"Just checkin', sounds like maybe you not so sure. French fryze?"

"Uh . . ."

"Dere's onion rings, too."

"Which is better?"

He shrugged. "Depends on you taste buds, bud."

"Gimme the rings."

"We're all out."

Now he got the full crooked stare. "You don't serve Italians or something?" I asked, my voice rising.

"Nah, you Eye-ties are okay; I even serve da *mavros*. Where ya think ya are, fella, Birmingham or somet'in? Wake up, it's nineteen-a-sixty-tree."

I couldn't help but laugh at his audacity. "Oh, that's rich coming from a Greek. So what gives with the onion rings then, chum?"

"It's Marco, okay? I just remembered I was out, all right? And who says I'ma Greek anyway?"

I was smirking now. "Your face, your accent, your occupation—your attitude. If you ain't Greek, mister, neither was Diogenes."

"Is dis Diogenes gonna come here and hassle me too?"

"Marco," I said in exasperation, "you're kind of a hard case, you know that?"

He leaned forward on his meaty knuckles, lowered his head beneath the glass, issued a growl that came from somewhere beneath Lower Wacker. "Guy wears a tuxedo to a hot dog joint and he wants to bust *my* balls?"

His sneer said he was ready to drop the apron, but then he relented, suddenly pressing his hands to his forehead. "Sorry, pal, forgive me. I'm havin' hard times here. My fishin' business went bust and the ol' lady left me. Took everythin' I had left to buy dis crummy dog joint with my brother Nick. Me serving sah-siggiz like some kinda *malaka*. Me—Marco Kabreros—I no canna believe it."

He choked up right at the end. Somewhere I felt a crocodile tear welling up inside.

"What happened to Skinny anyway?" I asked.

"Skinny got fat, had a grabber." He clapped his hands together, flourishing his eulogy with an, "Ohhhh!"

The tear receded.

"That's tough," I said, frowning.

"We all got it tough. Here's your dog, buddy. Forty cents."

"Thanks, Marco."

I took the dog and grabbed a stool along the rail, chuckling over the encounter. The guy really was a hard case, but there was something likable about him beneath all the bluster. Just another palooka trying to make it in the big town, taking his lumps but answering the bell for the next round. Greeks, Negroes, Irish, Jews, Poles, paesanos: They were good people in Chicago—wore their hearts right out there on their workshirts. I missed 'em. Missed their grit, their honesty.

I wolfed the dog down, lingering on the fiery taste of the sport peppers and the tangy accent of the celery salt. You can't get stuff like that in L.A. Out there, donuts and chiliburgers are the daily eats. It's tragic.

I started to walk away, stopped, signaled to Marco. He looked out. "Yeah?"

"That's a good dog, Marco. Top shelf—better than Skinny made."

He nodded once. "Damn right. T'anks. Enjoy your show, fella. Dat new *Chez Paree* is openin' tonight. You goin' to catch Vic Damone down there?"

"Uh-uh," I said mischievously, "Frank Sinatra."

"Who you kiddin', *vre* ? He ain't in town tonight."

I threw my hands up. "Okay, he's not. Be seeing you, Marco."

He waved me off, muttering as he turned back to his smoking grill while I walked away with a smile on my mug.

I was back at the hotel by 6:25. Frank was out front, signing autographs and posing for pics, a dark blue limo idling nearby. As I walked up to it, a smoked glass window slid down in the front, Jilly's kisser appearing from the darkness. He motioned me to the back. I opened the suicide door and slid in. Our eyes met in the rearview mirror.

"Sorry, Jill."

"Forget it. That was dumb of me."

"Yeah, but I overreacted." I reached forward, patted his arm.

Frank got in, closed his door, looked around. "What—you didn't bring us anything?"

"You didn't eat in there?"

"Frank Sinatra does not eat fish eggs. Christ, I'm starving, too. It's your fault, Joe; you hadn't a gone all sissy on us, we coulda landed at Meigs and eaten a proper meal at Tufano's—ohh, that eggplant parm' they got!"

"Jill," I said, "turn right on Astor, then right on Division."

"What for?"

"So I can get you guys a Chicago dog. Best in the world—better than those horseshit ones you guys eat in New York, for sure."

They both started to raise a ruckus. "Don't squawk, you know they're better. And we'll be in and out in two minutes. Besides there's a guy there I'd like you to meet, Frank. He could use a pick-me-up."

Frank Sinatra had endured many insults over the years, but skin-flint was not one of them. Through gratuitous use of gratuities, he'd earned a reputation across the globe as a big tipper, maybe the biggest. I guessed he'd take to Marco and chew the fat with him a little, then leave him some more fat in the way of a juicy tip.

He did just that, pressing a C-note into the hard-luck fisherman's hand as they shook good-bye.

Then we were off for the performance hall. I glanced back through the rear window as we pulled away, spied Marco leaning in the doorway underneath the neon sign, big bill in his paw and a touched-by-an-angel look on his slack-jawed face.

7

The Villa Venice was a great big, cheesy dago joint with columns, Roman statues, and even gondolas that carried guests along a canal through the lobby. Far from downtown Chicago, it had spent many years in slow decline until Sam Giancana had bought it and pumped a few fistfuls of fast cash into it. Frank, Dean Martin, and Sammy Davis had played the backwater club's grand reopening the year before, making a huge splash in Chicago with their weeklong engagement. There had been much speculation in the press about why the "Chairman of the Board" and his drinking buddies would play such an out-of-the-way venue, quite possibly for free, but Frank's explanation on the ride in had pulled the curtain all the way back for me.

We slipped in the back way when we arrived so no one would get wise about Frank's surprise show. Sam Giancana had sent a bottle of champagne to Frank's dressing room in advance. Jilly popped the cork and poured, then handed us both glasses as he grabbed one of his own.

"Sure you want to drink that?" I asked Frank as he raised his glass.

He stopped short, eyeballed me over the rim, gave it a little thought. "Ahh," he concluded, "it's all right. I've been too jumpy. Drink up."

We clinked the glasses together, drank the bubbly. It was rich, clean, and dry. "Ohh," I said, "that's good stuff. What is it?"

Jilly snatched up the bottle, read aloud. "Voo-vee Click-qwat. 1953."

"That's Momo," Frank said. "He always gets me a good bottle from '53—'cuz that's the year I won my Oscar for *From Here to Eternity*. See, Joe, these Outfit guys aren't so bad."

"Sure, sure," I smiled. "Like the guys in Havana, right? Good eggs to the core."

He stared back at me, chastened, his slow nod acknowledging the unsaid: that without my intervention during an attempted hit that same year, he never would've won his Best Supporting Actor award—not unless it was for playing a corpse.

We killed another thirty minutes in the dressing room. Frank loosened up his voice, however that's done, and Jilly loosened up his brain with the rest of the Veuve Clicquot. I took it light so I could keep a watchful eye on things.

A couple of message boys dropped in at different times, checking on Frank's needs and informing him his rehearsal would begin after the first act began so the noise would not give him away. Frank asked one of them to summon Miss Claudia so he could say hello. The messenger returned three minutes later and reported that the lady was too busy preparing for her show to come out, but that she sent her thanks for the large bouquet of flowers. She also said she looked forward to meeting Mr. Sinatra again after his performance.

"I'll be damned," Frank said. "Can you beat that?"

"I like her already," I chimed in. "Any gal self-assured enough to tell Frank Sinatra to hold the phone is okay by me. What gives with this Miss Claudia anyway—you sure she isn't your new flame?"

"Flame, yes. Mine, no. I'm too busy anymore for that stuff. Vegas, movies, recording studios . . . I hire my girlfriends these days," he said with a wink.

"You should be less busy."

"Nah, it works for me. Besides, I think maybe Claudia is your type."

"*My* type?"

"Yeah, beautiful—but a little sad. Like she's got a secret or something. C'mon. You'll see."

"No no no—leave the lady be. You heard the kid, she goes on in a few minutes."

"Ahhh," he said, waving me off.

I stepped in front of the door, put my hands on my hips. "You. Sit. If she's all that great, I want my first impression to be a good one."

Frank shook his head at me contemptuously. "Okay, you win. Let some small-timer tell Frank Sinatra what's what. Thanks . . . pal."

He grabbed a chair, futzed around for about five minutes with various objects on the dressing table, grumbling about respect. I walked away to shake the empty champagne bottle. Frank jumped up abruptly and made for the door.

"Like hell that gal's gonna make us wait; I set her up for this gig."

He was ten steps ahead of me by the time I hit the hallway. "Slow down, Frank," I whispered. "Get back here—you'll blow my chance."

"I'm gonna blow this brassy broad's ear out is what I'm gonna do," he replied, rapping loudly several times on her door. I arrived just as it flew open.

And there she stood, cross-armed in the doorway, oozing carnality in a green silk robe, a screw-you smile blooming beneath impossibly large almond-shaped eyes. The rest was a blur of swirling dark tresses, Alpine curves, lips lush as mascarpone.

She had it. All of it. Even the little bump in her nose was adorable.

"Claudia Cucciabella," Frank said, leaning in to kiss her, "*buona sera, signorina!*"

She gave him just that much, holding perfectly still while he planted one on each cheek, her eyes burning holes middle-high-nowhere above his shoulder. She was hotter than Rome in August, but she kept it simmering just beneath the surface.

"*Per favore, Francesco,*" she began, her Neapolitan accent rising and swooping like a flock of starlings, "I *am* 'appy to see you, *amore,* but I must finish my preparations and get dressed." She brought her hands together in prayer, shook them gently. "*Ti prego, ragazzo.*"

It was world-class work. Frank bought every piece, his wrath cooling away but quick. "Come on, *bella bambina*, just say hi to my pal Joey here. He's a very close friend. I've been wanting you to meet him."

She frowned at him, gave me an eye roll, held out her arm, hand extended down at the end. "*Ciao, Giuseppe. Un piacere.*"

The words were fresh out of the icebox. I was half surprised they didn't stick to her tongue.

"Nice to meet you, too, *signorina*," I said in the native tongue, hoping it might ingratiate me with her. It went over like garlic gum—there were nuns who'd given me more play.

She stepped back, closed the door halfway. "Okay, Frank, I see you boys later, wish me luck. *Ciao, bello.*"

She held that last note an impossibly long second, the way only they can. It was still hanging in the air as the door clicked shut.

Frank and I made mean faces at each other back in his dressing room until he left for his warm-up. I was pissed that he'd botched my intro to Claudia, and he was pissed that I was pissed. On his way out he asked, "You gonna stick around for my show or keep sulking in here?"

I put my fist in my mouth, bit a knuckle. He stuck his tongue out in response.

That made me smile ever so much. "Yeah, okay, I'll watch you out there—that's what I'm here for, right? Now get the hell outta here. Break a leg, an arm, whatever."

Jilly went out. Frank followed, stopped in the doorway. "Claudia's going on in five, the boys have you set up good in front. Give her a shot, she'll come around."

"I dunno, I think my hand's still freezer burned where she touched me."

"Just do it. You were right, I shouldn't have bothered her. Happy?"

"No. But thanks."

He slipped through the door.

"Hey . . ." I called out.

Half his face peeped back through the opening. "Yeah?"

"Everything else okay?"

"Yeah. I feel a lot better just having you here. We'll have some fun tonight after the show—like old times."

"That'd be nice."

"Yeah." He went out and closed the door, whistling brightly as he walked away down the hall.

8

People were still filing in as I took my seat at a front table. I ordered a bourbon and water and leaned back, scoping the room. The place was maybe half full but filling pretty quick. I thought I saw a mobbed-up guy or two, but no one I knew by name.

The lights went down and the curtain came up just after eight, the quartet in the middle looking rather small on that big stage, most of which was hidden in the darkness. First, the guitar began; then, the piano; and, finally, just a hint of horn playing a familiar-sounding tune, jouncy but subtle. Anticipatory applause broke out, followed by . . . nothing.

Two beats later, a spotlight lit up the far corner. I swiveled around as Claudia materialized from the darkness, flat crushing it in a red dress that broke the fire code in at least ten places. Eyes expanding, I dialed in as I waited for her to tear into some popular standard for her American audience.

But she didn't.

Her lips parted and an unexpected sound escaped: mellifluous, elegant, seraphic. Undeniably Italian. Then I realized what the band was playing: A *stornello*, an Italian folk song, this one a story of love denied.

And it was beautiful. And she was beautiful. It was all so very beautiful.

I put my drink down, then my chin. One on the table, the other on my hand, although I wasn't really sure which went where. The only thing I knew was that I was smitten. Right there, right then. Smitten.

She finished the song smartly, without flourish or melodrama, treating the work with respect. The applause was warm but less than I expected, my own contribution the loudest. Claudia's eyes met mine ever so briefly as she scanned the crowd, beaming.

She followed with "*Al Di Là*," and "*Nel Blu Dipinto Di Blu*." Beautiful songs both, especially in the native tongue, but I was hoping for another *stornello*, or even a tarantella after she'd set the bar so high. But the crowd had come to see the cornball headliner Anthony Di Scungille, not Claudia. Her sizzle had kept them in line so far except for a couple of shouted requests for her to sing in English, but her sublime charms were utterly wasted on those *contadini*.

She threw them a couple of bones anyway, doing a pair of songs in Uncle Sam's vernacular. That brought the crowd back just long enough for her to close with "*Grazie, Prego, Scusi*" and the up-tempo "*Tu Vuò Fa' L'Americano*," which got 'em on their feet at the end, me first.

The arctic routine I'd gotten earlier was already forgotten. It was no longer possible for me to be an uninterested observer; her talent was just too compelling. And I loved the courage she'd shown by opening with the *stornello* and performing most of her work in Italian. It might not have been career smart, but it showed a strong heart—and head.

I guess maybe it runs in the blood.

9

Jilly and I shot the bull at the table between acts, both of us doing the slow eye sweep around the room as various Outfit guys trickled in. Jilly pointed out this guy and that as they sauntered down to the lower tables, mistresses in raccoon and rhinestones sparkling on their arms. Rocco "the Parrot," Jimmy "the Monk," Joe "Yak," Willie "Potatoes," "Milwaukee" Phil—the whole alphabet soup of killers was there, even reputed overboss Tony "Big Tuna" Accardo.

"Jill, what's the big deal tonight?" I asked. "Frank and the whole pack were just here doing shows a month ago, right? How come the entire Chicago mob is here again?"

Jilly shrugged. "Guys like to see Sinatra sing . . . what can I say? Besides . . ." His voice trailed off, head swiveling slowly side to side.

I leaned in. "Yes . . . ?"

"The Quonset Hut is open tonight."

"Quonset what?"

"Hut. A gambling joint just up the road. Sam runs it. A mint."

I made a discreet wave at the mobsters. "But aren't these the guys who usually do the fleecing? What's their angle?"

Jilly smiled at me. "C'mon, Joe, you know anything they lose is guaranteed, same as Frank is at the Sands. They just sorta stimulate the pigeons, if you get me."

"Oh, get I do, Jill. Remind me to keep my roll in my pocket."

He smiled broadly. "Just enjoy the scenery, it's top shelf. Use your money for that." He actually winked on that one, as if I didn't understand the setup.

"I've got another play in mind, thanks, paesan."

"*Buona fortuna* there, *amico*; nobody gets anywhere with that one, not even Frank."

I sat back, crossed my arms, grinning. "So that's why ol' Francis said he thought she'd go for me. He wants to watch me crash and burn, too. Maybe he won't feel so bad that way."

Jilly looked on like the Sphinx, said nothing. But that nothing said a lot.

The house lights dimmed twice, signaling the imminent beginning of an intimate evening with Anthony Di Scungille. I'd already heard the screams on his records; I didn't need to visit the scene of the crime to know something was going to die up there.

"See you later, Jill, I'm goin' for a walk. Meet you back here at ten."

"Okay," he said, nodding. "I'll be here."

I slipped downstairs toward the dressing rooms, hoping to get a chance to congratulate Claudia on her performance. The guy at the door knew I was with Frank and let me pass. As I neared her room, I made out a heavyset guy in a hat at the door, a bouquet of red roses behind his back. There was a brief conversation I couldn't hear, then he went inside and the door closed behind him.

I stood there awhile feeling stupid, arms at my sides. "Day late and a dollar short, Joe." I sighed as I turned and headed back out.

At least I had a good seat for a Sinatra show, I told myself. The night still held the promise of that.

10

Villa Venice management waited a good fifteen minutes after Di Scungille finished burning the popular songbook on a pyre before making the surprise announcement about Frank. Anyone dumb enough not to notice that half the house was still hanging on to their seats lost their own to the mob fringe and friends who slithered in when they made for their cars. There were some protests and a dustup or two, but out was out, especially with that crowd.

I met Jilly back at the table just as the lights went down. The air was popping with excitement, hushed whispering rippling through the overwhelmingly Italian American crowd. I looked all over but didn't see Claudia anywhere in the audience.

A comedian came out to pave the way, making several ribald comments at the headliner's expense before introducing him as, "The one and only . . . Mister Frank Sinatra!"

A roar rolled through the room when Frank strutted onto the stage and tore into a two-fisted version of "I'm Gonna Live Till I Die." The band was all over it, too, the brass coming down in ingots as Frank nailed the ending. He owned that crowd when he walked in, but after that, he could have loaned their own mothers to them at three points above the vig.

The show, including a couple of monologues, ran a tight sixty minutes and closed to thunderous applause. We were all still on our feet when Frank came back out to perform an encore. He cracked a few jokes first then said he wanted to perform a brand-new song that Jimmy Van Heusen had written for his recently completed film set in Chicago.

"Before I begin," he added, "I just want to acknowledge a gentleman in the audience. He isn't gonna get up, but he knows who he is—and how much he means to me. He's a wonderful friend, and believe me when I tell you, I wouldn't be here without him." He held up a rocks glass, saluted the room. "Joe Bones, God love you, this song's for you. Welcome home, dago."

I sat up in my chair, nodding ever so slightly to acknowledge Frank's tribute, the first he'd ever given me in public. I was fully aware that he was sending a not-so-subtle message to certain parties in the audience as well as thanking me, but I couldn't help the mile-wide grin that broke out on my face as he finished the short intro and then launched into the song, bringing a roar from the crowd as he began with the words, "This . . . is . . . my . . . kind of town, Chicago is . . ."

11

Backstage, there was the usual glad-handing and clowning, but Frank cut it off quickly. "Okay, boys," he said, "it's already past eleven, time to go over to the Quonset Hut and let slip the bones."

What followed was a two-minute ride in a shuttle bus to a parking lot behind the nearby Flamingo Motel. At the far end there was a large half-moon building, maybe a hundred by one fifty, hidden in plain sight behind several dump trucks and tractors. Other than the blacked-out windows, the Quonset Hut looked fairly inconspicuous in the setting, its corrugated sides shining flatly in the moonlight. But what went on beneath them was anything but dull.

Inside, several hundred people were swarming around roulette wheels, blackjack tables, and craps games, cigarette girls and cocktail waitresses weaving amid the throng on the plush carpeting, their wares well distributed throughout the packed room. Everything vibed Vegas: the noise, the energy, the occasional shouts of triumph.

"You gotta be kiddin' me," I said to Frank. "They do this right here in the open?"

He backhanded me on the chest. "Which one of us is from Chicago anyway? The feds know all about it, but they want to get Sam on something bigger than this. And they aren't gonna blow all their hard work by pinching us for playing cards, dig?"

"Dug. As long as it stays on the hush, all is well. Same as it ever was here."

"Precisely," said Frank as he embraced an Outfit guy and planted a kiss on his cheek, before patting the other several times.

"Joe, I have to grip and grin with a few guys. See you in a bit. Ohh . . . And if you get the urge to throw the dice, Chuckie Sparrow here tells me table number three is the way to go. *Mi capisci?*"

"*Sì,*" I said, nodding. "I understand. You okay?"

He glanced at Chuckie then back at me. "You bet."

"Okay then, I'll do just that."

I wandered the room awhile watching the sheep get shorn. They seemed happy enough though, probably considering it just the price of admission to breathe in air that Frank Sinatra had exhaled. I played some cards, got burned. Then I sauntered over to table three and laid down a five-dollar chip.

My luck was better there, unnaturally better, I realized after rolling two sevens and three elevens in a row. A biscuit in black satin sidled up to me, slid an arm around mine. "You're a lucky guy tonight, aren't you?"

I eyefulled her, made her for talent. The too-bright lipstick sealed it. "Aren't you a bit cold in that lil' thing, dear?"

"I know how to get warm if you do, handsome."

I couldn't help but smile; she must have been working volume. "Do you, now?"

"It's close," she said, some odd kind of earnestness coming through her pitch.

The croupier announced, "No more bets, folks. Shooter, are you ready?"

Then I felt long-distance heat on me, scanned the room, spied a pair of chestnut eyes interrogating me from eighty feet. Claudia.

She looked away when I smiled at her. I didn't care, though, now that the odds really did seem to be turning in my favor.

A gambler along the side of the table bleated, "Hey, buddy, you shootin' or what?"

I turned. "Huh?"

"Is the shooter playing or passing, sir?" the croupier asked.

"Oh yeah, I'm playing—just not here. Cash me out."

There was a groan from the rail buzzards who'd been riding my win streak. I looked at the dubious gains, handed a ten-dollar chip to the croupier. He nodded in thanks.

A voice said, "What's the play, lover?"

It was the bordello number, still clutching my arm. She began to walk with me as I stepped away from the table.

"Here's the play," I said, pressing two more chips into her gloved hand, "Take a break, honey, go buy yourself a coat. You look like you were a nice girl once."

She didn't know whether to smile or slap me, but she put the tokens in her purse just the same as I moved off across the room, my eyes on a lady in a red dress.

Jilly waylaid me halfway across the floor. "Frank wants you to say hi to Momo."

I frowned, started to strike a posture. But then I realized that the best place to take the temperature of the room regarding Sinatra might be right by Giancana's side.

"Lead the way, Jill," I replied through a forced smile, nodding toward the far corner where Momo was standing with the other hoods.

We walked together toward the big-boy section of the room, passing a phalanx of made guys on the way. They gave a series of chin nods or smiles to Jilly, but I didn't know any of them. The only one I recognized was the big guy with the flowers I'd seen outside Claudia's room. I didn't know where he fit in, but I didn't like it much. Somehow, I could have sworn I knew him from somewhere.

Frank was telling some story to a couple of éminences grises in the mix. I patted his shoulder as I passed. Then I came face-to-face with the mob chieftain. "Mr. Giancana," I said, "how you doing?"

"*Tuttabon*," he answered. "Christ, I ain't seen you in a while,

Buonomo—I thought you was a ghost." He found that funny for some reason, issuing a single cluck at his own comment.

"Not yet, but it's not for a lack of trying by some people."

Neither one of us laughed at that one, although Jilly smiled nervously.

"Maybe you should take it easy then. I heard you half strangled one of Carpaccio's guys today."

Behind Sam, I could see the flower guy angling through the crowd, edging closer, his eyes aglow.

I flexed my neck. "Guy was out of line."

Giancana looked at me, his face stone serious. "He was right, you know—about O'Hare, I mean."

I could feel my face flushing, reminded myself I wasn't dealing with an underling here. Sam Giancana wasn't very big physically, but I knew that he was one of the most ruthless killers the Outfit had ever spawned.

"Sam, I knew Butch O'Hare—"

He waved his cigar vigorously side to side. "Nahhh. Not the kid, the old man—Edward O'Hare. Easy Eddie, we called him. He *was* with Capone."

"Says who?"

"Says me. I used to work for Capone back in the wild days, and I'm telling you I saw ol' Alphonse and Mr. O'Hare get into that bulletproof Cadillac of Capone's together more than once. They'd parley in the car so no snoops could overhear 'em."

"Yeah," I conceded, "I remember. O'Hare was his lawyer or something, right?"

Giancana flashed that killer's smile at me. "Aaat's right, he was his lawyer—and a *lot* more."

"But that's got nothing to do with Butch. He was a stand-up guy. Had a Medal of Honor and went back into the fight—because he was better than his old man and he needed to prove it. And that's something *I* know, Sam, because I knew *him*."

I could see the flower guy's ears perk up. He was definitely eavesdropping on our conversation now. I glanced over at him, back at

Sam, then said loudly for effect just to see what it would get me, "And I can tell you this too, Sam: The next son of a bitch to pop off about him won't get *half* strangled."

Jilly's eyes went lunar. Heads spun, including Frank's, but Giancana just threw his head back and laughed out loud. "All right, all right," he said, motioning down with his hands, "let's let it go at that. The kid was all right. I didn't mean no disrespect to him."

Giancana had thrown me a bone, so I played fetch. "Okay, I'm sorry about the ruckus, Sam. I don't want any trouble, I'm just here to have some laughs with Frank anyhow."

He nodded in acceptance, pulled on his cigar. The guys around us turned back to their conversations, but there were still a few look-overs. We shifted to safer ground, made some small talk about Frank's show. Frank drifted by, leaned over Sam's shoulder, basking in the attention. If there was anything up at all, Sam didn't betray it. He glanced back at Frank, grinned broadly, then jabbed a finger in the air in my direction. "Did ya catch Di Scungille's show, by the way? He could be the next Sinatra."

Frank's eyes rolled above his smirk in anticipation of my response.

"He's no Sinatra," I said. "Maybe the next Jerry Vale. Now, that comedian who introduced Frank . . . What is it . . . Bobby Weyze? He had me in stitches. And that Claudia Cucciabella? She's fabulous. She could fill any club in town. Let her open for Frank here next time he's back, why don't ya? Get her some real exposure."

"I don't know," he said, rocking his head. "Who wants to hear Italian anymore?" He hooked a thumb at Frank, "Dis guy, Dino, Bennett, Como—they all sing in English, right? Besides, I just own the joint, I don't run it. You wanna talk to her manager? He's around here somewheres."

He started to look around, but I waved him off. Why the hell would I want to get her ensnared in their web anyway? Frank's drinking buddy Joe E. Lewis had lost half his throat getting out of the Outfit's clutches, and Frank himself had been the source of innuendo about the mob strong-arming Tommy Dorsey to break his contract for decades.

I decided to quit while I was behind. "Nah, skip it, Sam. Now, if you gentlemen will excuse me, I'd like to convey my admiration to that lady in person."

"Is that what they call it dese days?" Sam said, what might have been a smile on his lips.

12

Claudia was alone at the end of the room next to the small checker-board dance floor, her eyes on her moonlighting band as they grooved through "Take Five." I watched her watching them, wondering what wheels were turning in her mind as the hypnotic rhythm riffed in recurring cycles. I stopped a few feet away, didn't speak. She glanced at me then back at the band, her stiletto tapping in time with the music as the piano soloed above the irregular drumbeat. I knew the piece, guessed that she did too since it had been a hit for Dave Brubeck.

I stood there, drawn into the music, inching toward the musi-cians, snake charmed by the inexorable beat, by the woman next to me, by the night itself. As far as I was concerned, the whole room was empty except for us at that moment.

The sax came back in then, followed by the cymbals, pulling the piece together as it closed like a receding tide, wave by wave by wave.

No one else seemed to notice, but we both applauded loudly when they were done, gaining the acknowledgment of the players. It seemed like a pretty good time to try my new luck out. I turned toward Claudia, grinned. "Lovely," I said.

She smiled at me, and I thought I saw the first crack in the iceberg. Then she said, "Maybe your prostitute, she would appreciate this too? Or your Mafiosi over there?"

That tore it. "*Basta!*" I said, throwing up my hands. "I just wanted to congratulate you on your show; I thought it was terrific. Jesus, lady, what did I ever do to you anyway?"

"I'm sorry . . ." she began, but I was already gone, checking my tux for signs of burned wool as I stormed off.

I went outside to get some air. The temperature had dropped enough that I could see my breath. Frank came outside a minute later, waving a Camel into the clean fall night.

"How'd it go, Romeo?" he asked.

I flattened my hand, rolled it upward then abruptly straight down.

"Shot down? Really?"

"Made a smokin' hole in the ground. Right"—I paused, pointing toward the back of the Quonset Hut—"over there."

He leaned over, nodded once. "Hmmm."

"Like you didn't know. That one kills 'em like Lucrezia Borgia—just for the sport of it. Heard she got you, too."

He flashed his veneers. "Yeah. Even me."

I waved a hand toward the hut. "Whaddya say we get the hell outta here, huh? The night is young and we've got some haunting to do."

"Way ahead of you, pal. Jill's getting the car. Next stop Rush Street. Suntan Charley's coming with, maybe some of the other musicians."

"Just musicians . . . ?"

"Good guys only tonight—no bad," he said. "Ohh," he added, "speaking of that . . . I talked to Sam for quite a while in there. Everything's all right."

I leveled a penetrating stare at him. "Sure about that?"

"Yeah," he nodded. "He says the take tonight'll be north of fifty thou for the show and the Hut. That's a lot of 'all right.'"

I made an exaggerated motion of my head, eyes wide. "Okay then. Well . . . let's get to haunting then."

"Sure. Just let me say some good-byes."

That usually meant fifteen to thirty minutes and at least one more drink, so I headed back inside with him to keep warm. I saw Frank's pianist, Bill Miller, standing alone, nursing a drink and holding up a post. Behind him, the four-man ensemble was regrouping after a quick break.

I gave Bill a nod, pointed at the quartet as they went through a sound check. We talked music shop awhile, killing time. Claudia was still watching the musicians from across the room, too. The flower guy was with her now, leaning in like a rider on a crowded bus. She wasn't having any of it.

I watched from the corner of my eye as I spoke to Bill, enjoying it at first with a bit of *sangue freddo*. Then it turned ugly. The big guy slipped a paw around her back then whispered into her ear. She spun around quick, slapping his hand away and thrusting her finger in his face, hot Italian words spilling out. It looked like a great time to cut in.

I excused myself and hustled across the floor, calling out a request to the musicians as I neared. Claudia and the masher were still squabbling when I arrived. She turned and looked at me, arms crossed, eyes narrowed.

Before she could speak, I said, "Would you care to dance, *signorina*?"

"*Ma non c'è musica*," she replied, surprised.

I placed a finger to my ear, bent the lobe just a little. "Listen," I said in Italian.

The gods were with me, the music beginning just then on my cue. Smiling, I held out my hand. She gave the big guy a nasty look then took it.

We took the floor as the *stornello* began, Claudia glancing up at me in perplexed curiosity as we began to sway in cadence. I hadn't danced one of those since I was a teen, but I was on the beat after a few bars. The jilted party fumed at the edge of the dance floor awhile before turning and stomping off. I knew the steps to that one too.

We didn't speak while dancing, just moved with the music, gliding over the parquet. I could feel the tension lessen in her with each step, the perplexed look on her face fading as she began to trust me. She was a wonderful dancer. I imagined she'd probably grown up in an entertainment family, performing onstage since she was a small child.

By the end of the song, I felt a confidence in the way she looked at me, like I'd made an inroad. I realized that I'd been too hungry earlier, too much like Frank. How could I blame her for assuming I was just another rake?

The music stopped. A solid round of applause followed from around the room. I held her for just a second on the floor.

"*Grazie.* You dance beautifully."

"*Grazie lei*, Joe. Sorry I was so"—she paused, searching for the word—"rude . . . before."

I touched a finger to my lips, hushing the thought, then surprised myself by asking, "Will you be joining us out tonight, *signorina*?"

She smiled at my repeated use of a term normally reserved for a woman a few years younger than her own midthirties. "*Claudia* is fine, thank you. . . . So is the *signorina, grazie.*"

"Claudia then. And tonight . . . ?"

Her lovely face wilted. "*Credo che no. Mi dispiace.*"

"Don't be sorry. Perhaps another time then?"

"Perhaps." The sadness Frank had spoken of seemed to be bubbling up to the surface. An awkward second or two passed, then she said, "Tell me something. . . . How did you know to request that song, '*Strada Del Bosco*'?"

I held up a palm. "I figured if your boys could play a *stornello*, they would know that one too."

"Yes, but how did you know that one was my favorite song?"

I grinned. What else could I do? "Just lucky, I guess. *Buona sera*, Claudia."

She nodded ever so slightly several times, the overhead light sparkling in her dark eyes.

"*Ciao, Giuseppe*," she said softly. "*Buona notte.*"

Claudia and I had traveled quite a distance together in just a few hours. Between that, Frank's new lease on life, and the forty bucks I'd cleared, it had been a pretty good visit to the Quonset Hut.

I took one last glance at her as I headed for the door, that swing in my step almost a bounce.

13

Chicago is a saloon town and a late-night one at that. There's a corner tavern in virtually every neighborhood from Edgewater to South Shore, and the lineup of heavy hitters along Lincoln or Rush is deeper than the Notre Dame bench. The nominal closing time at all of them is four a.m., but that's subject to what might best be called caprice, especially if a shift of off-duty Chicago police officers is tearing one off. For the diehards, they start up at five in Cicero, making round-the-clock benders a demented possibility. Some epic runs were said to have lasted better than a fortnight.

By West Coast time, it wasn't too late for dinner, so we headed down to Gene and Georgetti's to grab a steak. Frank, Bill Miller, and I climbed into the first limo, Jilly at the wheel. Three other cars full of musicians and hired help fell in line. We didn't arrive until well past twelve, but they'd stayed open late just for Frank. The ribeye was to die for.

We were cooking rather well ourselves when we left the steakhouse, but the burning of the city that followed made the sack of Carthage look like a wienie roast. Mr. Kelly's, the Cloister Inn, the

Gaslamp Club, the Coq D'Or—bing, bam, boom—one after another we knocked 'em down, Frank holding court like the king of the city at each one as the fire rose higher into the night.

We crashed into the Green Mill about three thirty, boilers stoked and making plenty of smoke. The joint was packed, the house band still laying down some serious action. It didn't take long before Frank was hauled up onto the stage for a quick medley of songs, including an ad-libbed version of "My Kind of Town," much to the delight of the crowd.

The better part of an hour of glad-handing and monkeying around later, Frank leaned into me at the bar.

"What'll we drink now, pally?" he asked.

I ran my tongue across my teeth, an odd thickness filling my mouth. "I'm thinkin' maybe hemlock; that's the only thing that'll stop the hangover I'm gonna have when I wake up."

"Nuts. Let's have us a Flame of Love—we've both been burned by that one." He stood up and waved at the bartender. "Pauly! Hey, Pauly, do ya remember how to make the Flame of Love? Great." Then his eyes fixed on something. "Say, Joe, take a look at this," he said as he bent over the bar top.

I looked over the rail, followed his finger to the trapdoor on the back bar floor.

"Ya know what that is, chum?"

"I think they call it a cellar."

He made a slurry grin, shook his finger back and forth. "Try again."

"How about you just tell me, Groucho?"

"Okay. It's a trapdoor, from Prohibition days."

"No shit?"

He shook his head once. "None. This place was mobbed up from the word go. You know this is where Joe E. Lewis got his, courtesy of Jack McGurn, that rotten bastard."

He had my attention now. I leaned in.

"Know what else?"

"Uh-uh."

"There's tunnels down there. The Riviera, the Uptown, this joint—

they're all connected. They even have an entire underground club beneath the Aragon."

"Get the fu—"

"It's true; I've sung in it. Ask Pauly Sitko here, he's been at the Mill since the thirties."

The burly bartender walked up, slid two cocktails in front of us, the burned orange-peel rub on the lip still detectable over the smoky air.

"He's giving it to you straight," Pauly announced. "The boys could move anything around through these tunnels: gin, whores, guns, guys on the lam. Cops come in one joint, everything moves over to the next. Mr. Capone liked it, too—just in case."

"C'mon, Pauly," I said, balking at his story. "Capone way up *here*? On the North Side?"

"Lemme tell ya something, pal." He pointed to his left, back toward the small exit door near the stage. "See that booth there, the first one in? That was Al Capone's booth. I saw him sitting there many a night. He liked it so he could watch the front door, and two or three of his guys could watch his back at the exit there. Believe you me, when he was here, *nobody* got in or out of this place."

Frank banged me on the arm. "Show him the tunnels, Pauly. This guy, you gotta show him things. He's a skeptic."

"Youse guys wanna go down there?" Pauly asked. "C'mon."

"How 'bout you just crack the hatch a little?" I said. "Tonight I'm not so skeptical."

Pauly took several steps, bent down, hauled up on an inset metal ring. As he raised the wooden trapdoor, a light activated underneath, revealing wooden stairs and shadowy walls far below.

Frank was up and over the bar in a heartbeat. He stumbled on the landing, but Pauly caught him in big tattooed arms.

"Okay, hero, you comin' or what?" Frank taunted. He winked at me, then he was gone. Three minutes later we had better than a half dozen people in the dank, musty space, tittering girls clinging to our arms in the dim light.

Pauly gave us a quick rundown, pointing out the different directions toward the other nightclubs and theaters in the area. "Dis one here goes to the Uptown next door. Dat one used to go to the Riv', but it's bricked up now."

"How about this one?" I asked, pointing to a darkened brick passageway crowned by a roman arch.

"Never been down it, but I'm told it leads to the Aragon."

Frank hugged a honey, said, "Crazy, ain't it?" Then he plucked a smoke from his gold case, added, "Well, Joseph, you always told me this was a connected town. Now you know how much."

I scratched my head, glanced around in the murk. "You think Ness got 'em for the taxes on these improvements?"

"Ohh, that's good, Joe, very good," Frank said, cracking up so hard that he missed Pauly's lighter twice, his demonic jag of laughter echoing off the subterranean walls in the flickering light. I had to blink twice then to be sure that it was Frank standing next to me, and not the king of the underworld, dread lord Hades himself.

The surviving souls grabbed breakfast at Lou Mitchell's then hit the hotel at sunup. I reminded Frank, as he staggered down the hall with two escorts, that game time was 1 p.m. at Wrigley Field, come hell or high water.

Then I drew the curtains, brushed most of my teeth, and rigged for silent running. I was probably asleep before my head hit the pillow.

14

The knocking began about noon. I rolled over, tried to read the squiggles on the face of my watch, looked around numbly. The phone was stuffed under my pillow, but I couldn't recall putting it there.

Then I heard Jilly whispering through the door. "Wake up, Joe, it's time for the game."

"Okay, Jill," I managed as the pain began to coalesce. "Gimme a minute."

I slid out of bed, lay on the floor, rubbing my face repeatedly. After summoning the courage to stand, I lurched off to the bathroom, huffed down a horse dose of aspirin powder, and did the shower/shave routine in about five minutes. Normally, I might have thrown on a sweater, my dungarees, and boots, but that whole Sinatra "thing" about dressing gave me pause. Reluctantly, I went upscale, hopping around like a crippled crow when I caught my foot in the wool slacks. I slipped into the tweed blazer, grabbed a tie, and stumbled off for the elevator.

Frank was waiting for me in the lobby, dressed smartly in a tan suit, brown hat, and orange muffler. He handed me a newspaper and a paper cup full of coffee, giving me the long once-over as he did while shaking his head in pity. "Jesus Christ, close your eyes," he said, "you're gonna bleed to death."

I fell into the back of the limo next to him and Jilly put her in gear, sliding niftily between a pair of police cruisers, blue lights whirling and sirens chirping out warning whoops. That was great for my headache.

A block down Goethe Street, Frank said, "We made the paper, you know."

"*What?*"

"Take it easy. There's no photo, just a notice in Huser's column about me being at the Pump Room with 'local war hero Joe Buonomo.' Nobody reads that shit other than housewives anyway."

"Actually a lot of people read that shit, Frank. Goddamnit." I wrinkled up my cheeks and tossed the paper over the seat at the back of Jilly's head.

"Hey—I'm drivin' here!"

"Yeah, pal, stick to it—and leave the public speaking to Cicero."

I saw Jilly's glass eye in the rearview mirror. The other one was out of sight. It looked funny; I couldn't help but chuckle.

"Feeling all right now, laughing boy?" Frank jabbed.

"Yeah," I said, "I'm fine. Let's go see some football. Hit it, Jill!"

That might have been a mistake. The Lincoln made a turn, then began speeding up well beyond the posted 30-mph limit, the engine winding up with a growl as Jilly's foot went down, police sirens wailing around us. I took a long sip of the coffee while I still could, scrunched down into the back of the seat, and dropped my Ray-Bans over my eyes, trying to maintain my cool as the car hit the on-ramp at fifty and began accelerating to takeoff speed down Lake Shore Drive.

15

Wrigley Field never looked so good, packed with fifty thousand Chicagoans just buzzing with excitement. It was a beautiful fall day, maybe sixty and partly cloudy. The air was crisp, the sky a brilliant cerulean blue.

The entire nation would be dialed in today to see Chicago's Monsters of the Midway knock heads with the Green Bay Packers for supremacy in the Western Division and the ticket to the NFL title game that bought. Both teams were eight and one and the Packers were defending champs, but the Bears were looking good and had already given Lombardi's boys their only black eye of the season back in September.

I caught what I could out west in the sports pages and the occasional highlight on TV: Atkins, George, and Fortunato punishing anyone who crossed the line of scrimmage; Marconi, Morris, and Ditka ripping off whole acres downfield with the football. It felt like one of those years—which made this one of those games. And with Frank's troubles in the rearview mirror that made this one of those days.

We slipped in the VIP entrance, shook a few hands, slammed a Bloody Mary, and headed down to the field, shouts of "Isn't that Sinatra?" and "Hey, Frank!" trailing us as the Andy Frain man led us to our box along the third-base side of the field.

The commotion that arose moments later eclipsed anything even Frank had generated as the Bears came running out onto the field, dark navy jerseys offset with orange stripes gleaming in the midday sun.

The Bears dominated from the opening kickoff, leading thirteen to nothing after one. Spirits were running high, especially in our box. Fortunato couldn't be contained, and neither could Sinatra.

When the gun sounded at halftime, Frank, Bill, and Jilly headed for the press box, and I dropped down to the concourse to grab a dog. The ballpark ones only came with mustard, but they were classic in their own way. While I was standing in line, a man waddled by with an unmistakable gait—one I hadn't seen in years. He was obviously older and slower, but there was no doubting who he was.

I dropped out of line to intercept him, almost shouting as I called out, "Sal! Ohh, Sal-eee!"

He turned as I came rushing up. It took him a long second before he made my face. "Joe? Joey Bo? Oh my God . . . How many years has it been?"

Then I had him wrapped up, smothering him in a bear hug that had him fighting me off from embarrassment. "Oh, watch it," he said, arms flapping, "People are starin'."

"To hell with all of 'em. You're my pal and I ain't seen you in a double dog's year. Lemme look at you."

I checked him over. The pleasant jowly face was the same: sleepy, dark eyes, bulbish nose, red-tipped ears. But there were additions also: hard lines on the forehead, bone-deep silver white in the close-cropped hair, marked heft in the figure—not that he'd ever been a guy to pass on an extra helping of mostacciol'. Sal had, in fact, long been known in the neighborhood both for his insatiable love of pasta and for his uncanny ability to use his police badge to get himself into any Chicago sporting event. Earlier than that, Salvatore "Big Horn"

Bencaro had achieved even greater fame for the enormous gold Italian horn he wore around his neck every minute of every day.

We'd been childhood running mates, and we'd stayed friends through the years, but the war and its aftermath for me had gradually pulled us apart. Although we'd often written each other when we were younger, it had been at least six or seven years since either of us had received a letter from the other guy. But the bond remained.

"How's everything, buddy?" I inquired, shaking his shoulder back and forth with gusto.

"Good," he answered in his understated way.

"And Gina—and your kids? You got three, right?"

"Good. All good, t'anks."

I beamed at him. "Still in the neighborhood?"

He nodded. "Oh, yeah, you know me. Right there on Fillmore, just down from . . . uh . . . you know."

"Yeah. I do."

We stared at each other a second, apprehension filling the blank space as we both saw what was coming next. Sal started to ask me the obvious question.

"You, uh, going by the old pl—?"

"Got a good seat?" I cut in, reversing field on him.

He rolled his eyes. "Uh . . . just kinda walking around."

I laughed heartily, happy to be taking the conversation in another direction. "The badge again? Always the badge."

"You know how it goes," he said, that patented sheepish look filling out his features. "But I gotta be careful, I'm a sergeant now."

"Well, guess what, old chum?" I said, putting my arm around his shoulder and steering him toward the concession stand. "We're gonna get a bite and a beer, and then I'm gonna put you in the best seat of your life—a free one I might add, Sergeant Bencaro. And you will *never* guess who you're sitting next to."

The Bears took the second-half kickoff and the mauling continued. You could see Lombardi ranting and screaming clear across the field, but what could he do? It was our day.

Secretly, I deeply admired the man for his brilliant leadership and strategic mastery of the game. But not out loud, and certainly not when he was playing the Bears. Why the gods had conspired to put that Italian genius in that Wisconsin wasteland instead of Chicago or New York I'd never understand. As if being born Catholic wasn't hard enough.

Frank and the boys came back early in the third with a couple of older sportswriters and a blonde of more recent vintage. Sal's eyes were so riveted on the field he didn't even notice them as they worked their way down the aisle. I chin-nodded Frank when our eyes met, motioning for him to sit in the open seat between Sal and me.

Buddy of mine, I mouthed as he squeezed by. Frank nodded, picking up on the gag right away.

He sat down next to Sal, bumping him brusquely on purpose. Sal spun around, prepared to pitch a beef.

"What goes, Joe?" he began, then jerked to a halt, transfixed, unable to comprehend the sight before his dilating eyes. Millions of Italian Americans adored Frank Sinatra, of course, gusting with pride at his famous voice and smooth style, idolizing him for what he'd done to make our people a respected part of the cultural landscape, but not one of them revered him the way Salvatore Bencaro did.

I had to grab Sal's hand and tug it forward, but finally he shook with Frank, staring in dumbstruck awe as he sputtered out, "This is the gr-greatest moment of my life, Mister S-S-Sinatra."

"You bet," Frank said. "Nice horn you got there, buddy. Very big."

It was a day to remember, all the way around. The Bears ripped chunks out of the Pack and spit 'em out, pounding the defending champs 26–7. And Sal got along famously with Frank, yukking it up, swapping stories, and enticing him into a sing-along of "Bear Down, Chicago Bears" at game's end that spread to the whole stadium. Everything was letter perfect—even a Sy Huser sighting didn't faze me.

When the final gun cracked, we all congaed out of the stadium and down Waveland Avenue amid the thousands, taking refuge from the feral storm in a corner of Ernie's Bleachers. We drank it all in, good cheer flowing like Old Style, current, honorary, and ex-pat Chicagoans celebrating among our brethren on a day of victory.

It was a glorious afternoon. The Bears were now a shoo-in for the title game, I'd found a long-lost friend, and Frank was as ebullient as I'd ever seen him. Happy days all the way around.

But as the sun rolled ever westward, shadows creeping like black fingers down the darkening city streets, I knew there was a reckoning coming.

It had been hanging over me ever since I hit town—since the moment I'd agreed to come on the trip, really. I'd been kidding myself about it all along, even after Frank had mentioned my name had been in the paper. Running into Sal cinched it. That was kismet, that one, and it stirred something long dormant inside me, something I could no longer smother down. I could feel it welling up all afternoon—hear their voices above the wind and the cheers, see their faces among the many thousands—my hope grappling with the dread, recriminations piling higher as I came to acknowledge what was indisputably at hand.

A reckoning many years in the making, often delayed by the storms and vicissitudes in my life, but ever destined to happen. A reckoning whose time had finally come.

And it lay back home where it all began.

On Taylor Street.

16

We stayed at Ernie's the better part of two hours, mixing with the sportswriters and glad-handers Sinatra attracted. A little after five, Frank leaned in and said, "Hey, Fortunato is gonna meet us for dinner at Twin Anchors. I think some of the other players are gonna come too. It'll be a gasser."

I was just putting flame to a Lucky. I glanced over at Sal, back to Frank. "Sorry, pal, this time I'm gonna have to pass."

"The hell you say," he grinned, cocksure and boozy.

"Not to worry," I replied. "Sal's gonna fill in for me, okay? You got your own private police detail for protection; all you gotta do is feed him."

He gave me a hard stare. "Whaddya talking about here? Did you not hear me? Joe Fortunato—your patron saint linebacker—is gonna join us for dinner at the best rib joint north of the Mason-Dixon Line. Of course Sal comes—but you're coming too. On this I must insist."

I zeroed in on him as I pulled in a lungful. "Not this time, Frank.

The coast is clear—you said it yourself. Now I've got something I have to do for me."

"Can't it wait?"

"No, sir," I answered. "Not any longer."

I blew out a cloud of smoke, tracking the curling white wisps as they roiled up toward the tin ceiling, searching for answers in them like some kind of gin mill oracle. "Twenty years is long enough."

17

Growing up, the nuns taught us that the handful of restaurateurs and merchants who arrived from Genoa in the 1850s were the first Italian immigrants to come to Chicago. Their success in business helped blaze a trail back across the Atlantic for the wave of their countrymen that followed, as any Genovese was only too happy to tell you. Over the decade following the Great Chicago Fire of 1871, the stream of immigrants increased as the city rebuilt itself. Within three decades, Chicago's hunger for labor, coupled with poverty and famine in Italy, had turned the stream into a tide.

They came from Arezzo, Castel di Sangro, Modena, Naples, Palermo, and a thousand other places. They came to Chicago to hack trenches, mine coal, lay bricks, forge steel, stitch fabric, peddle fruit, and toil for the railroads. They came to a distant city across the sea for "bread and work." And their labors helped build that city into a metropolis.

Italian neighborhoods dotted the Chicago landscape when I was a kid. All told, there were better than a hundred thousand Italian Americans in Chicago at that time, flung out across the city in ghettos and small pockets, divided by region of birth but connected by soul. Grand and Western was mostly Sicilian with some Pugliesi. Twenty-Fourth and Oakley was Tuscan. Way out on the west side, Melrose Park was Neapolitan. Distant Chicago Heights and Blue Island were said to be heavily Italian also, but those we took on faith.

But the biggest and best-known area by far was the Taylor Street neighborhood on the Near West Side. Although largely Neapolitan and Marchese, the bustling enclave opened its arms to my father, a boy of thirteen who arrived alone from the hills of Emiglia Romagna in 1899. Just a few years later, it welcomed my mother, a young girl from Naples who had emigrated with her entire family.

On Taylor Street, they met and married, lived and worked, pledged allegiance to their new country and raised their five children as Americans.

On Taylor Street, I would always be home.

18

From Wrigley, I grabbed the "L" at Addison and took it downtown. The game crowd had dispersed so I had the car almost all to myself. The scenery had changed a lot over the years, but the *clack clack clack* of the wheels on the tracks and the screech they made in the sharp turns took me back.

Below me, people were walking dogs, gathering near taverns, or scurrying home with grocery bags in their arms, just as always. Fragments of apartments zipped by as the elevated train churned on, lights snapping on in eye-level living rooms as people came back to settle in for the evening. Night fell over the city as I rode south, closing in mile by mile on a rendezvous long delayed.

Before long, I was in the Loop, marveling at the sheer number and size of the new skyscrapers as I rolled through the deserted downtown. I made the change at Jackson and took the Congress line west, counting down the stops to Racine Street, practicing what I would say, fidgeting in my seat, wondering what twenty years of war and wandering had done in the eyes of those who knew me once.

My plan was to hop the streetcar at Racine and ride it down the last half dozen blocks. I'd always loved the electric cars as a kid. For a nickel, you could go clear across town—and get a transfer. It took a couple minutes of looking around before I was forced to accept that the streetcar line I'd put Butch on so long ago wasn't there any longer. Then I realized that I hadn't seen any lines downtown, either. That I hadn't seen any *anywhere* in Chicago.

Things change.

I walked instead, the six clangs of the church bells letting me know I had just enough time. Strange sights greeted me at every turn. The el train had run the length of another new expressway where Congress Street had been. I had learned about that one from a letter my sister had sent me, but it was still startling to see how it bisected the old neighborhood, completely dividing families and neighbors with its stony gray coldness, thousands of cars barreling through a space once occupied by churches and parks and homes and vibrancy. It was quite disturbing. Other things were worse.

In the distance, concrete monoliths rose like giant pillboxes near Halsted Street, sterile mercury lighting silhouetting their incomplete forms. Around the structures, cranes with steel jaws sat poised for their next attack like mechanized carnivores. Beneath them, a mass of construction vehicles huddled in an ad hoc lot on Harrison amid the ruins of demolished businesses. In windows everywhere, I saw signs protesting something called the Circle Campus. A chill ran through me as I traversed the darkened streets. Much of it looked the same, but something deeply troubling was afoot in my boyhood home.

Things improved as I got farther south. There was a sense of normalcy to what I saw, the brownstones and bungalows the same as ever, maybe even polished up a bit. Other things looked different, like the trees in Peanut Park or the corner cobbler's shop now turned into a market, but they were still recognizable as something held together by a neighborhood fabric, still part of the whole. By the time I reached Taylor Street, I was breathing easier. The sight of Chiarugi's hardware store and Scafuri's bakery heartened me. But as I walked the final blocks, the uneasiness I'd felt at the football game rose inside me again, ambivalence and doubt about what I was doing flooding through me. I fought through it, pressing ahead past the last brick walkup buildings, past where the Colozzos and the D'Alessios and the Fiores lived, to the one I knew best.

The stoop was deserted, a single roller skate and a pockmarked baseball bat lining its steps. The door was open—it always was. I stopped, composed myself, peered through the glass. Then I turned the knob and pushed the door inward.

The redolence of Italian cooking filled the air. I drank in the scents like the marooned returned to civilization: the garlic, the rosemary, the sopressata, the gravy, the baking bread—age-old smells that permeated the house. I stepped lightly through the darkened hallway, not a soul in sight save for the images on Kodak paper on the wall. The graduation shot of me in my navy whites stoked the fires of memory, transporting me back to 1940. My idealistic smile spoke volumes.

But there were other smiles—ones on the faces of children I didn't know, and on people I knew who had passed away. Everything felt utterly surreal, like a dream I'd had a thousand times before.

I heard voices down the hallway. Walking slowly, I made my way to the dining room, my heart beating faster with each step. I stopped just shy of the doorway, peeked in.

They were there. My sisters, my brothers, my aunt Teresa, my uncle Nello, children, spouses. That pleasant murmur of anticipation that precedes the meal flooded through the room, adults sipping wine, children sneaking hunks of bread. I tried to enter, but my feet wouldn't move, my mouth wouldn't work. I just stood there frozen, watching, chest pounding.

The kitchen door swung open across the room. A woman backed in, holding a pot in her oven-mitted hands. She set it down on the table, lifted a wooden spoon full of gravy, stopped, looked across the room.

At me.

I could see her squinting through black-frame glasses as she struggled for recognition.

I stepped in, breathing shallowly, staring at her face. She was older, so much older, those regal features weathered, the coal-black hair now gone to smoke.

"Who'sa that over there?" she asked. "Louie? Louie Esposito—is thatta you, you old rascal, you?"

Heads turned around the room. Somebody gasped.

Then she got it. A hand flew to her mouth. The wooden spoon hit the floor, clattered in the stillness.

I took another step, struggling for my voice.

"Hello, *Mamma*," I said finally. "I'm home."

19

Pandemonium is not quite the word I'd use to describe what happened next. It was more of an abject shock, accompanied by dull paralysis. Nobody moved, they just stared, openmouthed and stunned, whispered *Ave Maria*s and *Oh my God*s the only sounds.

My mother began to cry, grabbing my uncle Nello's shoulder for support as her legs began to go. Then my sister Carmella was up and out of her chair, throwing herself upon me as the droplets began to fall, her arms binding me tight. My sister Francesca hit the pile a moment later, then my mother, clutching her rosary as she kissed me, black rivulets streaming down her face. My own eyes remained strangely dry. I just couldn't compel the tears to fall.

Nobody said anything that made any sense for a good five minutes, just a lot of bilingual gibberish and the invocation of many saints in dialect as we all danced around in an impromptu tarantella. Finally, my uncle Nello restored some degree of order, waving his hands in the air several times and commanding, "*Zitto, zitto tutti*— everybody quiet!"

We finally took our seats, but the melodrama ran on, the girls refusing to let go of me until Carmella had to go running off to make sure the chicken wasn't burning. Somebody's kid got scooped up and handed to me. She jerked her face away when I tried to kiss her and everybody laughed. It was all tremendously heartening, but it was simply happening too fast. Deep inside I knew it couldn't last.

Then I saw my brother Fabrizio sitting at the far end of the table, his brow furrowed.

"You're late," he said.

"Uh-uh," I said, fighting back with a grin, "Sunday dinner's at six thirty—I'm just in time. Come give me a hug, *fratello*."

"You're twenty *years* late, Joe. Don't be fooled by the smiles; not everyone here is that happy to see you."

He got up and walked out, fading into the gloom of the hallway, a flat, unpleasant silence descending over us all, faces falling like dominoes around the room.

Now, Fabrizio had earned the nickname "Incendio" when we were kids due to his temperament—this was a guy who could start a fight in a phone booth, maybe even get the pope to take a swing at him. But I understood his anger. My visit wasn't going to be some Campari and caviar affair on the veranda, and it shouldn't have been. I'd stayed in touch by the occasional letter over the years, but I hadn't set foot in my family home since I'd been back on leave in the summer of 1944. That wasn't something you got a pass on, not from anyone.

I'd actually gotten as far as Union Station when they mustered me out after VJ Day. As a big-shot navy ace, I rated a private berth on the train instead of the bench the other fellas got. There was a celebration planned for me too, even a parade from what I understand. It was going to be some kind of a big deal.

I never made it out of the station.

I'd been slowly falling apart ever since Pete died. He was my best friend, and I'd left him alone in combat—an unpardonable sin. That crushing guilt, and the permanence of coming back to a world I felt I no longer belonged in, brought all my anxieties to the fore, state by suffocating state, as the train churned homeward. Something about stepping out in the first familiar place pushed me over the edge.

They took me to Hines that night, then shipped me to a bigger VA facility in Washington a few days later. They kept me a few months until they were sure I was safe around the razor blades, then they cut me loose. That time there was no parade.

I kicked around DC awhile after my discharge, putting the pieces back in place, brick by brick. When news broke in late '46 that Chiang Kai-shek needed contract pilots in his battle against the Communists, I slipped away, back to China.

Back to the fighting, back to the killing, back to what I knew best.

It was a long, long time before my war ended.

20

Dinner made things a lot easier. God, how I missed the way my family ate. Last night's steak had been heavenly, but the table before me looked like the Feast of the Assumption: lemon chicken, bracciole, anchovies, risotto, baked garlic, squash, and a bucket of polenta just begging to be slathered in my mother's gravy. My dad was northern Italian, but my mother was all Neapolitan, and she still made the best red sauce in the neighborhood, which drove all the *Calabrese* and *Siciliani* crazy. Hey, the woman had a gift.

By the time we'd polished off the third bottle of Uncle Nello's wine, everyone was feeling pretty relaxed. Everyone but Fabrizio, of course. His black eyes never left me. Some of the girls had started to clear the table when he said, "So . . . Joe . . . is there anything you want to tell us about your world travels?"

Carmella was resting her head on my shoulder. I pulled my arm away from her and eased her up, took a deep breath, let it out. "Yeah, Fab, I do."

He pulled a section of the *Tribune* out, slapped it on top of his plate, Huser's byline facing up. I felt my eyes close involuntarily as my face crinkled up.

"Wanna start with your 'pal' Frank Sinatra here?"

There were a few, *What?*s around the room and several blank faces. Uncle Nello kept smiling benignly behind his horn-rim glasses, but everyone else just looked perplexed.

I stared at Fabrizio a long, hard time, looked over at my mother, then around the room. "Send the kids outside," I said. "And let's have a pitcher of water, huh—I'm going to be doing some talking here."

There was some shooing and shuffling, along with a whine or two and the clatter of plates being cleared. The spouses politely begged off from the discussion. Then it was just my mother, *Zio* Nello, *Zia* Teresa, and my brothers and sisters in a silent dining room. I fished out my Luckys, shook one free, then hit it with the Zippo and took a deep pull. Circling the room with my eyes, I marked each face, sensing their concern, their curiosity, maybe their sense of loss for me. Finally, I let out the smoke, then cleared my throat. It was time.

I did all the talking for the better part of an hour. There were some gasps, some tears, even a few laughs as I filled in the blanks. The war, my breakdown, China, my friendship with Frank. I even told them about Helen, my ex-fiancée—most of it anyway. In the end, I gave them a fair accounting. Not everything, but a fair accounting. My mother didn't ever need to know the rest.

And when I was done, I stubbed out my third cigarette and closed with words I couldn't have imagined speaking just two days earlier, "When I shipped out with the Flying Tigers, I figured I'd be gone six months, a year at most. No way could I foresee being away from all of you for so long—or what happened to me out there. I just . . . I just hope you can find a way to forgive me. . . . Maybe even remember when you loved me."

I threw down the last of my water, folded my hands awkwardly in my lap, and looked up. "That's it."

Unsteady gazes met mine across the table. My mother mumbled silently as she worked over her rosary like she was trying to make the Second Coming occur in our dining room. At my side, Carmella dabbed her eyes discreetly. Across from her, Francesca wept openly. My youngest brother, Jimmy, sat perfectly still, his hands flat on top of the table, his big brown eyes the size of chestnuts.

Then Fabrizio got up, his face grave. He stood at the end of the table, stone still, breathing slowly. After some length of time, he fixed his eyes on me and began to speak.

"Joe," he said, "you are the eldest. The rest of us grew up admiring you for your hard work at school, rejoiced when you won the Golden Gloves, burst with pride when you went off to college. You were our hero long before you became an ace, but when you did that, too, you elevated our family, our neighborhood, our whole race in the eyes of this city."

He looked around the room, surveying the faces of the family he now led. "And when you came home the way you did, we bled inside for you. Hid our shock, closed our ranks. Took it when we could, fought when we couldn't take it any longer, but always we stood up for you.

"Then *Zio* Emilio passed away. We waited for you then, but you didn't come home. And then our own father became ill and finally died—and still you couldn't be found. That was *unacceptable*," he said, his voice cracking, "but we waited for you. And finally, we began to marry and have children . . . and still you didn't come."

He paused several beats, lowered his eyes. "But by then we were no longer waiting for you."

I nodded mutely as each charge was levied, pangs of shame and regret stinging my still tearless face as I awaited the sentence.

"But, Joe," he said, stepping forward, "you are *still* a Buonomo. And although we have many questions, you will always be one of us." He looked down at me sternly, stuck out a wooden hand. "Welcome home."

I cocked my head to make sure I'd heard him correctly. After a long delay, I rose uncertainly and took his hand. Fabrizio leaned in as we shook, speaking tersely underneath his breath so the others couldn't hear. "You only get this one chance."

Then Uncle Nello proclaimed that this was as good an occasion as there would ever be for *grappa* and reached for the bottle and glasses in the cabinet. My mother tried to protest because it was Sunday, but she was heavily outvoted, and soon we were all chugging down shots of the fiery liquor.

The shouts of "Cent'anni!" and "Viva i Buonomo!" we let out were probably heard all the way over on Damen Avenue.

21

My brothers and I headed out to the front stoop about nine. It was getting chilly, but my mother rustled up my father's old camelhair coat and threw it over my shoulders. Jimmy said that with the collar flipped up close to my graying hair, I even looked like *Papà* in it. That image was priceless.

Zia Teresa dragged Zio Nello upstairs a few minutes later, then my oldest sister left with her husband, the guys' wives, and all the kids. Carmella and Tommy had moved out to Melrose Park a few years earlier, but everyone else was within walking distance.

"How come so far away, Carm?" I asked as I hugged her goodnight.

There was a trace of pity in her smile. "You've been away, Joe. A lot of things have changed. You'll see."

"I noticed some things I didn't like on the walk down."

"It's gonna get worse. The boys will tell you."

I cocked my head. Fab and Jimmy nodded, a sad resignation in their faces.

"Okay, Carm. Goodnight, lil' sister."

She blushed, touched a hand to my cheek. "*Buona notte, Joe. Ti voglio bene.*"

The sound of those words was strange, yet very welcome.

"I love you, too, sis."

When everyone had left, it was just me and the boys on the steps, like it was a thousand years ago. Fab pulled out a Camel, torched it.

I pushed him gently. "Still smokin' those coffin nails?"

He just made a face, waved it in the air. "You're still a Lucky man, I see."

"Sort of, I guess." I turned to Jimmy, waved the pack at him. "Kid?"

"Oh come on, Joe," he said. "You know I don't smoke."

"Guess I forgot."

He took one and stuck it over his ear anyway, his curly black locks holding it tight.

We burned our smokes and said nothing, rocking gently in the cold night. But the warmth of my brothers at my side could have held back an ice storm. There were a million things to discuss—names to learn, stories to hear, bonds to rebuild—but at that moment, all of us understood the simple gift of sitting there in silence, just feeling it, not talking. Just waving at the neighbors passing by on their walks, exchanging pleasantries.

Finally, Fabrizio stood up. "Gotta work in the morning. I'm a foreman now at the factory—can't be late."

Jimmy said, "Me too. Gotta help Maria put the kids down. I'm up at five myself. Even senior residents get long hours."

I spun my head ninety left, then right, smiling at them both. "Foreman. Doctor . . . you guys done good."

"We've done all right," Fab said. "But we don't pal around with Frank Sinatra."

I could tell he was playing, but jabbing the needle in just a little too. "You wouldn't like the hours—or the work."

He gave me the ol' stinkeye for that one.

We said our goodnights and I promised to see them the next day after work. Fabrizio stopped halfway down the stoop, turned to face me. "I meant it when I said you've got just one chance, you know."

I met his gaze, his lidded eyes unblinking in the darkness. "Yeah."

"People are going to have more questions as time goes by, resentment will probably grow. Years have passed. Decades."

I frowned, knowing he was right. "I had to start somewhere."

Jimmy was standing out on the sidewalk, the streetlight backlighting his body. "Let's go, Fab," came from the vicinity of his shadowy form. Fabrizio turned, nodded, then looked back up at me. He pointed two gloved fingers in my direction and shook them, his face suddenly a sheet of slate. It was my father's look.

"Don't screw this up," he said in a cold, biting voice.

Then he turned and walked off. I watched the two of them go off into the night together, their shadows slowly merging into one, the clip of their heels fading away on the sidewalk as they headed toward their homes, their families, their proper lives.

I leaned hard against a pillar several minutes, ruminating on what might have been. Then I popped back into the kitchen to kiss my mother goodnight. It was a good ways back to the hotel and I didn't know if the trains still ran all night.

"Where you think you're going?" she demanded.

"Huh?"

"You're staying here tonight; Cesca already made up your room."

"*My* room?"

She gave me her famous, *How did I raise this much of an idiot?* look. "Your room, Giuseppino. Uppastairs, on the left."

"You mean you *kept* it for me?"

She shook a hand in the air. "Of course not. But Carm and Tommy took the kids to Melrose, so now it's empty again. Whaddya think, we made some kinda shrine out of it?"

"Oh, Ma . . ." I said, grabbing her and kissing the top of her head, smelling the olive oil she still put in her hair. I admired her for several seconds, warmth spreading inside me. Then I declared, "I think I'm gonna take a walk."

"*Una passegiata?* Take that coat you were wearing—it's cold out there. And don't be out too late, I'm gonna lock that door at eleven. *Mi senti, figlio mio? Alle undici.*"

A warning finger waved before my eyes as she said it.

I shook my head, laughing as I walked out. "Oh, *Mamma*, you know you never lock that door."

22

I took the steps in twos and bounced down Fillmore toward Ashland, passing brownstones and chalked-out hopscotch courts on the
way, blued living rooms reflecting *Candid Camera* and *Bonanza* on
the brown leaves that clung to the branches of the elm trees. The
television glow was new, and so were the cars for the most part, but
everything else looked the same. The lights were out at the Bencaros
as I made the right at the block's end, but I was sure that Sal was up
to his eyeballs in highballs with Frank someplace.

Reaching the next corner, I made another right and began the
long stroll. I always loved Taylor Street at night: the quiet storefronts, their wares dangling out of reach behind darkened windows;
the neon tubes glowing in script in front of the taverns; the couples
strolling with young children; the old men pulled up in chairs near
the bocce court, admiring the girls as they walked by and telling
gentle lies about their younger days.

I wandered absentmindedly for several blocks, past Racine
toward Halsted, toward the cranes looming in the night. So many
things had happened in one day, in one evening. Emotions were

colliding inside me like Fermi's particles, setting off chain reactions of memories, of *what if?* and *what's next?* I felt at home on my old street, content even. I'd seen one guy twice already, but so what?

The lights were still on at the Café Napoli across the street. Just to be safe, I went in and ordered an espresso from an older gentleman. His olive face and prominent nose made me suspect he was from the old country. His voice made it an airtight case.

Before I knew it, I'd slipped into the local dialect we'd spoken on the streets as kids, a blend of Neapolitan and Marchese.

"Many years here?" I asked, clipping words off at their ends like so many cigar tips.

"*Troppi*," he said, the long, flat line of his mouth turning down at the corners.

I stole a glance out the window, spooned some sugar into the small cup he'd poured me, making a tiny vortex as I swirled it down to the bottom of the black liquid. "*Ma perche?*"

Signor LoGuardio went on to detail for me exactly why he had "too many" years in America. Following his arrival full of hope just after the First World War, he'd witnessed the whole long slow slide: the changing morality he'd seen develop in the neighborhood, the decline of respect for the family and the elderly, the abandonment of the traditions of Italy.

"*Quello bastardo*" Mayor Daley was held up for special condemnation for conspiring with others to build the University of Illinois's new campus in the heart of the century-old neighborhood, the perfidious act, he said, specifically designed to destroy the community and thwart the growing political ambitions of its people.

I put down the espresso in two quick slurps, then listened quietly as he vented, his diatribe matching the bitterness of the coffee.

When he was finished, I weighed what he had said, then asked, "*Allora* . . . now what?"

"*Italia*," he said flatly, smacking his hands together like he was brushing off chalk. Pointing with an outstretched finger, he indicated that the mobsters nearby had sealed the deal by putting too big of a *mordito*, or bite, on him for too long.

One of the very unfortunate realities of Italian life on either side of the ocean was the ineradicable grip crime families had on the citizenry. The 'Ndràngheta, the Mafia, and the Camorra back home had also made the Atlantic passage, tucked in like so many steerage-class rats in the bowels of the steamers that had brought another million honest, hardworking Italians to Ellis Island and beyond. Once here, they spread as vermin do, bringing first the Black Hand then La Cosa Nostra to New York, Philadelphia, Cleveland, Chicago, and any other place they could sink their claws into, bringing the ills of the old world to the new. It was something I knew far too much about.

I thanked the gentleman for the coffee. Reaching across the counter, I clasped his hand and placed my other on his shoulder, gazing at weathered brown eyes between bushy silver eyebrows and a matching mustache. I told him I hoped he'd find a reason to stay, if only to help hold the line. He nodded affirmatively but without much energy. I wished him well, scanned the street in both directions, and headed out.

23

As I came out to the sidewalk, I spied a couple of young kids three doors down, sitting on chairs outside a windowless business. I knew the setup, made the place for a "social club," a closed-shop operation where Outfit guys cooked up their schemes and sharpened their knives. This one went way back; I could remember the punks from the Taylor Street Crew and the Forty-Two Gang doing their hugging and kissing rituals as they met out front in the old days.

Seeing the kids was disturbing enough since they were only about twelve, but when I recognized one as my nephew Johnny, I went into low orbit.

Johnny's *oh shit* look gave it all away as I double-timed over. He whispered something to his partner as I neared, then turned to face me.

"Don't you move," I ordered the other kid. "Not one step." I cocked my head, struggling to grasp what I was seeing.

"Uncle Joe—"

"*Zio*," I spit out. "It's not uncle, it's *zio*, okay? Don't you kids talk Italian anymore?"

Johnny's eyes were baseballs, fear lining his small voice as he said, "Z-Zio Joe. I can ex—"

"No, you can't. You kids are leaving with me right now. We'll sort it out with your fathers."

Then a cocksure voice mused from the doorway, "Something I can help you with, mister?"

I looked over. A potbellied man in an unbuttoned hunter's shirt, dago tee and gold necklace underneath, stood looking down at me with no small measure of scorn.

"There's *nothing* you can help me with. This is my nephew. These kids are leaving with me now and they aren't coming back."

"That so?"

I stepped toward him, pulling Johnny in behind me. "*That's so*," I said.

He made a slow move toward his waistband. A man inside cut him off. "Get in here, Carlo. And put your hands down, you idiot." Then the man called out, "Is that you, Buonomo?"

That caught me off guard. After an unsuccessful moment trying to figure out who it was, I replied, "Who wants to know?"

A familiar killer grin came swimming toward me from the darkness inside. Vinnie Bo'palazzo leaned against the door frame in a smart powder-blue suit, smirking like he'd invented the look. "How'd you know we were looking for you?"

"You're not looking for me; you're looking for what I used to be."

He shook his head, smiling at no one in particular. "No," he said, "I'm pretty sure the boss wants the you of today, not the relic."

He held up a finger. "Wait right here, please," he said, then swam back into the murk.

Grabbing the kids by their jacket lapels, I pulled them in close. "You two, get home now or there will be hell to pay. *Mi capiscono?*"

"*Sì. Benissimo,*" Johnny said.

He and his running mate slunk off. I watched them until they made the corner, then I turned to face the social club, contemplating just what affliction my past was conjuring for me now.

There was nothing inside that club that I gave a rat's ass about. But I knew that whatever this "boss" guy wanted had to be refused straightaway so there wouldn't be any lingering idea that we were going to be chummy.

Bo'palazzo came back to the door a minute later and motioned me into the club. A clutch of brutish guys gave me the once-over when I walked in. Carlo, the dumb guy, frisked me. After that, Vinnie led me through the dim room past a table where the guys were playing cards.

When we reached the back of the room, Vinnie knocked on a shabby door, said, "He's here."

A deep voice rumbled back through the wood, "Send 'im in."

Bo'palazzo swung the door open. Out of habit I checked behind me, then entered. My eyes flared when I saw the man inside. It was the flower guy who'd been pestering Claudia the night before, the one I'd cut in on by asking her to dance.

"*You're* the guy in charge?" I said, scanning the rest of the room.

"Carpaccio. Fiorello Carpaccio. Come on in, siddown," he said, waving Bo'palazzo out with his hand.

"*You're* Carpaccio?"

"Didya maybe mistake me for Marcello Mastroianni?"

"Uh . . . no."

"Have a seat," he offered.

The door closed behind me. "I'm good standing. I won't be here long."

"Ahh, come on, sit. Let's tawk a bit. Don't worry, dis ain't about dat little fracas with my guy yesterday."

Carpaccio's voice rumbled like a locomotive gathering speed, his Chicagoese so thick it practically broke off in slabs. He gestured at a chair. That was the first time I noticed how big his hands were. Big and gnarled like a pug boxer's—or a guy who'd worked heavy labor for a long time.

I took a seat in the office chair across from his desk, the floorboards creaking beneath me as I lowered my weight into it. The room stank of sweat and cigarettes.

The guy across from me was definitely no movie star. Overall he was large, but maybe gone to seed a little of late, though plenty of avoirdupois still bulged through his rayon shirt along with a forest of black hair at the collar. The mane tapered off just a bit into beard stubble that looked like it had made it to five o'clock by midmorning. He had no neck whatsoever, and the head that sat atop that missing neck was too round and filled out with large, mushy features that came together like a three-car pileup. Cold, flat eyes gazed out at me from below the rim of a tired brown porkpie pulled low on his forehead.

Looking at him, I got that same vague tinge of recognition I had the night before. I'd seen this guy somewhere before. Long, long ago.

Carpaccio shook a Marlboro out of a pack, stuck it between his dark lips. "Want one?" he mumbled as he tossed the pack down on the desktop.

I shook my head.

He grabbed a large cut-glass lighter with a brass top and thumbed the switch several times until a little flame sprouted from the wick. Then he scorched his smoke and sucked in a healthy dose, our eyes never wavering from the other's the entire time. He pushed himself back from the desk with his feet a few inches, then leaned back in his chair and exhaled a grayish plume from the side of his purplish mouth.

"Dey tell me you used to be some kinda hero."

I scratched my ear.

"Dey tell me you were one of dem fighter pilots."

"Still got the wings in a closet somewhere."

"Dey tell me you knew Butch O'Hare."

"Me and two thousand other guys aboard ship."

I started to look around the little room out of boredom, taking note of the bricked-in windows peeking out behind peeling wallpaper.

He jabbed two fingers toward me, slinging off the nascent nub of cigarette ash on the desk. "Cut the crap. You knew him."

I was over the whole stupid game already. "So what? Is that why I'm in here, to tell you Victory at Sea stories? He was a guy I knew during the war. Now he's dead. It's been twenty years. What the hell do you want?"

"Ten million dollars."

I could feel the double take as I made it.

His brutal face cracked into a grin, cigarette-stained teeth glimmering as his lips receded. "Ha *ha*! Thought that would get your attention. You wanna hear a little story, flyboy?"

"Sure, I'll bite, church has already let out."

I grabbed a smoke of my own, snatched his tchotchke of a lighter, and flamed it.

Carpaccio belched out some more smog, and then he really started blowing smoke.

"Gino said you came unglued when he insulted O'Hare da other day. How many guys would bum-rush a member of a crew over something like dat? Dat's interesting, dat got me to t'inking."

"That must've been when I saw the lights dimming last night."

He took the barb. "Stay wit' me here, huh? So last night, I hear you tawkin' wit' Mr. Giancana, him sayin' he used to see Mr. Capone drivin' around wit' O'Hare's old man—a guy *everybody* knew worked for us."

"Until he caught a hundred stray bullets at the track."

Light danced in his dark pupils. "Exactly!" He sat up, leaned forward, his mouth cracking open like a panting bulldog. "And why do you suppose dat happened?"

"Maybe he kept banging in sick after St. Patty's day. C'mon, Carpaccio, I don't know. Get to the point here, would ya?"

But he didn't. Instead, he launched into a rambling story that covered more ground than the Union Stockyards—with twice as much bullshit. It began with some basic truths: Easy Eddie O'Hare had started out as Capone's business partner in some Chicago racetracks in the '20s, eventually becoming one of his lawyers and financial advisers. After Capone drew his famous eleven-year hitch in prison for tax evasion, he eventually determined that O'Hare was the insider who had sold him to the feds. That doomed Easy Eddie, who was gunned down after leaving his office at Sportsman's Park just one week before Capone was released from prison in 1939. All of this had been well covered by the Chicago papers in its day.

But then Carpaccio ventured into muddier terrain, alleging that O'Hare had hidden much of Capone's money throughout the city in various caches while Scarface's appeals played out, purportedly filching millions for himself in the process. He further averred that O'Hare's own secretary, Toni Cavaretta, was acting Outfit boss Frank Nitti's lover, and that she tipped the mob off to the time O'Hare would be driving home the night he died. With O'Hare out of the way and Capone mentally incapacitated by venereal disease, Nitti then had a clear path to any of the former boss's spoils.

With Cavaretta's help, Nitti may have been able to find some of it over time, but there was only so much she could have known. When Nitti drew a long prison stretch of his own, he took a "suicide" bullet through the brain in March of 1943 along the Illinois Central tracks. Butch's death in combat later that year ended any possible leads to the treasure. Many had searched since, but no one had ever struck paydirt.

I think that was supposed to be the big revelation, the *Eureka!* moment where I saw it all, where all the tumblers lined up and the great big vault door just swung wide open.

Maybe I was dense.

"So the money's gone, right? How much could there have been anyhow?"

"No!" thundered Carpaccio. "For Christ's sake, do you understand what I'm tawkin' about here? Do you know how many millions of dollars Capone stashed before he went up? Da guy had houses from Peoria to St. Paul," he said, highlighting the geography for me with a sweeping gesture of his nonsmoking hand. "Dey say Johnny Torrio took bags of money—millions—when he quit da rackets. Believe me, Big Al learned from dat. Sam Giancana once told me he saw one of Capone's joints up in Wisconsin dat had a safe full of fuckin' gold bullion and escape tunnels dug out underground. Dis guy was da greatest operator anybody ever saw, God rest his gangster's soul."

Some of the tumblers were starting to line up for me now. Tales of Capone's largesse were legion when I was kid. I'd seen him get out of a car once on Taylor Street when I was eight or nine. The older boys were jumping and pointing, the way the bobbysoxers did a decade later for Sinatra at the Paramount. The guy had that kind of star power. He controlled the entire city, and there was no doubting he'd acquired vast sums of money in his vicious surge to the top. I remember him handing dollar bills to neighborhood kids as they flooded the street, nearly stampeding me in the crush before I found sanctuary on a lightpole. That was a memory I hadn't recalled for the better part of thirty years, but it came to me then as Carpaccio spun his web.

"Hey, you listenin' to me?"

To my chagrin, I realized then that I'd been sucked in, my cigarette burned halfway down to my knuckle. I should've known better.

"Yeah, I'm listening," I said, "but it's all bunk. I'm sure Capone's boys found every penny he squirreled away, especially after he came out of the pen in a diaper."

"Dat why you was daydreamin' there, Buonomo?" His grin was all-encompassing now. "Come on, you know you wanna believe it."

"I believed in La Befana once, too. If your 'treasure' is so big, then why doesn't your overlord, Giancana, have any interest? Maybe because he already cadged it all?"

His head shook vigorously. "Nah, I tawked to Sam about dis last night; he thinks it's all gone, too. He said he looked on and off for a long time before givin' up."

"Well, there you go," I scoffed.

"But Sam doesn't have what I have."

"And just what in hell is that?"

He flicked his cigarette onto the floor and mashed it with a hoof then pointed a beefy finger at me. "You."

I stood up. "I'll be leaving now. Don't worry, I'll see myself out."

Carpaccio unleashed a simpering laugh. "You don't remember me, do you?"

"Not before last night."

He grinned, raising a hand to the weathered hat on his head. "It took me a while, too. First, da t'ing with Gino—dat didn't mean too much. Then I see you wit' Sam, hear some guys whispering your name. I kinda thought I knew you, but it still didn't connect. Den you get loud with Mr. Giancana and bird-dog my date and I ask myself, what kind of *coglione* is dis guy packin' here? Finally, one of my guys shows me your name in the paper today, and as I'm reading the words 'war hero,' it hits me all at once—so to speak."

He slowly tipped his hat back, revealing his massive forehead. High up in his balding hairline there was a pinkish slit. It ran jaggedly downhill toward his eyebrow, darker and uglier where the sun had weathered it. A battle scar—the kind you might get from getting hit with a beer bottle in a brawl.

I felt a chill growing deep inside me.

"O'Hare," he continued, "some local guy, a bar . . . way back during the war . . ."

He rubbed those massive hands together then, stared straight across at me.

I froze as the recognition swept in. *The Vernon Park Tap.*

He broke into a big, broad grin. "Now you got it."

I could feel my cheeks flushing. "You were the guy at the bar," I whispered.

"Been a long time, pal," he growled. "And dat's how come I know you was tight wit' O'Hare." He flipped a digit up to his temple. "'Cuz I heard youse two tawkin' da night you gave me *dis*."

His eyes were burning, nostrils flaring wide as he relived the beaning.

He had me way back on my heels. I sat down again, began playing for time. "Okay, so that was me. What of it? You guys got tough, we defended ourselves."

"Fair enough . . . We can make that part right some other time. Right now, I'm more concerned with discussin' how O'Hare was tawkin' about how he used to come up here in the summers and hang out with the old man, go fishing and sailing on the lake, take in some ball games—shit like that. Like that dog-track hustler was da father of da year or somethin'."

"A real *mensch*, I'm sure. And you want to go from *Boy's Life* stories to Butch telling me how his father stole millions of dollars from the most feared man in America?"

Carpaccio spun his hand around in the air several times. "You guys was reminiscin' about his dad, and you was . . . whaddya call it . . . comrades? Who's to say he didn't confide in you? Who better to trust with a secret like dat?"

I was incredulous. "And because we spent a few weeks together, he'd tell me about something that outrageous? If he even knew himself, which I doubt *very* highly. He was no fan of his father's business life, I can tell you that."

"See, he told ya dat much. I bet there's more."

I held my palms up, shook them. "Are you pulling my chain here? What do you want from me? I've got nothing for you on this."

He stared across at me, breathed heavily through his mouth, licked his dark lips. "All right, it's a long shot. But just t'ink about it, huh? Capone's dead. O'Hare—da bot' of 'em—dead. Nitti, Cavaretta, dat greasy pig Guzik, anyone connected to Capone—dey're all dead. You may be the last link to da money. If you remember anyt'ing, anyt'ing at all dat helps me find it, you'll be very handsomely rewarded. Be a nice way for you to square yourself for dis, too," he said, gesturing toward the gouge on his scalp.

I scoffed at him. "Count me out. I never heard of a partnership with you guys that didn't get notarized with an ice pick anyway. You wanna look for the lost gold of the Incas, go right ahead—but leave me out of it." I sat straight up, pushed my chair back. "I've enjoyed this trip down memory lane. Now I'm going to see that my nephew got home and let his father know where he was so he never sets foot in this place again."

"Nice kid, isn't he?" he said, breaking into a smile. "Be a shame to lose him."

His grin was three degrees beyond the pale. I could feel my pulse quickening and my face ratcheting down, but I didn't give in to the anger that was building inside me. Across the desk, the big gangster stared at me, his slit-smirk revealing his pleasure at successfully pushing one of my buttons.

"My offer stands," he said. "You can reach me here." He ginned up a particularly malicious leer. "And don't worry, I know where *you* can be reached too."

My hands went to his desk. Leaning forward on them, I said very quietly, "You just crossed the line right there. Leave my family out of this—all of us."

Carpaccio sneered back at me silently, his gaze fixed, his eyes unblinking.

I stood up. "Don't think that because I've been away I've forgotten how things work here. I was raised in these streets, Carpaccio . . . the Chicago way."

I turned around, opened the door, stopped, looked back at him. "Sorry about your face."

Then I left, walking wordlessly past the room full of felons and out into the cool quiet of the Taylor Street night.

24

I processed things out on the way back. There was no good way to spin Carpaccio's connection to Claudia or his innuendo about my family. On the other hand, both of us had made it patently clear we wanted nothing whatsoever to do with him, something even his simian brain would have to acknowledge. And I had just emphatically rejected his fool's-gold fantasy as well. Like a nearby hornet, he warranted a wary eye, but as long as we all kept our distance, things would probably be okay. I was only in town a few days anyhow.

Sufficiently assuaged for the time being, I had a bit of a chuckle at myself. Only I could go for a simple reminiscence walk in the old 'hood and get invited on an archaeological dig with the Outfit.

Francesca was waiting in the front room when I came back. She didn't actually have a candle in her hand, but it was nice to know there was a light in the window for me just the same.

We sat together at the kitchen table awhile and talked. One of the bulbs in the overhead fixture was burned out, same as always, but the dim glow was nice, almost a made-to-order sepia. It cast a pleasant hue over us as we tried to fill in all the empty spaces, wishing through the years and her tears that things had gone differently.

Just before she went up to bed, she said, "By the way, I dug out an old keepsake earlier. You gave it to me when I was a girl. I hadn't seen it in years."

I could feel myself beaming at the thought of the unknown curio—I'd brought home many from my travels during the war. "Do tell. . . ."

"I left it on the nightstand next to your bed. You'll know it."

She leaned down and kissed my cheek. "I can't believe you're here. . . . I never thought it would happen."

"I never dared to dream it myself."

"Funny you'd say that," she said, giggling as she turned to leave.

"How come?"

But she'd already darted out of the room, slippered feet pattering up the stairs as I sat alone beneath the light of the single bulb burning in the kitchen.

Upstairs, I tiptoed into the bathroom and got ready for bed. There was a note from Francesca underneath a brand-new toothbrush. I slipped into the bedroom, grinning at some familiar items that had made it through another generation of use. The White Sox pennant was still there, faded and curling, just like their aspirations did each summer.

Sports teams always took me back to being a kid, and I lay there smiling as I surveyed the old ballplayer photos, books, and bric-a-brac before snapping off the light. As I reached for the lamp, I remembered Cesca's promised surprise.

And there it was, right next to my hand, the snow globe I'd brought from Oahu so many years ago. I picked it up and shook it, watching the white sands settle around the plastic Diamond Head and Waikiki Beach for the umpteenth time.

I turned it over and gave the little brass key a couple of cranks. The notes were as mechanical as always, but still evoked the hypnotic sound of the Pied Pipers as the apparatus clunked through its tiny gears.

Replaying the words from memory, I lay down in the dark under my own family's roof for the first time in twenty years, the conjured singers in my head cooing "dream, dream, dream," in mesmerizing harmony. The nostalgia snuck up on me, struck like a bolt to the heart, penetrating deeper inside me than anything else that night had.

It was then, for the first time, that I wept.

25

It rained overnight. The noise awoke me sometime around four. I lifted my head off the pillow in disorientation, then lay back down when I remembered where I was, comforted by the awareness of my surroundings. The muffled sound of the falling drops ran steady on the rooftop. I listened to it for a long time, replaying all the events of these very busy last two days in my mind, water beating down, washing through the downspouts, flowing through the streets into the sewers.

Something had changed in me since I'd hit town, something palpable. I wasn't some furtive, distant vagabond anymore. I was a part of something, something I'd always been a part of, something I'd lost sight of. I was a member of a family. And it was up to me to reclaim my place in it.

When I closed my eyes again, I knew that I'd be staying on awhile.

At home.

Francesca was off to school by the time I came down at seven thirty, but Zio Nello was at the table with his coffee and the newspaper when I ambled into the kitchen in yesterday's clothes. My mother was at the stove frying up last night's polenta with some pancetta and eggs.

"Morning, *Mamma*, that smells like pancetta. Put me down for a pound, I haven't had that in ages."

"Not until you say good morning to your zio. Forget your manners?"

I smiled at the mild chastising. Nothing had changed in her world it seemed.

"*Buon giorno, Zio Nello*," I said.

His eyes were already giving away his smile, but when he dipped the paper to acknowledge me, I caught his full, toothy grin. I'd missed that.

I gave my mother a kiss then sat next to my uncle and planted one on him too. His face smelled faintly of citrus and clove, same as ever. The smell took me back.

"Where's Zia Teresa?"

He smiled to himself. "In bed—grappa."

I grinned back at him. "Sorry."

He shrugged. "Whaddyagonnado?"

Pointing at his paper, I asked, "Whatcha readin'?"

"Yestaday's *Daily News*. They got this new kid . . . Royko . . . writes a column once a week. He's a comer."

I nodded in earnest. "I'll check him out."

"Yeah. Dis one here's about Hull House."

"Oh?" I said, leaning forward on my elbow. "What about Hull House?"

"They been tearin' it down, Giuseppino. That's what all them bulldozers and cranes are doing over there on Halsted."

I laid a finger on the center fold, tugged down on the paper. "Whaaat? Tearing down Hull House? I practically grew up there— that's where I learned how to box. What goes on here?"

Zio Nello frowned heavily, inverted *V*s forming at his forehead and mouth. He spoke very quietly in Italian. "There are many evil things happening here, Giuseppe. Many."

I couldn't believe what I was hearing. Hull House: a school, a gymnasium, a home—a community—to tens of thousands of impoverished immigrants since 1889, a place Jane Addams had willed together through grit and pluck, a civic factory where people learned English and other skills necessary to succeed in America. And they were tearing it down? For what?

The pancetta was still terrific, but breakfast wasn't so great after I'd digested that news. I slurped a second cup of coffee after I ate, brooding over the destruction being wrought around my family home. Then I got pissed, grabbed my dad's coat, and bolted for the front door.

I flew over to Halsted Street, darting through the park and the puddles on the way. The ruins began long before Halsted, however, many of the cherished buildings having already fallen to Daley's wrecking crews. My heart ratcheted up a little higher in my throat with each turn of my head.

Where a learning institution that had sprouted as an endemic part of the neighborhood had stood, there was an endless field of fallen bricks, crushed mortar, and snapped beams, with contiguous destruction strewn out for whole city blocks like the cinders of cities on wartime newsreels. It was stupefying.

As I stood aghast amid the wreckage, I saw a woman in a wool coat and a head scarf half a block down, walking among the demolition crews, hectoring them but good. She was trying to hand them what looked like petition cards as they filed past her to their site, but they either declined to accept them or ducked her entirely. She wasn't very big, but she towered above the men, her voice ringing out in the cool morning air above the distant rumble of freeway traffic.

"You men are destroying our homes, our community, our way of life. How much are they paying you to commit this crime? What will you do when they come for your homes?"

I stood stock-still watching her admonish them, diminish them. When the last of them had scurried past her, she perched herself on a mound of detritus across the street, staring them down as they cranked up their instruments of destruction. A block down, a wrecking ball began swinging in the gray morning dampness.

I found myself walking toward her, drawn to her, compelled to know who she was. I stopped several yards away, looked up at her as she stood hawklike on her rubble roost, peregrine eyes boring into the workers across the street, arms swept back behind her.

"Good morning," I called out.

Her head cranked around and down. Her face was Italian, but the voice was all Chicago. "Come ta help?" she asked.

"Came to see."

"Like what you see?"

I shook my head.

"So you came ta help then?"

That made me crack a smile. "Sure. How?"

A hand fluttered down. "Help me offa these bricks."

She wasn't much older than I was, but it had to be difficult to navigate the pile in heels. I took her arm and helped her to the street. After she stepped down, she composed herself, adjusted her scarf, then stuck out her hand again. "Flo Scala," she said without fanfare.

"Joe Buonomo. Nice to meet you."

She studied my face, her eyes flickering back and forth as she took in my features. "You the fella made all the headlines during the war?"

I nodded.

"I know your family, Joe. Good people."

"Thank you. I don't remember any Scalas, I'm afraid."

"Giovangelo," she said. "It was Giovangelo before I got married."

"Ohhh, sure, your father's the tailor, right? I used to get my slacks hemmed there way back when."

She got right down to brass tacks. "Well, he's gone now—so's his shop. They bulldozed it a few months ago, along with Granato's"

"Granato's? The greatest pizza joint in the new world? Gone?"

"Gone. Knocked flat—just like they're gonna do to all these places here if we don't stop them somehow."

Mrs. Scala then detailed the recent demise of the Halsted-Harrison end of Little Italy. In 1961, the city had declared by fiat that they were going to raze whole tracts of the neighborhood to make room for the new University of Illinois Circle Campus despite the fact that the area around the abandoned Dearborn Station was readily available and much closer to downtown.

Florence and others had organized the community and fought back with a march on the mayor's office, sit-ins, protests, and every other available resource, battling the mighty Daley machine to a standstill, month after month. All of City Hall's dirty tricks—threats, intimidation, even the bombing of her home—couldn't make her give in. When the board of Hull House capitulated to the city in what Florence called "an outrageous sellout," she and her colleagues sued. But after going all the way to the Supreme Court of the United States, the residents and merchants of Halsted-Harrison—the people of the city of Chicago—lost. Lost their homes, their businesses, their very sense of civic identity.

As she spoke, the wrecking crews went about their grim business in the background, smoke belching from their bulldozers as they ground their way through the remnants of a neighborhood like tanks on a battlefield.

The scene and the story were disheartening, but I found myself energized by this small woman's courage and heroism, her unyielding sense of dedication to her neighborhood and her people, which she pointed out now included Mexicans, Negroes, and a handful of Greeks displaced by the Congress and Dan Ryan expressways. A great warmth welled up inside me for this woman who wouldn't admit defeat even as the wreckers gouged through houses behind her, walls falling with thundering crashes amid roiling clouds of dirty white dust.

When she was done, she asked me, "And you, Joe, where have you been all these years, through all this battle?"

I looked away briefly, then back into her eyes. "I've been away."

"Where?"

"After the war, I stayed overseas a few years. Been in California most recently."

"Overseas? That where you lost your razor?"

I rubbed my stubble self-consciously. "I ran over here when I saw the paper. Guess I'll have to shave when I get home."

She just eyed me. "So what do you do out there in California, pick grapes?"

"Uh-uh. I run a freight company, fly boxes from A to B."

"Got a wife out there?"

"No."

"Kids?"

"Uh-uh."

She gestured with her hands. "Anything?"

I just shook my head silently.

A certain sadness filled her eyes. She didn't say anything for a while, the booming of the bricks a background basso profundo to the unsettling silence between us.

Then she said, "Well . . . you've been moving all those boxes around out there, Joe, but what are you really building? What do you really have?"

I didn't have an answer; the impact of her words was as jarring to me as the wrecker's machinery.

Sweeping my hand across what had been Hull House, I asked her, "But, Florence, if you've lost this battle, if even the Supreme Court came down against you, what else *can* you do? Why are you here handing out leaflets?"

She got a little exasperated. "We lost *this* round, but if we don't keep fightin', that Judas Oscar D'Angelo will help City Hall take the rest. They want to expand the medical complex over on Damen, ya know. And take a walk through Bronzeville sometime this week—if you can find what's left of it. Ask those people what happens if you don't stand up to this bully Daley."

I nodded as she spoke, realizing that we had a great deal in common. My admiration for her must have shown. I could feel my face winding up into a smile as I signed on for yet another lost cause.

"Okay, Florence. I'm in."

Mrs. Scala and I spoke another twenty minutes or so. I agreed to meet her at a citizens' meeting that night at Our Lady of Pompeii, then we said our good-byes. After that, I headed over to Café Napoli to make a couple of calls, one local, one long distance.

The long-distance call was first, collect, to the Nighthawk Aviation hangar in Long Beach. It was early, but Sean Parker, the hard charger I'd hired the year before, picked up on the second ring. I told him to let my partner, Roscoe Montgomery, know that I'd be gone a few more days and that we'd need a temp to pick up my share of the flying. Sean said he didn't think Roscoe was going to like that. I told him Roscoe didn't like much of anything.

The second call, to the Ambassador East, was shorter. Frank was out, but I left a message that I wouldn't be flying home with him Tuesday. I also asked him if he could get a certain party's phone number for me.

I hung up the phone and smiled to myself as I thought over the two phone calls and last night's decision.

Things change indeed.

26

When I got home, I saw Sal, gold horn dangling low, sitting on his front porch three doors down nursing a cup of coffee. From his slumped posture and closed eyes, I gathered that he was nursing a bit of a hangover, too. I walked over, hopped up the steps, slapped him gently on the thigh.

"Hiya, Sal, how'd it go last night?"

His eyes cracked open, blinking several times as he came around like a bear emerging from winter. "Hi, Joe. Madonn' that Sinatra is a wild man—we were at the Playboy Club till four in the mornin'. The Playboy Club!"

"Gina talking to you this morning?"

He shrugged. "Might be a few days. She'll get over it."

"Bang in sick today?"

"Nah, actually I'm off the next coupla days, but I'm gonna need to stay out of the house awhile till Gina cools down. You free?"

I nodded. "You bet. Let's hang out a bit, you and me. Like the old days, huh?"

"Okay. But maybe let me snooze here awhile?"

"Sure, pal. Sure. I'll get cleaned up. You get some rest." I patted his leg again, then walked quietly away, wondering to myself if he'd come to terms yet with the enormous expansion his world had undergone in the space of a few hours.

The old claw-foot bathtub still didn't have a showerhead, so I took my first traditional bath in many a moon. I went ahead and soaked in it awhile, reflecting on all the events in my own life in the last twenty-four hours. Sal Bencaro wasn't the only guy on my street getting his universe taffy pulled.

Reveries came to me as I unwound in the warm, soapy water, my head on the curved enamel edge of the tub. Everything from grade school to boxing at Hull House to schoolyard chums to old flames drifted by. Inevitably, I got to the war, and the time I'd spent on tour with Butch, thinking about the things we'd talked about.

I remembered telling Butch about the small skiffs we used to rent for a buck a day from the park district to sail on Lake Michigan. He lit right up, telling me he'd done the same with his dad on his visits to Chicago in his teen years. Both of us wondered if we'd all met by happenstance years earlier.

That was something I couldn't dismiss from Carpaccio's wild claims the evening before: He definitely knew some things about Butch O'Hare and his father. I didn't let on about it, but it made me begin to ponder the connection between O'Hare Sr. and Mr. Alphonse Capone. I began to give more thought to the possibility that some of those spoils might really be locked away somewhere in the old Windy City, and if I did indeed possess some cryptic knowledge of their whereabouts.

There was a rap on the door, then my mother's voice through the wood. "You asleep in there, *figlio mio?*"

"No, *Mamma*, just daydreamin'."

"Well, when you're done with the mermaids and back on dry land, I left you some clean clothes—no son of mine is going about in dirty underwear."

"Okay, thanks. Whose are they? Don't tell me you kept mine?"

"Whadda you care? Maybe yours, maybe your father's, maybe

Fabrizio's—I dunno. Just put 'em on, okay? They're plenty clean, I washed 'em myself."

My smile looked up at me from the water's sheen. "Okay, *Mamma. Grazie.*"

But she was already down the hall, on to the next project on her list.

I scooped myself out of the water, grabbed a towel. As I shaved and dressed, I decided that I had a new project on my own list to investigate. If I was going to stay in the family home, I was going to have to earn my keep.

27

Sal was still on his front porch, head resting on a propped hand. He woke again when he heard my heels clicking on the walk. He looked better than he had before but still a few bricks shy of a load.

"Ready to go, Sal?"

He yawned deeply, nodded. "Yeah, sure, what do you have in mind?"

"A beef sandwich at Al's—sweet and hot—then we hit the road in your flivver."

"Mmmmm," he mused, "juicy beef. Sounds good. Where we going?"

"Twenty-second and Michigan."

He scrunched up his face, looked over at me. "The Lexington Hotel?"

"Still there?"

"Yeah. God-awful dive anymore. What do you want there?"

"Answers, dear Sal, answers. Come on, buddy, walk with me," I said as I took his hand and pulled upward. "I've got a little story to tell you on the way. . . ."

*   *   *

There was just one thing Carpaccio had confided in me the night before that made me think any treasure had ever been hidden in the Lexington in the first place, let alone remained today. As proof of his rambling tale, he had produced a letter postmarked January 1942 that young Lieutenant O'Hare had purportedly sent to Toni Cavaretta on the eve of his shipping off to war. The last line of the letter stated that should anything ever happen to him she should "check the Lex," for the key to his father's affairs. The Roman numerals *IV*, *MI*, and *C* appeared together without explanation at the bottom of the page just above the signature.

I'd laughed openly at that point, telling Carpaccio the letter was vague and could've been made up by anybody at anytime, but I knew Butch to be a prolific letter writer, and I did recall discussing his father's "business dealings" in very general terms. He was under no misapprehensions about the nature of his father's life—or its end. If the story of the letter were real, the affairs Butch mentioned would very likely have pertained to his father's dealings with Capone, not more mundane family matters. As his former secretary, Cavaretta might well have been the best person in town to attend to any ongoing legal or real-estate holdings O'Hare Sr. had, especially if Butch had no inkling she'd been disloyal.

I still couldn't imagine that there'd be even a hint of O'Hare's effects—and certainly no treasure—left over in the old grand dame hotel. Not after three decades of made guys scouring every brick of what Big Horn said had become first a bordello, and now a transient flop. And it's not like some Outfit player was going to call WGN to report that he'd found Al Capone's missing millions anyway. If they were gone, they were gone, and that was that.

But I didn't have anywhere else to start and had a whole day on my hands, and maybe, just maybe, I'd latch onto some clue while I was there. Sal and I would make the whole thing an adventure anyhow, just like when were latchkey children. It would all be harmless fun. Kid stuff.

28

During the years that Al Capone ran Chicago like a feudal city, he and his men inhabited large parts of the swanky Lexington Hotel on South Michigan Avenue, including the entire fifth floor. The newspapers made frequent reference to his fortified enclave just off the lake, a place no one was allowed to enter without being observed by Capone's tommy gun–packing men. Exterior photos of the hotel had been published often enough that I could recall its appearance from memory, but very few of the interior ever got out. If ever a modern king had lived in a castle keep, it had been Capone at the "Lex."

The Lexington still stood at the corner of Michigan and Cermak, but it hadn't fared any better than Capone in later life. A hobo's camp of bottles and trash littered the street out front, and many boarded-up windows blighted the building's ten-story face like so many gouged-out eyes beneath the tattered blue awnings. A bum slept in a stupor on a ventilator grate just down from the once elegant Venetian pillared entrance.

The decline of the former high-end neighborhood shocked me. South Michigan Avenue—known as Motor Row for its dozens of beautiful rococo auto showrooms—had been a grand destination once. Now it was a slag heap.

Big Horn was twitching a little as we approached, his cop instincts on high alert, his head swiveling from side to side as we entered the lobby of the derelict hotel. I wasn't as concerned as he was—it was broad daylight and it was just another dead-end dive. I'd seen a whole lot worse. The revolving door was jammed so I pulled open a gilt glass and wood door, held it open for Sal, and then stepped inside.

The place smelled like dirt. And booze. And a lot of other things, none of them good. The few bulbs that still worked in each of the chandeliers augmented the grayish light from the overcast skies flooding in through the dust-streaked lobby windows. Still, corpse-like figures sat alone on battered couches in the recesses of the lobby, paper bags clutched tight in sinewy hands, vacant eyes staring out into another reality.

The toll on the Lexington Hotel for the sins of the Capone era had been as absolute as it had been enduring.

In the middle of the room, a fat guy in a bellhop's jacket was viciously dressing down an older wino from behind his bully pulpit of the front desk. When he saw us staring, he called out, "Youse guys want something?"

"A minute of your time, sir," I requested, stepping toward him, dragging Sal in tow. Reaching the nicked burlwood countertop, I looked it and him over, noting the cigarette burns on the wood and the acne scars on his cheeks. "You the clerk, or the bellhop?"

"Clerk, bellhop—manager, too, until he comes back from gurgling down his lunch. We ain't exactly operating on an unlimited budget here." He eyed us both as he spoke, clearly making us for something other than transients.

"Does your boss know you push your clientele around like that?" I asked.

"Those rummys? That's all they understand, Dudley Do-Right." He waved a condescending hand toward me. "Now look, it's six bucks a night—or the hour—don't make no difference to me how long you stay. Weekly rate's thirty."

Sal leaned over the counter, into the clerk's space. "What do you mean, 'by the hour,' pal?" he inquired in a low growl.

The tub made a snarky face, put both hands on the counter, the sheen of his greasy skin jaundicelike in the gloom. "C'mon . . . middle of the day? No bags? Youse gotta be a coupla fairies. Don't worry, it's all right by me. We don't ask no questions. Just pay your six bucks and get on with it."

Sal's arm shot out like a piston head, slamming into the clerk's forehead badge-first, his other hand grabbing a hold of Tubby's bow tie and yanking him forward.

Sal closed to three inches, spoke low. "Chicago police, shit-knocker. You ever say anything like that to me again and I'll bury you under this crud-strewn floor."

He shoved him away when he was done talking, pulling the clerk's tie loose in the process, the undone ends flitting down on his shirtfront as he recoiled. I'm pretty sure I could see the imprint of a shield between his narrow-set orbs.

"I'm terribly sorry, Officers," he sputtered. "I had no idea. Youse guys never come in here. H-h-how can I help you?"

Sal looked my way, played up the police status I'd just been accorded. "Detective?"

I gave the hapless bellhop the five-second disgusted look, taking in his porcine features and grimy clothes. "What's your name, slob?"

"Freel. R-Robby Freel."

"That German?"

"No sir, Irish. Sout'side Irish."

I eye-checked Sal, spied his smart-ass grin, and heard him scoff, "Figures."

"Okay, Freel," I said, making it up as I went, "here's how it goes. We're looking for clues to an old murder one of Capone's guys pulled way back. We're gonna need to take a look into that room of his."

Freel stared at me, his lips repeating my words, bewilderment spreading over his fat face. "Capone? Al Capone? That was thirty years ago. You puttin' me on or some'tin'?"

I straightened up, flexed my chest, took in a deep breath. "You obstructing justice, Freel?" I reached into my coat pocket for nothing in particular, watched him squirm.

"No!" he almost shouted. "No, Officer, I'm not. I-I'll get you the key to that room right away. I've got a guy downstairs who can help you. He's just some dumb moolie—lights the boilers, keeps the elevators running—but he was here back in the Prohibition days, I've heard him talking about it. 'Course you never know with a shine, the way they lie and what."

"Freel . . ."

"Yes, Detective?"

"Shut up. One more crack like that and I'm coming over that counter for you."

He nodded silently and rapidly, the thick gears in his brain struggling to grasp what he'd done wrong. Whatever low-end torque they generated wouldn't comprehend the nature of the blows I was itching to rain on him anyway—hard lefts on behalf of my partner, Roscoe Montgomery, a decorated Tuskeegee airman, and hard rights for the broken wretches in the hotel he so obviously enjoyed cowing. It was best that he just shut his mouth. But I still kind of hoped he didn't.

Freel picked up a house phone and dialed, then wet his lips and smiled nervously as it rang six or seven times. To his obvious relief, someone finally picked up on the other end. "Vernon, get up here right away. No, right away . . . please," he begged the party on the other end of the line.

It took a full three minutes for anyone to appear, Freel shuffling papers, straightening pens, and retying his tie twice while Sal and I eyed him from fifteen feet, mumbling low to ourselves about the state of the hotel, its inhabitants, and its help. Finally, a thin, older gentleman in a crisp blue uniform appeared from a service elevator and began to walk our way, gray head down as he crossed the lobby in a deliberate cadence, a pronounced hitch in his gait.

"Yes, Mistah Freel?" he said when he arrived, fatigue, perhaps an edge of contempt in his rich, husky voice.

"These men are detectives, they need to examine Mr. Capone's old rooms. Please take them up to the fifth floor and assist them in every way possible."

The man in the janitor's uniform turned to face us, a little dubious of two Italian detectives in Daley's Chicago. Savvy, veteran eyes interrogated ours, brown irises still sharp despite the seven-plus decades on the deep-seamed eyelids, a hard-earned suspicion evident on his coffee-colored face.

"Vernon Pryor," he said at length, nodding just slightly as he spoke.

I held out my hand. "Detective Buonomo. This is my partner, Detective, uh, Horn."

My outstretched mitt seemed to confuse him. Sal, too. After some hesitation, Pryor shook it, our eyes meeting as I took in a grip far firmer than his lean frame suggested. He shook with Sal also, and from the awkwardness of it, I could tell that Chicago policemen didn't generally shake hands with the public—at least not the Negro public.

I caught Freel watching too closely and froze him with a glare. Then Sal, Mr. Pryor, and I headed toward the elevator bank, Sal grabbing a glance or three behind him as we passed in front of the shabby grand staircase and navigated the hazards of what had once been the King of Chicago's royal foyer.

29

The elevator was in better shape than could have been expected, although its inspection certificate was two years out of date. Mr. Pryor said that he maintained the elevators himself—motors to mahogany finish—but inspections were "outside his purview." I liked his use of that word; it hinted at a refinement unanticipated in a custodian. I appreciated the pride he took in his work too, although it was tantamount to putting a streetwalker in Chanel in that place.

What the doors opened to on the fifth floor, sadly, was definitely not a French salon. Once-rich wallpaper dangled down in irregular curls, water-stained plaster flaking down to the floor from the exposed walls. Hair curlers, cigarette butts, tin cans, and whiskey bottles littered the hallway, and a drunk was lain out on the floor so stone cold that Sal had to check him for a pulse with one hand while holding his nose with the other. If Capone himself had been on the other side of door 530 with a cocked Thompson at the ready, it still would have been a damn sight better than the hallway.

But when Mr. Pryor turned the key and pushed open the door into the run-down suite, the only life inside was a pigeon sitting on a sill in the large cupola, taking shelter in an open window from the light drizzle now spitting down outside.

We went over the room in detail for about twenty minutes, Sal grumbling the whole time that it was a waste of effort. Unfortunately, he was right. Too much time, too much decay had occurred. Mr. Pryor told us what he knew of the room—he said he'd begun working at the hotel as a steward in the late '20s—but other than the fascinating bricked-over passageways Capone had built as escape routes, there wasn't anything original left in his quarters save the green and lavender bathroom tiles. The room had been picked clean and made over several times. The furniture, the furnishings, the paint, the carpet, the curtains—everything from Capone's time was gone. The only thing left was history, and the things the mind imagined thereof.

Still, there was a presence in the room—a remnant of life. A life of great reach, of great magnitude, of great evil. I stood in the doorway assessing it all after the others had left. From this suite, the most famous criminal in American history had handed out decrees of life and death at the height of the Roaring Twenties. What parties, what meetings, what riches, what dreams this musty, ruined room had seen in its day. I could almost hear the laughing voices, the clinking scotch glasses, the tinny sound of King Oliver on the record player as the dark czar of the Jazz Age celebrated his life and his times until the stars hung low in the sky.

Mr. Pryor was eyeballing me when I stepped into the hallway and pulled the door shut behind me. I was rather dispirited at finding nothing and I guess it showed.

"Are you really a detective, suh?" he asked.

I pushed a smile through pursed lips. "No. But my friend here *is* a police officer. Are you really a janitor, Mr. Pryor?"

"Vernon. And I am now, but I had a long, successful life in between my tours at the Lexington—down in Bronzeville where a colored man could make a decent living once. That was before they chopped up the neighborhood, put those housing projects and that school in."

"They got your neighborhood too?"

"Yes, suh. That mean you're from over there on Taylor Street, Mistah . . . ?"

"It is actually Buonomo. Joe. Yes, I am originally. Been gone a long time though."

He snorted through his nose, made sort of a laugh. "You go away again and they'll snatch your home like mine—just you watch. That Daley doesn't send any bulldozers through Bridgeport, you know, just everybody else's neighborhood."

"Maybe we should send a bulldozer through Daley's house," I opined.

Vernon laughed out loud. "Ha! I'd like to see *that*! I'll do the driving, Joe."

"You're on, brother."

Vernon Pryor had a certain undeniable charm. He'd clearly been done a bad turn or two along the way but was still soldiering on. And while he'd been living up north for decades, occasional traces of the rural South wafted through his smoky baritone as he spoke, enriching both his timbre and his vocabulary. In any event, he spoke a far better brand of English than anyone else I'd encountered in the last few days.

As we waited for the elevator to wend its way down from above, the hum of the machinery growing louder as it neared, Vernon said, "Just what is it you're really looking for here? Because you sure as hell aren't interested in solving no murdeh."

I shoved my hands in my pockets, faced him. "Honestly?"

"Yeah."

"I'm looking for clues to Al Capone's treasure."

His face stretched a solid inch, forehead rising as he took in my words. "Mmmmhmmmm. Why didn't you say so? We keep the treasure in the basement. Cash, gold, jewelry, guns—it's all there, just waiting for someone with the right claim check to come get it."

The elevator dinged as Sal shot me a thunderstruck glance, his eyes opening far faster and nearly as wide as the rumbling door of Mr. Otis's automatic lift. I shook him off, smiling sardonically, well aware that Mr. Pryor was putting us on.

"Okay, Vernon," I said, waving him onto the elevator behind Sal, "so there's no treasure here—I get it—but is there anything down there to see? Vaults? Tombs? Hieroglyphics? I think I still have my old decoder ring if it helps."

He didn't answer, just pushed the bottom black button on the stack. As the door closed and the car began its descent, Vernon looked at Sal, and then at me, smiling in anticipation. "Let's just go see, shall we, boys?"

30

The bowels of the Lexington were just about as bowely as they come. Massive, moldy, dank, decrepit, and dark—positively stygian beyond the short throw of the single workman's lantern mounted on the bare brick wall above the elevator.

"Damn," Vernon muttered. "Forgot my torch and the breaker's tripped again. Come on y'all, I'll have to go reset it."

Senses primed, I pushed Sal ahead and followed Vernon into the depths. The last thing I saw as we cat-footed into the gloom was Sal's hand going to his service revolver. Then the basement swallowed him up. Somewhere in the emptiness, I heard a low whooshing sound, rhythmic yet undulating. The hairs on my neck raised as the unnatural sound rippled throughout the darkness.

"I gather you know your way around here pretty well, Vernon," I said wistfully.

There was no response.

I called out again. No soap.

"Vernon . . . ? Sal . . . ?"

"Right here, Joe."

A flick of my Zippo lit an orange halo around my buddy in the coal-dark cavern. "Where the hell is Vernon?"

"Dunno."

There was a dull click somewhere. I could feel my knees buckling as I went into a defensive stance. A second later, a row of hazy, yellow lights flickered on overhead, one after another like stoplights in sequence, down the entire spine of the low ceiling. Fifty feet away, Vernon stood next to an open breaker panel in the wall, smiling in the half-light of one of the bulbs.

"I got it now, fellas. Over here, I'll show you all around."

Vernon led us down toward the far end of the basement. As we walked, we passed between numerous rows of concrete pillars running laterally across the basement into the murk. Halfway down the immense basement, I noticed a set of metal double doors, faint flickers of flame escaping along their edges and the gap between them where they bowed open. Then I understood what the whooshing sound was.

"That the boiler room in there?"

"Yes, suh. My office is in there, too. Plenty warm on those cold winter days when the Hawk comes out."

That was something about Chicago I didn't miss: a winter wind so biting the locals called it the Hawk. I shuddered just a little thinking about all those bitter days trudging through snowbanks when I was a kid.

A hundred feet beyond the boiler room we came to the short end of the building. Spaced out in twenty-foot intervals in the center of the brick wall were a half dozen recessed storerooms with arched frames. Vaults.

I felt a low-watt tingling as I surveyed them. Storerooms in the basement of the very hotel where Capone had lived and run an empire. They almost certainly had contained some of his goods at one time, possibly Edward O'Hare's as well. But what they contained now I could only guess since they were all sealed up tight with concrete plugs from floor to vaulted ceilings.

Even Sal's eyes were alive. I could picture the images dancing behind his pupils as he speculated on what lay just a few feet beyond. It was impossible not to thrill like a kid on a treasure hunt looking at those rooms, not to dream of the wealth they might have once contained, not to hope that someone somehow had neglected to empty them.

Vernon took care of all that. "What you thinking?" he queried, unable to suppress his smirk.

"I'm thinking I'd like to know what's behind those concrete plugs. Is this where Capone kept his spoils?" I asked, gesturing with my index finger toward the nearest one.

Mr. Pryor's guffaw cut through the vast space, echoing sharply off the cold masonry. "*Spoils?*" he asked incredulously. "This was no treasure vault—it was a liquor locker. They kept thousands of cases of that bathtub gin down here. Now that's somethin' ol' Vern could use right now!" He laughed again, slapping my shoulder as he did.

"So there's nothing back there?"

Vernon made a dubious face. "Ohh, I don't know. . . . Maybe a paint bucket or two. After Mister Capone went up, we used to use the vaults for storage. . . . That is, until those Treasury men sealed them up. Said they didn't want any more of Capone's boys using the place. That's the last time they've seen the light of day."

I'd known it was ridiculous to even hope, but once I'd actually gotten down in front of the vaults, the temptation to dream ran away with me. I struck a Lucky with my lighter, then kicked at the concrete plug in dejection.

"Oh, don't feel too bad, Joe." Vernon smiled. "You had to know there was nothing down here."

I exhaled some smoke, frowned. "I know, Vernon, I didn't really expect it to be that easy. I was just hoping to find some clues to anywhere else Capone might have salted it away."

He scratched the stubble on his chin, thought a second. "Well, there are a couple of tunnels down here I can show you. Maybe there's some clue there."

"Tunnels?"

"Oh yes, there's tunnels scattered all over this place. Some of them like the ones I showed you upstairs, but others down here running off every whichaway."

"But these can't be the Loop freight tunnels. They don't run this far south."

Vernon shook his head. "No, suh. These tunnels were dug by Mistah Capone. Some were for sneaking the gin in and out, others were escape tunnels. He even had one that connected to his old headquarters at the Metropole—two blocks away! His men were always burrowing around down here; this place was literally honeycombed with those tunnels."

As I started to speak, Vernon raised a hand. "Now, mind you," he cautioned, "most of them are bricked up or collapsed. There's just two that I know of still open. Like to see them?"

"You bet. You're in charge of the expedition, Dr. Pryor. Lead away."

"Oh boy," he said, "half an hour with you guys and I'm a doctor already. Can't wait till we find that treasure—I might become a world-famous professor of archaeology."

"I'll make sure your name gets in all the papers so the IRS can come get its fair share. Of course, the Treasury boys may take the lot of it first."

His eyes expanded again. "IRS? G-men? Tell you what, how about you just send me a thank-you note with a couple thousand in it—on the QT."

I took hold of his sloped shoulder. "How's this? If Sal and I find any treasure, I'll buy you a new house to replace the one the city flattened. Good?"

He grinned at me, a gold tooth gleaming in the dim light. "That would be fine, mighty fine. It won't save Daley from the devil's dogs, but it would be just fine by me even so."

We turned and began walking, Vernon hitching along with his hobbling gait, Sal trailing along reluctantly behind him, and me in the rear, musing quietly on the hardships of a life spent with a hellhound on your trail.

31

We stopped at the boiler room on the way so Vernon could grab his flashlight. He pushed open one of the iron doors, banged it into the wall, and then fished out something with his foot to hold it open.

"Wait right here, fellows; I'll get my torch. It's a good one with a handle and that big light on the front—army issue."

When he returned, I gestured toward the doorstop that I'd been staring at the last fifteen seconds. "What's that, Vernon?"

"What's what?"

"That thing you propped the door open with?"

He cocked his head, pointed at the same spot I had, closed an eye. "*That?* It's a doorstop, Joe. We call it that on account of how it *stops the door from closing.* You foolin' with ol' Vern here?"

Sal cut in. "That's no doorstop, that's a bocce ball."

"Well, it's a doorstop now. Been knocking around here forever, I put it to good use when I came back to this grand old lady a couple of years ago."

He tapped a finger to his temple, winked at me.

"It goes way back?" I asked. "Really?"

"Oh yes," he nodded. "Mr. Capone, he loved him that lawn bowling. Those whiskey runners used to play it all the time down here when they were waiting on a shipment. Now let me show you those tunnels."

We walked off across the basement, Vernon's flashlight arc cutting a dancing beam on the unevenly lit cement floor as we made for the opposite side. I took a last, curious glance at the boiler room, shaking my head in amusement at Vernon's revelation.

Al Capone. Lawn bowling.

Go figure.

The first passageway Vernon showed us was smack in the middle of the wall, just an innocuous door frame with a corridor right-angled off behind it. Vernon waved his torch into it, pointed it into the distance as we entered the old bootlegger's passage. A hundred feet in, the corridor dead-ended at a crude wooden staircase, a bricked-over doorway looming at the top of the steps. And that, as Vernon said, was that.

The other tunnel was clear at the north end of the building, its entrance cleverly hidden behind a water main access door beneath a stairwell that led to a bricked-up exit. That alone stirred my blood. Vernon had to produce a large key with unusually cut teeth to unlock the camouflaged entryway. He stuck it in the hole set in the middle of a brace of raised letters, gave it a firm twist to the left, and pulled the brass door open. Mystery was in the air as we stepped inside the cloistered chamber.

The passageway beyond was much narrower than the first one, and cut right through the foundation wall of the Lexington. This was an actual excavated tunnel, not just a converted corridor. After three minutes walking and two more foundation walls, I figured us to be a solid city block away from the Lexington. But there was nothing other than scattered bottles, rags, the occasional section of loose pipe, and a dead rat along the way.

We eventually came to a plywood slat propped against the wall and anchored by a pair of cinder blocks. I could feel a cool rush of air around its edges. Intrigued, I leaned close to Vernon, excitement undoubtedly gleaming in my eyes.

"What's all this about? What's on the other side of this opening?"

White teeth shone against darkened gums. "I figured you'd want to see this. Go ahead, push that board out of the way."

I muscled away the cinder blocks then turned the panel ninety degrees to the side, revealing a three-foot opening chiseled through the brick and mortar. Vernon handed me his flashlight, and I played the light into the cleft. A jumble of bricks lay scattered on the floor around the opening, suggesting that this tunnel, unlike the others, had been concealed in its time. Crouching down, I stepped through, just grazing the top as I did. The space was very dimly lit via a sewer grate far above. I swept the open space from side to side with the light to get a better look. A wry smile came to my face as I did.

Familiar sights from my childhood roustabouts greeted me: a latticework of iron support girders, limestone-lined walls, hoary cobwebs cluttered with dust, and a pair of narrow-gauge rail tracks, wending toward a three-quarters oval tunnel in the distance. We were in one of Chicago's underground freight tunnels, used since the 1800s to move coal, freight, and mail to the towering downtown structures above.

A dozen yards down, a shape loomed on the tracks—a hopper car—just like the ones Sal and I used to bag rides on below the city.

"Sal, do you see that?" I said, advancing toward the scaled-down coal carrier. "It's one of those old freight cars. Man, did we used to raise Cain on those things!"

"Right, Joe, only now I'm a cop, and I get paid to send kids like us to juvee for stunts like that."

I waved a hand at him. "Oh come on, killjoy, let's check it out."

He said something I couldn't hear as I crunched my way across the rubble toward the tracks, making big sweeps with the light as I advanced just to be sure we were alone.

The car was standard issue, right down to the Chicago Tunnel Company stencil on the side, but it hadn't moved in years judging from the rust and accumulated dust clinging to its iron surfaces. The hopper bin was empty of course. The tracks it stood upon just sort of began about ten feet from the wall opening, a stack of wooden ties demarcating the end of the line. It was obvious that the rail spur was either an ad hoc adjunct to the old system or just a place where the line petered out—it was already several blocks farther south than any part of the system I knew of.

I walked the tracks to the lip of the tunnel, the open room narrowing down to the typically tight clearances present on the many miles of underground trackway cut through the soft midwestern clay. Exhilarated, I aimed my beam deep into the tunnel and peered as far down the egg-shaped passage as I could. Ghost sounds from three decades past filled my ears as my eyes scoured the subterranean passage, my heart hopelessly seeking a relic, a clue—any sign at all—of Al Capone's presence in this ancient railway that ran unseen far beneath the city's spires.

But it was not to be. There wasn't anything more down there to see than there had been in Capone's room or the vaults. I cased the tracks and the subbasement for another ten minutes until finally Sal's protestations and the sense that I'd been a bit overindulgent with Vernon's time forced me to admit there was nothing more to be gleaned. It had been entertaining, but we were just chasing phantoms.

Chagrined, I gave up the quest. "Okay, guys, I'm done. We can go."

Almost inaudibly, Vernon said, "Sorry, Joe."

I think he wanted to believe, too.

One by one, we ducked into the hole and stepped back to the other side. The last thing I glimpsed before I slipped through was an overturned wheelbarrow off to one side of the opening. "Some treasure," I sighed as I stooped down, leaving my childhood memories behind me.

Vernon went as far as the elevator with us, saying he'd probably catch hell from Freel if it looked like he'd been with us for such a long time. I handed him back his flashlight, giving it a good lookover for the first time as I did, noting its sturdy construction and olive drab Bakelite shell.

"Wow, this *is* army issue—and old too. How long you have this thing, Vern?"

"Since the Great War. Something works, you stick with it."

I looked him over in a new light. "You don't say?"

"I do say," he countered. "Gentlemen, you are looking at one of the last of the Buffalo Soldiers. Fought in the Mexican Expedition with the Ninth Cav, then transferred into the Ninety-Third Infantry in '17 so I could take a whack at those Huns. Served my country with distinction in the Argonne Forest."

Gesturing at his game leg, I asked, "That where you got that hitch in your step?"

Vernon looked at me, his eyes interrogating mine. "Yeah," he said, his voice almost a whisper. "Fightin' for America. Of course, the army put us Negroes under French command—heaven forbid those white soldiers would have to actually associate with the men dying alongside them in the mud."

Neither Sal nor I spoke. We just gave him his moment, seconds passing slowly in the cool air.

"I'm sorry, fellas," he said at length. "It's an old wound, but it still burns from time to time."

I understood. I couldn't possibly feel it the way he did, but I understood, and I was pretty sure the wound he was referring to wasn't the one in his leg. I looked deep into his tearing brown eyes, wishing I'd known a few more Vernon Pryors in my life.

"Thank you, Vernon. From one vet to another, thank you."

"Army?" he asked hopefully.

"Uh-uh. Navy—flew in the Pacific."

"See much action?"

I exhaled, nodded once. "Yeah."

"Thought so."

The elevator chimed. We all shook hands again, and then Sal and I stepped on. I waved good-bye to Vernon as the door rolled shut, leaving him alone in his underground empire. As we chugged upward, I heard him shout out, "Don't forget about that house!" before breaking into a hearty cackle.

Freel was talking to some other scuzzball at the counter when we emerged from the elevator. Their backs were to us so they didn't notice us approaching. The pride of the South Side was making a loud declaration to his companion about finding "that lazy nigger Vernon after those two cops leave and kicking his black ass back to Africa."

This time, I went over the counter for him.

32

All in all, I was pretty sanguine on the ride back. We'd come up empty at the Lexington, but I'd never expected to find anything anyway. At least Sal and I had gotten some kicks out of the deal and met a stand-up guy in Vernon. Besides, the drizzle had let up while we were downstairs, bright yellow gobs of sunshine now bursting through the scattering clouds, chasing off the chilly morning and ushering in a warm fall afternoon. My knuckles were a little sore, but that was a good kind of hurt, considering.

The last thing I said to Sal as we rolled down Roosevelt and made the right at Loomis was, "It's just as well we didn't find anything. I could use some downtime anyway."

That didn't work out the way I'd planned.

It isn't every day that you come home to find Frank Sinatra in your living room. He was parked on the couch, gray fedora canted back on his head, one of my nieces seated on his lap, another eagerly awaiting her turn. My mother was sitting next to them, dictating what he should write in their autograph books. Jilly was off in the hallway with my aunt Teresa, looking at family photos.

"Hey . . . there he is!" Frank exclaimed as Sal and I walked through the door. "Now, no cutting, Joseph; you boys will just have to wait your turn for autographs."

I nodded at Jilly, bent down to kiss my mother, and then dropped onto the edge of the couch next to her. "Who's this, Ma?" I asked. "A traveling rainmaker?"

She just beamed, gripping my arm tightly. Frank leaned over toward me, put a covering hand to his mouth. "Nice of you to drop in," he jabbed. "Thought you were coming to my trailer shoot this morning. Maybe you could call once a month or something—if it's not too much trouble?"

"Whaddya talkin'? I did call."

"Maybe you shoulda called again. A girl's wondering . . ." he retorted.

"Who . . . ? Vanessa or Gianna here?"

"What?"

"Who's wondering what?"

He waved a finger at me. "No, no. Not these lovely young ladies. A big girl . . . name of Claudia."

I could see my mother's eyes. She knew something I didn't.

Leaning over, I whispered, "Oh yeah? And what might she be wondering?"

"When the hell you're going to ask her to dinner. Sorry, girls, remember, that's a bad word—we shouldn't use it."

The children giggled.

"But that's why I asked you for her number."

"That won't be necessary any longer," he countered.

Tilting my head and stealing a glance at my mother's conspiratorial smile, I intoned, "And why not?"

"Because I brought her with me—she's upstairs talking to your sister."

"*Here?* Uh, now?"

"Mmmhmmm." He jerked a thumb over his head. "Get to work, Casanova."

Rising, I could see the mirth in Frank's smile. I tried to reach behind my mother to whack him as I got up, but he just managed to duck out of the way.

Claudia was with Francesca in my sister's room. A brace of family photo books lay on the bed between them, another one open in Cesca's hands. They were speaking Italian.

"*Ciao, signorine,*" I announced as I entered the room.

"*Ciao, Giuseppe,*" thrummed Claudia.

"No school today, sis?"

Francesca made a face. "With Frank Sinatra in your house? I took the afternoon off as soon as *Mamma* called. I just came up a minute to show Claudia your navy scrapbook. I didn't think you'd mind."

I didn't mind. I liked that Claudia was interested. "I was much better looking then—the white uniform helped."

I got an eye roll from both of them for that one.

Leaning down between them, I peered down at the old leather binder my sister was holding. Photos of me aboard various navy vessels and in the cockpits of several aircraft stared back at me. So did my old flame Iliana, wearing my flight jacket and showing off her lovely smile. *God, Iliana. How did that all slip away?* I asked myself.

Before I got an answer, Cesca flipped a page and there it was: a photo of me and Pete, our arms around each other's shoulders, big-league smiles on our faces.

I could feel myself locking up, an instant sadness rising within me. Francesca caught my freeze, glanced down at the page, flopped the book shut. Claudia must have detected something, but she didn't let on.

Straightening up, I summoned a smile. "Claudia, I'm so happy to have you in our home. . . . It's a very pleasant surprise."

We made small talk about Frank's movie-trailer shoot and the typically impulsive Sinatra decision to rush on over to Taylor Street to find me afterward. Then Francesca made an excuse to sneak out of the room in order to leave us alone. I winked at her when she looked back at me on her way out.

With Sinatra afoot, I knew I had to act fast. Otherwise, he'd find us and announce where and when he'd gotten us all the best table in town, and how we must—must—go to that spot for lunch.

"Like the family?" I inquired.

"Oh yes, Joe, I like your mother. Your sister too. They both invited me to come visit here anytime. Is important to me because I'm here all alone in Chicago."

"How convenient," I replied.

"How do you mean?" she asked, her face twisting.

"That way I'll know where to find you." I showed some teeth to sell my pitch.

She smiled a decorous little smile in return but said nothing. Those Italian girls—they show you a lot from a distance, but the closer you get, the less you see.

Downstairs, Frank had broken into song with Zio Nello manning the piano. We hustled down to check it out. A dozen or so family and neighbors had gathered by this time in the living room. Sal had located Gina and had her locked tight in his arms. It appeared that Ol' Blue Eyes had gotten him out of Dutch.

I sidled up behind his ear, hissed, "Need a favor, Sal."

"Yeah?"

"I'm slipping out, can I borrow that Nash of yours?"

Without looking, he slipped his hand into his coat pocket, hauled out a set of keys, and dropped them into my palm. His eyes never wavered from Frank, his head never moved. Neither did Gina's.

If Sinatra's spell could work for Sal, I figured it could work for me. I walked back to the base of the stairs, reached out, and gently tugged on Claudia's pinkie.

She looked over at me, grinning cautiously. Frank Sinatra was doing the singing today, but I channeled Chet Baker instead. "Let's get lost," I whispered, flashing the car keys.

She mulled it over a second, looking to my sister for reassurance. Francesca nodded subtly. Claudia broke into a broad grin. "Sì . . . andiamo!"

I took her hand and we scampered down the hallway and ducked out the side door.

Frank was breezing through "High Hopes" for the children when we left, regaling them with the improbable optimism of "that little old ant."

That ant wasn't the only one with heightened expectations.

33

I had no idea what I was doing with Claudia, but I couldn't stop myself. Truth was, even three years after everything with Helen burned to a cinder in Baja, I was in no shape to expose my heart to the cruelties of *amore*, but something about Claudia drew me to her. Clearly, she was hard to reach and more than a little old-fashioned. She also lived fifteen hundred miles from Southern California and carried some kind of hidden weight inside her. I suppose that would pose a problem for someone who was easily deterred.

We ran back down Roosevelt, then banged a left at Central Station and started up Michigan. The temperature had risen to the low sixties, warm enough that we actually had the front windows down, the sounds and the smells of the city livening up the drive. Catching that first look of afternoon sun on the brilliant blue water of the lake, I recalled the sights along Chicago's grand lakefront esplanade. "Ever seen Buckingham Fountain?" I inquired.

Claudia shook her head. "Only in a postcard."

Just like that, I had a plan. Three blocks up, I turned east on Balbo. We caught a red light at Columbus, but that was a nice spot for recounting the enormous cultural significance of General Italo Balbo's arrival at the 1933 World's Fair with his magnificent squadron of flying boats. Millions of Chicagoans attended the spectacular Century of Progress exhibition on the lakefront that summer and fall, but *all* of the Italian community flocked to the lake to see the great amphibians that had crossed the Atlantic from Rome in a remarkable demonstration of Italian airmanship and daring. It was the seminal event of my youth and inspired me to become something more than a bricklayer's son, to dare to dream of being a pilot.

"He was *fascista*, you know," Claudia said bitterly, the hardships and folly of the Mussolini years resonating clearly in her voice.

I raised a hand in acknowledgment, slapped it back on the wheel. "Yes, I know he was no saint, dear, but we didn't understand that then; we were just kids happy to have a reason to be proud of our heritage. It wasn't so easy to be Italian back in those days."

"I understand. I'm glad you were proud, Joe—and I'm glad you became a pilot too. Your family is very proud of you."

"That's nice of you to say."

"*È ironico, no?*" she mused, looking out the window at the cars zipping by and the lake beyond, surging waves cresting as they neared the shore.

"*Che?*"

"That we needed Italian American soldiers and pilots like you to save us from those monsters Balbo and Mussolini in the end."

I nodded in assent, knowing that there was a list of the boys lost over there on a church wall in every Italian American community back here.

The light turned green. I gave way to a bus and then made a left on Columbus. Changing the mood, I pointed out the large street sign honoring the famous Genovese sailor/explorer. "At least there's a hero who's held up over time—nobody will ever kick ol' Christopher Columbus around."

"How could they?" Claudia replied with a laugh as we moved up the street toward one of the city's most famous landmarks.

Clarence F. Buckingham's eponymous fountain was one of those places Sal and I used to escape to on summer nights to meet girls from outside the neighborhood, frantically chewing Sen-Sen to cover the smell of garlic from our mothers' cooking. In summertime, you could forget about finding a parking spot anywhere near Grant Park, but in mid-November, it was a snap. We got one just short of Jackson then catty-cornered through the tree-lined park to the center where we beheld the massive sculptured fountain shining resplendently in the afternoon sun.

Much had changed since I'd last been in town, but the fountain was exactly as I remembered it. Even closed for the winter, the enormous Beaux-Arts masterpiece inspired reverence with its wedding-cake layers and muscular bronze sea stallions at each corner. Despite the surprising warmth of the late fall afternoon, just a few other people were traversing the vast open plaza or admiring the fountain. But the solemnity of Grant Park at that moment only served to heighten the austere majesty of Mrs. Buckingham's gift to the city in her late brother's honor.

"*È magnifico*," Claudia declared, running a hand across the smooth pink marble lip at fountain's edge.

"Mmhmm."

"But where is the water?"

I gazed out toward the cold depths of Lake Michigan a hundred yards away, last night's rain and the shifting wind kicking up the surface of the inland sea a bit.

"It's too cold now, that's why it's dry. But you should see it in the spring when they turn it back on—the lights and the water are amazing."

Funneling my hands up and outward, then letting them fall slowly, fingers spread wide, I imitated the motion of the fountain at play.

Her lovely eyes grew even larger as she conjured the image in her mind, a gleam of white shining behind crimson lips. "I hope I will be here to see it. But the winter is long—and very cold I hear."

I turned to face her, stepped closer, took her hands in mine. "Cold days are coming, my dear. Let's enjoy this sunshine while we can. It'll be dark soon."

Claudia looked up at me. "Okay, Joe. You be my guide; show me around town. I haven't been out too much since I arrived here."

"Okay, *Beatrice*," I said, offering my arm.

She smiled knowingly at my nod to literature, slipped a hand under my arm, grasping my bicep. As we set off toward the lake-front, I could feel the corners of my mouth curling in pleasant anticipation. It felt good to have her on my arm. Damn good.

We crossed Lake Shore Drive and strolled along the lakefront, quietly admiring the day, lustrous waves cascading against the seawall in splashes of turquoise. First the Chicago Yacht Club, then Monroe Harbor came and went as we worked northward, me pointing out the landmarks I knew and both of us "wowing" at the ones neither of us had seen, like the two concrete cylinders rising like giant corncobs on the north bank of the Chicago River.

Native son Nelson Algren had famously described Chicago as a "City on the Make," a few years earlier. While it had always been that, it was clear to me that now it was also becoming city in full bloom—modern construction and conveyances jostling cheek by jowl with the old in pure Chicago roughhouse style, somehow everything settling in together in the end: the beautiful, the brash, and the just plain brutal. There was an energy to it. A hunger.

At length we came to Navy Pier, a mammoth, half-mile-long quay ramming straight out from downtown toward the Michigan shore seventy-odd miles away. A servant of many masters in its life, the pier was the current home of the University of Illinois-Chicago, the so-called Harvard on the Rocks. During the war, the navy had actually docked two training aircraft carriers at the pier, teaching navy fliers how to land aboard ship in a safe, inland environment. The carriers were long gone, but the sight of their former mooring place stoked my interest to see yet another old haunt, especially one with such gorgeous views of the city skyline from the far end of its long reach into the lake.

Pointing toward the raised towers on the east end, I said, "Claudia, the city looks amazing from there. Have another mile in you?"

"Oh yes, let's go see."

We passed under the University of Illinois marquee hung high on the brick-walled entrance and "matriculated" on campus, filing past the dozens of converted classrooms housing hundreds of students at lecture. We stopped briefly to buy a candy bar and a coffee at one of the snack bars then set off for the distant east end of the pier, taking in the sights outside along the south walkway, which ran past the freighters moored on the wall. Dozens of longshoremen swarmed around a ship of the Swedish Chicago Line, its overhead cranes jockeying pallets of unknown goods to the wharf below. A whistle blast warned of the advance of a locomotive, its big diesel engine rumbling low as it nudged forward with a line of empty cars soon to be filled with foreign wares.

Eyes darting, heads moving, we observed the machinations of the metropolis at work: grunting, heaving, shouting, gesturing men doing some of the millions of daily tasks that kept the city's heart beating. Near the end of the walkway, we cut through the auditorium full of milling, chattering young scholars and slipped outside again onto the promenade fronting the open lake, whose roiling blue-green water crashed upon the breakwater beyond in great spume-capped waves.

Claudia gaped in awe as she glided toward the rail at water's edge, pirouetting twice in graceful three-sixtys, captivated by the panorama of water, wind, and sky. The smell of sea life and industry hung heavy in the air, the great lake freighters, the pier's paired Italianate towers, and the jutting silhouettes of distant skyscrapers dominating the vista, the ebbing sunshine warming our faces as we marveled at the brawny big city canvas.

"Oh, Joe, is fabulous," she cried. "*Che bella vista!*"

I saw my moment. I took it.

Grinning, grabbing, I snatched hold of her hand and spun us

around, then put my shoulder into the rail, pulled her in, and kissed her. Not long, not heavy, but with purpose.

Oversize brown eyes regarded me with surprise for a second, blinking rapidly as the sensation registered. Then she kissed me back. Brother, did she ever.

It was a wonderful moment—the first I'd had like it in years. I held her close, looking into her probing eyes, beaming, knowing. You could feel the magnetism between us, damn near hear it hum. You know when you know, and I knew we both knew. The kids walking by with the big smiles on their faces knew too.

Even the man who was following us had probably figured it out by then.

34

I'd first seen him at the fountain but didn't think much of it. I spotted him again as we crossed the Lake Shore Drive Bridge and still didn't sweat it—lots of people take that route when they're out walking. But the third time, way out on the end of the pier, especially with the way he'd ducked behind his newspaper when he saw me looking at him, that's when I knew he was a tail. He wasn't very good at it, but I figured just maybe he was a reporter or cameraman who'd followed Claudia from Frank's shoot, hoping to get a scoop on another Sinatra romance.

Claudia wasn't aware of any of it. Her back was to the man, her eyes on me, those great luscious lips mere inches away, glistening in the sunlight. Man, was I in a classic Buonomo fix now.

I wanted to keep kissing her, to see where this thing was going, to feel like a complete person again for a few short minutes. But there was the guy, glancing furtively toward us from behind his *Chicago American*.

To hell with him, I decided. Guy gets paid to watch—I figured I'd let him earn his money.

"Beautiful city," I declared. "*Una bella città, no?*"

"*Sì, Joe, bellissima.*" Her eyes danced as she spoke, the sunlight behind her lighting up her chestnut hair. Her voice was soft and low, the cooing of a dove.

I kissed her again, this time longer.

We stayed there a few minutes more, holding hands, admiring the rhythm of the water, lost in that fog that comes over you in those moments. The sun dropped down behind the clouds and the temperature dipped, but I hardly noticed.

As we gazed out on the undulating surface of the lake, Claudia made a funny face. "What is that?" she asked, pointing toward a small concrete structure rising from the lake's depths several miles away.

"A crib," I said.

"*Ma che cos'è?*"

"A pumping station. They send the drinking water into the city from out there. There's three or four of 'em—been there for ages." Skimming the horizon north to south, I stopped momentarily on the other stations. "See the others?"

"Chicago must be even more beautiful from there, no?"

"It is," I replied, recalling those long summer days spent sailing around the cribs on the park district sloops. "But they won't let you on them. The city is kinda touchy that way."

Claudia just nodded absently, still staring out over the water, the eternal allure of the sea claiming another soul. Then she made just the faintest of shivers. I took her hand, said, "Let's head back, okay?"

She nodded, kissed me quick.

"Have a dinner plan, *cara mia?*"

"Your mother's maybe?"

"Let's find out," I said, steering innocuously toward the man with the newspaper, who buried his nose in the editorials as we neared. I smirked at him as we passed, but he didn't look up.

Several steps later, I leaned in close and nonchalantly said, "Claudia dear, I think a paparazzo is following us. I've been watching him awhile."

"*Paparazzo? For me?*"

"Well, you did sing before Frank the other night. And I bet he had press coverage at the trailer shoot today, right?"

"Yes . . . lots of it."

"So somebody probably followed you to my house. Maybe they thought I was Frank when we snuck out, figured they'd get a nice scoop."

I was soft-pedaling it, but I didn't want to alarm Claudia, and I didn't really know who it was anyway.

"Wanna lose him?" I asked with a grin, making a game of it.

She smiled uncertainly, then said, "Okay, sure."

We sauntered a little farther down the pier then quickly slipped through an open doorway into the hallway. I signaled to pick up the pace. Heels clacked on the linoleum as we hotfooted past classrooms full of collegians. When I looked back, I saw our man well back in the hallway, arms pumping as he double-timed down the corridor as softly as he could manage, the echo of his footfall still betraying him.

Fate intervened at that moment. A long clang sounded in the emptiness of the chamber, signaling the end of a class period. Claudia, giggling a bit, looked up at me, knowing what came next. "Shall we run?"

"Not yet."

There was a lot of shuffling and the groan of chairs on floors as hundreds of students got up in their classrooms. We kept walking.

Backlit shapes appeared behind opaque panes. The tail picked up his pace.

"Now?" she asked.

"Wait . . ."

Doors swung open throughout the hallway. Students in dungarees and skirts began filtering out by ones, then threes. The man behind us realized what was happening. He began to run, a steely determination on his face.

"Now!" I said.

I grabbed her hand and we took off like rabbits, bobbing, weaving, giggling as the wave of humanity closed in around and behind us. We made maybe a hundred yards before the crowd slowed us to a crawl, then we had to shuffle forward for the next three minutes. I caught one glimpse of our man in the mass. After that, he was gone.

We made a quick turn at the entrance and cut back sharp to the pier's edge, where a growing throng of university kids were gathering along the rail to smoke. Claudia was laughing the whole time. I tried to smile to reassure her, but I had begun to have serious doubts that the man was a photographer. We hid in the crowd facing out until I saw the tail come barreling out the front doors, panting heavily through clenched teeth. I got my first good look at him then, and he sure as hell wasn't Alan Funt.

Nothing was funny any longer.

That did it for me. I'd been getting the feeling I was being followed practically since I hit town. And I had my fill of it.

Speaking low in Italian, I said, "Claudia, listen to me. That guy is no photographer. I'm going to draw him out and find out just what the hell he wants. I need you to stay here with these kids and keep out of sight."

Her face drew tight. "No, Joe, don't—"

I was already off, marching out into the open, heading toward the shadowy workspaces beneath the freighters where I could brace the guy out of sight now that the workday had ended. He was still near the front entrance, head spinning back and forth amid the teeming crowd. Finally, he picked me and gave chase. I quick-hoofed it toward the ships, hopped the train tracks, and ducked between two of the many rows of huge crates stacked along water's edge. Flattening up against the wood, I lay in wait, hands at the ready.

I could hear him closing in, coat rustling as he scurried over.

I readied myself to pounce.

There was a sudden scuffle of feet then, followed by a pronounced "Ooof."

Taken aback, I leaned out beyond the edge of the crates, saw a blur in motion.

It was the man—tumbling sidelong off the pier—arms flailing, a latent cry trailing behind him as he hit the lake headfirst and disappeared below an eruption of water. Behind me, I heard scampering feet, spun, caught a flash of a brown suit as it vanished in the crate stacks. I broke into fast pursuit through the maze of boxes.

The man in the water came up to the surface then, dazed, struggling, shouting for help. The shrill tweet of a police whistle rose in the air a moment later. Emerging from the crate stacks, I saw the man in brown darting into an open workbay in the pier, then spied a life preserver on the wall of the foreman's shack in front of me. The man in the water cried again for help. He didn't sound too much like a tough guy now.

I clenched my fists, slowed to a stop. "Damnit!" I shouted aloud over the dilemma. Then I grabbed the life ring off its mount, walked back to pier's edge, and flung it down at the waterlogged tail, trying my best to bounce it off his head.

People were rushing in toward the sound of the commotion, the police whistle nearing. I took a last look at the guy as he clung to his float, wondering just who the hell he was, then darted between the crates and out of sight as people began to arrive on scene.

Claudia was standing along the rail where I'd left her.

"What's going on, Joe?" she queried.

"I have no idea whatsoever," I said tersely, "but we should leave right now."

We struggled upstream against the hundreds moving the other way toward the "jumper" in the water.

Claudia's eyes were locked wide. Her connection to Carpaccio came to me suddenly—his attentions on her the other night, his disappearing into her dressing room. I still wasn't sure the tail was his guy, but Claudia's reaction told me there was more at play than I knew. And now there was another party involved as well, one motivated enough to shove a man into the lake.

"*Amore*," I said, "did you happen to recog—"

Her eyes were distant. "I . . . I have to go, Joe," she blurted out. "Now."

She broke away, hustled across the old trolley line, hailed an idling cab. I went after her, took hold of her shoulders. "Claudia . . . baby . . . don't go!"

She shook her head, struggling in my arms. "No, Joe, let me go.

I'm sorry. Don't get mixed up with me. *Mi dispiace. . . .* Let me go!" she pleaded.

I felt my fingers slacken. Claudia wrenched free and slipped into the taxi. A moment later it was off. She glanced back as the car merged into the evening traffic, a navy glove to her mouth. Then she was gone.

I just stood there in numb shock, watching her go, yammering throngs rushing past me in the other direction to see what the big deal on the pier was all about, all of us utterly confused by everything that was going down.

35

They were pulling the half-drowned man out of the water when I left. That was the last I saw of him. It was also the last I saw of Claudia that day, dashing my faint, foolish hope that she might have decided to meet me back at the car. But other than the deserted fountain, the only thing waiting for me was a three-dollar parking ticket for violating a rush-hour traffic zone. Figured.

I leaned across the roof, ran my fingers through my hair, brooding as the encroaching grayness of the evening settled in. Things were not so jake in Miss Cucciabella's world. Mine either.

I checked my watch. It was nearly six; the day had gotten away a little. Then I remembered that Florence Scala's meeting was at seven at Our Lady of Pompeii.

"Shit."

It was time to scratch gravel. I jumped in the Nash and pointed her west, putting the afternoon's disturbing developments behind me for the moment. I had plenty of other things at home that needed taking care of anyway.

~

There was hell to pay when I walked in. Fabrizio was bent that he had missed Frank's visit. Jimmy was pissed about the deal with his kid and the social club. Francesca said that before Frank left, he had done no small amount of grumbling about me ducking out on him again. And my mother wanted to know what I'd done "to offend that nice girl so badly that she didn't come back."

Fortunately, Sinatra had a plan to fix most of it. Everyone was ordered to meet at Slicker Sam's out in Melrose Park at eight for a feast. It worked on several fronts: Jimmy and I could talk there over wine, Fab could meet Frank, and I could put in some face time to keep Ol' Blue Eyes quiet. But it didn't put me—or my mother—any closer to Claudia. In any event, I said I was going to be late.

That brought on a chorus of protests from all quarters.

"Wait a minute, wait a minute, *wait* a minute," I said, holding a stop sign up against the onslaught. "I'm going to Florence Scala's meeting tonight. Surely you all want to join me to help fight for our neighborhood."

"*Our* neighborhood?" razzed Fab. "Where the hell were you the last two years while this was going down? I don't remember seeing you at any sit-ins."

Jimmy chipped in with, "Joe, we went to a lot of those meetings—what did we get? City bulldozers on our front lawns. It's over. Forget about it. Nobody beats the Machine."

Even Francesca went along silently, glum resignation on her face.

I turned toward my mother. She threw up her palms. "What can you do, Giuseppino? We've been fighting, but Daley is too strong."

"Listen," I countered, jabbing out with my finger. "Don't tell me we have to take this lying down. I'm sorry I wasn't here before, but I'm here now, and I'll do whatever I can to stop them from destroying our community."

Jimmy threw his hands up, muttering, "You don't understand, Joe."

"Maybe I don't, but there will be no defeatism in this family while I'm around. *Papà* would never have stood for it—and neither will I."

"Twenty years gone and now you're just gonna snap your fingers and fix everything? Just like that?" Fabrizio retorted sharply.

I looked at my brother, fully aware that he was referring to more than Florence Scala's campaign. "No, Fab, we can't fix anything overnight. It's gonna take hard work, maybe years of it. But if we all pull together, we just might make it."

Fabrizio looked on coldly, arms crossed. The small reflexive smile he cracked a second later threw me.

"Okay, Joe," he said, motioning back and forth between the two of us, "let's you and me go to the meeting, huh? Then we'll meet everyone else out in Melrose. *Va bene?*"

I scrutinized his face, not sure if he was playing it straight or pulling my leg. "You serious?"

His look said he was. He wasn't given much to humor anyway. "On the level, Joe. She's a gutsy lady, Florence, and she's done a lot for this neighborhood. If she's still in there swingin', I'll hear her out one more time. They've taken enough from us already."

"All right, brother. That's what I wanted to hear." I walked over to him, offered my hand. "*Grazie.*"

He squeezed my hand surprisingly hard. He was thawing; I could feel it.

Before I knew what I was doing, I had grabbed him, pulling him close to me. He stiffened up, unprepared for my act of tenderness, still struggling with his emotions. Finally I felt him relent a little, start to hug me back. Over my shoulder, I saw my mother beaming at us.

It's a start, I thought as I held him tighter than I had since he was a kid, and then tighter still.

36

The old Lady of Pompeii looked pretty much the same as Fabrizio and I approached through the park, leaves crunching beneath our feet as we crossed the darkened lawn. I'd spent a lot of time in that church growing up, and it felt good to be headed toward it, my own estrangement from the teachings notwithstanding.

I didn't recognize the priest who greeted us at the door. He smiled at my brother though and shook my hand warmly when Fab introduced us. Florence greeted us inside, said she was pleased to see us both. Fab and I went around the room briefly as I remade some old acquaintances and established some new ones.

Florence gave it to us straight from the get-go: The City, having won in court, was going to put its thumb in the collective eye of those who had tried to stand up to it. The Hull House battle was largely lost, as was the fight to protect the homes and businesses on Harrison-Halsted. Now the City was coming for the homes near the Congress Expressway to expand the medical complex around Pres-St. Luke's Hospital. Whole residential blocks were going to be gouged out if the citizens couldn't find a way to stop the Machine.

Given enough time, Daley might level the whole neighborhood and sow the furrows with salt. That was the Chicago Way, all right, but it wasn't much fun being on the wrong side of it.

The meeting broke up about eight. Fab and I hung around awhile, chatting with Florence and a small crowd of others. I was impressed with the way my brother spoke, his passionate and articulate encomium about what the neighborhood meant to him resonating deeply within me. I felt very proud of him just then, realized what a fine man he'd grown into.

Florence made us both commit to knocking on doors to rally the troops the next couple of days. It was going to be an uphill fight, but I'd been in a few of those before. Thanking her for her dedication and courage, Fabrizio and I finally dashed out about 8:15. As we parted, I invited her to dinner to meet Frank, but Florence demurred, saying she had far too much to do at home to go "cavorting about with that libertine Sinatra."

Jilly was waiting outside the church in the limo per Frank's orders. Rush hour was over, but it still took twenty-some minutes to get out to Melrose Park.

Things were already in high gear when Fab and I got to Slicker Sam's. The joint was bursting like overstuffed manicotti, waitresses struggling through the crowd, platters of baked clams and mostaccioli held aloft above the fray on sturdy, upraised arms. Bartenders were taking shouted orders behind the smoke-shrouded bar, ice clinking into glasses, Chianti corks and beer bottle tops flying through the air as girls hustled the highballs and vino to the thirsty mob. Above it all, a terrific Dick Contino solo was jumping right out of the jukebox, the old accordion maestro layin' it on but good. It was actually fairly restrained for one of Frank's affairs, but it was still the biggest Monday night they were ever going to have at Slicker Sam's.

Hours later, as the party slowly ebbed, I sat with my brother Jimmy at the end of a long table, the waiters scraping up the last of the crumbs from the cubic ton of antipasto, salad, clams, eggplant parmesan, garlic bread, grated cheese, and tiramisu the customers had scarfed down. Cigarettes burned in piles of ash in green cut-glass ashtrays around us, a forty-five selection by the guest of honor now playing in the bar, couples moving in starstruck rhythm around him as he danced with Francesca.

Jimmy looked at me, grinning in disbelief at the smoldering ruins of the *festa*. "This how it always is with him?"

I shook my head. "Not always. There are some dark times, brother. Very dark."

"And tell me about Cuba again—how you two came to be buddies? I'm still a little fuzzy on that."

I chewed on his words, wearing a happy face while I struggled with the turmoil within. He and Fab had to know the full truth about my past. Nobody else did, but they had to, especially with Carpaccio loose in the neighborhood. "It'll take some explaining. . . . There was some trouble. . . ."

His brows veed down, questioning eyes narrowing beneath them. "Yeah . . . ?"

A waiter came by, changed out the ashtrays, asked if we wanted a coffee. I shook him off.

"Tell you what, Jim, I'll bring you and Fab up to speed soon—just us though, okay?"

He nodded.

"Let's get back to last night. Did Johnny have anything to say to you about it?"

"Glad you brought it up. I think he came clean. Him and Tommy—the other kid—they're pretty close, okay? *Culo'camicia*, you know?"

"Yeah."

"Well, Tommy's uncle is in that crew. He got the kid started doing some odd jobs for them, cleaning the place up, making food runs for the guys, stuff like that."

"That's how it starts."

He waved a hand. "Don't you worry, Joe. I put an end to that. Johnny's not leavin' the house till summer—and then only if he has a job. A real job. I know exactly how much trouble those guys get into. I grew up in the neighborhood, too, you know."

I reached over, clasped his hand, looked into his eyes. "I'm glad you do. Don't *ever* let your boy get mixed up with them. They're the worst people you could ever imagine—don't be fooled by that veneer of friendliness."

He regarded me intensely a long moment. "So tell me something then, big brother."

I'd sensed it coming. "Go ahead."

"How come Johnny says he saw you go in there last night after you sent him home?"

I flicked my Zippo, bent slightly forward over the flame, drew in a drag from the fresh cig. Looking up at the ceiling, I blew a long plume of smoke out, turned back toward my brother. "He thought I could help him with something."

"Why would he think that?"

"Because there was a time I might have. A long time ago, Jimmy. And never again. Do you understand me?"

He didn't say anything, just eyed me uncertainly.

Fabrizio came over to say goodnight. He looked as happy as I'd ever seen him. An extra shot of espresso tomorrow morning was a small price to pay for the night his family had enjoyed.

As he walked out, I glanced over at my sister dancing away beneath the hanging wine bottles. Her shy smile belied the excitement I knew she felt, her dark eyes reflecting the sparkle from the red and green lights above her. Maybe she was a little dazed that she was dancing with Frank Sinatra, but her gaze seemed to be fixed on me.

She truly was a beautiful girl. But seeing her there in that fuzzy light brought another sloe-eyed beauty to mind, one I'd last seen speeding away from Navy Pier several hours earlier.

Over in the far corner of the room, two rough and tumblers were conferring, their saturnine features obscured in the dusky light. I'd been concerned about them at first until I saw Frank jawboning and backslapping with them. Over the course of the evening, I'd come to realize that, like my sister, they seemed to be watching me more than Frank. Like the events at the pier, it was just another sign that the wheels of things I didn't yet understand were now in motion. Where it was all headed, I hadn't a clue.

37

Sal was having coffee with my mother and aunt when I came down-stairs a little after seven. He launched the day's first shot before I got through the door.

"Thought you were gonna be up there all day, Sleeping Beauty."

"*Buon giorno, Zia Teresa. Buon giorno, Mamma,*" I said. Sal got the dagger eyes.

"*Vuoi café, figlio mio?*" my mother asked.

"*Sì, Mamma. C'è colazione ancora?*"

"Ohh," interjected Sal, "whaddya mean, 'breakfast'? We gotta get goin' here." He tapped his watch heavily several times for emphasis. "Frank'll be waiting."

I scrunched up one half of my face, turned in his direction. "Going? Where?"

"To take Frank to Meigs Field. Aren't you gonna see him off?"

I had hoped to spend the morning with my family. But it wouldn't take that long to drop him at the lakefront airport. Besides, I had several suits he'd paid for hanging unused in a closet up on the top floor of the hotel that I had to pick up.

I had a couple of important questions for him as well.

"Give me ten minutes to shower up—if I can beat Zio Nello to the bathroom."

"Hurry it up," Sal grunted. "I can't be late. I'm not some fly-by-night freight jockey who just drops in whenever he feels like it."

That was the second shot of the morning. That one drew blood.

Somewhere along the way, Sal had gotten ahold of Frank's limo, which put me in the back of a Lincoln Continental being driven by a twenty-year member of the Chicago Police Department. I'd been for rides in the back of police cars before but never in one with a minibar and cigar box.

Bill Miller and Jilly went ahead to the airport in another car with the bags while Frank and I grabbed a coffee in the hotel. Sal refused an offer to join us, feeling duty-bound to stay with the car. He was solid, that guy, even with the jabs.

I sat down across from Frank on a deep couch in the Ambassador's lobby, squishing down in the rich, brown leather. Frank was wearing a killer Glen plaid sportcoat, the blue top pattern matching his tie and his eyes perfectly.

Those eyes were just a touch rheumy, though, and I knew that the extended partying caught up even with him on occasion.

"Nice jacket," I offered.

"Thanks. Yours are still upstairs, unless you're just going to go on wearing that same outfit you've got there for the rest of your life."

I turned up my palms. "My mother washed the shirt and pressed the rest for me."

"Love that lady. Love your family, Joseph. Can't believe I had to track you down over there like a missing person. Like you were ashamed of them or something."

Shaking my head, I set him straight. "Nah nah, it's the other way around, Frank. I wasn't sure I could ever face them again, not after what I'd become."

"Know what that makes you?"

"Uh-uh."

"A first-class imbecile. A man has a family that good, he can tell them anything."

I slugged down some coffee, replaced the cup on its saucer with a little click. "You're all heart, Sinatra."

Frank checked his watch. "Eight o'clock. Time to make tracks. You comin' with, or stiffin' me again?"

"Comin' with. I've got a couple of questions for you on the ride over." I made a couple subtle head turns, said, "Too many ears here. Just let me get my clothes and I'll be right down."

A French-cuffed hand danced before my eyes. "Skip it. I got you the room for the whole week. I figured you might have some business here." He flashed me a conspiratorial wink. "Lord knows I did."

"Thanks, pal."

"Don't worry, it's all comped anyway."

A few brief waves and handshakes later and we were in the Lincoln. The sun was breaking bright and clear above the lake as Sal turned the car eastward down Goethe, the morning chill's hold over another very late Indian summer day slipping away.

During the drive, I told Frank about my afternoon with Claudia, and also about how abruptly she departed. Then I asked him how much he knew about her. He said he knew very little actually, but he liked her and loved her talent. He also said he got a kick out of her refusing his overtures. That one he made confidential.

I sat back in the limo, trying to get a read on her. My face must have given me away.

"You're hooked, aren't you?" Frank said.

"Like a marlin."

"Can't say I blame you. There's a lotta bait on that hook."

I nodded, grinning.

He whistled low. "Some siren she is."

Shaking my pinched fingers together, I inquired, "Speaking of said siren, what goes on with her and that *mammalucc'* Carpaccio anyhow?"

Frank swooshed a dismissive hand. "Maybe he buys her nice things, maybe he reminds her of her father. Who really knows what goes on in a broad's head, huh? But I know for a fact he hasn't gotten his fat lips around that hook yet—she told me so."

That was heartening. And probably true based on what I'd seen. But Carpaccio was a problem still.

The car came to a stop at a red light. Frank lit a smoke. I decided it was time to ask my second question, this one a little more involved. "Hey," I said, "about this Carpaccio . . ."

Frank dragged on the Camel, chin-signaled me while muttering a little "Uhh?"

"I need a little favor."

"Anything."

"We met the other night. Didn't go well."

Frank tilted his head. "How so?'

"Carpaccio wanted me to help him with something."

"Ohh, watch out, he's slippery—even Sam says so. Who do you think I was worried about the night we came in?"

"I figured, but there's nothing there."

He tapped the stations of the cross on his forehead and chest. "I know that now, thank you."

"And don't worry, I told him I didn't want any part of anything he was up to."

"So it's settled then."

"Yeah. Except . . ."

His eyebrows curved. "*Except* . . . ?"

I fumbled with my hands a little, trying to get the words right.

He whacked my arm with a quick finger flick. "What? Except what?"

"Well, Carpaccio runs that neighborhood . . . and my family lives there."

"Did he threaten them? One phone call, Joe. It's done."

I threw my hands up in protest. "Whoaaa—what kind of phone call are we talking about here?"

Frank cut me a look. "Whaddya mean, *what kind*? Three days ago I was sweating my own funeral and now you think I go around ordering hits? Jesus!"

"Mea culpa."

"Accepted. And I meant a phone call to Sam will get Carpaccio to heel."

"That I can use, thank you."

"As soon as we get to Meigs, I'll call him. Carpaccio should know better. I'll talk to Sam and that will be that."

I exhaled in relief. "I'd appreciate that. I'm a big boy; I can answer for my own sins. But my family has never been involved with that shit, none of 'em."

Sal pulled over into the turning lane, traffic zipping past us on the right side. Frank blew out some more smoke. "The rules are the rules, Joe. Families are off-limits. Especially yours." He drummed his fingers on his vest. "Especially to me."

"I really appreciate that, Frank."

He just nodded and patted my hand, his chain-link gold bracelet pressing softly on my wrist, his eyes cold blue in the smoky morning light.

The kid from Kansas had the jet opened and ready when we pulled up, Jilly muscling the bags on board when we walked into the small, clean-line terminal at the lakefront airport. Frank immediately commandeered a phone and called Giancana's house, but someone told him Sam was out. Happens.

Frank promised to call him again when he got to the desert. Then Sal and I walked out with Frank onto the ramp, past the watchful eye of a CPD sergeant and captain, no doubt special detail to see our famous friend safely off. The sergeant made a little hand wave and wink toward Sal as we went by, then pointed him out to the officer, who'd leaned over in apparent curiosity.

I gave Jilly and Bill handshakes and waved to the pilot as Frank conducted a nice chat with Sal, pressing an embossed calling card into his hand and demonstrably ordering him and Gina out to the desert at their earliest convenience. He passed on the stiff American ritual of the firm handshake and gave each of us a hug and kiss on the cheek. His grip was tight as I thumped his back.

~

Sal and I climbed the stairs to the observation deck above the flight line and watched the Learjet crank up and roll off toward the far end of the short runway. While we hung over the rail, I motioned to the two police officers on the ramp. "You got noticed down there, pal."

"Don't I know it. I took the detective's exam again last month—third time. Think this won't help me when the results come out?"

"What? It's not based purely on the score here in Chicago?" I quipped.

Sal just rolled his eyes at me then looked downfield as the Lear spooled 'em up for takeoff. I had some apprehension about the length of the surface since the little jet seemed long on vroom and short on brake, but they just flashed by at midfield, nose raked, gear folding into the belly as the shriek of the turbine engines whistled through our ears. The flash became a blur and then a speck.

I turned toward my old running mate, bumped his shoulder, gave him a grin. "Pretty good show, huh?"

He didn't answer, just stared up into the sky at the dissipating trail of black smoke streaking up and westward, the look on his face that of a kid who'd just discovered that every impossible, hopeless thing he'd ever wished for could be his.

IV

38

Sal and I walked back toward the Lincoln together. He was doing an ants-in the pants routine about having to drop the limo off and be somewhere else, but I wanted to walk around a bit—I had a lot of Chicago to reintroduce myself to and I wasn't far from downtown. As a kid, I'd made sojourns around town that lasted from sunup to sundown, reveling in coming of age in such a wide-open playground, drawn by the lure of the sharpies, big shots, crash-outs, flimflammers, impresarios, street-corner emperors, and out-and-out bastards, all of whom flowed along on that relentless hustler's tide that coursed through the city like the river that split her.

I sent Sal off, telling him I'd catch an el train back home from the Loop. He impugned my intelligence then headed for the car. I wrist-flicked the Zippo and toasted a Lucky as I began my stroll, a wry anticipatory grin on my lips as I wondered how long it would be until I caught that first whiff of the eternal mystery and vice of the Midway and the boulevards.

About ninety seconds as it turned out.

The Lincoln was still easing around the corner of the parking lot when the window of an idling Imperial slid down next to me. A man in the driver's seat looked up from behind black sunglasses and removed a hand-rolled cigarette from his mouth. "Need a lift anywhere, friend?"

I kept walking. "No thanks, Mac, my mother told me not to take rides with strangers."

I took three more steps then stopped flat while my brain caught up with what I'd just seen. The Imperial coasted quietly alongside a second later.

I turned and looked inside. The man had a dark face with strong features and piercing black eyes that stared at me above the frame of his glasses. He wore a fine maroon fedora on his head, but underneath he had thick dark hair—lots of it. One of his hands rested casually on top of the steering wheel, the numerous silver rings on his fingers studded with jade and turquoise. They were rather striking, as was his face, which I made for American Indian, but neither garnered as much of my attention as his dark brown suitcoat and the jet-black pistol at his side.

"Why don't you get inside?" he said.

39

"Maybe you've got the wrong party," I offered, stalling.

He smiled at my moxie. "Please get in, Mr. Buonomo. The gentleman I represent is quite interested in meeting you."

I gestured toward his weapon. "Alive or dead?"

"He definitely wants you alive. It's a matter of some urgency."

"Like the way you urgently chucked that fella into the lake yesterday?"

His lips formed a flat line. "I have no idea what you're talking about."

I shrugged. "Sure you don't. Well, what's with the gun then? All you can do with that thing is shoot me, and then—say what's your name?"

"Ronnie."

"*Ronnie?*" I asked, more than a little incredulous.

He sighed. "We're not all named Crazy Horse, you know."

"Sorry."

"If you only knew how often I get that."

I nodded. "I didn't mean to offend. Okay . . . listen, Ronnie. . . . So I run away and you drill me . . . now what have you got?"

"Seven more shots. How about you?"

I grinned at his retort despite my circumstances, placed my hand on the back door's chrome handle, pushed in the button.

"Say, Ronnie . . ."

"Yes, Mr. Buonomo?"

"Joe."

"Joe then."

"Tell you what, you put that piece away and I'll get in. But before I do . . . you tell me just exactly who I'm going to meet, and why."

Dark lips pursed in the side mirror as he debated the wisdom of my request. He took a chance, sliding his gun into his shoulder holster. Then he leaned out and said, "You're going to meet his eminence McBride, Grand Chief of the Fraternal Order of the Potawatomi."

I stared straight ahead, utterly nonplussed. After some time I managed, "An Irish Indian, huh? Screw you too, bub."

"It's on the level. He is one heavy fellow. Come along and see, won't you?" He leaned farther out, goosenecked his head back and forth, then, whispering for no apparent reason, said, "He can make you stupid rich—beyond your wildest imagination."

That again. To think I'd spent my whole life jocking planes across the globe hustling sawbucks when every guy I'd left behind in Chicago was just dying to fill my arms with stacks of millions—fresh pressed, razor cut, and banded with ermine.

But I found Ronnie rather enigmatic and his promise compelling, if more than a little absurd. I'd gone out looking for intrigue and gotten a box of it Special Delivery—I couldn't really walk away from it now. Truth was, I'd probably have gone almost anywhere with him at that point, even Cleveland.

I threw my hands up, climbed into the backseat, and pulled the door shut. "Hell's bells, why not? Let's go see the chief."

The drive was short, just over to where Michigan Avenue meets the Chicago River. The water was sparkling blue in the morning light as we drove across the bridge. It occurred to me belatedly that I might be bobbing in that water later if things didn't go over so well with the Grand Pooh-Bah.

Ronnie pulled over just north of the river, one building beyond that old crank McCormick's gothic eyesore. I rolled my window down and stuck my head out, squinting from the glare cutting through the slits in the wall of high-rises.

"This the place?"

He nodded. "This is it."

"You coming?" I asked. "I think I like you, Ronnie. Besides, I may need that piece of yours if the chief doesn't take a shine to me."

He shook me off coolly, but he appeared to be trying to repress a grin as he did it.

I got out, balanced a hand on the car, and craned my neck up, scanning the amazing details of the sand-colored skyscraper as my eyes worked upward. Arabesque reliefs, carved warriors, minarets, and all manner of other embellishments stood out on a stepped-back ziggurat culminating in a magnificent gold dome high above me, glittering like a sultan's cache in the bright morning sky.

The old gal still packed the wow thirty-five years on. I remembered it being a big deal when they opened the building up in the late '20s. The papers reported it to be some kind of opulent—rich carpeting, an amazing swimming pool, a bowling alley, and even a shooting range. But it wasn't the sort of place working-class Italian kids ever entered—not the Medinah Athletic Club, no sir.

40

The pride of the Medinahs went up in 1929 to effusive praise and obsequious press, mere months before the stock market took the express car down to the subbasement, carrying a good part of the club's wealth—and membership—with it. A building conceived to flaunt the position and power of its esoteric overlords had, in very short order, become an albatross around their necks. If memory served me correctly, it had been shuttered and sold off by the mid-1930s.

Easy come, easy go.

The ornate entrance and its gilded metal doors still looked imposing, but one of them opened easily enough when I pulled on its handle, as did the revolving door in the marble-clad entrance beyond.

The lobby was deserted. No doormen, no receptionist, no passersby. Nothing. I puzzled over that a moment, then, recalling Ronnie's directions, I moved on across the floor up to the second-floor landing.

The reception may have disappointed, but the building did

not. It began with an elegant curving staircase of gray marble that wended upward beneath colossal Corinthian pillars, then gave way to a carpeted landing with a bank of burnished brass elevators watched over by carved falcons on alabaster perches. It was an impressive entrance, but the exotica really hit high gear in the sitting room beyond.

Stone reliefs of Abyssinian lions met me as I entered and stood before a beautiful Moorish fountain atop yet another plushly carpeted staircase, a stream of water gurgling down blue Spanish tiles into a stone catchbasin below. Medieval images of saints and kings in prayer graced alcoves and ceiling panels, wrought-iron chandeliers hanging down above them. I stood gaping as I took it all in: the marble benches inlaid with heraldry symbols, the detailed figures sculpted into the pilasters, the gilt crosses and crowns on the walls, the metalwork, the columns, the mahogany beams. The full weight of the power and wealth the Medinahs once possessed hit me then. Their former home commanded respect. Lots of it.

I'd waited about two minutes when an elevator chimed. A little man in a doleful gray suit stepped out, looked over at me, and quietly said, "This way please, Mr. Buonomo."

I walked over and peered into the elevator. The jockey-size guy was alone. Stepping in, I took a place behind him and waited for the doors to close.

"Quite the place the old Medinahs have here," I ventured.

"Had, sir. Had," he corrected me without looking back. "Their profligate ways were their undoing. The FOP is now the rightful steward of this property."

"The 'fop'?"

"The Fraternal Order of the Potawatomi," he answered with a measure of pride.

"So you guys own this whole building?" I asked, as the car started its rise, trying to reconcile their Little League antics with the kind of money and power required to leverage such a property in the heart of Chicago's business district.

"Not exactly," he said sadly.

His response was still hanging in the air when the elevator came to a stop. The doors opened onto a hallway. We crossed it, turned down a narrow cleft, and entered a second elevator, this one much smaller than the first. As the door closed, the valet inserted a small key into the brass panel and pushed the only button, unsurprisingly marked *PH*. Intrigue built as we soared upward into rare air seldom breathed by the city's hardscrabble workforce. The door opened, and the little guy gestured silently with his hand. I stepped out of the elevator and into a dream world.

The domain beneath me was spectacular, its rose-colored walls lined with fabulous oil paintings and soaring walnut bookshelves, its vast marble floor bedecked with acres of rich Persian rugs. At the far end of that run, flames danced inside a massive stone hearth, the crackle of the logs clearly audible from the staircase. In between, the large central hall was packed chockablock with statues, candelabras, suits of armor, birdcages, Indian headdresses, spears, daybeds, a grizzly bear, glass display cases filled with ephemera, and hundreds of other items large and small. Far above us, a stuffed condor, poised forever in full flight, completed the inventory. I felt like I'd stumbled into the central holding warehouse of the 1893 Columbian Exposition.

Below me, in the center of that trove of antiquities, a man in a purple smoking jacket stared up at me. "Welcome to the exalted realm of the sacred Fraternal Order of the Potawatomi," he said.

I guess I stood staring just a little too long, taking in the ossifying splendor of the chamber, the unusual-looking man in the middle of it, and the word jumble of a name he'd just thrown at me. "Come, come, lad," his voice boomed out then. "Let's have a look at you. And a drink then, too. Come on down, won't ya?"

Nodding, I grabbed the wide mahogany banister and sauntered down the carpeted stairs, daydreaming like a kid in a toy store as I went. Scanning the room as I walked, I made my way toward the curator in the velvet robe. We met in the center of the room, above the inlaid image of a compass rose. He took East; I got West.

The man drew a bead on my eyes, held out a hand. "Jack McBride," he said as we shook.

Jack McBride was no ordinary cat. Tall with a stocky build, he would have commanded great respect himself once, but gravity and time had done their mischief. He was on the handsome side still, with solid Gaelic features and a wild mane of tousled white hair that was rather thick given his age, which was absolutely Methuselian. His right eye was a startlingly compelling aquamarine; the left was hidden behind a black silk patch. Both were set off against a pale Irish complexion that apparently saw little sunlight despite the loftiness of his quarters. No one had the panache to pull off a purple smoking jacket, but he'd managed the silk ascot rather well. The ram's head walking stick in his left hand, upon which tilted his considerable mass, was well over the top but a sartorial home run nevertheless.

So leaned the great Chief McBride before me: imperfect, raffishly dignified, and decidedly not Indian.

"Whiskey?" he inquired.

I noted the time on a huge grandfather clock clicking rhythmically nearby. "Perhaps a tad early for me."

"Horsefeathers."

McBride began calling out for the man who'd brought me up on the elevator.

The little fellow in the threadbare suit came hustling on the third call. "Yes, Chief?"

"Fix us a couple of drinks, man. Whiskey for me and whatever Mr. Buonomo is having."

"Coffee . . . splash of Jameson's."

The chief eyed me suspiciously. "Trying to suck up to the old Irishman, are ya?"

There were hints of a brogue in his speech, but I suspected his lineage was quite local. "You sound a lot more like a Chicagoan to me."

He snorted. "True enough—but with pure Irish blood." He clapped me on the shoulder and gave me an approving grin. "All right then. Let's have a sit and get on with the particulars."

We dropped into a pair of outrageously high-backed leather chairs. McBride smiled at me, said, "Now then, would you like to hear a story, Mr. Buonomo? A fantastic story dating to the eleventh century that strains credulity but is nevertheless true?"

I smiled back. "No."

"How's that?" he blurted out, his eye dilating.

"Let's talk about the money. Looks like you've got a little to throw around."

"Less than you think, I'm afraid."

The little man arrived with a tray holding a tall tumbler of whiskey and soda for McBride and a black coffee mug with an enameled coat of arms for me. He placed them on the table between us, nodded subserviently, and then backed away. I picked up the drink and sipped, savoring the guilty pleasure of the whiskey so early in the morning.

"How's your drink?" McBride asked.

I raised the glass. "That's good coffee, Chief. Mind if I smoke?"

"Not at all."

"Thanks," I said, pulling one out. "You gonna tell me about the money now?"

He shook his head. "I don't think so."

"Okay. How 'bout you tell me how you came to be the leader of the Potawatomi tribe? Last time I checked, there weren't any teepees in County Cork."

"County Galway. And there were never any Indians in the Order, no real ones anyway. That wouldn't have passed muster in the old days."

"You've got a real one now, don't you? His gun looks plenty real too."

"Well, times change, you know. Ronnie's grandfather and I went way back, and his great-grandfather was one of the original signatories on the land purchases of the Order. Now, are you going to listen to me or what?"

I looked up at the condor, sighed. "Fine. To the Magna Carta if you must."

McBride sat up, took a breath. "What would you say if I told you that you were brought here today to help the Order recover a treasure dating back to the time of the Crusades?"

"I'd say you've been watching too many Bogart movies."

A cold eye met mine. "Christ, Buonomo, would you work with me a little here?"

I relented, held up my hands. "All right, all right. But I'd like to get home to see my family today, so would you please tell me just what the devil I'm doing here?"

McBride quaffed down some of the glory of Ireland and cleared his throat. "Are you familiar with the story of the Knights Templar?"

"The basics."

He gave me the CliffsNotes just to be sure. The twelfth-century rise of the mythic papal army, their epic battles in the Holy Lands, their betrayal and persecution by King Philip of France, their reemergence alongside the Knights of St. John on the Island of Malta, and their five-hundred-year stint as sea raiders on the shipping lanes of the Mediterranean, a run that ended only when Napoleon evicted them from the island in 1799, scattering the last remnants of the mythic order on the four winds, where, McBride averred, they remained to this day.

I stubbed out my cigarette nub in what looked to be a solid gold ashtray. "Excuse me," I interrupted, "but just what does any of this have to do with an Indian tribe on the banks of the Chicago River?"

He held up a hand. "I'm getting to that. Now, can you imagine, Joe, what sort of a fortune one might build from half a millennium of plundering the high seas?"

"Quite substantial, I imagine."

"Gasp inducing."

"But if the Order disintegrated . . ."

"It didn't," he corrected, "it exists still—in many quarters. The Freemasons, the Rosicrucians, the Illuminati, the Medinahs who built this palace, the Potawatomi—we have different agendas, but we all flow from the same holy wellspring."

"What about the Elks?"

"Come now," he chided with a shake before resuming his aggrandizing. "And if our treasure and our power were ever reunited . . ."

His eye wandered off to distant places then, trumpet flourishes undoubtedly sounding inside his head. "Nations would kneel before us!"

I knew what was coming next. I had been in the presence of no small number of madmen over the years and knew one by his throbbing temples when I saw him. A meeting with a garden-variety sociopath like Carpaccio seemed positively ducky in comparison at that moment.

"And all you need from me is . . . ?"

"That which will unite us all again in one Holy Army."

I looked askance at him, offered, "The head of St. John the Baptist?"

The ancient Hibernian's head swiveled back and forth several times. Then he leaned forward, pushing off with the ram's head cane until we were nearly face-to-face, his rumpled hair a billowing mass of clouds, that crystalline eye sparkling like a gemstone as he quietly whispered, "The Merchandise Mart."

I half choked on my Irish coffee. When I'd finally managed to gather myself, I cocked my head to the side and asked, "Did you just say the *Merchandise Mart*?"

"You bet your ass I did. The largest building in the world—four million square feet of capitalism—the centralized hub of wholesale trade in Chicago. Right down the street from us, and all of it mine."

"Thought so. You're completely crazy, aren't you, Jack?"

"I am a driven man, that's for certain. And I aim to have what was once mine."

My jaw opened, but I couldn't get any words to come out.

"That's right, '*once mine*,'" he said definitively. "Stolen from me by a onetime partner who became a full-fledged criminal overlord."

"Oh my," I managed.

"One of your kinsmen, Buonomo. Born of New York but made famous in this very metropolis of Chicago."

It began racing toward me then, like a well-aimed bullet.

"And this is where you come in. . . ."

"Oh no," I said, foreseeing the response.

"Oh yes," he smiled. "Alphonse Capone."

All around me I could feel the air getting heavy. There he was again: the legendary gangster. A man I'd never met—dead almost twenty years—yet someone to whom I was beginning to feel inextricably linked. And I knew then that somehow, somewhere, our paths were going to intersect.

It was not a particularly good feeling.

41

Despite knowing better, I went ahead and asked the question. "The holy descendants of the Kingdom of Christ in league with the crown prince of bathtub booze? You gotta be kiddin' me."

"Afraid not."

McBride went on to elaborate on his earlier declaration that the Fraternal Order of the Potawatomi was a modern face of the Knights Templar. After their exile from Malta, many members had made their way to the new world with a substantial amount of the vast treasure, gradually breaking off into different sects scattered throughout the Americas. The founders of the Potawatomi had pooled their considerable resources into a Chicago land-holding company in the 1830s, buying up large tracts of the then-burgeoning city from the Indians along the banks of the river, making a killing in the process but losing sight of the original aims of the Order amid the rush of wealth, privilege, and manor.

"So everybody still got rich—uh—richer. What's the problem?" I asked.

He gave me a weary look. "You know what followed. Arrogance, greed, hubris. Foolish petty quarrels, a hundred destructive lawsuits, a slow siphoning away of the Order's wealth in bad land deals and damage settlements, member pitted against member, family against family, squandering all we had built. After the Crash in '29 we were left teetering on the brink of insolvency."

"And that leads to Capone how?"

"He offered us a way out."

"Come again?"

"We went into business with him. It began easily enough when he was still fronting for Johnny Torrio. You know this has always been a swindler's town. From the first commandant of Fort Dearborn to Hinky Dink Kenna and Bathhouse John Coughlin to that clown Mayor Thompson and every hustler and whore in between. Everyone has always been on the take here—*everyone*."

I swigged some bootleg coffee, gestured for him to continue.

"Business with Capone was quite lucrative for a time—and we had nothing whatsoever to do with Mr. Capone's turf wars or gunplay. We only helped facilitate his transactions when the financial institutions—"

"Oh," I interjected, "you laundered his money."

"Yes. Basically."

"Sooo . . . the Merchandise Mart then?"

"Our last great property. Capone stole it, the son of a bitch."

"How do you steal an entire building?"

"Just how you think. By illegally acquiring title to the land beneath it."

Like Carpaccio before him, McBride now went into an elaborate story whose provenance belonged to the fowl and bovine orders, explaining how Capone and none other than Marshall Field III, scion of the department store founder and onetime member of the Potawatomi, had conspired to steal the deed to the entire city block the Merchandise Mart was built upon. There were many purported twists and turns and much palace intrigue, but when all was said and done, Field was the de facto owner of lot and building, and Capone, the title holder, the deed locked inside one of his many vaults.

"And after Capone melted down, how could you ever know what became of it?" I asked.

"I wouldn't have, but Eddie O'Hare tried to peddle it back to me when he was trying to clear town back in '39. Said he had it stashed with some other things that he'd stolen from Capone."

"And . . . ?"

"And the Syndicate blew his brains out on Ogden Avenue."

"All right, with O'Hare and Capone out of the way, couldn't you go to the County Records office and prove you guys owned the land?"

"We tried. Got laughed out of there every time. After the swindle, Field had one of his cronies on the inside at the clerk's office record it as a sale to him—claimed it had been his family's all along. A classic Chicago scam."

I couldn't help smiling. "That's funny, you complaining about a scam."

He glowered at me silently.

"And you couldn't fight that in court?" I queried.

Jack's eye doubled. "In *this* town? Against the word of the Field family? Come on, Buonomo, you know the score."

I nodded back at him as the dead-end scenarios played out in my mind. "Had you cinched up tight, didn't they?"

McBride covered his face with his hands, sighed deeply. "A title worth a gazillion bucks—the foundation of a restored Order of the Potawatomi—locked up somewhere in a hidden safe in a basement God knows where."

A silence fell over the room. We stared at each other across the coffee table. McBride sighed again.

"How's your coffee?" he finally asked out of courtesy.

"Shit tastes like whiskey."

He showed some teeth. We both chuckled. "By God, I like you, Buonomo," he declared. "I knew I would."

"I like you, too, McBride. I'll be sure and send you a valentine."

"Ohh," he countered, "not in this town. That's bad luck you know."

We both laughed some more. I was surprised to realize I was falling for the old bullshitter. He was totally nuts but quite charming.

But I still didn't see his connection. "So, Jack," I asked, "what can I, Joe Buonomo, *freight pilot*, do for you? I'm not in real estate, I don't have any political connections, and I'm sure as hell no lawyer."

McBride grinned broadly. "Don't kid a kidder, Joe. You know, and have known, certain people in your lifetime—namely Frank Sinatra, Sam Giancana, and the son of the man who gave Capone to the feds, one Edward 'Butch' O'Hare."

His knowledge of that surprised me, but all I gave him was, "And?"

"I was curious about you after I saw Sunday's paper. But when Huser's byline on Monday morning referred to you as 'Sinatra's mysterious aide-de-camp,' I became *very* curious. So I tapped some of my contacts, and did I ever get some interesting reports on your activities after the war. I also learned all about your air freight business, and its acute need for capital enhancement these days. Apparently, you owe a substantial amount of money to some rather unsavory fellows."

I nodded in acknowledgment. His sources were good—and high up. "First off, Huser's an idiot. I'm not anybody's aide-de-camp. Nor am I a batman, a valet, a manservant, or anything else other than a freight pilot. But I am Frank Sinatra's friend, and friends help each other out from time to time. You got that?"

McBride looked at me blankly. "Fine. Huser's an idiot—the whole town knows that. But you are close to Sinatra, were seen talking to Giancana the other night, and spent several weeks traveling with the late great O'Hare Jr. during the war."

"Let's say you're right about those things. What's that add up to for you? Because it's dick nothing for me."

McBride got a little piqued. "Now look, this isn't some pitch for a soda jerk's stipend we're talking about. There's an enormous amount of money at stake here—twenty-five percent of which would make you very, very wealthy—so much so that I doubt rather highly that you'd ever climb into another grease-caked flying boxcar again."

I drank the last of my coffee and whiskey, scoffed out loud. "This ain't my first air derby, McBride. Your land claim is malarkey—compared to yours, Captain Streeter's was etched into the city's bylaws. And what makes you think I'd want to go around town digging through rose gardens looking for Al Capone's blood money anyway?"

McBride broke out laughing. "Oh, come now, stop being so cagey. You aren't going to tell me Carpaccio sent you to the Lexington Hotel yesterday for high tea, are you now? That's right, I know you met with him, and I know you scoped out those empty tunnels too. I've got reach, bucko."

I had to smile at him, tongue against my teeth. The old bird had made me but good. Either Ronnie was a much better tail than I'd given him credit for or someone at the hotel had tipped him off, but either way the chief had shown a significant acumen for discovery.

"Okay, McBride, cards on the table."

"Now you're talkin', Buonomo," he said, whisking his hands together rapidly.

"I am not working for that miscreant Carpaccio, okay? But I did take a look at the Lex on a whim. There's nothing in that old rattrap."

The glee in the old man's face was irrepressible, the iridescence in his eye positively electric in the morning light. "Of course not! But that's the first place everyone looks."

"And also my last."

"Oh, Mulligan stew! I know a freebooter when I see one. You aren't giving up that easily."

"Well, I have no idea whatsoever where I'd look next."

The ram's head cane cracked the marble. "But I do."

I threw my hands up. "But you must've scoured all these sites time and again over the years. What do I have that you and your men don't?"

McBride hefted the cane, pointed the horns right at me. "A crusader's heart, a Chicagoan's brass, and personal contact with Butch O'Hare within the confines of this very city."

"Look, Jack, I don't know . . . Maybe there's something to it, but I don't want to get mixed up with Carpaccio or any other sewer dwellers. I just want to see my family for a few days before I leave town. That's it. Just this once I'd like to be one of the good guys again."

McBride chortled derisively. "Not in this town, you won't. There are no good guys here—only the corrupt and the less so. This is the City of Chicago—the hustler's Valhalla—and we make no small plans here. Here we work, we brawl, we scheme, we grift, we rip things free with our bare hands, day after savage day. You want to laze about on the porch in the afternoon sun with a martini in your hand? Try Naperville. You want to elbow and claw your way to enough gold to make Solomon weep? Cast your lot with me— here—in the City of Big Shoulders."

While I was grappling with that Barnumesque pitch, McBride reared back and heaved another from deep left field. Lunging forward out of his chair, he latched onto my wrist and pulled himself toward me until we were face-to-face again, the booze on his breath as bracing as his words.

"Joe," he said low, "what might Florence Scala do with a million dollars? Is it blood money then if it saves your neighborhood? Your church? Your family home? You can do all that and more if you find that deed."

He was good, McBride. Really good. His smug grin said it all. He had me, and we both knew it. As the words sank in, I gazed deeply into that crystal ball of an eye, silently noting the glittering flecks of gold floating in the blue-green iris. Grasping his fingers, I pried his hand free, took it firmly in my own, and pumped it fervidly. "McBride," I said, "you've got yourself a quest knight."

42

There was, of course, zero chance for success. For starters, McBride's hoping that Butch had ever told me anything useful was as completely insane as his desire to keep the Order alive. And everything that Carpaccio, Vernon, or McBride had told me cemented in my mind the infinitesimal chance that anything of whatever spoils there had ever been could have survived hidden for thirty-plus years with every Mafioso in town looking for them. But when he mentioned Florence Scala and my neighborhood, he hooked me up to the gills. Treasure hunts for mobsters were bunk, but home and community were other things altogether. Those were worth fighting for, worth bleeding for, no matter how lost the cause. And winning a place back in my family's heart rated everything I had left to mortgage. Everything.

Convinced of my earnestness, the old Celt produced a map of the city circa 1930 and proceeded to point out dozens of circled places on it known to have been speakeasies, safe houses, haunts, or hit spots of Capone and his lieutenants. Some of them I remembered from my youth. Most I had never seen.

The Lexington Hotel was there, of course, along with the Metropole, the Hawthorne, the Alton, and the Drake. The baker's dozen of speakeasies ran from the lakefront to Cicero and included Kelly's, the Edgewater, and the Green Door, among others. The rest of the list consisted of a smattering of no-name pool halls, clip joints, cathouses, bungalows, and three Extra Edition headliners that stood out like a ball bat at a baptism: the flower shop on State where Dion O'Bannion caught a six-pack in the boutonniere, the Clark Street garage where seven men were famously shot to hell and gone on St. Valentine's Day, and the bullet-scarred facade of old Holy Name Cathedral, where the boys literally blasted St. Paul's epistle off the wall the day they took down "Hymie" Weiss.

It was all there: the whole crimson, caterwauling history of Prohibition Chicago right at my fingertips—all her sins and secrets enticingly near, yet decades out of reach. As usual, the Italians and the Irish were fighting for the same prize, but for once, we just might have been on the same side.

43

As properly briefed as I could be for such an endeavor, I thanked Jack for the whiskey and told him I'd get started right away. He wanted to send Ronnie with me, but I told him I'd be going it alone. He raised quite a stink, but I insisted. Taking the map and his phone number, I offered McBride my hand and promised to be in touch. Then the jockey and I rode the elevator back down from the sky to the more concrete realms below. It really had been one hell of a morning.

I began to walk down Michigan, still trying to grasp exactly what had just transpired up in the ether. The shrill sound of a car horn jarred me as I crossed over by the Wrigley Building and I realized, belatedly, that I'd walked against the light. I turned at the curb, glanced back at the Medinah building and the brooding cluster of Sumerian warriors on the parapets. Once again, at the staircase that led to lower Michigan, I stopped and gazed back at the enigmatic figures. They were only limestone carvings, but at that moment they seemed very much alive, sculpted eyes marking my steps, immutable lips letting slip indecipherable whispers that swirled around me in the brisk air as I took the metal stairs into the under-city below.

Down on the substreet, I flagged a taxi and took a tour of the city as a precaution against another tail. Fifteen minutes later, I jumped out on North Avenue, slipped down Dearborn, and zigzagged through the Gold Coast to the Ambassador East.

I went up to my room, kicked my shoes off, lit a smoke, and lay down in bed, reflecting on the escalating mess I was making of my life.

I stayed in bed a long time. The radiator cycled on and off and the room darkened as cloud cover set in over the city. Newsreel footage of Al Capone flashed before my eyes: the smiling press conferences, the brazen admissions, the plain-sight audacity with which he throttled a major American city.

New currents ran into my stream of consciousness. The O'Hare conundrum, its puzzling connection between a war hero's father and a criminal overlord defying any reasonable explication, the cryptic *IV MI C* code daring me to crack it, taunting me when I failed. Images of American Indians emerged next, followed by conjurings of riotous frontier days I'd read about in school, then by myriad other fragments of this run-on weekend, all of it jumbling together like a Sunday crowd on Maxwell Street.

Singers, mobsters, trapdoors, mysterious codes; a long-ago dustup in a tavern; a new beginning with my family; the raucous confines of Wrigley Field and the quiet alleys of Taylor Street; the black depths of the ruined Lexington and the shimmering heights of the Medina's tower of Babel; O'Hare and Capone, Sinatra and Giancana, McBride and Carpaccio. None of it fit together much as I lay there, but all of it was so very Chicago.

The late nights and the early whiskey caught up with me. Claudia's face came to me as I drifted off. I only snoozed a few minutes, but all my dreams were of her.

When I awoke, I decided it was time to start looking for connections. I started by picking up the phone and dialing Claudia's number. The landlady picked up and said she was out, but she took a message for me. After that, I changed into the dungarees and flannel shirt I'd worn over on the plane, gave my razor the day off, and then jumped the "L" back to Taylor Street.

*　　　*　　　*

Sal was out, but I caught my mother at home heating some of Sunday's leftovers for lunch. Properly sated and repeatedly kissed, I set out. Grabbing the clipboard and the latest petition that Florence had given me at the previous night's meeting, I told my mother that I was going to knock on neighborhood doors and renew some old acquaintances. That part was absolutely true.

What I didn't tell her was that I was also going to be visiting some other locations outside the neighborhood, places on a map given to me by a mad Irishman.

44

I worked the neighborhood for a couple of hours, enjoying some wonderful reminiscences with retired shopkeepers, laborers, and housewives. Many of the doors closer to Harrison were opened by Hispanics, a few by Negroes. Every resident, whether they believed we had a prayer of succeeding or not, expressed their support. Some of the faces on Taylor Street had changed since my time. The soul of the neighborhood had not.

By midafternoon I had worked my way back home and dropped the clipboard off. Then I poached a bicycle from the basement, pedaled south on Damen, and started crossing places off a map.

It didn't take me long to realize how silly it all was. No one was going to let some unshaven stranger on a bicycle into their home, so I concentrated on the businesses instead. But almost all the places I visited had long since changed hands. Of the few that hadn't, only one had anyone present who had worked there during the Capone era. The septuagenarian bartender with whom I shared a beer didn't tell me a damn thing that could help me, but I enjoyed watching his eyes light up as he recounted dubious anecdotes from the halcyon days. That was the extent of my success.

By the time I left his tavern, the streets were getting dark. I headed home, pedaling slowly in the gloom despite the cold wind, reveling in childhood memories of trekking across the cityscape on whatever shit-box bikes we'd thrown together that week. At one point, I thought an old Cadillac was following me. Just to be safe, I cut down an alley to lose them, but I figured I was only seeing things anyway.

I got home around six and flopped on the couch. My mother and aunt were busy in the kitchen, so I kicked my shoes off and relaxed, moving more pieces around in my mind, trying to make some sense out of Carpaccio's and McBride's wild dreams. Nothing really fell together and I chuckled a bit at the inanity of it all.

"Whaddayou laughing about over there?" a familiar voice inquired.

It was Zio Nello. He'd come quietly down the stairs in his slippers. I gestured for him to sit next to me, patting him on the thigh when he sat down. "*Ciao, zio*," I said, taking the hand he offered me, holding it in mine.

We looked at each other awhile, smiling gently.

"Where you been alla these years, Giuseppino?" he asked me, "Your *mamma*, she missed you *molto* you know."

The question was rhetorical. "*Mi dispiace*," I replied.

A long silence passed, the ticking of the wall clock the only sound, our merged pulses and the rise and fall of our chests the only motion in the room.

My father's brother looked over at me. "You gon' stay awhile this time, *ceracatore*?" he said, using an Italian word for "wanderer. "

"*Sì.*"

He leaned over, kissed me on the forehead, squeezed my hand. We sat some more, still not talking. Just sitting, holding hands, enjoying our moment. Me, Zio Nello, and the ticking clock. It was nice.

Sal dropped in after dinner. We made some patter in the living room with the family, then I steered him outside with my eyes. I flamed a smoke on the porch and hot-boxed one for him even though I still had my lighter in my hand. It just seemed like the thing to do, a nod toward long-ago days.

We went for a turn around the block as I detailed the McBride encounter for him, his *Are you kidding me*s getting louder each time he repeated them. By the end of the fourth block and an espresso at Café Napoli, I had revisited the Carpaccio meeting as well, unconvinced that the mobster and the mick were cohorts, but flabbergasted by the apparently citywide notion that I was the missing link to Chicago's long-dead *capo massimo*.

Sal shook his head in disbelief at me when I was done. "Can't you just come back home for an easy week or two without turning the whole city on its ear?"

"I don't know, buddy, these things just happen to me like this. I've learned to roll with it. I want nothing to do with Carpaccio, but the McBride thing intrigues a bit. Whatcha doin' tomorrow—working?"

He grinned in satisfaction "Uh-uh. I'm off. I already told you that, but you never listen."

"So you're saying . . ."

He sighed heavily, slapped his thick legs with his hands. "That I'm free to go treasure hunting tomorrow. Me and my long-lost crazy friend who's come back to town to remind me how much fun I've missed out on in life by playing it straight."

I beamed at him. "Attaboy, Sal-ee pal. If we aren't careful, we just might get rich."

Claudia had phoned while Sal and I were out. Francesca took the call. Her smile told me I had good news waiting on the other end of the line. It was all I could do to wait for the wheel to spin back from each digit as I rang up her number.

This time, she picked up. She said she couldn't make the dinner invitation I'd extended but offered me some great news instead: Frank had scored her a gig in Uptown at the Green Mill. She'd be doing several performances every night through the weekend.

"That's marvelous, Claudia. When do you start?"

"Tomorrow night. Maybe you can come if you aren't too angry with me? I'd like to talk with you. . . . I'm very sorry about the other day."

I swung a triumphant fist. "Yes, yes, I'd love to come. How about tomorrow? How about all of them?"

She giggled. "*Mille grazie, Giuseppe.*"

"My pleasure. Be great to see you."

We exchanged a few more nervous pleasantries then rang off. She seemed a little hesitant still, but I was delighted for the opportunity to see her again. I fully intended to catch every show if it was all right with her.

That set the rest of my week: mornings volunteering for Florence, afternoons on McBride's fool's errand, and evenings at the Green Mill in search of something of real value. The old Irishman was definitely right about one thing: Chicago was a city for big dreamers. It was all there for the taking.

But he never said anything about the price.

45

The mercury had dropped daily. Sunday had been downright balmy, Monday just a little less so, Tuesday things had turned cooler, and Wednesday morning was just plain blustery.

I was up early enough to see Francesca off, same as I had when she was the student and not the teacher. She still looked like a kid to me as she trundled off in her long wool coat and scarf, dark hair trailing out beneath a knit cap, but my mother reminded me she'd had her share of suitors over the years.

I lingered over coffee in the kitchen, my mother and I filling some of the gaps we'd papered over with hugs and kisses thus far. She foxed a little more out of me than I would have liked, but I managed to grab the clipboard and head for the door when things began to get sticky.

"Giuseppe," she said to me as I slipped away, "we've needed you around here alla these years with *Papà* gone. *I* need you. Understand?"

I paused in the doorway, met her penetrating eyes. "*Sì, Mamma.* I understand."

*　　　*　　　*

I meditated on her words as I walked the once-familiar streets, weighing what I'd built in California versus what I'd lost in Chicago, as if there were some scale that would so easily balance out on one side or the other. Each solid step, each cold exhalation, each newly familiar sight beckoned me homeward, but a growing freight business, the half dozen people who worked for me, and the ties I'd made on the West Coast all compelled me to return.

At ten thirty I headed up to Café Napoli for a warm-up espresso, the morning's business done. There, I waited for Sal and studied old Signor LoGuardio's face between glances at my map, planning the afternoon's lark that just might help me make it all work out.

The first location I chose was a long way off, relatively speaking. 7244 South Prairie Avenue was a sixty-block hike, and although the Dan Ryan freeway Daley had just rammed through Bronzeville was finished, we took the side streets so I could reminisce a little. Logistically, starting at the farthest point south made sense because we'd be able to work our way back to Taylor Street throughout the day. Instinctually, it was even better, for 7244 South Prairie Avenue was the one place that Chicago's famous crime boss had always returned to throughout all his years of roving, pillaging, and hiding out. It was the place Al Capone had called home.

When Capone had first begun to make it big with Johnny Torrio, he did what any up-and-comer would do: He bought a home for his family. Through his many changes of headquarters, vacation homes, and the occasional stretch in stir, the one constant was the family residence where his mother, wife, son, and sister lived. The last member of the Capone family had packed up years earlier, however, and legions of fortune seekers had no doubt scoured their way through the unassuming brownstone in the ensuing decades. Accordingly, we went in with low expectations.

They were met.

The old Lithuanian gent who answered the door was actually quite informative and more than willing to give us a full tour of

the property, including the basement, the attic, and the backyard.
A kind request—and a flash of a CPD badge—worked wonders like
that. He seemed to be quite proud of owning that piece of Chicago
history, soiled though it was, and especially thrilled to be showing it
to a police officer. We looked over, we peered into, we asked myriad
questions. We got squat.

After an hour of no great revelations, we left. As we pulled away,
Sal said he knew a good barbecue place near Back of the Yards
where a cop could grab lunch on the cuff. I checked my watch, said,
"You bet," catching a flash of a big dark car in the side mirror as I
did. I watched it out of curiosity for a few seconds, but it slid into
a parking space down from Capone's house just as Sal went into
a soliloquy about the "incredible brisket" they had at the place we
were going.

I shrugged. Lunch was calling. Barbecued beef sounded good
to me, too.

46

The brisket was a little dry for me. Sal thought it was fabulous. But as my father used to say, "There's no accounting for taste."

After lunch, we decided to split up to cover more ground. I stayed on the South Side while Sal continued on to the town of Cicero, a former Capone stronghold just west of Chicago. The Cicero sites were particularly dubious, but Sal knew the town well, so at least I could tell McBride I gave it a shot. I supposed I was going to have to tell Jack about my partner at some point, but half of nothing being nothing, I was pretty sure I could float his share.

My first two stops were dry wells. After a quick map check, I jumped a bus on Archer and bailed out at Chinatown. Then I hoofed it east along the fringes of the old Levee District, a place of staggering vice whose bordellos and saloons had giggled and roared for blocks at the turn of the century. Just a hurled brick from the decrepit Lexington Hotel, this part of the neighborhood was even worse off, the fixed stares I got from a couple of young Negroes letting me know I was running hard along the edge of the color line. At Wabash, I turned south, tramped another block, and then stopped and gazed up at the site where an emperor came of age: the Four Deuces Club.

Cribbing its name from its street address of 2222 South Wabash, the Four Deuces had been Johnny Torrio's headquarters as well as the most notorious nightspot of the mid-1920s, with plenty of pleasure or pain to be experienced depending on your altitude. The upper levels were well known as a gambling hall and den of sin, but popular lore from my childhood had it that the basement was a mob inquisition chamber where rising star Capone and his crew put the pliers to many an unlucky man, none of whom were ever seen again.

When Capone took charge of the rackets, he moved his head-quarters west to Cicero, and the Four Deuces fell into disuse, quickly achieving the status of haunted house for kids on a dare. One day around 1928, Sal and I worked up the courage to jimmy a side window and slip inside, but ran out screaming with our hair on fire when a wino threw an empty at us. We laughed all the way home. I hadn't laid eyes on the place since.

Time had done nothing to improve it. The windows on the upper levels were shuttered; those on the first floor, boarded with plywood, as was the entranceway, although enterprising vagrants had peeled one of the sheets back enough to allow entry. I stood before it a good minute peering inside, listening for any sounds as my eyes adapted to the murk. Then I flexed the spray-painted board a few feet and slipped past its nail-studded edges into the legendary house of iniquity.

Enough gray light entered through the naked window frames for me to clearly see the beer bottles, cardboard beds, and aban-doned clothing of those too forlorn to fear the phantoms of Prohibi-tion, but there was going to have to be a downright aureole for me to spot anything remotely related to a clue. Still, the legend of the place was intriguing enough to draw me farther inside.

Picking my way through the effluvious ruins, I reached the skel-eton of a back wall. Beyond it, there was what might have been a covered patio in its day but was now just an open-air mud patch leading off to an alleyway and the elevated train tracks above. The whole of the lot was strewn with junk and a couple of burnt-out areas marked off with loose bricks. Graffiti on the back wall paid a cryptic homage to the genius of Allen Ginsberg above a brace of Night Train bottles.

But unless the fortified admirer had scribbled a note somewhere reading "This way to Capone's loot," it was just another dead end, albeit one laced with perverse nostalgia.

Failing to spy any evidence of divine aid, I right-side-upped a fruit box, sat down, and shook out a Lucky. I sat and smoked awhile. A commuter train rumbled by in a dirty green-and-white blur on the elevated tracks then vanished. A truck on Wabash rattled the upstairs window frames as it passed. A police siren wailed somewhere in the distance. Other than that, it was silent in the Four Deuces. Just me, my thoughts, and the psychic echoes of the spirits.

About my fifth drag, the smallest of creaks sounded behind me. I turned, jumping up into a defensive crouch, hands at the ready.

What I saw made me want for the ghosts.

47

There were two guys. One big, one bigger. They were Italian American, but a quick look at their faces told me they hadn't come to invite me to the Knights of Columbus pancake breakfast.

I gave it a shot anyhow. "Howdy, boys," I offered. "Don't worry, I didn't drink any of your derail stash here."

The big one wasn't much for humor. He pulled out a revolver, aimed it at my chest.

The bigger one walked up to me, drove one into my solar plexus. I went down in stages into the muck, giving up my brisket along the way.

The pain was all-encompassing, bright red fuses burning their way along nerve endings as they raced toward my brain. As I lay there retching and gasping, the big one said solemnly, "Mr. Carpaccio says your Easter egg hunt is over unless you start doing it for him."

After three attempts, I finally managed to catch my breath well enough to sputter, "The hell you talking about? They told me . . . this was . . . O'Bannion's flower shop. I'm here . . . here for the begonias."

The bigger guy smiled. "That's funny, they're out of season."

"Shut up, Tony," the big guy said.

Tony nodded.

"Tony," he said then, "pick up that brick. Mr. Buonomo is a little unclear on our instructions."

The big guy clamped onto a nasty-looking number, hefted it up in his hand. I struggled up to my knees, spitting out phlegm and vomit, trying to summon any energy at all. "Easy there, boys," I wheezed, holding up a hand.

The big guy looked at me, some faint hopefulness registering in his face. "You gonna play ball?"

I got up to both hands on my knees, hunched over but coming around. "Yes, yes," I replied. "Now . . . if you guys will just tell me where the begonias—"

"Tony!"

The brick went up over his head.

A shot whistled out through the courtyard. The masonry fell into the muck. Tony fell alongside it.

The big guy spun, looking for a target. I launched myself into his back, forearm first, and we went down in the mud together. Fortunato would've been proud of my technique.

Then a very low but firm voice said, "If it is your wish to die today, Mr. Leonardi, I will happily grant it."

Leonardi and I looked up into taut sienna features and eyes like onyx, a gleaming automatic mere feet from our faces.

"Ronnie," I exclaimed through puke-smeared lips, "how nice to see you."

48

Turned out that Mr. Leonardi did not want to die that day. Neither did Tony, although any aspirations he might have had as a shot-putter ended with the .45-caliber round Ronnie blew through his scapula. The two of them limped off together through the courtyard, mud-caked and bloody, the big guy holding up the bigger, Ronnie following them all the way with his weapon at the ready. The hoods fell into a dark blue Sixty Special, their filthy suits doing nothing for the tan interior. I realized then it was the car I thought I'd seen following me on Tuesday afternoon, then again on Prairie Avenue. As the big sled glided away down the alley, tail fins slicing by like tiger sharks on the prowl, I realized belatedly that I was in way over my head in some very troubled waters.

Ronnie and I made our way back through the gutted club. He stopped at the edge of the courtyard, taking in the measure of the place. "Guess we just added another chapter to one of the most infamous places in town," he mused, rather pleased with himself.

"Bully for you," I replied, wiping some slime on a wall. "Now let's get the hell out of here before those guys come back with reinforce-ments."

Then I headed off for the front door, shaking off mud and pick-ing my way through the rubble, stealing out of the Four Deuces Club with my tail between my legs for the second time in my life, swearing out loud that there would never be a third.

Ronnie drove us north in the Imperial. He let on that McBride knew about my room in the Gold Coast, so there wasn't any harm in head-ing over to it. I could shower up and mix a drink in peace there, which was infinitely better than the hell I'd catch from my mother for coming home covered in mud anyway.

Once we'd reached the safety of the Loop, I had Ronnie pull over at a pay phone on Clark. It took me a fistful of dimes to run Sal down at the old Hawthorne Hotel, one of the Cicero spots he'd gone to check. It was highly unlikely that anyone was going to hit a cop, but I told him what had happened and warned him to ease on out of there and get home.

I got my third dirty look from a passerby as I hung up the phone, the middle-aged secretary type haughtily informing me, "If you've got the money to be buying drugs on the telephone, you can damn well afford a bath somewhere."

It's a tough town.

Ronnie was mum on the way to the Ambassador, deflecting my questions about McBride or flat out ignoring them.

"Listen, Ronnie," I declared as I got out of the car, "I'm going upstairs to take a shower, and I'm not the only one who's gonna come clean here. You tell McBride he better have some answers for me about just what in the hell is going on here or he's gonna need a new Sir Gawain. Savvy?"

He nodded silently.

"By the way . . . thank you. You probably saved my life back there."

Ronnie tipped his head, a faint curl appearing at the edges of his mouth as he put the car in gear.

The Imperial rolled away as I entered my four-star hotel caked in muck, gaining admission only because the doorman recognized me. If Sy Huser had been present, he could've written another whole column about me judging from the startled glances cast my way as I rushed head down for the elevator.

49

The steam felt good. I stood in the shower a long time after the mud had washed away, letting the hot rivulets stream over me, the warm vapor soothing sore muscles and vacating a cluttered mind. I did some reassessing of my situation while I was in there. A long, hot shower is good like that.

The hotel had those fancy Phonetel answering machines, but the message light remained dark in the bedroom when I peeked in. I shaved my face then slapped on some bay rum. The phone didn't ring. I got dressed anyway.

It was only Wednesday afternoon, but I put on the Saturday night suit—the midnight blue one—and paired it with a narrow navy tie with thin brown stripes. The day had been for shit, but the night still held promise. I figured I might as well dress for it.

Gina picked up over at Sal's house and put him on the horn. I told him to pack it in for the day. He said he was packing it in for good—how could I blame him? Then I asked if he wanted to catch Claudia's show tonight, but he said he couldn't make it till Friday. We said good-bye and hung up.

I puttered around another five minutes waiting for McBride to check in. He didn't.

"Screw him," I muttered, then went out, closed the door, and rang for the elevator. Didn't matter anyway, I was all done with his crusade, too.

I stepped out in the lobby and made for the revolving door, figuring I'd catch a movie at the Esquire, then grab the elevated to Uptown. Claudia's first show was at nine and I had no problem being early.

Halfway to the exit, a voice called out behind me, "Where the devil do you think *you're* going, laddie?"

I stopped, smiling sardonically as I turned to face Jack McBride, cocked sideways in the doorway of the Pump Room. The old rogue grinned at me, unabashedly resplendent in a gray houndstooth suit and forest-green turtleneck sweater, a tall glass of something that probably wasn't mulled cider in his hand. "Come on up and have a drink with me, you sharpie," he commanded.

I extended a hand at the entrance. Instead of shaking, McBride clapped me on the back hard enough to make me miss a step.

"You got some strength there, old boy," I observed.

"They don't let Nancy boys play quarterback at Michigan, you know."

I ran my tongue against my back teeth, sizing up the old fossil. "*Michigan?* Really?"

He took a deep swallow from his glass, wiped his mouth with the back of his hand, and then stated with more than an inkling of satisfaction, "Varsity. Three years. 9-0-1 in '09. You can look it up. I tell you, Buonomo, you'd be amazed at what the old Irishman has done in his day."

"Has he sold anyone else out to Carpaccio?"

His eye narrowed, the white brow above it angling down with it. Then he put a heavy arm around me, steering me through the doorway. "Come inside," he whispered. "Let's not be so chatty among the hoi polloi."

We walked up to the first booth, a big, plush affair with a RESERVED card on top. McBride slid onto the curved leather seat then picked up the card and chucked it over his shoulder. "Boy!" he shouted out to a passing waiter. "Let's have another drink here."

A waiter in a red jacket came over and stood at the ready.

"What's your poison, Gawain?" he challenged.

I cut him a glance, turned toward the waiter. "Whiskey neat. Scotch and soda for King Arthur here."

The waiter nodded with a smirk and departed. McBride turned to me, grasped my hand, and looked into my face with purpose. "Damn crazy business, this waylaying people in broad daylight."

"Care to tell me about it?"

"What's there to tell? You got in a fix, Ronnie saved your corned beef and cabbage. You're welcome, by the way."

"Oh yeah . . . thanks. Thanks for having me tailed again. Thanks for running me all over town from one ruin to the next. Thanks for leaving me out there like a bird on a wire to get plinked. Thanks for—"

His fist came down hard on the table, rattling the glassware. "You didn't think it was gonna be a goddamn walk in fields of clover, did ya? There's a lot of money at stake here, and some other folks want it—bad enough to kill for it. It isn't my fault you stuck your snoot into the Lexington the other day, you know? You hadn't done that, we might not be dealing with these, these . . ."

"Mobsters?"

His voice dropped to a murmur. "Shhh . . . nobody uses that word up here in Potter Palmer land. Didn't Ronnie put Carpaccio's thugs on the run anyway? Oh, he can shoot that fellow, a dead aim he is."

"Nuts," I sneered. "You're crazy if you think you can outmuscle the mob. Your boy probably just started a war." I cupped a hand to my ear. "Where's your cavalry, McBride? 'Cuz I sure as hell don't hear any bugles. All we have is one Indian, one crazy old man, and one damned fool smack in the middle."

"Oh, I've got heft, my boy, and it's not all in my waistband. Carpaccio has a hammer—I have connections. He's got guns—I've got clout. What do you think rates higher in this town?"

The waiter arrived, put the drinks on the table. McBride feigned patting for his billfold several times. I made a face at him, handed the waiter a fin, waved him away.

"Guess we'll chalk that up to clout, huh, Jack?"

He bit his lips, said nothing.

Then I hoisted the glass, eyed McBride, and threw down a gulp. I let it run down and in, way back in the gills, easing back a notch as the liquor hit home.

It was good stuff. I held the glass up again, examining the contents, noting the color and the purity.

"It's something, isn't it?" McBride said.

"What's that?"

"Whiskey, my boy. Al Capone made a fortune on it. These gangsters like Carpaccio—they weren't always so stupid and clumsy, you know. Capone was a genius. An evil one, mind you, but a genius nevertheless."

McBride's eye was alive now, his voice stoked in a growing timbre as he began to wax rhapsodic on days long gone. "He built an empire on whiskey, a vast, multitentacled octopus—the Syndicate, they called it. That syndicate ruled this entire town and half the criminals in America. And Capone ran it. Politicians, police, probies, distillers, importers, bootleggers, reporters, lawyers, accountants, gunmen—they all depended on him. He made hundreds of millions of dollars doing it."

McBride leaned way in, cut his voice to a conspiratorial whisper. "And he left it all behind—for you and me to find."

The old man was electric now. His ramble down memory lane had taken thirty years off him, and the smell of greed was as pungent as the corn mash in my glass.

I listened to everything he said, turning it over several times in my mind.

At length I asked, "Is it just me, Jack, or does this whole Capone thing infect everything it touches—like the clap he died from? Because the only thing I've found so far is man's limitless ability to delude and corrupt himself. What good is this treasure if it costs you your life or your soul? I mean, I'm at it two days—*two days*—and I'm already neck deep with the mob. I'm done with that shit; I don't have any more time to waste on them. What time I do have could be far better spent with—"

"Florence Scala?"

There she was again. Florence, and the fight against Daley and his minions. Good and evil. As clear-cut as a razor swipe.

McBride conjured up a puckish grin, pulled a cigar out of his pocket. He bit off the tip and spit it on the Pump Room floor. I hit the Cuban with my lighter, watching the old man roll it over and over and over as he took several deep draws, the tobacco flaming brightly to life between us.

He exhaled a dirty little cloud. "Buonomo," he said avuncularly, "this is what you do, son. This is what you are. Stop running from your past—embrace it. You put your neck on the line for Uncle Sam a hundred times and what did you get? A couple tin medals. Then you did it for Chiang Kai-shek for a few yuan. Now you do it for Frank Sinatra for God knows what. You *are* a crusader—same as the Knights Templar—but even they got rich in the bargain. C'mon, Joe, get smart. Help the old Irishman out. Help your family out. Help . . . yourself out. Play for the money—just this once."

He paused, a smirk betraying the mirth he was suppressing. "Hell's bells, why not? Right?"

He laughed quietly to himself, took a long drag from his torpedo, and leaned back, hands behind his head.

I stared long and hard at the Mephistophelian figure across from me in the booth, features obscured by the roiling smoke but that gold-flecked eye sparkling like a doubloon, that ancient face gleaming with its light as it broke into the long, deep curve of a very knowing smile.

50

Having just witnessed McBride's Oscar-caliber performance, I scratched the movie off my list, electing to grab a quick bite instead after our drink. I went down the street, ducked into Skinny's, eye-checked Marco Kabreros behind the glass.

"Hey, how ya doing, *vre*?" he called out over the counter.

I touched a hand to my bruised gut. "Been better."

"Ahh. Maybe it's da weather. Turnin' chilly out dere."

I glanced out the window. "Yeah. Looks like."

"Youse wanna coffee maybe? Warm ya up."

I thought it over a second, shook him off. "Just a dog. I got a belt in me already—startin' early today."

He nodded knowingly. "I got somethin' for dat," he declared, as he reached underneath the counter. He checked the window then pulled out a bottle of ouzo, brandishing it proudly between us.

I grinned at him. "Tempting. How's da coffee anyway?" I asked, hearing the local dialect in my speech again for the first time.

"Lousy. So . . . cup'a coffee, splash'a da good stuff then?"

I pointed two fingers at the counter. "Hit me."

He poured some brew into a white ceramic mug, floated a slick of the Greek hooch on top, pushed it all toward me. Then he made himself one, too, sans java.

He raised his cup. "*Yamas.*"

"*Salute,*" I replied.

We drank.

He put his cup down, wiped his mouth. "Nice suit," he observed.

"Thanks. Guess who?"

"Figured. You some kinda manager or somethin'?"

I took another sip. "No. Just a face in the crowd."

He scoffed at me, waved his hand.

"Say . . . this 'coffee' ain't bad, Marco. How much?"

"Who you kiddin'? You bring Frank Sinatra to my joint, he dukes me a centurion, and you wanna pay twenty-five cents for a cup of loaded coffee? C'monnnn! On da house."

"Thanks."

"Think nutin' of it. Coupl'a more tips like that and I can get my fishing business up again."

I looked up at the many black-and-white photos of Marco and some other fellows on the wall. They were workingmen, smiling with pride at the large fish either in their hands or packed in ice-boxes on an old trawler, their slimy aprons and grimy flannels proof enough of the hard work done.

"Whaddya got there, coho?"

He nodded. "Yeah. Lake trout, too. Even chinook sometimes. Yep . . . those were soooome days."

His voice trailed off as he faded into a reverie.

I left him out there awhile, then reeled him back, "That your boat?"

"Yeah," he said, returning to shore, "the *Pelecanos*. Good boat— damn good boat. She's impounded now at Chicago harbor, just rotting away. I'll get her back, though. . . . One of these days."

He started off into another daydream. I brought him back again just long enough to get a char dogs and fries then headed out to catch the Howard Line "L."

A familiar Imperial was idling out front on Division Street. It was getting so I expected it.

I walked up, climbed in the front seat, shut the door. No one even had to show me a gun.

"Where to?" Ronnie asked. "Mr. McBride said I should offer you a ride."

"Did he now?" I replied, only mildly surprised. "Well, take me to Uptown then," I said. "Got a date with a lady."

51

Traffic was already picking up. We started on Clark, jogged over to Lincoln. Ronnie said it was faster even though it ran farther west. I would've taken the Drive, but who was I to argue anymore?

I enjoyed the sights, the neon warming to life as evening set in. Ronnie and I made some small talk as we wended north. He turned out to be pretty thoughtful for a guy who threw people off piers.

Ten minutes in, we passed the Biograph Theater, forever linked to the demise of John Dillinger, a criminal less accomplished than Al Capone but perhaps even more adored by Depression-era America.

We turned right on Ashland, caught a light. I took in the storefronts, the people, the cars, the pulse of the city. A battered facade a few doors up drew my eye. It was an easy seventy-five years old and none too well maintained. *The Wigwam* was painted on a small marquee in faded multicolored letters beneath a badly weathered bust of an Indian chief, his splintered gray eyes overseeing the liquor stores and pawnshops of his dominion. A sign in the glass said, "Big chief make war on high prices. Him declare nickel beer night at Wigwam every Tuesday! Heap good deal!"

I looked back inside, caught Ronnie interrogating my face. There was an awkward silence. The light changed. Ronnie tapped the accelerator and we drove off, leaving the chief behind to his station. A guilt-edged pang of emotion rippled through me.

"Ask you something, Ronnie?"

He braked suddenly for a stoop-backed old woman who had darted into the street, glanced over at me, his eyes inviting the question.

"Do you ever feel that—"

"Yes," he replied. "Every day."

"But still you work—"

"For an organization that stands in living mockery of my people?"

"Well . . . yes."

He looked across at me. "And yet I do their heavy lifting? Take out their trash, if you will?"

"Yeah, that too."

The Indian regarded me solemnly, pushed in the cigarette lighter in the center console, fingered his chin.

"It's complicated."

We rolled on another block without speaking.

"McBride is a better man than you may think," he said. "His family goes way, way back with mine."

"So you come from a long line of indentured servants?"

The stare he gave me was cold and deep. "It isn't like that. You know how this town works—you're in or you're out, and we Potawatomi have been out since 1833. No one gave a damn about anything we ever had except our land. At least the McBride family gave us a halfway decent buck for it—most of it was stolen in broad daylight. Need the history lesson?"

The cigarette lighter popped up. I offered him a Lucky. He waved me off curtly, drew a hand-roll from a slender wooden case, touched the lighter to it.

"I'm okay on the history, Ronnie; I went to school here."

He took in some smoke. "You mean you're okay on the white man's version."

"Easy there," I shot back. "We both know the story of this town begins with the boosting of the Potawatomi lands along the river. Even as a kid I could see through the mythology."

He exhaled, grinned ruefully. "Mythology. That's good. Thought only we Indians had myths."

"You know what I mean—that Manifest Destiny horseshit. And knock off the self-pity. You don't strike me as much of a victim."

He chuckled. "Touché."

We went back and forth awhile, the litany of broken treaties, lies, and outright theft laid bare. But Ronnie also took pains to point out how the Potawatomi, the Fox, the Sauk, the Algonquin, the Illinois, and other tribes had taken land from one another repeatedly in the preceding centuries. It was all part of one continuum to him. In the end, he was less concerned with the wrongs of history than the exigencies of the present.

"It's true my people have endured great hardships," he concluded, "but still we have endured."

He swept a sinewy hand across the breadth of the windshield. "This is the world we've been accorded. I make my way in it as best I can." Ronnie's hand drifted farther back, a lone finger pointing directly at me. "Same as you."

There was another prolonged silence broken only by a honking horn somewhere. Then Ronnie added, "My family is none too particular about how I get the money I send them anyhow—they're too busy trying to get through the day."

"Family?" I asked.

He stubbed out his cigarette in the ashtray, blew smoke through his nostrils. "Out west—Iowa. They put us across the river, where no one has to see us. Far from 'civilized' people, far from 'Checagou,'" he said, an ironic grin twisting his mouth as he uttered the original name for the land upon which Fort Dearborn had been built.

"Like it out there?"

He gestured dismissively. "Ahhh. It's okay—I go sometimes, but I'm more of a city guy. I was raised here. This place is in my bones."

"Even so?"

He nodded. "Especially so."

We crossed an intersection, passed a city park, its withered grass choked with leaves from fallen maples, its small grounds deserted.

"Get lonely much?" I asked.

"No," he answered softly. "But it's funny you'd ask that."

"Why's that?"

"Because I do have an Indian name, actually. Orphaned Bear."

"I'll be damned. That some kind of prophecy? You all alone here?"

"Oh no, never. We're still here in spirit you know—Osceola, Mohawk, Winnemac, Washtenaw, Wabash," he said, smiling as he ticked off street names on his fingers.

I cocked my head, grinned wryly. "Planning on a comeback?"

He shrugged. "Anything is possible. Chief Ottawa rose up once. Black Hawk, too. You want a prophecy? The way this country and the Russians are going at it, we could all be gone soon."

He had a private laugh with himself then mused aloud softly, "Who knows, maybe wild onions will bloom here again one day."

My Indian guide and I rolled on into the cool blue Chicago evening. He said very little the rest of the way, but that thin smile remained planted on his dark lips, a brief sparkle of vermillion glimmering in his faraway black eyes as the last flash of twilight extinguished in the west.

52

Ronnie let me out at Wilson. I had some time to kill before the first show, so I wandered up Broadway, peeking in storefronts. I passed a beat-up saloon called Ballinger's, its shamrock-festooned signage proudly proclaiming the owner's Celtic heritage. Back came McBride.

I ducked in and ordered a shot and a beer, trying my best to drown away the Irishman and get back to thinking about Claudia.

It took a little while, but the rye and the pilsner did what they were supposed to do. Soon enough, I was revisiting my brief interludes with Claudia, musing pleasantly over a Lucky on the promise of things yet to come. About the eighth time I checked my watch, I decided it was time to trade my barstool for one up the street at the Green Mill.

Some no-neck at the door tried to tell me I was too early, but Pauly Sitko saw me jawing with him and eagerly waved me in, shouting for the bulldozer to ease up.

Pauly greeted me with a solid handshake as I pulled up to the barstool closest to the stage. "Hi, Joe, what'll it be, kid?"

"Hey, Pauly." I nodded back toward Mister Five by Five. "What's with the talking gorilla?"

He waved a hand like a ham hock toward the door. "Ahhhh. Some new guy, first day. He ain't gonna get to be old around here, I can tell you that."

I puzzled over that one a second.

"So what's it gonna be?" he asked. "Flame of Love? Rusty Nail? Old-fashioned?"

"I dunno, maybe a water. I got a couple—three—down already."

"Screw you, too, pal. Come on, whatcha drinkin' already?"

"Okay . . . Schlitz or something. I've got a date meeting me later and I don't wanna get sloppy."

He chuckled at me. "Christ, you're a grinder just like that Sinatra, aren't ya? I shoulda known."

"Nah. This one's a nice girl. From out of town."

He thought it over, shrugged his leathery face. "Sounds all right, I guess."

"She sings a little . . ." I added, throwing in a wink.

He looked at me, cheesing up to his ears, "Get oudda here! Signorina Hubba Hubba? You dirty dago!"

I minted a return grin. "Like you didn't used to take 'em in threes, you old Polack hustler."

He spun a coaster onto the wood, slid a frosted schooner of Dorfer on top of it. "Try this. Best German beer in this crooked Irishman's town."

I pulled my money clip out of my pocket, tossed it down on a bar top with the history of Chicago gouged into its nicked and burned surface. Pauly cut me off with a wave.

"Your money's no good here tonight, pal. The blue-eyed Sicilian tipped a gino on a three-hundred-dollar tab the other night. You're home free, kid."

"That's Frank for you."

Sinatra was out of town now, but it was shaping up as a Frank kind of night: a show at a legendary club, a date with a beautiful woman, the run of the bar, and the friendship of the tender. I smiled at my turn of luck. In just a matter of hours, I'd improved my hand from Four Deuces to four aces.

53

Claudia's first set was little more than a rehearsal, but I got that lump when I saw her come out onstage. Those red lips parted sensuously when I gave her the high sign with my smoke hand, but I stayed at the bar, letting her concentrate on her performance.

She tore it up—for the fifteen people on hand—but I had a feeling Frank would pack the joint with a "be there or else" commanded audience of friends for the ten-thirty show. Sure enough, they began to trickle in by ones and twos as her set progressed. By the time she closed with "Arrivederci Roma," the place was close to half full.

She took several bows and disappeared offstage. Pauly sidled up behind me, leaned down on burly arms extending beneath his rolled and braced sleeves, and said ever so gently, "She's somethin', brother. That kid could go places."

Leaning back, I gave a pat to his tattooed bicep. "Maybe with me."

I felt a hand on my own arm then. I turned, and an angel kissed me. I'm pretty sure I hadn't melted since the fourth grade when Mia Di Laurenzo planted one on me behind the auditorium curtain, but I got pretty soft around the edges just the same.

"*Ciao, bella,*" I purred. "You were great up there."

"*Grazie,*" she said, holding her smile awhile. She might not have melted either, but I'm pretty sure she blushed.

We kicked it around a bit as a crowd filed in. I got so caught up chatting with her that I missed a chance at a good booth for the second show.

"*Mi dispiace, amore,*" I said in chagrin. "Looks like I gotta watch this one with Pauly again."

"No, Joe," she said, tugging at my hand, "I get you the best table on the side—so you can see and I don't get too distracted watching you."

Claudia stood up and we walked toward the front of the darkened room, she unashamedly squeezing my hand on the way. She led me to the first booth on the right-hand side and proudly pointed out the handwritten RESERVED FOR JOE BUONOMO sign on the table.

"Okay, gotta go now. See you soon, okay?" she said.

I wanted to smooch her one right there but thought better of it. Instead, I blew her a kiss and wished her good luck.

She smiled, and then she was off. A waitress in fishnets and red satin came by a few minutes later with a cocktail I recognized from its sweet odor.

"Pauly says you'd be wanting one of these," she said above the gathering din. "He called it a Flame of Love. Smells like burnt orange or somethin'. Says to tell you that you are one lucky son of a bitch."

It was hard to disagree.

People kept pouring into the place as we neared the appointed hour. By the time Claudia came on, they were two to three deep behind the bar. Frank had delivered as usual—and there were too many familiar faces from the Villa Venice for it to be a coincidence. That wasn't necessarily a good thing considering the company.

Her show came on as scheduled. I sat back in my private booth, taking it in: the flaming torch singer in the emerald dress, the captivated crowd, the Beaux-Arts paintings and the voluptuously curved woodwork in the smoky room, the bite of the whiskey I was now working over, the stirring sound of Claudia's strong voice. It was a helluva scene. I was maybe drinking a little too much, but I needed to vent off a blast or two and I was a long way north of my troubles on the South Side of town.

Claudia scorched the joint, closing out to a big ovation from the crowd. I couldn't be sure about *their* sincerity but had no doubts about my own. After she took a bow and blew a few kisses, she came right over to my table. I stood and let her slide in, then took my place at her arm. She told me there wouldn't be a third nightly show until Friday, but that she wanted to see the hard jazz quintet coming on next. I caught fishnet and satin's eye and ordered a bottle of Prosecco for which, of course, I was not allowed to pay.

I proposed a toast to Claudia' success, and we settled in for the next show. The five-man band came in hot and kept cooking, serving up one hard-driving bebopper after another. The night just kept getting better. Soon enough, the Prosecco was bottom's up. I'd mixed several types of booze by then, and lots of it, but I was still riding skyward.

The band took a short respite to tune their instruments between pieces, the horn player delving into a story about Benny Golson, then riffing into a monologue about some cat who "was into the horses and very much against manual labor."

Claudia took the moment to make a quick dash to the ladies' room. As the door swung shut behind her, the drummer smacked his stick once and the piano player launched into a two-chord refrain. The bass kicked in next, then the saxophonist came in over the top with a smooth, familiar groove. I rolled right with the wave, feeling the music, riding the high.

Fishnets arrived at the table with a bright red smile, then placed another bottle on the table. I took one look at it and begged off.

"Thanks so much, hon, but tell Pauly I'm halfway to the stars already."

She shook me off. "He didn't send it."

I felt my eyebrows arching. "Oh?"

"No. The gentleman over in Booth One—by the back door there—he sent it."

She pointed across the room. I sat up high, my eyes following her hand through the murk to a half-moon banquette, my head still bouncing lightly to the killer vibe of the quintet as I sought out some generous fan or friend of Frank. At first, I could only make out a coven of steely-eyed men, tight faces blued by the stage lights and smoke pall. Then a man in the middle cocked his chin toward me and waved casually. I smiled as I squinted to see who it was, then sucked in my breath when I did.

Forty feet away, from the depths of Al Capone's former roost, gunmetal eyes glared at me with an intensity that cut right through the indigo gloom, the teeth beneath them glinting like a scythe on Vinnie Bo'palazzo's cold, hard face.

54

If ever there was a message in a bottle, Bo'palazzo had sent it. I knew his boss had a connection with Claudia, and his crew had tried to massage my temples for me earlier in the day, so it was unlikely a coincidence that the boys were present in numbers.

Then again, Frank was good with those people, and they weren't going to make a move in a crowded club; that stuff went out with Capone and Bugs Moran. Maybe they were just there to watch the apple of Carpaccio's eye for him. Mob guys get jobs like that.

I gave Vinnie the cement face while I sat there weighing the thing out in my head and sobering up quick. The odds for either scenario weren't evenly matched, but there was a reasonable possibility for either case. In the end it was a push.

I decided to push back. Running wasn't going to work, not with Claudia being booked for a week—and it wasn't my style anyway. I was cruising on jet fuel by that time and feeling flinty, but it wasn't the time or place for a fight either.

There was, however, nothing wrong with improving my hand. I snagged fishnets at the next table and asked her to pop into the restroom and tell Claudia to meet me by the bar. That got us out of the corner, and a lot closer to the front door if anything broke bad. The narrow space between the bar and the nearby wall booths, crowded with customers as it was, would whittle down Bo'palazzo's operating room if he did try a muscle play.

When fishnets went into the restroom, I got up and walked to the front of the club without looking over. A nice-looking young couple at the bar eagerly agreed to take my booth in exchange for their seats along the rail. I parked myself on one of the brown vinyl chairs, leaned across the wood, and signaled with my hand. Pauly smiled when he saw me. The big Pole walked over, ignoring several drink requests as he came, stopping across from me and raising both hands, palms up.

"Table service not good enough for ya?"

I swiveled my head. "I might be in a spot. Got some unfriendlies in the club. I think it'll be okay, but I'd feel a lot better with you watching my back. Whatsay?"

"Like you even had to ask," he answered, leaning down to eyeball something beneath the bar.

"Thanks, pal."

"Natch."

Claudia arrived in short order, after stopping along the way to talk with several people offering congratulations. When she finally made it to the bar, her face betrayed no alarm. That was just as well as I had no interest in upsetting her where she worked. Best-case scenario we'd have a drink, chat a little, and slip out into a cab without interference from the Outfit. Who knew, maybe they were just there at Frank's request too.

My plan worked.

For about five minutes.

I did my part, sitting quietly on my stool, nursing an ice water and killing a Lucky as we watched the musicians play another Jazztet standard, my hand on top of Claudia's, both of them resting on her hip. Then one of Bo'palazzo's heavies drifted over a few seats down the line, whispered into some guy's ear, and took the seat that opened up. Pauly was watching. Our eyes met for half a second. Maybe the guy saw, maybe he didn't.

I leaned over close to Claudia, whispered, "What do you say we get out of here, *bellissima?*" into her ear.

She turned, surprised, her large brown eyes interrogating me as she pleaded, "Can't we stay until they are done?"

I chewed my lip, stole a glance toward the door, caught the bouncer eyeing me a little too closely. Clouds parted in my head as the adrenaline began to trickle somewhere inside me, the dull taste of iron crowding out the whiskey on my tongue. "I think we better go."

She crossed me up then. "Bo'palazzo? You worry about him? He's just here to watch me—like always."

"Well, he doesn't look like much of a music lover to me."

She sipped her drink, smiled bitterly. "He watches me for Carpaccio."

I gestured with both hands. "Would you mind telling me what the hell that guy has on you? There can't be any way that you'd ever be interested in him, I know that."

Her top lip flattened as those almond-shaped eyes curved into ovals. "*Quel animale?* Don't make me laugh."

I moved in close, squeezed her wrist. "So what is it then? What could there possibly be between you two?"

Claudia pulled her hand away, smacked it on the bar in frustration, her face screwed up tight. She turned toward me suddenly, spat out, "*Un contratto*, okay?" Then she looked away, pounding the bar softly with her fist several times.

"A contract? That's what this is about—a singing contract? Can't you break it?"

She shook her head with a short, violent twist. "No! Listen, my family didn't have any money after the war—*niente*—and many mouths to feed. When I was fourteen, my father made a deal with a man in Naples to promote me. A powerful man, Joe, a *very* powerful man. *Mi hai capito?*"

"*Camorra?*" I asked, broaching the name of the fearsome Neapolitan mob outfit.

"Sì," she replied ruefully. A shiny dab beaded up in the corner of her eye. "I work many years in shitty clubs, but the Camorra never gave me a chance, even though I begged them to help me or let me go to America. When they are finally convinced I won't make it, they let me go, but they sell the contract to that pig Carpaccio. So now I am in the 'beeg time' in America, but still they own me, same as always."

She palmed a tear before it could fall, gazed emptily into the mirror behind the bar. "Same as it will always be."

"Jesus Christ."

"Now you understand, ahh?" she said, the hard edge of recrimination plainly evident in her voice.

"Yeah. He takes half of what you make over here. You break the deal, they go after your family back home. But listen, baby, Frank went through that. He could—"

She chopped me cold. "Frank Sinatra has no control over these people whatsoever. His 'great friend' Giancana, do you think he pays Frank for these appearances he puts in? That is a laugh! Frank is a big shot, sure, but he's just another puppet on a very long string. This I promise you. I know."

She turned and faced the bar again, sitting perfectly still except for the very small shakes of her head she made as she silently cursed the Fates.

The quintet was still bopping in the background, the occasional clink of a glass or muffled chuckle rising above the low buzz of the crowd. Cigar smoke and good cheer were in the air, the Green Mill cooking as usual. It might have been a great night for everyone else in the house, but just then I couldn't stop the floor from falling away beneath me as the weight of her words sank home.

We sat in silence for several minutes. Claudia asked me for a cigarette, the first one I'd seen her smoke since we'd met. I lit it for her and watched her pull on it several times as she stared vacantly at the band. She ordered a shot of Canadian Club from Pauly, hammered it, then backed it with another. I stuck to my ice water. There was nothing more to be said or done at the moment.

Finally, she turned to me, took my hand, kissed it. "*Grazie, Giuseppe*, I am sorry to be mean to you."

"*Stai calma, bella,*" I chided gently, shushing her. "Frank's a little more independent than you think—and he's got a friend named Jack whose brother Bobby has some serious pull. We're going to straighten this thing out with Mr. Carpaccio. This I promise *you.*"

I leaned over and kissed her lightly on the cheek, clasped her hand. She kissed me back. Once gently, and then again, like she did at the pier. If there'd been a check to pay, I'd have called for it right there.

Then a voice behind me sneered, "Oh, isn't that *sweet*? Mr. Carpaccio's gonna love this little romance."

There was no need to turn around. It was Bo'palazzo, the roach in the punch bowl.

I turned my head the three inches it took to give him the knife edge of my eye. "Blow, Vinnie."

His chortle rang like a Klaxon above the music. "You're in no position to be handing out orders, Buonomo."

Some unknowing guy in the crowd shushed him loudly.

I spun around and eyed the pin-striped Mafioso and the shark-skin duo behind him, one of them Leonardi of Four Deuces infamy. "You talk pretty big with those piano movers behind you, don't ya, Vin?"

He jabbed a finger into my shoulder. "And you talk pretty big behind Frank Sinatra, flyboy."

Things were unspooling fast. I was drunk, and he looked as if he'd been hitting the tiger's milk pretty good too. The testosterone was flowing like the Old Style in there. It was only a matter of time.

In the mirror behind Bo'palazzo, I caught a flash of Pauly's image moving in.

I slapped Vinnie's hand away hard. "Listen, *faccia di cazz'*, I stand in *front* of Sinatra, not the other way around. Who stands in front of you when things go down, tough guy?"

Bo'palazzo's sneer faded into a contemptuous smile. "We all stand together."

He made a sweep of his arm. "The boys here stand with me, I stand with Carpaccio, Carpaccio stands with Giancana. And, just in case you forgot how things work in our world, a Giancana trumps a Sinatra any day—hands down."

I gestured toward Leonardi. "You're down a couple of cards already by my count. Your Giancana trump didn't help them. Maybe you might wanna fold this time."

"Don't you worry," he grinned. "Tonto will get his, too. You both will."

Claudia tried to intercede then, but I was past that. I put a hand on her shoulder and gently pushed her back. People on either side of us had begun to move away as well, Vinnie's simians stepping into the vacated spaces. I could hear my voice rising, feel my pulse pinging like sonar.

"We can talk about that tomorrow with Momo. But right now, I am trying to have a drink with a lady. Just leave me and Miss Cucciabella the hell alone and we can all go on our way tonight."

Bo'palazzo sucked in his lower lip, exhaled hard, fixed me with a wicked stare. "For a guy with a playmate who belongs to us, you certainly have a lot to say, Buonomo. You might want to think about keeping that big mouth of yours shut and not saying anything at all about Mr. Giancana—for Miss Cucciabella's sake and your family's."

That tore it. I shoved two fingers in his face. "You go anywhere near her or *anyone* in my family and I will air-drop *chunks* of you on Sam Giancana."

The shock hit him like a slap to the face. He recoiled at my words, reaching reflexively into his jacket.

Vinnie shot a look toward his henchmen then back at me, charcoal eyes fully dilated, cold rage burning in them as he struggled to control himself. Though his lips barely moved, I heard his gravelly words as they ground slowly past his teeth, "Don't be so sure Sam won't take you down just because you're Sinatra's boy, 'cuz, brother, you just earned it right there."

I glanced down at his chest, at the butt of the pistol in his hand peeking halfway out of his suit coat. Several nearby patrons were actively pushing away now, their eyes wide with concern.

Pauly whispered something to Claudia I couldn't make out. I

knew I should stop, but we were already so far beyond the line by that point.

I scoffed at Bo'palazzo's bluff, laughed in his face. "You gonna use that thing? Here—in a room full of people?"

Vinnie fingered the gun in his hand, stole another glance at his backup. Then he relaxed his arm, still maintaining a loose hold on his piece.

I stepped in close, nose to nose, looking over his lavender dress shirt and polka-dot tie. "Then put it away," I whispered, "you fucking *clown*."

This is where everything went sideways.

55

Bo'palazzo went for his weapon. I popped him with a straight left before he broke leather, snapping him backward.

The other two came at me, guns up. I heard Claudia gasp, then Pauly yelling my name above the fray as what Thursday's *Daily News* would dub the "Uproar in Uptown" broke free.

In the mirror, I saw rapid movement behind the bar. I ducked fast, catching a glimpse of Pauly sweeping down with a bat like old number 8 of the White Sox. He clocked Leonardi and the other guy with one clout, dark blood spraying out as they both buckled amid the roar of a pistol and the shower of splinters that erupted from the wooden light fixture an instant later.

The gunshot galvanized the house. What had been a grooving, buzzing throng exploded into a Chinese fire drill, the music cutting short like a jerked needle across a 78 as the musicians dove for cover, screaming people stampeding for exits, shoving everyone every which way, bodies tumbling down amid the chaos.

Pauly was up and over the bar, driving his war club down on one of the goons with a thud so profound you could feel it. I clawed my way upstream along the rail, reached for Claudia, took a hard overhand hook from the bouncer that staggered me. Pauly wheeled, buried the Louisville Slugger in Five by Five's gut.

A hoarse rush escaped the bouncer's lungs. He went purple, wavered a beat, and then just kind of hung there, his mouth making little gasping sounds. I drove one into the side of his fat head and he just folded down like a Murphy bed between us. He hit the floor and then he didn't move.

Other pockets of fighting had broken out across the room. They might have been Frank's guys, they might have been Vinnie's, they could have been anyone's really. Couples were darting between the pugilists, desperately trying to reach the exits. It was a Pier Nine brawl by that time.

Leonardi struggled to his feet, his nose in a new zip code. There was a crash of breaking glass and a spray of whiskey, then dark night veiled his eyes. Claudia emerged behind him as he fell, broken neck of the CC bottle in hand, her eyes blazing like Pallas Athene's on the plains of Troy.

The hand to hand went on and on. Bo'palazzo was against the far wall, trading punches with some bohunk in a bowling shirt. I kept trying to get a poke at him, but somebody would either crash into one of us or I'd have to grab Claudia to keep her out of harm's way as she kicked and flailed at Carpaccio's crew. Twice, I picked her up and tossed her on the bar. Each time, someone grabbed me from behind and tried to go Greco-Roman on me.

It might've gone that way all night, but then there was a wail of a siren, the screech of tires out on Broadway, and the shrill pitch of a beat cop's whistle as he burst in the side door on Lawrence. Prohibition couldn't have been any wilder.

Pauly and I froze, staring at each other like kids caught smoking in the bathroom. "Joe," he yelled, "the trapdoor! Straight out at the bottom, you'll come up in the Aragon. Take Claudia! Go now!"

I was over the woodwork in a heartbeat, signaling Claudia to follow me, scooping her up as she slid across the ancient bar top and into my arms.

Bluejackets were pouring in through the front door now, nightsticks high as they whacked at all comers, shoving fleeing bodies back inside, felons and citizens all one and alike to them. I gaped at the calamity for a second then grabbed the iron ring in the floorboards and yanked up hard. The light came on, revealing the stairway below.

I snatched Claudia's hand, reached back up to the counter for a fifth of Four Roses, and then ducked down into the abyss, pulling the trapdoor down hard behind us as we descended from the mayhem into a netherworld of shadows and silence.

56

It was tomb quiet down there. Above us, there was muffled yelling and banging and the howl of sirens, but all was still below. Only our labored breathing broke the quiet of the dank air.

We caught our breath, looking wild-eyed at each other and at the dim cavern around us, still coming to grips with what we'd just seen and done.

"Are you all right, baby?" I asked.

"I think so," she said, examining her hands.

"Come on," I whispered. "Let's get out of here before the cops come looking. They've gotta be wise to this dodge after all these years."

I grabbed her hand and started off down the corridor that ran under Broadway overhead. The stairway light faded away fast, so I pulled out my Zippo and spun the wheel as we scurried on, yellow-orange luminescence appearing at my fingertips.

The glow illuminated the mildewed brick archway above us, then an old iron door off to one side like the one Vernon had led us through in the Lexington. And like that one, it had the letters *CWW* in raised letters on its surface with a keyhole inside.

"Chicago Water Works," I mused under my breath as I stared at it. "What does it mean?" Claudia inquired.

I looked at her, back at the door again, then shrugged. "Nothing. Just an old water department access door. We better keep moving—it's at least another block to the Aragon."

I held up my lighter and we set out again. After several steps, I could hear Claudia giggling. It was not the reaction one might normally expect in those circumstances. I turned, gazed into her eyes.

"Oh, Joe," she exclaimed breathlessly, "that was so much fun I cannot believe it! I hate those *bastardi* so much! So many years of them preying on me and my family. It felt so good hitting and kicking them!"

Now I knew we'd be needing a long sit-down to make that thing right, but nobody had died so far as I knew, and Bo'palazzo had had it coming. Tomorrow was another day, one that would require cooler heads and Frank's assistance, but right now we were running scot-free in an underground tunnel with a half bottle of bourbon and the shank of the night in hand.

I held the Zippo close until I could see Claudia's face. Her hair was mussed, her features sweaty, her mouth wide open as she gulped in air. She looked fabulous.

I knew we should have been hustling out of there, but it had been such a long day already. I'd been threatened, gut-punched, dipped in mud, shot at, and roughed up in a brawl. Suddenly, I just didn't care too much. I took a country pull of the bourbon, handed the bottle to Claudia. She took it and drank deeply, flashed me a feral grin, her dark eyes burning bright in the flickering light.

Her lipstick was smeared. I smeared it some more. Then it was all up for grabs, our hands clutching for each other. I snapped the Zippo shut, jamming it in my pocket as we fell against the wall, the musty darkness of the cavern swallowing us whole as the night closed in around us.

57

I awoke at dawn in the Ambassador East, Claudia at my side. Clothing was scattered around the room like the after-Christmas sale at Carson's, an empty bottle of Four Roses skewed sideways on a nightstand. Two crushed Luckys lay in the ashtray, a crimson splash on one. I grinned deeply as I played it all back, although my jaw ached a little when I did.

The message light was blinking red in the darkened room, a flare shot from the outside world into our den of tranquility. Maybe it had been there when we came in—I couldn't really recall. It occurred to me that at some point I would have to see who it was.

I gazed down at Claudia as she slumbered next to me, her hand resting on my arm. Dark ringlets of hair ran off in curlicue tangents around her face and shoulders, her supple body rising and falling with the rhythm of her respirations under the fine sheets.

I reached over to the phone, hesitated, my hand hovering above the message machine as I rethought my move. Then I extended a finger, gently spun the telephone ringer to OFF, and lay back down.

"Screw the messages," I murmured as I melted into the goose-feathers and closed my eyes.

There'd be a headache later—and some hell to pay. There always was.

Like I gave a tinker's damn at that moment.

58

Room service rang at nine. Breakfast got a little cold on the table.

The coffee was still strong and hot when I poured it, a heavy-viscosity jolt back to the world of the living. I played back the messages while Claudia took a shower. I suppose MacArthur had received worse at Corregidor.

The first was from Frank and contained multiple obscenities, some of which contained hyphenations I had never heard. The second was from my brother letting me know how upset my mother was that I hadn't checked in all day. The third was from my partner, Roscoe, who had apparently been taking grammatical notes from Frank.

I put the phone down, drained my cup, trying to stem the pulsing tide building in my temples. It was early in California, but I knew he'd be up.

"Hi, Frank. How's the sunrise over the mountains?"

"Fuck the fucking sunrise! Good God, Joe, what the hell happened there? I got Carpaccio jumping down my throat at four o'clock this morning. Do you know how . . ."

I put the phone to my chest, closed my eyes, listened to the muffled ranting until it tapered off.

I put the phone back to my ear. "You done, Albert Schweitzer?"

He exhaled heavily. "For now."

"Okay, first: enough with the yelling already. I don't work for you. Go yell at George Jacobs or Jilly or someone else who gets paid to take your bullshit. You got me?"

He didn't say anything for quite a while. Finally, somewhat chastened, he apologized. "All right, Joe, I'm sorry. But that call worried me. Carpaccio says you started a brawl with his crew, said there was shooting, cops, a real full-fledged riot."

"There *was* shooting. One of Bo'palazzo's Boy Scouts pulled the trigger—and they tried to kneecap me yesterday afternoon, too, so let's not have any Goody goddamn Two-shoes crap from that side."

"Jesus. Are you all right?"

"I am, thank you. Well, no. . . . My jaw hurts a little. . . . But other than that, I'm fine. So is Claudia."

"Glad to hear it. I gather you two are getting on pretty well."

The bathroom door cracked open. Claudia slipped out wearing some steam and nothing else. She grabbed a robe from the closet, smiled at me from across the room. "Thanks," I said. "And, yes, we are."

Frank shifted gears. "So you know about this contract business with her that Carpaccio mentioned to me this morning, right?"

"She told me last night," I replied under my breath. "She's going to need your help with that one. You got any juice?"

"Yeah. Believe me, I know a thing or two about mob contracts. Pretty sure I can help."

"Good. How 'bout you start by getting Sam Giancana on the hot line? He's the key to all our problems here."

"Been trying. Left six messages over three days so far, even sent an urgent telegram. I've never had a problem reaching him before. Something very big must be up."

I closed my eyes again, mashed the phone against my ear in frustration. "Here's hoping we ain't it."

"No, I actually came away from Chicago feeling very good. I'm pretty good for business, as you know."

He went on to tell me what a cinch it was that Sam would have my back, how the whole thing would get straightened out by the weekend even if he had to fly back to Chicago, et cetera, et cetera. My mind began to wander.

Claudia was still on the other side of the room, fiddling with the rabbit ears on top of the television and finishing her coffee. Her hair was wet and she wore only the robe but she still looked great to me. I studied her quietly as she sipped and fiddled, fiddled and sipped, murmuring inaudibly in the native tongue.

Frank was saying something, his voice buzzing in my ear like an insistent gnat.

"Hey . . . you listening to me there?"

"Yeah."

"Anything else to report? I gotta hurry over to West Lawn. . . . We're filming a scene in a cemetery today of all places."

"Yeah."

"Well . . . what?" he demanded.

"I think I love her, Frank."

"Oh, Christ. Are you certain?"

"Sh-boom sh-boom."

"Here we go again."

"Yeah."

"I'll try Sam again before I go."

"That'd be great."

The call to Frank brought some relief. That left Roscoe and my brother. Roscoe gave me a boilerplate ration of grief, some of which I even had coming. I reminded him that most of the days off I'd taken over the years could hardly be construed as leisure time, so I was long overdue for an actual vacation. He called me a few more names before hanging up, but his heart didn't seem to be in it.

Addressing my brother's message wasn't going to be as easy. For starters, he was at work and I wasn't going to bother him there. Additionally, he'd said some pretty inflammatory things and it was just as well if we didn't talk until later. The next call was the more important one anyhow.

"*Ciao, Mamma.* I'm sorry for not calling last night, I've been very busy."

"*Giuseppino . . . Grazie a Dio!* Your brother just called me and said there was some kind of a shootin' at the Green Mill last night. *Stai bene, tu?*"

"*Sì, tutt' a post'*—I'm fine. Claudia, too."

I heard her sigh, visualized her making the sign of the cross for the ten millionth time. When she came back on the line, her voice was surprisingly firm and composed. "You know your brother says you are a *pecora nera*, that we shouldn't have anything more to do with you. I tell him not to talk this way, that you are a fine son, that we are all so happy to have you back."

"*Grazie.*"

"But *figlio mio . . .*"

"*Sì?*"

"I'm beginning to wonder . . ."

"*Mamma . . . aspetta . . .*"

"Please, son, please don't fool around with those bad people. We love you, and we missed you more than you can ever know, but please do not bring evil into our *casa.* If this is the price of you coming home"—she paused, composing herself—"it would be better if you had not come at all."

Her words sucked the air out of me. I fumbled for a response, came up empty. In the silence, I thought I heard my mother sniffle. I had wanted to ask her if I could invite Claudia to Sunday dinner, but it was no longer the right moment to ask that. It was no longer the right moment to ask anything at all.

I clutched the receiver, holding quietly on the line. After a painfully long silence, I said, "I understand. Good-bye, *Mamma.*" Then I gently cradled the phone.

I dug out a cigarette, lit it, and walked to the window, cracking it open an inch at the bottom. Claudia was singing softly in Italian in the bathroom. I leaned into the frame, laid my bruised knuckles on the sill, watching the smoke escape outside into the cold air.

Down below, cars rolled south on State, in the general direction of Taylor Street—and my family. In the concrete miles between us,

Marcos Kabreros hawked his hot dogs while Vernon Pryor limped silently through the belly of the Lexington Hotel and Florence Scala waged her heroic, hopeless battle against the city. On either flank, Jack McBride and Fiorello Carpaccio were closing in like rogue highwaymen, their gold-blind aspirations portending malevolence. The spaces in between were filled with memories of my lost friend Butch O'Hare, tantalizing fragments of long-ago conversations flitting through my mind but never coalescing into clear memories.

Above it all, an apparition hung in the ether above the city. From bungalow chimneys, skyscraper ventilators, and steel-plant smokestacks it rose, kite-dancing and swirling in the leaden skies, unseen but ever sensed.

And I knew that omnipresent specter was the mocking, grinning ghost of Alphonse Capone, dead set that his gilded treasures would remain his, and his alone, forever.

59

Claudia wanted to return home to her apartment. I convinced her to stay at the hotel until Frank had squared our little mess from the night before. The sobered-up fear of Carpaccio she felt was readily apparent in her face, and as the details of the night before returned to her, she quickly agreed to remain inside.

The manager set her up in a suite on a lower floor on the hush. That would keep her off the street and out of sight of any of Carpaccio's crew if they came looking. It was no long-term plan, but it would do for the day.

After she was settled in her room, Claudia called up to let me know she was okay. I told her I'd be down soon. Then I depressed the hook and released it, cradling the phone under my chin as I sipped cold coffee while dialing the operator. It was time for me to make some more calls. They were a quarter apiece, but what the hell, Frank Sinatra was paying.

I tried Sal first, but Gina said he was out. Next, I tried the Green Mill to thank Pauly and make sure he hadn't been put in the can, but no one picked up over there that early in the day. That left McBride.

"My, my, but you're a pistol, Buonomo," he began. "Busted up the whole goddamn North Side last night. You really are a tall, bold slugger, aren't you? You've gotta be getting close to something to have those boys in such a tizzy."

"Jack . . ."

"Mobsters, gunshots, sirens, paddy wagons—"

"I can't do this."

"Just like the good old days! Eighteen arrests, but of course not you, bucko. You're too— What did you say?"

"I said I'm out. This scavenger hunt of yours is out of control. Florence and I will have to get by without the millions—they aren't worth a damn thing to me if I'm dead."

"The hell you say! You can't quit on me—we've already settled this. You're going to—"

"Quit. I'm sorry, Jack. Say good-bye to Ronnie for me. I'm going to miss him. You too, old man."

"Nobody quits on Jack McBride! We've got a deal."

"I gave it a good try. But it's a mirage—there's nothing here. Nothing to see, nothing to find, nothing valuable of any kind—just a lot of Outfit guys with guns."

"Don't tell me you're afraid of those guinea brigands, damn you. I'm not afraid of Joe Kennedy, so don't tell me you can't handle that hog cutter Carpaccio."

I sat up, perfectly still. A cold sliver formed somewhere deep inside me, grew into an icicle running the length of my spine, crept outward throughout my body.

Joe Kennedy. Just the name numbed the senses.

"Did you just say 'Joe Kennedy'?"

"I did at that. What of it?"

"Joe Kennedy, the father of the president of the United States?"

"Of course that one!" McBride harrumphed.

I could feel my fingers going cold on the receiver. "What's he got to do with this, Jack?"

"He owns the Merchandise Mart. Everybody knows that."

Moisture began to form on my upper lip. "I thought you said the Field family owned the Merchandise Mart."

"They did—but they sold it to Kennedy in '46. Who gives a buffalo nickel who owns it? I own the land beneath it—and that makes it mine!"

"Oh God . . ."

Memories, deep black memories from Baja, awoke inside me. Dust clouds, machine-gun fire, the shriek of a warbird. Rockets, roiling smoke, blistering heat.

Helen.

Chaos and bone-deep terror. Despair and impenetrable sadness. All of it all over again all at once.

"You still on the line, Buonomo?"

I shook myself free from the grim flashbacks. "Jack . . . Jesus . . . You gotta listen to me. Do *not* get involved with that man, do you hear me? You don't know what he's capable of. Do not ever cross him, you *will* live to regret it—but not very long."

"Now you get this straight, mister—"

"No, you get this straight. You're a fun guy, McBride. I enjoyed this little game we played, at least until the mob got involved. But the Outfit is paper-fucking-dollies compared to Joe Kennedy. You don't think a man with his power, his connections, can bring the hammer down on you? His son is the president, for Christ's sake, his other son is the attorney general. Did you not see the Bay of Pigs on TV? The Cuban Missile Crisis? Don't even think of playing games with those people, Jack; they will disappear you so fast it'll leave a vacuum!"

There was a long silence on the line, the faint hum in the connection the only sound. I thought maybe I had reached him. I was wrong.

"Well, well, well," he chided. "So you're deserting the old Irishman in his hour of need, are you? Joe Kennedy? A Paddy bootlegger trump Jack McBride? That's a load of rubbish! Well, just you watch, mister, *these* Potawatomi ain't too square. We've got reach—big reach. Joe Kennedy, my ass! We'll see who gets his Irish up—just you wait and see."

"Jack . . ."

There was a click and then a dial tone.

I held the phone numbly at the end of my outstretched arm, the dull hum of the ring tone in the empty room droning like the wail of an ambulance in the dead of the night.

I racked the receiver, stared absently through the window, stunned dumb by what I'd just heard. I glanced back at the phone one last time as the eventualities hit home.

"So long, Jack McBride," I eulogized. "You were a hail-fellow-well-met."

60

I took another hot shower. My world needed more clarifying. Fast.

Fires were breaking out all over the prairie now—before long, they'd be too big to stamp out. The one McBride was playing with could sear the whole city a second time if Kennedy brought the big heat. I'd seen what that man was capable of and I didn't want any part of it. I really hoped my words had had some impact on Jack.

And I really, really hoped he left my name out of it if they didn't.

I finally got around to picking up last night's clothes off the floor. Somebody's blood was all over my shirt, and the suit smelled like smoke and booze and perfume and tunnel mold. The tie had gone missing. That left me the charcoal gray suit with the narrow lapel. I pulled it out of the closet, paired it with a pale blue shirt and an indigo tie.

I started out for Claudia's suite. While I was waiting for the elevator, I remembered my smokes and dashed back to my room. The phone was rattling inside when I got to the door.

Frank.

It rang three more times while I was fumbling with the key, turning the knob, and rushing across the floor. I was certain the line would be dead when I picked up.

It was much worse.

"Dere you are," Fiorello Carpaccio teased. "I figured you might be hanging out at Sinatra's digs."

"What do you want?"

"Nutin' much. Just a few hours of your time."

"Do we really need a sit-down over this? You talked to Frank, I did too. Everybody made bail, right? Let's just bury the whole thing. . . . I'm all done with any more treasure hunting. Trust me, I got your message."

"You ain't done just yet. You got one more little favor to do for me."

"A *favor*?" I scoffed. "I don't ever want to have anything more to do with you guys, all right?"

"*Tsk tsk*," he sneered. "That's gonna be too bad. Guess I'll just have to send my guys down to Alton without you."

"*Downstate?* You bet your ass you will. I got nothin' for those cornpone hamlets."

He laughed disingenuously. "All right . . . But it's funny, isn't it?"

"What?"

"Me finding this lady after alla dis time. And to think it was you that tipped me off. Kinda serendipidous, wouldn't you say?"

"You're a regular Lucky Luciano, Carpaccio. Good-bye."

"Okay, Buonomo," he chirped, "if you don't wanna come, I'll just let my guys talk to Mrs. O'Hare all alone. I'm sure they'll have a lovely time with the old girl."

61

The Fates are strange kittens. When you're buried on the schneid, they can flip you an ace. But it can just as easily be another deuce, too—you just never know. They love, they hate, they pitch pennies with your face on them—that's divine intervention. Either way, you deal with it. In this case, the deal was raw.

Carpaccio explained that his guys had taken note of me telling Frank about Mrs. O'Hare coming to the airport rededication back in April. A simple library visit did the rest. As luck would have it, the newspaper writeup identified her as Mrs. Selma O' Hare of Alton, Illinois, a river town just north of St. Louis.

Knowing Carpaccio wouldn't hesitate to employ any form of persuasion necessary, I had little choice but to go along to try and protect her from harm. The next train to St. Louis left at noon, giving me just enough time to say good-bye to Claudia and grab a taxi over to Union Station. The last thing I told her was to stay put and not let anyone in.

I waited out front a couple minutes for a cab to arrive. The weather had turned from blustery to brutish, an early winter wind swirling down from the north in great vrooming gusts that howled through the narrow clefts between the buildings. Styrofoam plates, hot dog wrappers, and crinkled leaves whirlwinded across the frigid streets as darkening skies closed in overhead.

As I stood there, I was thankful for my father's overcoat and the black fedora Frank had insisted I take. November had arrived in full, and it had ridden in on the wings of the Hawk.

62

The cab let me out on Canal Street. I stood in place on the sidewalk for several moments as I took in Union Station's massive limestone dimensions for the first time since 1944. Dark memories from that turbulent time began bubbling up as I started toward the huge Greek columns and the wood and glass entrance doors beyond.

I stopped, took a few uneasy breaths underneath the oversize red lettering far above me, then reached for a cigarette, reflecting on what had been the low point of my life at the time. A check of my watch told me there just wasn't time for a mental handholding session. That stuff would have to wait. I put my Lucky Strikes back in my suit pocket, took the last three steps, grabbed the brass handle on the nearest door, and pulled hard.

Then I was inside, gliding down Tennessee marble steps worn low by millions of tromping feet, decade upon bustling decade. The staircase brought me into the Great Hall, an epic, hundred-foot-high chamber based on ancient Rome's Baths of Caracalla, whose majesty still inspired awe.

I stopped still, took in the imposing splendor of the hall. The shell of the epic public space remained unchanged, but the interior elements had metamorphosized. Gone were the rafts of forty-eight-star flags, the enormous war bond banners, the cadres of milling soldiers and sailors. The only familiar trappings were the double rows of long wooden benches and the newspaper stand at the edge of the room.

Scanning the crowd, I walked slowly into the center of the hall, the clicks of my heels scaling the lofty, colonnaded walls then echoing back down to the floor where they mingled with the murmurs of people on the benches. I pressed on through the under-street tunnel into the Grand Concourse, another massive chamber beehived with hundreds filing toward or away from trains. The concourse was also largely the same, but the site of the USO where I'd once sought refuge from a collapsing world was now a candy and nut kiosk. I chuckled silently at the irony.

I leaned against one of the crosshatched support girders, searching for a face I didn't want to see. Far above me, the ornate clock between the glass skylights stared down indifferently on the timeless scene, black hands crawling inexorably toward the departure times of the Southwestern Chief, the Dixie Flyer, and the City of New Orleans, trains whose names spoke of the vast sweep and many faces of the nation.

I waited and watched as long minutes clicked by, shifting my weight from foot to foot on the hard stone floor. Maybe I should have been relieved, but instead the waiting brought on anxiety. Anxiety over Claudia's well-being—and my family's also. Anxiety over the hash I'd made of a weekend getaway. And anxiety over the demons clutching at me from my past, trying to drag me back to that bleak day I'd experienced in this very station so long ago.

Fuzzy announcements periodically cut the air. Passengers scurried by with suitcases in hand. I stood alone in the middle of the grand rail hub, watching as impassively as the clock at the crisscrossing thickets of ordinary Americans going about their business. Even among them I remained apart.

Three men dressed like Outfit guys appeared in the tunnel. Any of them could've played tackle for the Bears. Carpaccio stepped out from the herd, a cigar lodged in his beefy hand. I walked toward the men, met them under the archway separating the Great Hall from the Grand Concourse. Nobody offered to shake hands.

"Rough night?" the big boss smirked. His breath smelled like White Owl and garlic.

Turning my face, I said, "Better than some."

He gestured to one of the men. "Jerry, give 'im his ticket."

An Acme-issue henchman reached into his coat, handed me a pass on the Abraham Lincoln.

"C'mon, walk wit' me over to track eight," Carpaccio entreated, head-shaking his guards away. "We only got a coupla minutes."

We turned, walked in tandem toward the south end of the station.

"Okay, Buonomo, here's how it's gonna be: You're going with my guy out to Hickville dere to find out what dat old broad knows—dere's gotta be something she can tell you."

"What if she can't? Should I just draw up a treasure map, tattered edges and all?"

He smiled, looked down at his highly polished shoes, shook his head. "Can't say I'd recommend dat. Look . . . You know I ain't sending you out for a ride. You'd already be swimmin' in the Sanitary Channel if dat was the case."

"Yeah," I said, brandishing my ticket. "But I see you didn't pay for round-trip. That doesn't exactly put me at ease."

"Perspicacious, ain't ya?"

I put my hands on my hips, shot him a look. "If I were so goddamn smart I wouldn't be standing here. But we're past that now, aren't we?"

"Dat we are, wise guy. But you can square dis whole little mess from last night if you help me here. All's you gotta do is squeeze dat nice little granny a little for me and everyone plays nice from here on out. But don't get tricky. It won't pay—not even a nickel, let alone millions."

We walked out to the platform and then down the tracks alongside a polished aluminum prewar train, the smell of oil and machinery heavy in the air, redcaps and train hands moving nimbly around their stations on the endless rows of parallel tracks as people boarded their cars. In a rapidly modernizing world, Chicago Union Station—a relic of the past—remained a place that worked, that breathed, that lived.

The great shining streamliner next to us still gave an impression of quicksilver speed and sinewy beauty even while idling, the low-frequency rumble of her big diesels reverberating throughout the covered shed with a hum you could feel through your feet. The conductor was calling "all aboard" above the din as the last stragglers darted down the narrow passageway.

I stopped at the next open door, put one foot on the step, dead-stared Carpaccio. "I'll do this—but only to make sure you guys leave Mrs. O'Hare alone. There's nothing she can tell either of us, but I'll go just to prove it to your guy—who is where, by the way?"

Carpaccio jerked a thumb. "He's already aboard. You'll find 'im in the smoking car." He paused, flashed a stillborn smile. "You've met."

"Yeah yeah," I nodded. "Now here's what you're going to do for me in return for this trip. You're going to release Claudia from that contract and leave her alone, too."

"Ha," he roared. "Dat'll be the day. You can play smack and tickle wit' her all you want, but I'm keeping dat contract. I paid fifteen grand for the rights to that little songbird and I'm gonna keep her. Her bookings are up lately thanks to your pally boy out west."

I started to react, caught myself. There just wasn't any more time for anything else.

The conductor beckoned me inside and began closing the door. I angled my shoulder out of the car, jabbed a finger through the grease-tinged air. "You'll let her go, Carpaccio. There's something *you* can make book on."

I leaned back inside. The door slid home between us with a click while Carpaccio and I made tough-guy eyes at each other through the window. The Abraham Lincoln's bell clanged several times, then the train began easing away, gliding out beneath the long covered portico, picking up speed, engines chuffing out heavier breaths with each passing rail.

Working my way forward, I found an open seat, tossed my hat on it, then passed through several other passenger cars and pushed the door to the smoking compartment sideways. There was a man at the far end reading the sports section. I walked up, stood across from him several seconds, lurching gently with the rocking of the accelerating locomotive as it powered through the chiseled cityscape of the South Side.

I read his headlines while I waited for him to look up. The Black Hawks had won again, Bobby Hull scoring twice more. The kid was unstoppable.

The fedora behind the paper tilted up. The sports page drooped.

"Well, whaddya know?" a regrettably familiar voice muttered as he ditched the coy act, a wide predatory grin and an incipient shiner gleaming above a slate double-breasted pinstripe and a black shirt. "Here we are—two strangers on a train."

He riffed through a few lyrics from "On the Atchison, Topeka and the Santa Fe," grinning smugly. He was off-key.

I turned my head slowly from side to side, frowning. "More like the 3:10 to Yuma. I'll be in back—don't crowd me, Bo'palazzo."

I pivoted on my heel and walked out of the swaying car. He was still murdering Johnny Mercer as the door slid shut behind me.

63

It was better than four hours to Alton, each one longer and lonelier than the last.

I spent a lot of the time thinking about Butch, recalling how he electrified the nation by single-handedly shooting down a fistful of Japanese bombers, his stunning audacity and courage undoubtedly saving his carrier from a severe mauling. Uncle Sam had been taking an extended ass-kicking in the Pacific up to that point, but Butch lit up the newsreels and our hearts with his Medal of Honor–winning flight. He made us proud. He gave us hope. He showed us we could win.

His good looks and humble, forthright manner hadn't done anything to hurt his popularity with a gaga American public during the extended PR tour that followed his famous engagement. The guy was just bedrock. Everyone admired him. Everyone. I'd always felt privileged to be his friend. His death in combat in late '43 was a body blow to all of us.

And now I was clattering south on a train with a miscreant not fit to kiss his tail hook, and we were going to see *his mother*. The thought of it made me sick inside. I swore to myself right there that no harm, no fright, no whit of apprehension would trouble the mother of my long-deceased friend while I remained on this side of the divide.

And I think Bo'palazzo knew it, too.

A car was waiting for us in Alton. An older Hudson Hornet: deep maroon and freshly waxed, noisy whitewalls and windshield brow. Even in the sticks, the Outfit guys couldn't resist the urge to put on the dog.

We rode in silence along the brick-paved streets, passing through the heart of the old riverfront city as the sunlight ebbed. Drugstores, dress shops, banks, taverns, churches—Alton had the look of a good, honest town. The kind of town that had given her good, honest sons to an overseas conflagration without hesitation, suffering her devastations behind closed curtains when the Defense Department telegrams arrived, little gold stars in the windows replacing the bright-eyed boys who'd once lived there. Boys with dreams. Boys cut short. Boys like Butch.

Chicago was no such town as Alton. She was big and brawling and painted and hard. But she, too, had sent her sons into the maelstrom—whole convoys of them—many thousands of whom never returned or came home crippled or broken beyond repair. Men who lived out their days drinking themselves off barstools in VFWs or sitting quietly in basements from Pilsen to Pullman, battling phantoms only they could see. They'd gone forth into that grinding maw while grifters like Carpaccio and Bo'palazzo had stayed behind to jimmy out hunks of people's lives with pry bars. People like Mrs. O'Hare. And Claudia. And ten thousand others.

A rage began to rise in me as I sat in the car stewing over it, a primal desire to put my hands on the mobsters' throats and suffocate the life out of them, an overwhelming urge to jerk the steering wheel hard—to dump us all into the churning Mississippi just below road's edge, willingly surrendering my own defiled life to rid the world of two of them. A fair trade all the way around.

But I had a family to protect, and Claudia, too. Taking us all out now wouldn't stop Carpaccio from exacting his revenge, or from sending another car to Mrs. O'Hare's house. So I waited, watching silently as the car pulled away from the turbid water, driving upward into the limestone bluffs where old Alton resided. I wasn't sure how things were going to go from here on out, but I knew I'd have to fix it so these men didn't ever come back.

64

We crested the cliffs, entering into the quiet neighborhoods atop the hills. At length, the driver turned down a tidy street of broad lawns and brick houses. We passed several old mansions that dated to the Civil War, their turrets, porches, balustraded balconies, and widow's walks in differing states of repair. The driver went down several blocks then stopped the car in front of a relatively modest Queen Anne, the duck egg–blue paint with cream trim exuding a cheery note not in keeping with the blustery fall day—or our mission.

Bo'palazzo told the other man to stay in the car. I took a few steps up the walk, turned, faced Vinnie. The brutish fall wind whipped through the elms above us, a few more reddish-brown leaves dropping with each gust.

He cocked his head, shoved his hands in his pockets. "Cold feet?"

I swiveled my head twice, gestured for him to follow me, headed to the edge of the walk, out of sight of the largest windows.

When he was standing next to me, I said, "You want to know what this woman can tell you about her son, right?"

He gestured with unseen hands. "Of course."

"So let me talk to her alone."

"That isn't going to happen."

"Just listen to me here, Vinnie. Two guys—one of them sporting a pimp suit and a black eye—crash this lady's sitting room and ask her to dredge through painful twenty-year-old memories. For what? Who are we to her? What's her incentive for telling us anything?"

"I dunno. Staying alive?"

"C'mon, goddamnit. You guys always go for the sledgehammer first. Look . . . I knew her son, I served with him. . . . We exchanged letters. Don't you think I can pass myself off as a guy just looking in on an old friend's mother better than the two of us can by plowing in there like Spartans on holiday?"

He scratched the back of his head, pursed his lips. "I see your point, but you could come out of there saying anything. Mr. Carpaccio will put me in the freezer if you get that treasure from under our noses."

I made a face, swatted his lapels with the back of my hand. "Don't be a simp. You guys have all the cards here. You said it yourself. I'm not going to cross you guys—not with my family living down the street. Whaddya got in your crew—twenty, thirty soldiers? I'm one guy. Think about it, Vinnie."

It took another five minutes to get him to see it my way, but I finally convinced him he had nothing to lose by letting me try honey first. We both knew they could always come back with the vinegar if they still believed Mrs. O'Hare could help them.

In the end, he agreed to wait in the car, but he tipped Carpaccio's hand when he said, "Just don't say anything in front of the driver on the ride back. We're keeping this thing on the QT for the time being."

His words chilled deeper than the wind whistling through the naked trees. For the first time, I knew for sure that Carpaccio hadn't included anyone but Vinnie in his scheme. That made perfect sense; he was threading a very fine needle by trying to operate under Sam Giancana's nose. The fewer people who knew anything, the safer— and the richer—he'd be. That's why he'd shed his muscle at the station. I realized then that it could only end one way for me as well— at least as far as they saw it.

I stared into Vinnie's dead gray eyes as I worked over his words, nodding numbly as the stakes ratcheted up to the limit in my mind.

Properly apprised of the situation, I made my way up the sloping walk to the front door. I stood still for several moments composing myself, trying without success to peer through the lacey thing behind the window. Then I took a deep breath, adjusted my hat, and pressed the buzzer on the cream-colored door. Twenty seconds passed before I heard footsteps on woodwork inside, followed by the sound of the doorknob turning an unlocked door. It reminded me of my own mother who never locked ours, either, even in Chicago.

The door cracked several inches. An elderly face looked out from the recess.

"Mrs. O'Hare?"

"Yes?"

"My name is Joe Buonomo. I was a friend of Edward's. I was hoping I might speak to you about him."

Her eyes flared, then she blinked several times through wire frames. She regarded me stonily, cautiously, her face suggesting she was debating if she ever wanted to open up that box again.

I said nothing, my insides knotting up as I stood still on the top step, Bo'palazzo's menacing presence well in mind.

Mrs. O'Hare fidgeted with the door handle as she looked at me. Then the smallest of smiles broke around the edges of her lightly lipsticked mouth.

"Yes, Mr. Buonomo," she said. "I think we can do that."

65

Selma O'Hare offered me tea, of course. I felt it impolite to refuse. We made some small talk as she prepared it while I looked around her parlor at the photos on her walls and lace-topped tables.

Several featured young Edward with his sisters, both of whom had grown into lovely women. A famous photo of Butch's wife, Rita, decorating him with the Medal of Honor in the Oval Office stood alone on the fireplace mantel, a note of thanks from President Roosevelt scribbled across the bottom. There was also a wedding photo of E. J. O' Hare and his bride, circa 1915, on a nearby table. It seemed Mrs. Selma O'Hare wanted to remember what had been best in her life, not bitter.

We talked about Butch, and also Rita, over a fine English tea. Rita had remarried and remained on the West Coast with her new family, far enough away to escape the clutches of Carpaccio, I hoped. It was pleasant conversation, and Mrs. O'Hare seemed to enjoy it, smiling in warm reminiscence of her famous son. Inevitably she got to *the* question.

"So what's brought you all the way to Alton, Joe?"

"I . . . uh . . . I'd like to ask a few questions about Butch . . . and his father . . . in Chicago." I bit the inside of my lip after I said it.

She looked at me a long moment, put her cup down delicately on its saucer. "I'm afraid there isn't much I can tell you, young man. Mr. O'Hare and I were divorced in 1927, you know. It isn't something I'd be inclined to discuss with a stranger, even a friend of Edward's."

"Yes, ma'am. I understand. But I'm wondering if you'd indulge me just a little, please. This is a matter of some importance. Frankly, there may be a significant amount of money at stake here."

"I do perfectly well with what I have," she said, clearly annoyed. "So do my girls. Whatever E. J. did in Chicago came at a very high price, as you must know. I don't see how having anything that came from those labors could bring anything but unhappiness to me and my family."

Emotionally, I was with her. I felt dirty just asking her to talk about it, but there were many things in play that Selma O'Hare didn't know—things I was taking great pains to keep her from ever having to know. Instinctively, I eyed the windows from time to time, imagining Bo'palazzo's lurking figure in the mulberry bushes outside.

"Please, ma'am. I'm truly sorry to be asking you this. Is there anything at all you might recall Butch telling you from that time? In a letter maybe?"

She exhaled gently, eliciting the tiniest of sighs from her furrowed pink lips, sad eyes narrowing behind her round glasses. "Joe . . . you seem to be a nice man, and I do vaguely recall your name from letters Edward sent during the war. I really believe you were friends."

I nodded like a schoolkid to the teacher, eyes wide, desperate for her approval.

She stood up slowly, straightened her dark dress, thinking something over. "All right then," she announced. "Please come with me to the den. I keep all of Edward's things there."

Mrs. O'Hare led me a cozy room at the back of the house with a rolltop desk and a wheeled chair with a well-worn leather seat. The maple bookshelves were neatly stacked with encyclopedias, years and years of *Harper's* magazine in sleeves, and hoary volumes of *My Book House* that brought a smile to my lips when I saw them. A globe in a standing mahogany frame dominated one corner of the room, a large wooden model of a US Navy ship the other. Outside, the last remnants of fading twilight skittered around the edges of the barren trees and peeked through the slatted blinds as cold night set in along the banks of the Mississippi.

The mother of my star-crossed friend retrieved a large box of letters for me, asked if I'd like to stay for supper, and left the room quietly.

Then I was alone with Butch, his words, his photos, his memories filling the decades and fathoms between us. The truth of it was I couldn't possibly have known him as well as I thought I did, but the war had compressed everything. You had to make friends or fall in love quickly then because so many of us didn't come home. Every emotion was magnified by the epic size and nature of the conflict. There was a gravity to those days I'd never felt since. Just seeing the censored letters with the wartime postmark gave me a warm buzz. For a little while, I even forgot there were two hardened criminals waiting outside for me.

Thirty minutes of sifting through letters and curios did not, however, bring me any closer to matters at hand. My mind was clear and receptive and brimming with warm recollections, but I'd seen scant correspondence between Butch and his father and nothing whatsoever related to my quest.

At the bottom of the box, underneath the letters, I dug up a pile of black-and-whites bound with old twine. As I withdrew them, the string broke, photos spilling out into the box and across the floor. I swore softly and stood up to retrieve them, cracking the tight links in my back as I did.

As I gazed down on them from my stretch, one of the photos caught my eye. I took a step, bent over to look at it more closely.

It was Butch and his father, E. J., on a daysailer sometime in the 1930s. The boat was tied up along a familiar-looking esplanade. A tingling began in my fingers as I reached to pick up the old Kodak.

A second photo was stuck to the back of it, held there by a water spot and time. I pulled them apart to examine the back photo. My mind began to race, silently mouthed words spilling over my lips.

In the photo, a teenaged Butch smiled at the photographer from the cockpit of the same sailboat. The boat was surrounded by water, but there was a skyline in the background—one like no other. "Me and Dad" was written on the back in fading ink.

Images from the past week began zipping through my mind, began fitting in place.

Eyes darting, I scoured the room, searching for anything that might help shed more light. The books, the globe, the desk, the naval academy graduation photo—the ship model.

"Mrs. O'Hare," I called out, almost shouting. "Mrs. O'Hare, can you come in here, please?"

When she came in, I was bent over the carved replica of Butch's aircraft carrier, peering over every detail of the large scale-model, scanning every gun mount, every arresting wire, every tiny plane affixed to its deck.

"Whatever is the matter, Mr. Buonomo?" she inquired with alarm. "You startled me so."

I turned, stared at her, energy crackling through me. "What can you tell me about this model?"

She gaped at me as if I were deranged, which I surely was at that moment. "Why . . . why it's a model that Edward sent me when he went off to the war. It's his ship, of course . . . The one he saved. The *Lexington.*"

"Yes. I know. May I pick it up?"

She hesitated. "Please be careful."

I lifted the carrier off its wooden base. It was heavier than I expected. I knew that meant something as I hoisted it up to the light, testing its heft in my shifting hands. "I have to ask you something I shouldn't," I said, "but I must."

"Well, what is it?"

"I think the flight deck can be removed. It's attached by pegs, not by glue. May I please open it?"

It was more of a demand than a request, but I waited for her to respond while I carried on like a madman, clutching the wooden model of the legendary ship to my chest. She said yes, but I would have done it anyway in another two seconds.

I placed the model on the desk and began gently wiggling the flight deck fore and aft, then side to side, just bursting with excitement. Mrs. O'Hare crowded in while I manipulated it, overcome by her own burgeoning curiosity.

One jostle, then another, carefully pulling upward on bow and stern all the while.

The carrier deck shuddered, then popped free lightly in my hands.

"Oh my," uttered Mrs. O'Hare as we stole glances at each other. "Whatever is inside there?"

I set the flight deck down on the desk, peeked inside the open hull, gasped silently.

And then I knew.

The way, the when, the where.

Everything.

66

It's a hell of a thing to get into a car with two men who may very well be planning to kill you. It's harder still when you believe you've just figured out the location of a treasure worth millions of dollars.

But there wasn't any way around it. If I somehow managed to duck out, they'd assume I'd learned something from Mrs. O'Hare, go right back to her house, and put the screws to her. And if I played stupid, they might just believe me and give me that swim in the Mississippi I'd contemplated earlier. That left me just one way to play it.

Vinnie was waiting for me in the darkness when I came down the walk, the Hudson gleaming behind him like a garnet in the crisp, black night.

"Long time in there, Buonomo." He flung a cigarette onto the lawn. "That's my fourth Chesterfield. I'm running out."

I kept walking, denying him a chance to get anything out of me. "Let's go. I want to see Carpaccio tonight."

His lids widened, the dull eyes inside flickering to life on the darkened street. "Remember, don't say *nothin'* till we get on the train," he muttered as I brushed past him and took hold of the sedan's door.

Then we were riding down the leaf-strewn streets of Alton in the Hornet's shadowy interior, dim dashboard lights betraying the furtive eyes and calculating minds within. A heavy silence descended upon us as we cruised down the setback rows of antebellum manses, rolled down the limestone cliffs, and slid out on the parkway, the old sled hugging the curves of the river flats like a slot car.

The driver made a left just past the huge grain elevators at water's edge and drove into the heart of bright little Alton. But we cut right through the buzzing neon of the downtown eateries and emporiums, heedless of the warm spaces and good cheer inside, pushing on instead to the little brick station at the far edge of town, toward a rendezvous with a night train.

We made it about ten minutes prior to departure, which was a good nine minutes too soon. I cringed when Vinnie went to the phone booth, knowing he'd tell Carpaccio I was on to something. I knew better than to try and make any phone calls myself, especially with the Hornet man at my side, hands deep in his overcoat.

I'd already made all the calls I needed to anyway.

The Ann Rutledge pulled in just after eight. She was another streamliner, an elegant anachronism in this day of muscle-bound locomotives and boxy passenger cars. This one even had an open cab on the back-end observation car, another rarity in the modern age. I climbed aboard and took a seat in a middle car of the lightly populated train. Bo'palazzo sat in the row behind me, way too close for comfort.

I turned, leaned over the seat back. "Hey, can't you give me a little room here?"

"Fat chance, Bonesy," he sneered. "You're not jumping this train on me. We're riding this one together—all stops. You get out before Union Station, it'll be in a hearse." He patted his chest where his gun lay underneath just in case I was slow on the uptake.

A couple several rows down whispered to themselves, then got up and left the car. I stared into Bo'palazzo's empty eyes, boring my contempt for him into his slate-colored pupils.

The *clang clang* of a bell sounded. Then the engine began its slow wind, impelling a hundred tons of aluminum along steel rails, first by inches, then by yards. Vinnie looked through his window, gave the wave off to the Hornet man, watched him recede.

He turned back to me and said, "Carpaccio said for you to tell me what you know. We got a long trip to kill, so why don't you fill me in on what the old lady said? There's something going on behind those eyes of yours, Buonomo. I can see it."

I nodded slightly. "Make you a deal, Vinnie. You don't try and strong-arm me again and I won't tell the conductor about that hog-leg you're wearing and get you tossed out in the next hick town we pass, okay? I'll talk to Carpaccio—and him only."

I gestured toward the back of the car. "Now you're going to give me some space like I asked."

Bo'palazzo gave me his Sunday best stare, his black-eyed face telegraphing the many injuries he burned to visit upon me. The mobster got up slowly, walked to the back of the car, and sat down, his eyes on my back.

He was right, of course. There was a great deal going on inside my head, and precious little time before things would begin happening. That left me just a few hours to figure out a viable plan.

The engineer hit the horn several times, tooting out jagged warnings as the train chugged out of the Alton yard. I cracked my neck, rolled my head sideways, peeking out the corner of my eye. Outside it was quite dark under the cloudy skies, yet Vinnie's washed-out face shone clearly enough in the window.

The downstate runner headed out, Burma Shave signs ticking by in crimson streaks as she put on the speed. Fuzzy cars and telephone pole blips zipped by my window, vanishing quietly into the prairie night, but Bo'palazzo's reflection remained with me, mile after glowering mile, an ever-present and wholly disquieting reminder of the things that lay ahead in the big city by the lake.

67

The time passed quietly. Despite the scowling visage in the window, I was able to revisit the deduction I'd reached at Mrs. O'Hare's house and fine-tune the plan I'd set in motion before leaving. It was all predicated on me getting off the train unseen in Union Station. How I'd pull that one off I hadn't yet figured out. Everything changed in Springfield anyway.

While the train was idling at the station, Vinnie sat down across from me.

"You know, I was watching you," he said.

"I was trying hard to look like a man on a train. How'd I do?"

His face grew tired. "Not here. Back in Alton—at the old lady's house."

I turned too suddenly. He smiled.

"That's right. I saw you right through that window . . . looking at those pictures, fiddling around with that model. I caught some of what she said to you. If you're thinking about checking that ship out, you better plan on bringing me and Carpaccio along for the trip."

I chuckled in his face. "Bring your scuba gear, Vin, she's been on the bottom of the Coral Sea since 1942. Got any other guesses?"

"Yeah—for you. Guess where I'm gonna be tomorrow if you don't come across tonight?"

"I'll start by ruling out the physics lab at the University of Chicago."

"The old lady's house. And it won't be to try out her chicken and dumplings, I promise you that."

His eyes began to twinkle as he pondered it. I knew he was trying to get a rise out of me.

"Leave her out of it, Bo'palazzo. She doesn't know anything."

The train had begun to move again, blocks of Springfield edging quietly past on either side of the car, the dome of the capitol a distant silver smudge against the deep blue night sky.

"You know Carpaccio was a butcher, right?" he said, grinning deeply. "His family still owns a shop—right there in the old neighborhood."

"You'll excuse me if I don't go right out and order some cuts."

"I can't blame you there—just imagine some of the things that have happened in there after close of business."

He smirked at me, made sure I knew where he was going. "I'm only an apprentice myself, but it's gotten so I can dress anything out pretty good."

He laughed silently inside, marking my eyes the whole time, tickled pink with himself.

I could feel the testosterone surging within me, the tension building in my fingers as I clutched the edge of the cushioned seat back. "You like that, huh, Vinnie? You get off on hurting old ladies, do you?"

Bo'palazzo showed all his teeth. "They aren't all so old. Some of them are much younger," he said, leering with clear intent. "So many poor little lambs out there in this dangerous world."

"Like who?" I demanded.

The hired killer grinned again, cut right to Hecuba. "Like Miss Goldenthroat. Like that little kid sister of yours. That's who."

I felt my face flush hot red, but I stayed cool, fighting down the urge to leap on him and beat his brains in with his own pistol on Miss Rutledge's plush velour seats. I bit down hard and met his cold stare, but I let it ride. I let it all ride.

Fully gratified, Vinnie stood up. The train lurched suddenly and he had to grab for an overhead railing to steady himself. I probably could have had him right there and taken his weapon, but it wasn't the right time.

He beamed at the development. "Not so quick to make a move without that bartender behind you, are you?"

I looked on quietly, avoiding his gaze.

Convinced that I was chickenshit, he declared, "I'm gonna go have a smoke. You go anywhere you want on the train, Buonomo—jump off for all I care. But you're gonna tell us what we want to know first."

He extended an olive-colored finger toward my nose, almost touching it. "Or it's off to Grandma's house I go tomorrow." Vinnie leaned down close, brazenly patting my hand as he snickered, "*Ogni agnello ha un macello.*"

Then he turned and shimmied through the gently rocking car, his smug grin on full display in the window as he made his way aft toward the smoker.

We had departed the state capital by then, city lights receding slowly in the darkness as the train rolled on through the ancestral lands of the Illiniwek. I remained rigid in my seat, sucking in shallow breaths as I steeled myself against the rising tide of fury within me, disturbing thoughts clouding my judgment.

Or perhaps clarifying it.

There were three ways to play it: The first was to tell Carpaccio what I knew, let him find the treasure, and spend the rest of my life waiting for two behind the ear. The second was to skip out on Bo'palazzo, score the treasure for myself, then use it to buy my way out of the bog in which I was slowly sinking. And wait the rest of my life for two behind the ear.

The third option was more concrete.

Bit by bit, the inevitability of where it was all headed became clearer. I debated it, grappled with it, rifled through the entire *Why me?* matrix. I didn't want to be that guy ever again, but there didn't appear to be anyone else standing in line for the job.

I knew the answer all along, same as I had when the war had come: Some of us just get chosen. It didn't matter what your life's plans had been, whose fault it was, or whether you felt it was fair or not. Something far bigger and more important than you was dictating the terms and your number had been called.

And the sooner you made your peace with that, the sooner you could go out and do what was necessary.

The streamliner bored on. In the quiet land outside, the harvest was over, Indian summer a distant memory. The warm autumn days, with their hayrides and barn dances and pageantry of brilliant ochres and yellows, had given way to hoarfrost mornings, ragged lines of fleeing birds, and the endless brown expanse of the fallow landscape.

I stood up, gazing out at the sere earth one final time. Barren roadways, darkened farmhouses, and row upon endless row of culled wheat fields flashed by outside like pages in a flip book, each image a portrait of rural solitude and emptiness.

All of them foretelling the desolation of the coming midwestern winter.

68

It was after ten when I went looking for him. Most of the passengers were asleep in the darkened seats; a few others lingered over coffee in the dining car. None of them paid me any mind as I worked my way through the train toward the last car. When I reached it, I grabbed the chrome handle under the stenciled OBSERVATION CAR sign and slid the door open. He was the only one inside.

My thoughts were of my sister Francesca, and my brothers and their kids as I moved through the compartment. A face like Claudia's beamed from the cover of a fashion magazine left on a tabletop, a flashback of her at my side blooming vividly in my mind.

I walked past him, pressed my nose against the glass rectangle of the back door, and peeked out. Bo'palazzo grinned at me as I went by, probably still musing on what he had in store for his little lambs. The muscles in my jaw trembled as I thought about it.

It would be nice to believe that the police could protect you from the Carpaccios and Bo'palazzos of the world. That was an understandable but dangerous fantasy. These were people who operated outside all boundaries of law and society, taking what they wanted from anyone they wanted, respecting only the rules of force and brutality. *Pesce mangia pesce* as they liked to say. Fish eat fish.

Well, so be it.

I grasped the metal door handle, pushed down, heard it click. In the glass, I saw Bo'palazzo regarding me quizzically. "Where are you going?" he demanded.

Turning to face him, I made a smoking gesture, waited. He gave me a knowing nod and signaled me to go ahead.

I stepped onto the metal platform and pushed on the heavy door behind me. The suction grabbed it, pulling it shut with a percussive *thoomp*. There was a din of rushing wind and the throbbing pulse of the big iron lady over the rails, but it was unnaturally calm in the vacuum of the slipstream. The night was jet black, the solid overcast shrouding the frigid skies like rolls of bunting. The pastoral air smelled faintly of fertilizer.

Bo'palazzo, thinking better of his decision, burst through the portal, hand in his coat, and took up a station across from me. "Wouldn't want you getting any crazy ideas all alone out here."

I leaned on the far side of the rail and turned toward Vinnie, pulling out my deck of Luckys. I shook one free, slid it between my lips, pulled out my Zippo and flipped the top open. "Me?"

Bo'palazzo drew deep on his own cigarette. He glanced at the butt and then flicked it over the rail, out into the empty space behind the train to a resting place among the rails and ties, a prize for some hobo to unearth.

"Cold out here," I offered.

"I guess," he retorted, the long white cloud he exhaled resembling the steam that puffed out of the old locomotives that once crisscrossed the West. "Think about what I said?"

"How's that?"

"You ready to tell me something now? We'll be in Chicago in a couple hours and it's better all around if I give the news to Carpaccio myself."

"Better for who?"

He scowled. "You—and your little lambs."

A horn sounded down the tracks. Our engineer followed suit.

"Ohh. The little lambs . . . of course." I turned to the side, leaned over the rail next to him, inching nearer as I did. I took a drag on my cigarette, exhaled. "You know, Vinnie, it's funny what you said back there."

"What?"

"You know . . . 'Ogni agnello ha un macello'—every lamb has his slaughterhouse."

"What about it?"

"My father used to say that—picked it up in the old country. See . . . they had this old guy in his village, Signor Alighieri—"

An oncoming freight train rushed up on the opposite tracks, the cars whizzing past like so many guillotine blades, mere feet away. I watched the mesmerizing blur of metal, felt the pull of the vortex as the rusty ore hoppers clattered by. Ten seconds later, they were gone in the night.

Vinnie looked across at me as he reached for a cigarette, turned over an empty pack, threw that over the rail too. "Nuts, I'm out."

"Have one of mine. Those Chestys'll kill ya."

He regarded me with suspicion. "Thanks."

"Don't mention it."

Vinnie dug in his pocket for his matches, lit one, cursed as it immediately flamed out in the wind. I extended my lighter, thumbed the wheel a couple of times. Bo'palazzo looked over skeptically, drilling holes in me with his stare.

He thought it over several seconds then leaned over slightly, one hand in his coat, and put his face near the flame, his eyes riveted on mine. His features glowed reddish orange above his cupped hand as he drew on the coffin nail, the bright fire illuminating the scuffed old Flying Tiger logo on my Zippo.

The train was approaching some other hazard. The engineer began tapping the air horn again, his signal blasting out in short staccato bursts as we neared the source of the caution.

"So what about this old guy, Alizerri?" Bo'palazzo mumbled through clenched teeth as he straightened up.

I put the lighter in my pocket, laid my hand casually on the grillwork above me. "Alighieri."

"Whoever the hell he was," he replied tiredly. "Get to the point—what about him?"

"Oh, not much. . . . He was kinda the wise man in my father's village, that's all. Quick with a quip, I guess. According to my father, he'd use that slaughterhouse expression whenever some big shot got taken down a notch. Hadn't heard it in years, until you said it back there."

"Is that it?" he asked, exasperated.

"No. He had others—lots of 'em. Wanna hear another?" I asked, a surge rushing through my veins as chemicals began to spike.

He sighed. "Sure."

"*Pesce mangia pesce.*"

He cocked his head, looked out blankly, working something over in his head. It seemed to click for him just then. "Hey, wasn't he . . . ?"

"Vin?"

He looked up.

"Say hello to Signor Alighieri for me."

Light gleamed in the matte gray eyes. His hands came up as I closed in, but he was far too late.

The train rolled into a bend. We fell hard against the corner rail, our arms entwined in violence.

The locomotive whipped through the turn, whistle blaring. There was a blur of winking red and the jarring of bells as the train crossed a rural highway. Bo'palazzo flailed hard for life, but my clutching hands found his tie, then his belt. I got him up on his back.

The train slashed through the intersection and plunged back into blackness. I summoned all my strength and heaved, flinging him over the rail. Vinnie's fingers tore at the empty space as he tumbled free, his mouth sprung wide in horror as yet another "soldier" gave the last full measure of devotion for his cause.

Miss Ann Rutledge and her string of silver cars thundered on, oblivious to it all, even the plaintive wail that briefly eclipsed her horn. It rose sharply in the night, echoing deep into the starless sky, then fell silent, lost in the rolling field of black ties that played out endlessly in her wake, one after another after another after another.

VI

69

The die was cast.

All good resolutions were now gone, as were the fair. Only the shitty remained. But that's the way it came down.

At least I still had all the way to Chicago to figure things out.

All ninety minutes.

By myself.

With the mob waiting for me at the station.

In the end, I still had Sinatra, which gave me Giancana—maybe. Frank would have to find him first, of course. Old Sam sure as hell wasn't going to be pleased that I'd red-lighted Bo'palazzo, but he'd be positively enraged if he found out that Carpaccio had been hunting around for Capone's loot under his nose. So I had that chip. More importantly, I knew—or thought I knew—where the money was, and that was the best insurance policy I could get with either Giancana or Carpaccio. Nothing would bring Bo'palazzo back, but he was a small meatball at a big banquet; things could be set right if I got my hands on that stash. Nothing said "I'm sorry" at a mob funeral better than a briefcase full of greenbacks.

~

The train hit Chicago at 12:44. I got out at 12:43.

With Vinnie gone, I was able to slip off the back of the observation car as the train slowed down during its approach to the station. Running low in the dark, I hopped four sets of tracks, then scampered up the far side of the platform and ducked into the station behind the two heavies waiting there. Allowing for some head scratching by the torpedoes, I figured Carpaccio might remain in the dark maybe five more minutes. After that, he'd be as hip as Kerouac.

I dashed through the deserted Grand Concourse and broke into the Great Hall on the fly, my head on a swivel. As I headed for the staircase to the street, somebody behind me shouted, "Dere he is!" So much for the five minutes.

I took the steps in threes, threw open the station door, and bolted out to the curb, needing that car to be there more than I'd ever needed anything. Spinning right, I spied a lone taxi already pulling out. I looked left, saw nothing.

My pulse quickening, I darted into the middle of Canal Street.

A pair of headlights winked in the darkness. A transmission clicked into gear. Then a muscle-bound Buick lurched forward, speeding my way. It was not the car I was expecting to see.

The metallic green sled roared up and screeched to a halt between the station and me. Fifty feet away, I heard the echoing of hooves as the heavies thundered up the marble stairs. The Buick's passenger window powered down. I peered inside at the driver.

He gave me back my stare. I froze for a second when I made his face. Through his window, I saw two men hit the stair top and burst out of the station.

The car door flew open. The man at the wheel looked up at me and asked, "You just gonna stand there all night admiring the car, or get in?"

I dove in and he balled the jack, ethyl surging through that big 401 when the pedal came down. The Electra cut loose with a banshee shriek, fishtailing crazily down Canal as I fumbled with the door, the sprinting henchmen shrinking fast in the rearview mirror.

The driver spun a hard left on Adams, downshifting in the turn as I slid across the vinyl into the door. The rebound put us nearly shoulder to shoulder. I leaned into him and gazed with disbelief into his dark eyes. "Thanks."

He nodded, checked the road, stuck out his hand. We shook. My brother Fabrizio smiled at me then and said, "Think you're the only guy in this family who knows how to jock around big iron?"

70

We cut up Clinton then ran west on Madison a half dozen blocks before heading back downtown, zigzagging north and east to make sure we weren't being followed. We caught a red light at the river. I thought about what lay ahead, had a sudden pang.

"As long as we're going by the back forty, Fab, can you swing by the Ambassador East for me?"

He looked over at me. "Thought you wanted me to drop you by the lake?"

"I know, I know, but I need to see Claudia."

"Sure you got time? It's almost one."

"We got time."

"All right, but those guys might be watching for us over there. Not too many cars on the street at this hour."

"Not too many cream-and-green Sherman tanks like this one, that's for sure."

"*Sherman?* Get with the times, brother. I drove a Patton in Korea."

I stared at him. "What the hell are you doing here anyway? I asked Sal to pick me up."

Fabrizio gave me the look. "Sal's watching the house. Whatsa matter, army guy not good enough for you?"

I shook him off, put an arm around his neck, kissed his cheek. "No, you're fine, just fine, brother of mine. You did great, thank you. Now just get us uptown, Audie Murphy."

The light changed. Fab turned left on Clark and drove north.

"Mom know anything?" I asked.

He shook his head. "Nah. Sal's over all the time. Brings another uniform sometimes. They drink coffee, bullshit with Mom and Cesca."

"Good. He bring anyone tonight?"

"Yeah. Colored guy. Nice kid. Sal says he's a good cop."

"I'll be damned."

He swatted my arm. "I told ya . . . times change."

"Yeah."

We hit the Ambassador just after one. Fab let me out a block away, and I slipped in quietly without detecting anything suspicious on the way. I hadn't told a living soul Claudia was there, but my heart was still in my throat. I'd called her from Alton but, of course, we hadn't spoken since. My nerves began jangling on the elevator ride.

The floor was deserted when I got out, but the light was on in Suite 805. An empty room service platter sat on the floor outside. I'd asked her to stay inside, so that was a good sign. As I approached the door, I heard a strange humming tone then smiled when I realized it was the TV. She'd probably fallen asleep watching the late show.

I slipped in the key, turned it softly, opened the door.

The room was empty, a test pattern glowing on the television screen.

My heart rate pegged. I ran to the bedroom, checked the bathroom and the closets. Nothing.

Maybe she went out for smokes, I told myself. *Crazy broad.*

I went back to the sitting room, spun around, looking for anything. The previous evening's dress and shoes were in the corner, so she'd gotten new clothes somehow. I didn't like that.

Then I spied something on the TV, speared on a rabbit ear. It was a piece of hotel stationery. I walked over, removed it, folded it out flat on the set top, praying it was from Claudia.

Then all I could feel were my knees buckling underneath me as I read the words:

Got your canary. The Lexington Hotel. Bring the key.

FC

71

I stood next to the buzzing television, palms to my face, as everything came crashing down around me.

Carpaccio had the upper hand now. Hell, he had all the hands. If I went to the Lexington and he brought his boys, I was a dead man. And if I bugged out, Claudia would be in an awful spot.

But if he stayed true to clandestine form and brought *only* Claudia, then I just might have a ghost of a chance.

I didn't tell Fab how bad it was. I couldn't. I just told him there'd been a change of plans and I had to meet a guy at the Lexington. He wasn't buying.

"Bullshit, Joe. Something's wrong here. What gives?"

"It's just a small wrinkle, Fab. I gotta go by the Lexington, that's all."

He pointed over his shoulder into space. "Why don't we just stop by the house? It'll only take a few—"

"Fabrizio. We are not stopping by the house. No one else gets involved. C'mon, I gotta go."

"But Joe—"

"Now, goddamnit, now!"

He argued with me the whole way. It made me proud of him, but it was no use. A block north of the hotel, I had him pull over. "Now, look," I said, pointing toward the hulk in the distance, "I'm going in that building now, and I'm going in alone. You are not coming with me. You have a wife, you have three children, you have the rest of our family to care for."

"And what about you?"

I stared into his face for what seemed like a very long time. "I have the life I have made for myself, Fabrizio. . . . And that includes this."

I paused, fought back the tightness I could feel in my throat. "I want to tell you something, kid brother. You did a great job with our family—and yours. I'm sorry I wasn't there for you all these years. But they were all so very lucky to have had you. You're the real hero in our family, Fabrizio—you always were."

He looked over, a tremor rippling through that slate-hard face. Then he threw himself onto me and we hugged each other like we did when I went away to the war. I didn't want it to end.

"Fab?" I finally said.

He wiped an eye brusquely, blinked some. "What?"

"Tell *Mamma* I love her. And Cesca—and everybody."

"Joe, whatever this is, can't we—"

"*Fratello?*"

"Yes, brother?"

"I love you, too."

I got out, took off my father's coat, and tossed it on the seat. Then I laid a hand on the car top, leaned back down, gazed into his eyes. "And one more thing. . . ."

"Yeah?"

"See you in the morning."

72

The Buick made a slow U-turn, stopped, brake lights glowing bright. I pointed a finger straight out, held it there until the car finally began to roll away. I stood there watching until the taillights faded out of sight down Michigan. Then I was alone on the darkened street.

I turned, facing the somber expanse of the Lexington, looking for some omen of good fortune in the gray, weather-beaten facade. I went inside.

The first thing I saw was Robby Freel's fat face smirking at me from behind the desk. His right arm was in a sling.

"You're gonna get yours now, Buonomo," he sneered as I walked up. "They're waiting for you in the basement."

They're waiting for you. They're. It was not the favorable sign I'd been hoping for.

I stopped at the desk, faced him.

"You don't look so good, 'Detective,'" he taunted. "Maybe someone down there can make it better for you—with one shot."

Just in case I hadn't picked up on it, he shouted "Pow!" after that, spraying little flecks of spittle on me.

I wiped my chin, regarded him across the counter. His nose was still red where I'd tagged him. I gestured toward it. "That hurt much, Freel?"

He touched it lightly. "Not as much as that hole you're about to get in your head, jerkoff!"

I shot my hand out like I was bagging a fly, snatched his beak, twisted as hard as I could. Something popped inside it.

He shrieked in pain, falling backward against the mail slots while clutching his schnoz, a splotch of blood spreading beneath his fingers.

I turned and walked away. Over my shoulder I suggested, "You might want to have that looked at by a doctor, Robby—I think it's broken."

I called for the elevator. Freel was still whimpering at the desk when I stepped in.

There had been no good omens in the lobby.

But I found one on the way down.

As I reached to punch the button to the basement, a hand slipped past mine and covered the panel. Recoiling, I spun around, looking up into two soft brown eyes. As the bronze door rolled shut, the man put a finger to his lips and silently mouthed a *Shhhhh*. As the elevator began its descent toward the basement, he flicked the stop button, jerking the car to a halt halfway down.

We had only a few seconds together before he powered her back up, but when I stepped out at the bottom, I had a plan.

And a ghost of a chance.

73

Carpaccio was standing in the middle of the basement, a large pistol in his hand. Carlo the dumb guy was behind him, holding Claudia by her arm. I had learned this on the elevator. It wasn't real good, but it was workable. Just two guys with guns against me—and Claudia in the middle.

But I had a Buffalo Soldier on my side.

I walked over to the big butcher, stopped fifteen feet away. He gave me "the look" every step of the way.

My eyes met Claudia's. She didn't look afraid; she just looked pissed. That was good.

"Where's Vinnie?" Carpaccio growled.

My heart began thumping underneath my jacket. I waited several seconds, reading his face. "He got off down-line."

Carpaccio cocked his oversize head and quietly demanded, "*Where?*" His guttural voice seeped like muck through the musty chamber.

I started into a stall, then gave up and just threw it out there. "Oh . . . mile marker ninety-nine maybe. I'm sure he'll turn up soon."

He pointed the weapon at me. "You fuck!" he shouted. "I'll kill you right here."

The thumps became drumbeats.

Big, Gene Krupa ones.

Rat a tat tat.

I needed some time. "And miss out on Capone's treasure?" I shot back. "I know where it is now."

"So do I! Vinnie told me. It's right here—in the Lexington. He said the old lady *told* you dat! Vinnie heard her. It's right here—and you've got the key. And if you want to see dis lady walk out of here alive, you'll take me to it right now."

He was coming unglued, sweat beading up on his husky brow despite the clamminess of the air.

Somewhere well behind him, Vernon Pryor crept out of the furnace room, crowbar in hand.

I shook my head from side to side, held my palms up. "I want to see all of us walk out of here tonight—"

"Dat's not open for discussion anymore."

His eyes were blazing now in the incandescent light. "You do not walk out of here, Buonomo. You die. An eye for an eye. You show me that treasure and *she* walks out, dat's all I'm offerin'."

Claudia's eyes bulged. She struggled to break free, but Carlo jerked her in line. I swallowed down a lump, felt cold beads forming on my lip and forehead.

"You're looking in the wrong place, Carpaccio. It isn't here. Kill me now and you'll never find it. Mrs. O'Hare can't help you either. She doesn't know what I know—she never will. I'm the only one who will ever know where it is, because I learned it from Butch."

"Horseshit! You're bluffing. Gimme dat fucking key! I'll blast you right now if you don't give it to me."

"How bad do you want to see me die, Carpaccio? Ten million dollars bad?"

Carpaccio stepped forward, shaking with rage, looking a whole lot like he was ready to pull the trigger.

Vernon was sliding up along the wall, fifteen feet behind the dumb guy, his hand edging toward a metal panel.

"I'm giving it to you straight, Carpaccio. I didn't realize it until I went there, but Butch O'Hare told me where it is twenty years ago. You can never learn what I know, and I'll never tell you unless you let Claudia go now."

Carpaccio clicked his jaws, taking several deep breaths while he thought it over. He looked back at her then over at me again. I didn't like how long he was taking.

Then he flashed a funny little smile. "Ya know, you've been one helluva lot of trouble for a very long time. It just might be worth the money to see you dead."

He raised the gun, pointed it at my face.

Vernon made a sudden gesture. The entire basement went black.

I dove to the ground, white flame erupting from Carpaccio's hand. A deafening boom enveloped the chamber a moment later, reverberating off the Lexington's brick walls like a broadside.

There was a thump in the distance. Carlo groaned, then a pistol clacked on the cement.

I rolled twice, launched myself at an angle into Carpaccio, his grim bulk outlined in the dark as he discharged his weapon again. I checked him hard up around the chin with my forearm and elbow. We both went down.

Scuttling feet rushed past me as I fell: Vernon and Claudia making a break the way we'd planned it.

Carpaccio was on his back squeezing off rounds in the darkness, muzzle blind from the flashes and bellowing with rage.

I was seeing spots, too, but I managed to scamper over to the opposite wall, getting my bearings from the exit sign above the far stairwell. I felt along, nearly blind, smacking pillars with my outstretched hands on the way, pressing on toward the end of the enormous basement.

Ahead of me, I could hear shuffling steps; behind, Carpaccio helping Carlo up. He was yelling, "Find dat panel, it's on the wall somewheres."

A small yellow glow bloomed ahead in the darkness. It was Vernon's Great War torch, largely covered by his hands, its small visible arc lighting his path. I did the same with my Zippo, sliding from pillar to pillar as they loomed up before me, clumsily working my way forward.

At the back wall, I joined the others in front of the water access door. I grabbed Claudia and held her close, shielding her as Vernon pulled the waterworks key out of his pocket and stuck it in the aperture. We were all panting heavily.

"I kick that son of a bitch Carlo in the face," she whispered triumphantly.

Down the hall, there was a chilling clack. The lights began snapping on, rushing our way bank by bank.

"Shit! Hurry, Vernon, open that door!"

"There they are!" Carlo yelled. Gunfire exploded again a heartbeat later, bullets ricocheting wildly off the mildewed walls around us.

Vernon turned the key smartly in the lock, then he flung the door wide, grabbed his flashlight, and dove through.

A bullet blasted chips of mortar off the staircase above my head, fragments spraying down on both of us. I grabbed Claudia's shoulders and pushed her into the opening, giving her a solid shove on the rear for good measure as I tumbled through and dog-piled on both of them.

We were all thrashing limbs as we struggled to get up, Vernon groaning in pain and clutching his game leg. I just managed to pull the door shut as another slug slammed into it with a prang that jolted right through my fingers. Large eyes shone clearly in the lantern light when I spun around.

"Vernon, can we lock this from the inside?"

"No, sir," he said.

"What do we do, Joe?" Claudia begged, clutching my arm with both hands.

"But—" Vernon continued, wincing as he reached in to his side pocket—"we do have *this*."

He stuck out his hand, turning his light to shine on it. My eyes flared. In his open palm, he proffered an ancient revolver, slightly rusted but plenty lethal.

"Take it," he said, handing me the weapon. "These old eyes don't see so well anymore."

"*É un miracolo,*" Claudia exclaimed.

"No. A Colt model 1917," he stated proudly. "Six shot, double action, fully loaded."

Stuttering feet were clattering on the cement outside as the killers worked their way closer, pillar by pillar. I stuck the pistol out the door, aimed in the blind, squeezed once.

The old Colt spit fire, the discharge erupting like a howitzer in a cavern. The footsteps outside skidded to halts.

I glanced back at Vernon. "You had this—and you used a crowbar?"

He looked at me, then beyond, rubbing his thigh. His eyes were somewhere far off. "I killed a lot of men in the Great War." His face grew tight, teeth grinding as he struggled with his memories. "I jus' got no more taste for it."

I understood, but I had no such compunction at that moment. Darting feet were on the move again in the basement. I pointed toward the sound of a footfall and fired. The boys hit the floor this time.

"That'll hold 'em," I said. "Vernon, didn't you say there's another way outta here?"

"Yeah, Joe, there's another passage. I can loop us around back to the furnace room."

I jumped up, taking hold of Claudia's arm. "Buddy, I need you to take that one—it's obvious you can't go on. Go back, and stay out of sight."

I pointed toward the tunnel he'd shown me on Monday. "We'll go the long way."

Vernon nodded. There was little time for further discussion. Carpaccio and Carlo would be on the move in seconds.

He stuck out his hand. I took it then embraced him, quick but tight. "Thanks, old soldier."

Vernon Pryor stood up ramrod straight, flashed me a regulation salute, those old brown eyes suddenly a half century younger. "We Can. We Will."

Then he went limping off down a narrow cleft between the walls, grunting slightly with each step, the last of the Buffalo Soldiers fading herky-jerkily away as his torchlight receded into the shadows.

74

Armed with a fifty-year-old pistol, a Zippo, and a chanteuse, I set off down the narrow tunnel toward the subterranean railway. Thirty seconds in, I heard the boys opening the waterworks door. I stopped, told Claudia to cover her ears, and fired off another blind round. I don't know what it hit, but there was a good deal of yelling at the other end. I figured it bought me a little more time.

We pressed on, dodging water pipes and jutting two-by-fours. I stumbled on a loose brick and went down, smacking my head on something on the way. A field of stars bloomed in the blackness, then I felt my thumb burning. I just managed to drop my Zippo as the flame seared skin.

As I lay wincing on the dirt, a gloved hand reached down and grabbed the hot lighter. Claudia held it up, pointing it forward. "*Andiamo*, Joe. They are coming still."

Behind us, I could hear their grunting, see the small dots of fire from the mobsters' own lighters as they clambered into the tunnel.

I got up, hunched low, rubbing my head with my blistered hand. The thought of ambushing them in the narrow space crossed my mind, but I had only three shots, assuming the old Colt even held together. It was better to forge ahead and use the gun to keep them at bay.

"Keep going," I whispered. "I'll follow you and help block the light."

Then we were off again, climbing through one foundation wall, pushing toward the next, desperately scrambling toward the end of the tunnel and the railway beyond.

Halfway toward the next wall, the Zippo sputtered. Claudia turned, her eyes bigger than I'd seen them before. "What do we do?"

"Keep moving. If it goes out, just press on. Put your hands out and feel your way. There's an opening at the end behind a board. Beyond it there are train tracks. We make those, we're home free."

Just beyond the second foundation wall, the lighter finally died and the tunnel went black. Claudia stopped cold, sucked in her breath.

"Claudia," I whispered, "remember the other day when we ran down the hallway?"

"Si, baby."

"We're gonna do it again. Put your hands up, feel the edges, and keep your feet moving."

I put a hand on her back, guiding her along, hoping that the other side was saving their bullets, too.

Before long, the faintest bluish edge of light appeared, growing bigger incrementally as we neared the opening. I knew that once I opened that board up, Carpaccio would be able to see our silhouettes. We'd have to be quick.

When we reached the end, I pushed the cinder blocks out of the way and took hold of the plywood slat. "Duck down," I said, "and when I tip this board, you go in and get off to the side. Run for the tracks, I'll be right behind you."

Just the outline of her head was visible as she nodded and said, "Okay."

Down the line, a small orange flame bobbed closer, a second one waving in and out of view behind. I heard Carpaccio murmuring, "Dere's some kind of light at the end dere, Carlo."

I spun the board to one side, helped her through.

"Dere they are!" Carpaccio yelled.

Gunfire burst out again as I slipped through. I tried to pull the board shut behind me but lost it when I hit the ground.

I spun to face the opening, laid flat on my back, pointed the weapon toward the hole and fired. Someone in the passageway groaned loudly then cried out, "Goddamnit!"

I didn't wait for a casualty report. Rolling, I cleared the opening, found Claudia behind the abandoned hopper car, and grabbed her hand, taking off over rock and rail toward the gray dab of light across the chamber.

I looked back once, saw both men wedge through the opening a beat apart, guns drawn. Carpaccio spotted us and fired wildly, his shot caroming off the old coal car as we struggled over the loose surface. Before he could get a clear line, we had made the safety of the tunnel mouth and begun scampering down the long straightaway ahead.

"You're gonna die, Buonomo!" the burly beef carver roared as he rushed on behind us. "I swear to God you'll hang on a meat hook tonight!"

His gravelly baritone thundered throughout the murky underground realm, reverberating off the high chamber walls and surging into the tunnel alongside us, matching our every step as we fled in a dead run toward a distant light a hundred miles away.

75

We ran full out. Then we ran some more, toward the light and as fast as we could, but Claudia was doing it in heels and a long woolen skirt. We'd probably started with better than a hundred-yard lead, but the sounds of their pursuit kept nearing. They'd shoot when they were close enough. Knowing that fat son of a bitch Carpaccio would probably drop dead from a heart attack just after killing us provided me with surprisingly little consolation.

We'd come a good quarter mile, the periodic dim overhead bulb the only illumination in the tunnel itself. The light at the end loomed closer even as our breathing became heavier. Claudia was struggling, missing steps, panting hard. I stopped running behind her, slid up against a darkened section of the wall, and dropped to a knee. "Keep going," I urged as I drew the pistol. "I'll catch up. Don't stop!"

The boys came on, shoe leather spanking cement. Neither would've medaled in Rome, but Carlo had moved into the lead as his boss faded, his strides long, arms pumping as he passed under a ceiling lamp toward his idea of glory.

I aimed for the center of his moving mass, waited until he was big enough to see clearly, then fired.

The old revolver exploded in my hand, the barrel caroming against the wall and clanging off the near rail on the bounce. Carpaccio dove for cover in the distance, but Carlo came on undaunted. I chucked the ruined weapon aside, grabbed my throbbing hand, and got up into a crouch, preparing to do what I could to delay him.

Carlo slowed, his steps out of rhythm. He looked at me queerly, braced an arm against the tunnel wall, and stopped cold. Then he fell forward, facedown on the tracks.

I was up and moving in a heartbeat, passing on the dicey chance for his weapon, moving out to catch up with Claudia instead. She was near the opening now, laboring visibly but still moving. I dug deep as I took off toward her, raggedly drawing in air and shaking my stinging hand at my side as I went, never daring to look back.

Carpaccio shouted something when he reached Carlo, then cursed me again and discharged his weapon several times, a bullet skipping off the wall beside me close-in. I leaped over the tracks to the opposite side, stiff-armed the wall, and surged on.

Seconds later, I was rushing into a large, open chamber. Just ahead, the north-south line we'd been running along junctioned into an east-west one at a big sweeping curve. Switching devices, lighted displays with colored bulbs, generators, and other large pieces of equipment dotted the room. There weren't any people in sight. No workers—and no Claudia.

I jumped clear of the line of fire, spun around. "Claudia! Claudia, where are you?"

There was no response. All I could hear was Carpaccio's raspy breathing as he lumbered forward.

A steady hum began to buzz through the air, then a low rumbling I could feel through the concrete.

"Claudia!"

She still didn't answer. She must have been hiding, too afraid to speak. I darted over to an iron door, tried the handle. It didn't even turn. I pounded on it. "Is anyone in there?"

The rumbling I'd felt grew louder. A light appeared in the east-west tunnel. I knew immediately that it was one of the old scaled-down electric locomotives that distributed coal and mail in open cars throughout the Loop. It was smaller than a house, but a helluva lot bigger than a breadbox and moving at a good clip—definitely not something you'd want to get hit by more than once.

I peeked down the north-south line. Carpaccio was staggering on, sucking wind, arms sagging from the weight of the pistols he now held in each hand. Behind me, the train was closing in fast, its headlight splashing the opposing wall with light. The beam fell on a recessed archway as it advanced, exposing Claudia's shock-white face. She looked exhausted and frightened.

I started across the tracks toward her, jerked back at the whistle of gunfire, throwing myself flat on the cement at the edge of the rails.

Carpaccio was bearing down on the opening, coming up on Claudia's side of the tracks. He hadn't spotted her yet, but he unleashed an especially evil leer as he targeted me.

"Almost dere, Buonomo," he growled. "Just you wait."

"The train," I shouted. "Claudia, jump on the train!"

Her almond eyes bloomed wide, frozen in the light as the automated locomotive chugged forward and leaned into the curve, a rolling wedge that would separate us from each other in just a few seconds.

I pushed off the floor with my hands, coiled up. The engine sped by, blue sparks dancing off the ceiling where the steel runner met the electrified rail. I leaped, grabbed the slats of the first cargo car, and hurled myself over the top rail, falling onto a coal pile at the bottom.

Scrambling up, I reached over the far side, thrust out my blackened hands. Carpaccio was twenty yards from the opening, cars clacking by as he pointed his pistols toward me.

"Give me your hand!" I yelled at Claudia, "Now!"

She stared at me, mouth agape, until it was almost too late. Then she summoned her courage, limbs springing into action as she darted forward like a deer.

I reached for her, heard Carpaccio shout something that was lost in the trundling creak of the switch rails and the whir of the wheels as our hands came steadily together, closing, closing, leather-clad fingertips grasping for mine.

Then I had her—for a split second.

She slipped free, outstretched arms hunting for mine, her mouth a stunned red *O*, as I hauled in, falling backward into the car without her.

The train rolled on toward the tunnel ahead. Claudia dropped away screaming, the empty space between us multiplying exponentially as I looked on in shock from a cloud of coal dust, a bracing angst in my heart and an empty white glove in my fist.

76

Claudia lunged for the next car in line, stumbled, the slats slipping past her hands as she tried to grasp the painted wood. I dashed across the shifting coal and vaulted the boards into the empty middle car, my momentum carrying me clear across the ten-foot bed and smack against the back rail.

The next car was the last. Claudia was crying in desperation as she clawed for it. She got her fingers around a post, swung her legs upward as the train carried her forward.

Carpaccio had found a fifth gear. He was sprinting full-out, hell-bent to get a hold of Claudia before I did. I read his intentions and threw myself up and over the railing, dropping onto the cardboard boxes and mail sacks below.

Claudia was still struggling to get aboard, legs flailing as she clung to the post. Carpaccio was reaching out for her, just a few yards away. I grabbed one of the boxes, heaved it over my head. It hit the wall above him and bounced away, but still forced him to duck, putting him a few steps farther back.

Claudia got one leg up on the bed outside the posts. Then she lost her balance, her upper hand slipping free. She fell backward, clinging wildly to the post—half on, half off—as the engine pushed into the narrow tunnel mouth.

The mob boss closed in, clutching for her trailing hand as it waved wildly. He'd have her in a second.

Reaching down, I hefted up a sack of mail, wound up like Warren Spahn, and slung it backward off the car with everything I had.

The mailbag sailed through the air and hit the butcher square in the chest, knocking him flat.

I whipped around, saw the first car entering the low tunnel. Bounding to the top of the pen, I reached down, grabbed Claudia's arm, yanked hard. "Come on, baby," I urged. "Come on!"

I could feel her muscles straining as she pushed up with her leg, hear her desperate exertions as she twisted toward me.

The second car whooshed into the shaft, darkness looming.

Leaning all the way over, I got my hands around her shoulders, hauled back.

Then she was in my arms, floating into the car. We fell together on the canvas bags as the low ceiling closed overhead, blackness blotting out the artificial light.

I caught sight of Carpaccio through the slats. He was still on the seat of his pants in the middle of the tracks, kicking wildly at the mailbag, frothing and foaming in rage.

We surged into the subterranean passage and chugged away rapidly, the oval shape of the tunnel framing Carpaccio in the fading light. The irate capo grew ever more remote in the distance, the rhythmic clacking of the wheels slowly subsuming his primal roars. Smaller and smaller, fainter and fainter, until finally he just wasn't there anymore.

We lay flat on our backs on the mailbags, gasping for breath, taking in great lungfuls of cool, life-sustaining air as our hearts wound down, our arms together.

"*Madre di Dio,*" she finally said. "*Che è succeso?*"

I rubbed my face with both hands, forgetting the coal dust in the darkness. "We got away, baby—that's what happened."

"That was *the* most fantastic thing that ever happen in my life," she declared.

I stroked her hair. *"You're* fantastic, Claudia. Beating up mobsters, leaping on a moving train . . . Wow."

"I was ballerina when I was young. Maybe that helps, hmmm?"

"Maybe."

I leaned over, found her lips. "Maybe this will, too."

We passed under a light. *"Dio mio,* you are so black!" she exclaimed, noticing my coal-smudged clothes and features for the first time. I looked at my hands, chuckled. Claudia began to giggle. Two minutes earlier, we'd been fighting for our lives; now we were laughing at grime.

I pulled her over on top of me, kissed her again, deeper.

The little locomotive zipped forward amid a comet's tail of sparks, passing beneath the unseen city blocks forty feet up. From my childhood sojourns, I knew there were signs posted overhead indicating the names of the streets above. Roosevelt, Polk, Harrison, Congress, Jackson—I'm sure they all flashed by.

I didn't see a one.

77

The train finally came to a stop at Adams. We crept off the far side
and slunk away in the shadows as a pair of night hands approached
the mail car. While they were slinging bags, we slipped across a
loading dock and into the subbasement of one of Chicago's behe-
moths. Four flights of stairs later, I kicked open a fire exit marked TO
WABASH and we stepped into an alley.

The night air was bracing, but the building blocked most of the
wind. Even still, little eddies of trash spun up periodically as we trot-
ted through the alley and across the short end of the block. Out
on Michigan Avenue, it picked up again, that north wind sweeping
through the broad urban canyons with gusto. Neither one of us was
dressed for the weather, but we had no choice.

Taking no chances, I checked both ways for headlights before we
lit out across the double-wide thoroughfare. Once across Michigan,
we cut north at the Art Institute, hugging the shadows below the
grand masters as we scampered through the garden. We ran east
on Monroe, crossing the Illinois Central tracks and arriving at the

north end of a Grant Park whose empty environs looked a lot less enticing than they had a few days earlier. Three minutes of duck-dodge-hide later we hit the lakefront.

Despite my late arrival, Ronnie's Imperial was still motoring silently in a dark corner of the Monroe Harbor lot. A whistle and a high sign later, Claudia and I piled into the luxury vehicle and shut the door, reveling in the warm air redolent of tobacco.

A man in the front turned around, eased an elbow over the seat, looked me up and down. "What's with the coal dust? Going Welsh on me?"

I held up my hands, turned them over. "Just a drop of the midnight oil, McBride."

He gestured toward Claudia. "That the Siren?"

"Singer."

"Like I said. Christ, she's a looker."

Claudia's self-conscious grin became a grimace the second McBride looked away.

"Never mind all that," I said. "Let's get down to brass tacks."

As I gave them the thirty-second rundown on the devolving situation with Carpaccio, Jack and Ronnie exchanged multiple surprised glances as the details emerged. Neither one blinked though.

Then I asked, "You pull the strings I asked about, McBride?"

He thumped the seat back. "Damn right I did—told you I had clout. The night crew took a powder, place is yours until seven a.m. Not a minute more, mind you."

I patted his arm. "Thanks. I'd better get started then. Coming with?"

He shook his head. "That's no place for a septuagenarian drunkard like me."

"Suit yourself. Ronnie?"

"Ronnie stays with me," he said before the Indian could answer.

"Why don't you let him speak for himself? I could use a man like him."

"So can I, what with the hornet's nest you stirred up."

"It's all right, Joe," Ronnie interjected. "I've got an obligation to Mr. McBride; we're partners in this thing. But thanks."

Jack made a sour face. "What gives? You've got your cop friend over there anyway."

My eyebrows shot up. "Sal?"

"That's the one. Been here for some time. Don't you know your own plan? You ain't inspiring much confidence here, *Rififi*."

I smiled through the jab, delighted to know Sal would be with me. "All right, it's settled then."

"Right. Come over to the Medinah as soon as you get back. Ronnie and I will keep a close watch on your little dove here tonight."

Claudia cut me a look, started to object. I eye-checked Ronnie in the rearview mirror. His nod told me things would be okay. Claudia raised a hell of a fuss, but I finally convinced her she'd be far safer overnight with McBride. She still turned her head away when I tried to kiss her good-bye.

Italian girls. Christ.

I got out, shut the door. McBride's window came down. "Remember . . . I put you on to this thing," he said. "Seventy-five–twenty-five, my way. And take a good look for that deed—It's got to be there somewhere."

I chuckled in derision. "Tell you what. . . . I find the head of St. John the Baptist, it's all yours. Any money gets split how I see fit. And if I see even a postcard with the Merchandise Mart or Joe Kennedy's name on it, I'm torching the whole works. We clear on that?"

He was all out of cards to play. He sputtered, caught himself. Finally, he bowed his head in resignation and sighed. "Please don't do that."

It was as solemn a look as I'd seen from him. I thought it over a second. "We'll see."

I gazed back toward Claudia. She was still sulking. "*Ciao, bella.* See you soon."

"*Vai, vai!*" she said bitterly, waving me away.

I turned, took a step.

"Hey!" McBride called out, a hint of mischief in his brogue. "Damn precious cargo you're leaving here, Buonomo. I wouldn't waste any time comin' back for her if I were you—I'll be showin' her how things are in Glocca Morra if you don't check in by eight."

"Get bent, McBride," I said, laughing at his boast.

The old man chortled back, gave me an exaggerated wink of his one eye.

I waved goodbye to all, then set off for the waterfront.

78

The City of Chicago mandates that all leisure boats be out of the lakefront harbors from the end of October until things thaw out again in May. That makes for a short season for pleasure cruisers, but Lake Michigan is no place to be fooling around when November's storms come calling.

The lake was choppy tonight, igloo-shaped whitecaps dotting the forbidding waves beyond the breakwater. But I had no intention of going *in* the water—and I wasn't going out on a pleasure boat anyway. I was taking the *Pelecanos*.

It wasn't hard to find her. There were only three boats in the harbor to begin with, and only one with a Chicago cop on board.

"'Bout goddamn time you showed!" Sal carped when I came down the gangway. "I been freezin' here an hour already."

"Yeah, no problem. Thanks for posting that guy at my mother's place."

"Got two there now, plus your brother."

He slung a familiar camelhair coat at me. "He said to give you this, you dumb Californian."

I closed my eyes, exhaled. "Bless you, Sal. I've got a real problem with Carpaccio now."

He regarded me warily. "How much of a problem?"

"Tell you about it on the way. Let's get this baby cranked up first."

"Where we goin' anyway? Benton Harbor? Michigan City?"

"Tell you *that* on the way too, old chum. C'mon, the Greek told me the key's in the aft locker. Help me find it."

It took a few minutes to locate the key, but the Chrysler Marine big blocks fired right up when I turned them over. I filled Sal in on the downward spiraling situation of the last twenty-four hours while they warmed up.

Sal collected the dock lines while I got the lay of the harbor and figured out a bearing to pick up once we cleared the breakwall. I took note of the large Coast Guard cutters tied up a few hundred yards away on the other side of the sluice gate. We were going out pretty early in the morning to pass ourselves off as a fishing boat, but I figured Sergeant Bencaro could run interference for us if it came to it. I still gave some thought to running dark but flipped on the navigation lights at the last second to make everything look normal.

That's one I'd like to have had a mulligan on.

79

The ride was rough, five-foot seas driven by a twenty-knot north wind that spanked the Greek's boat broadside, sheets of green water periodically breaking over the port bow and spraying back over the pilothouse. I had no problem with it, but Sal was over the lee rail within five minutes. Fortunately, Marco Kabreros was right: the *Pelecanos* was a good ship. Steady, stout, and well powered.

The trip wasn't that long anyway, maybe thirty minutes at the eight knots we were making—and not across the lake to the Michigan side as Sal had speculated. Just a fraction of that distance, in fact.

In Chicago, the word *crib* refers to one of several in-lake intake stations that provide fresh drinking water to millions. Their foundations were sunk well offshore via caisson in the 1860s, when the polluted water at land's edge became too foul to drink, their extensive connecting pipes channeling clean, cold Lake Michigan water inland to the legendary Water Tower and other pumping stations. These low stone edifices dotted the horizon from Evanston to Hyde Park—origins and function unknown to most of the populace—

mysterious castles or coastal batteries in the minds of children like me who gazed out at their fuzzy images from the beaches on shimmering summer days.

But the cribs were wholly visible from any lakefront building that topped five stories—and almost certainly from the roof of the Lexington Hotel as well. An enterprising man like Al Capone might have conceived of the remote citadels as the ultimate bastion for hiding his whiskey—or treasure—in plain sight, justifiably proud of his own cleverness. The man who clutched an entire city in his vise-grip fists could surely have exerted control over a pumping station run by the Chicago Water Works, a department—like most other municipal entities—honeycombed with men in his employ. And after Capone had fallen, an equally enterprising man might utilize these same cribs to hide the spoils he'd plundered from Big Al's cache.

A man like his *consigliere* Easy Eddie O'Hare.

There had been fragments of things—conversations, memories, intuitions—jumbling around in my head all week. What I discovered at Selma O'Hare's home crystallized them all.

During our time together, Butch and I had often discussed our love of sailing, even making a plan to do so at his next duty station in Hawaii if the stars aligned. He was an expert seaman, as was his father. And it was Edward O'Hare Sr. who had taught Butch how to sail—both in the numerous bodies of water around St. Louis and on the windward shore of a lake the Ojibwa called the "Great Water."

In the town beside this lake, Edward O'Hare had made his fortune—and sealed his fate. There, too, he had shared time with his teenage son, on and around the water, even taking him to an intake station on their day-sailing trips, having become so casual about his visits that he took his son's picture from a stone landing several miles from shore, his point of vantage as unmistakable as the land beyond.

In that photo, stretching out behind young Butch's smiling face, was a vast curving elbow of what was once sand and prairie, home to the Algonquin, the Sauk, and the Potawatomi, later the men of

Fort Dearborn, and finally the stampeding generations of hustlers, swindlers, and squares who'd come to inhabit what a white-haired poet had dubbed the City of the Big Shoulders.

Chicago.

Once it hit me that the "Lex" Butch had referred to in the letter Carpaccio showed me was not the Lexington Hotel at all, but his ship, the USS *Lexington*, I understood what he meant by "check the Lex for the key to my father's affairs."

It wasn't so much code as it was impossibly arcane. No one who wasn't standing in that room in Selma O'Hare's home, looking at that wooden model, armed with that statement would have figured it out. Even then, it only made sense because I had spoken to Butch about his trips on Lake Michigan and learned from that dog-eared photo where he had alighted. And then, on top of all that, what I found inside the aircraft carrier was only significant for me because I had seen those same markings earlier in the week: the raised-letter CWW of the Chicago Water Works.

Seeing that, in conjunction with all the other clues, put me very close. But the markings on the key inside the ship were my Rosetta stone. Anyone else looking at the sets of Roman numerals etched into the brass shaft would likely glean nothing from the numbers *4*, *1001*, and *100* in series.

But to me the meaning of the clue was indisputable—*IV MI C* wasn't a number sequence at all. It was a place.

The Four Mile Crib.

80

None of this guaranteed that I would find anything more than an empty storeroom—if even that—among the many locked doors inside and out of the Four Mile Crib. This was only an eleventh-hour gambit in a week full of ghosts, bricked-up chambers, and busted flushes, just one more forlorn prayer flung into the wind in a city that ate hope for breakfast.

But it was all I had. I was at full-on war with Carpaccio now. Even Frank couldn't sway Giancana if he wanted me hit. Money was the only answer. It always was with the Outfit, and the Outfit had always been what Chicago was about.

I picked up the flashing red beacon on top of the crib about half a mile out, holding course until the damp stone sides began to glisten dully in the blackness, working my way slowly toward the landing on the southern face of the weathered cut-block redoubt.

I put the helm over as we neared the crib, brought the *Pelecanos* in bow first, lighting up the landing with her spotlight. It was tricky in those seas, but Sal got a line on a piling on the second pass. I jumped out and lashed her fast fore and aft, waves breaking against the stones below me, splashing up on the concrete at my feet. Then I put my hands out and hauled Sal onto the pavement, where he sat mopping his brow, oblivious to the wetness and the smell of dead fish.

"Think anybody's here?" I asked him.

"No way. My cousin Ralphie works for the department. Somebody high up makes the call, you think some city worker's gonna ask any questions? This job is major patronage gravy—nobody's gonna blow this deal."

"Yeah. But what about the door? You think it's open?"

He struggled to his feet, recovering well enough to be exasperated already. "Joe, this is the city of Chicago. If your guy has any juice, the shift got pulled and the door got left unlocked. That's how it works here, remember?"

We marched over to a pair of large, rusty iron doors set flush in the casement wall. I placed a hand on the circular handle, looked back at Sal.

"Well . . . Open it already," he prompted, looking plenty eager himself.

I pulled on it hard. It gave with a groan and swung forward, dim light from the recesses spilling out onto our windy, wave-swept perch.

"Told ya," Sal trumped.

Then we stepped inside, out of the blustery elements and into the dead calm of the deserted crib. I began to pull the door shut behind me. Then, in the wind outside, I thought I heard a cry. It sounded like my name. I wheeled, stopped cold at what I saw: Claudia was running across the landing, waves nipping at her heels. "Joe! Joe—*aspetta!* Wait for me! Don't leave me out here!"

She'd stowed away while Sal and I were getting the boat ready, probably hidden in the captain's berth below. I was flabbergasted.

She ran up, threw herself into my arms, shivering. "Don't be mad with me, baby. I couldn't stay with that crazy old man—I want to be with you and Salvatore."

I wanted to be angry with her, but the move was right out of my own playbook. Sal and I gawked at each other for a second, then he shrugged, "'Nother set of eyes at least."

I wrapped her in my coat, hugged her close, kissed her forehead. "All right," I said, "now we're three. Let's get started."

And so we set off to find the treasure a deranged mobster had told me about that allegedly lay behind the door that fit the key I'd found in a wooden ship in an old lady's house three hundred miles away in rural Illinois.

And we were now out on a dark and stormy night.

On a water intake station.

In the middle of Lake Michigan.

Alone.

Hell's bells.

81

We entered into an empty brick-walled crew quarters, picking up the pair of workers' lanterns left on a dining table along the way. The complex's radiant steam heating was a welcome change from the chilly air outside, the warmth emitted through the floor an immediate boon to our cold, damp bones. At the far end of the quarters, we stopped in front of a door marked INTAKE ROOM in red-stenciled letters. I smiled again at my companions, opened it, and stepped through.

The sight that greeted me was familiar—but only from childhood readings of Jules Verne. First, a narrow brick passageway, crowned with an arch. Then a large circular chamber beyond, roughly sixty feet in diameter, punctuated by stacks of glass block windows every ten feet through which daylight surely fell at a better hour. A few spartan offices and a minimal amount of furnishings filled out the near side of the room, wall-mounted clipboards containing reams of paper detailing whatever tasks the crew wouldn't be getting around to tonight. That stuff was all pretty routine.

What made it so peculiar, however, was the fact that the intake room was essentially an inverted bowl on top of the water, the great majority of its open space occupied by the lake itself. Other than the catwalk ringing the wall's circumference, the room was an open sheet of flat water ten feet below floor level. That water looked every bit as fresh and as cold as the turbulent lake outside, but inside it was as placid as a martini on a Pump Room tray.

Sal explained the little he'd learned from his cousin about the operation of the complex. The crib itself was fixed to the bottom by its caisson. Offshore hydraulic pumps drew lake water into the cribs, carrying it past filtration screens then into the large intake pipe at the base of the open bay. The pipe then led down into the lake bed and ran submerged several miles into the waterworks's pumphouses ashore.

It was all quite fantastic, the dim lighting, steady hum of distant pumps, and extreme isolation all heightening the science-fiction feel of the setting.

We all stared in silence at the strange scene, our minds processing the physics at work as our eyes pored over the hardware. Despite having been previously ignorant of the process, I had an immediate appreciation for the Civil War–era engineering that had created a water delivery system still in use a hundred years later.

All of which was well and fine, but it wasn't going to open any doors on any imperial treasuries. I was going to have to stick a brass key into a lock to do that. And that meant some good old-fashioned looking around.

"Claudia, Sal, we need to get cracking," I said as I pulled the key out of the inside of my suit jacket and held it up. "See the unusual shape of this thing, two outward-facing teeth, each one on its own shank?"

Sal's eyes doubled up as he fixated on it. "What *is* that?"

"It's a key, Sal-ee pal. One that may lead us to everything we've been hoping for."

Claudia reached out and touched it, running her index finger down its length, smiling at the strangeness of it, just a flash of pink appearing between her teeth. "It's, how you say? Med-eye-evuhl?"

"Medieval. Yes, it is." I swept out my arms, "Now . . . let's find out where the hell it goes before the king gets home. We need to split up to save time. Claudia, you take the crew quarters; Sal, check outside between the seawall and the building here. Try every door you see, every cabinet, every closet, every storeroom—who knows where this key fits. Okay?"

"Okay," they both agreed.

"Let's go."

I grabbed a lantern, handed the other to Sal, walked toward the crew quarters.

"*Dove vai*, Joe?" Claudia inquired as she walked with me.

I pointed toward the double iron doors. "I'm going outside, to look along the outside of the seawall. See you soon."

The wind was bracing and the air damp, but I was on a mission. It was pushing four thirty now, and a new crew was due at seven. This was likely the only time McBride's contact would be able to pull off that "storm relief" stunt. Chicago tolerated a lot, but you didn't want to try the same trick twice, "Don't make no waves," being a well-known figurative dictate of the Chicago Code.

The nuances of that code kept nagging at me as I worked my way around the slippery curving contours of the crib's protective seawall amid some very literal and rather large waves, each treacherous step putting me a little farther out on the ledge but no closer to the door I'd hoped I'd find. A particularly big swell broke beneath me, icy water soaking my trousers up to the knees as I clung to the wall like a starfish, cursing like a longshoreman.

The cold shock did it.

They didn't need to hide anything.

One was Al Capone, the other his lawyer. Who in hell in the Water Department was ever going to question them? Those guys didn't skulk about; they walked in shouting orders, if anyone was even there when they arrived. "Urbs in Horto" might have been the official city motto on some charter somewhere, but "Go big or stay home" was the only ethos the people here had ever known.

That door, I knew then, was inside the building if it was anywhere.

Despite my rising excitement, I managed to make my way back around without falling in. Before I went inside, I double-checked the *Pelecanos*'s lines. When I looked up, I thought I saw a light on the water in the distance. It was way too early to be the morning crew, but if it was, Sal was going to be working his badge and the phone something fierce. I stared at the spot for a long time without seeing anything again. Reassured, I went inside.

That's another one I wish I could redo.

82

I rounded up the others and gathered them in the intake room. Neither of them had turned up anything remotely relevant, although Sal had gotten a hold of an Italian sausage sandwich in the fridge and was administering the coup de grâce to one half of it.

"Listen," I told them, "we're short of time. There's nothing outside, nothing between the walls, and nothing in the crew quarters. Know why?"

Heads turned silently. Sal burped, covering his mouth a moment too late.

"'Cuz it's in here in plain sight—in this room. It's gotta be. Because when Al Capone or Edward O'Hare came here, this room was empty—just like it is now."

I gestured toward Sal. "I thought about what you said earlier. You were right. Jack McBride isn't the first guy to ever order a crib crew off-shift. Torrio, Capone, O'Hare, Nitti—they all could've done it. Those guys had major clout, and clout talks in this town. Bullshit and everything else—including city workers—walks."

The energy and urgency of the opportunity so close at hand was amping me up, my temples beginning to pulsate, my voice spiking like Rockne's at halftime as I spoke. "You two following me?" I demanded.

Again the heads moved, this time up and down.

"Good," I declared, thrusting the key up high. "Now let's go find that damn door!"

Claudia worked the near side, Sal the open electrical closet down a small flight of stairs. I took the catwalk, scanning every inch above and below the metal bars as I worked my way around the circle. Doors got slammed, pipes got banged on, drawers got rifled. Minutes flew by on winged feet. No one found a thing.

A little before five, Sal called out "Hey Joe!" from the brick passageway. I whipped around from the far end of the catwalk, eyeing his big frame in the archway to the crew quarters.

"You got something, Big Horn?" I yelled, excitement and hope surging through me. Claudia stopped searching too, her attention rapt on my buddy.

He shook his head sideways. "Oh . . . no . . . I just wanted to know, didya want the other half of this sandwich? I'm getting hungry again."

I threw my hands over my head, then bit a knuckle. I started to curse him.

Then I froze in place.

As I looked at Sal across the room, I caught the water intake pipe in my peripheral vision. Behind it, underneath the lip of the overhanging floor, I saw . . . something. I started forward slowly as if entranced, then faster.

Sal cocked his head, cheek sticking out to one side with a mouth full of ground pork. "Whu izz id?" he mumbled.

There was a ladder on the side of the water pipe. I followed it down with my eyes, to the narrow slit behind it.

Claudia saw it on my face. "*Ma che fai?*" she asked excitedly.

I didn't say a word, just smiled dumbly. Some things you suspect, some things you guess at, and some things you just know.

Hopping over the rail, I called for one of the lanterns. "C'mon, c'mon!" I urged as Claudia ran it over.

I took it, climbed down several rungs, hung the light into the dark space behind the pipe. You might've built Soldier Field in the time it took my eyes to adjust.

But then there it was. Not a door, but a passageway. I swung around off the ladder, stepped onto the crosshatched steel flooring, my heel clicks echoing in the tight space. I leaned back, looked up. The faces above me were alive with curiosity.

"What is it? What do you see? Is there a keyhole?"

"Let you know in a sec. Hang tight."

I shined the lantern down the passageway. Yellow light fell on a rusty iron surface twenty feet down. I walked toward it.

It was a door. The door had no handle, but it did have a pair of inch-long holes in the center.

In the middle of the letters *CWW*.

Senses afire, fingers tingling, I withdrew the key from my pocket, placed it against the door, pushed it in.

The teeth fit.

I held my breath, twisted my wrist. The big lock opener turned, each of its two shafts rotating in the curved channels next to their respective holes. Tumblers clicked inside with a pronounced *thunk*. The door cracked open almost imperceptibly.

My heart skipped.

I took a very deep breath, pulled back on the key, the iron door swinging open on rusty hinges that might not have been opened in thirty years.

The others were yelling above me. "What is it?" they cried.

"I heard something click, Joe!"

"For God's sake, tell us!"

"Ten more seconds," I shouted.

I waved the light into the inky space, stepped inside, the smells of mildewing cardboard, corroding metal, and the inland sea suffusing my nostrils. As my eyes adapted, I began to make out shapes in the room: sections of pipe, canvas bags, scattered crib detritus. So far I was ice cold.

I stepped inside, brought the light to bear on the objects beyond the installation gear. Suddenly, I got a lot warmer.

The light fell on stacks and stacks of Canadian whiskey boxes, leather ledger books piled on a wooden bench, a roulette wheel—Prohibition bric-a-brac all, but none of it terribly valuable except to the Chicago Historical Society.

I pivoted again, aiming the lantern into the very back of the room, swinging it left then right. The light hit an off-white shape about the size of a barrel. I stepped forward, training the beam on it. I realized then that the object was a burlap cloth, and that it was covering something. Something worth covering even in a hidden locker.

My senses crackled.

I closed in, breathing heavier, grinning crazily, a wild rush of excitement pulsing through me. Greedily, I ripped off the cloth, pinpointing the light in the dank air, my mouth open wide in anticipation as I beheld:

Bocce balls.

Whole sets of them, stacked up like twelve-pound shot on a brass monkey, eight to a rack, ten racks total.

Lawn bowling sets. Like the ones Vernon told me Capone's boys had used.

I'd bet my life on this gamble.

And I'd gotten bocce balls.

83

I'd been sitting on the floor several minutes before Claudia finally entered the room.

"Ha-loooo?" she called out.

"Here," I replied dejectedly.

"What did you find? Why didn't you answer us?"

I made a wry face, held up a green ball, adjusted the light so she could look at it.

She took it, turned it over several times, made a puzzled glance. "Bocce." She sighed. "Heavy, no?"

"Maybe Capone exercised with them," I said, smirking. "Well, maybe there's something else in here worth a buck or two. Let me know if you find any mummified heads."

We began to rummage through the junk, Claudia singing softly in Italian while I ruminated on my looming problems with Carpaccio, wondering how things could possibly get any worse.

Then they did.

A shout arose upstairs from the intake room followed by the report of a large pistol. A man groaned then fell.

"Stay here—don't move!" I whispered.

For want of a better weapon, I grabbed a bocce ball then rushed down the narrow passage, clambering up the ladder steps by twos.

I stuck my head up at the top just high enough to see, scanned the room. When I saw my childhood pal lying near the catwalk clutching his chest, I forgot myself.

"Sal!" I cried, standing upright on the top step. "Sal!"

He looked over at me, tried to shake me off. But he was too late.

A large man stood in the brick entryway, smoking weapon pointed my way, dark eyes glowering in the half-light of the crib.

Like a bad penny, Fiorello Carpaccio had turned up yet again.

"Buonomo!" he shouted in glee. "I *knew* I saw you in dat boat. Good t'ing Vinnie told me you said somet'in' about Monroe Harbor on the phone—got dere just in time to see youse go by."

He advanced through the archway, gun first, stopped twenty feet away. For the first time, I noticed a red sheen on his jacket sleeve. I realized then that he was the one who'd called out in pain in the tunnel; he was the one I'd winged. There wasn't a lot of blood, and it was too high up to be serious, but it was something.

Across the room, Sal groaned weakly. His head sagged to the floor, his hand falling limp.

"Sal!" I shouted again. He didn't move.

White rage flooded through me, clouding all reason. I reared back, whipped the bocce ball full force at Carpaccio's head. As I did, I saw an orange blip from his gun, felt a quick jolt in my gut and a ringing reverberation in my hand.

The hurled ball struck the bricks above his head, dropped straight down, and wobbled crookedly away across the floor.

I looked down for a hole in my entrails, saw nothing. It took a second, but I realized the bullet had struck the steel ladder that I was leaning upon, the impact causing the zing and the vibration I'd felt. I'd been spared, but only for another second.

Carpaccio came forward, incredulous. "Jesus Christ, dat missed? I've never had to work so hard in my life just to kill someone."

He lurched toward me, the big automatic in his hand. He stopped ten feet away, almost drooling, eyes hungry with hate. "I'm gonna

334 · JOHN SANDROLINI

shoot you in dose oversize balls of yours, den I'm gonna dress you out with my knife," he seethed. "Any last words?"

"Yeah," I murmured through my amazement, "I know where the treasure is."

He snickered. "Dat's good. You are consistent, aren't ya?"

"I'm looking at it, Carpaccio."

He blinked, lowered his head. "Come again?"

"At your feet, Blind Lemon. Take a look."

And there, just a yard away from the mob boss, lay the fractured bocce. The casing had cracked when it struck the wall, a good chunk of it splitting off. A shiny, half-moon dome pushed up from the broken ball, like a chick's head peeking out of an egg.

But it was no chicken inside that ball.

It was the solid gold core.

84

We both stared in awe at it, everything now clear as a winter's morn. Capone, well known to have gold bar, coin, and jewelry stashes throughout the Midwest, had melted down some of his treasure into balls and had them packed in fake bocce casings. In an era when violin cases, iceboxes, engine blocks, stuffed bears, and even corpses had been filled with guns, hooch, or loot, it was hardly out of the ordinary for him to have sought another way to hide something.

But it was still ingenious. And likely even more ingenious for Easy Eddie O'Hare to have transported them out of the Lexington via underground railway to a waiting boat tied up along the river.

My mind made lightning-quick calculations: my best guess of the price of a troy ounce of gold, the number of troy ounces in a pound, the weight of that ball in pounds.

Times eight balls.

Times ten racks.

Plus the *pallini*, the little object balls.

It wasn't ten million dollars, but it was a whole helluva lot of money.

And now I was looking at the only thing between me and that bocce ball bonanza: a very angry mob capo and the very big axe he had to grind.

Sal moaned lightly from across the room. He was still alive. The only thing I could do now was offer Carpaccio all the gold if he'd let me help Big Horn. But that would expose Claudia. And with the gold in hand, there wasn't one reason in the world for him to let us live and better than a million not to.

Carpaccio stooped to pick up the ball, held it up to the light, his eyes reflecting the brilliant sparkle of the very precious metal.

I didn't have time to cook up a plan, I just started talking.

"Listen, that man you just shot is a Chicago cop. His partner knows he's here with me."

He kept staring at the ball in his big, scarred hand, enraptured.

"Carpaccio! Are you listening? He dies and you get the chair."

He looked up. "Huh?"

"Let me help him. You keep all the gold. I don't care, just let me help my friend."

"Where's the rest? Down there?" he asked, pointing with his weapon.

"Yes. I'll bring it up. You're going to need my help loading it on the boat."

He took aim. "Nah, I'll load it myself. The fisherman I hired can help me." He chuckled at his cunning and good fortune. "Funny what fifty bucks and a gun'll get ya in this town."

"Uh . . . would your fisherman be the one I hear motoring away, probably on his radio alerting the Coast Guard?"

"Whaaaat?" He took a step backward, turned his ear toward the crib entrance, listening intently to the fading sound of a boat motor. "Son of a bitch!" he shouted.

I grinned. "You might've wanted to give him a hundred. Looks like we're partners again."

"Like hell we are. Gimme the keys to your boat!"

"It doesn't have a key, it has a marine ignition system. A lummox like you could never figure it out—you won't even find the fuel switch. You shoulda spent a little time in the navy, you might've learned those kinds of things in your spare time aboard ship."

He spit out a raft of profanities. It sounded like one of the big boys in the ape house in Lincoln Park letting loose.

I was stalling for time, flat out lying. There was no such thing as a "marine ignition system," at least not on the *Pelecanos*, whose key was in my pocket. But Carpaccio didn't know that. And any time my bluff bought me was more than he was giving me. Every second was a chance to turn something else in my favor.

"Look," I said, stepping off the ladder, hands up, "I'm going to help my friend. Then I'll go down and get the other balls—there's a whole rack of them. We're doing this my way—you go down there, I take the boat and leave you here."

He parted my hair with a shot.

"We're going down there together—you first. I've had it to *here* with your tricks," he growled, gesturing toward his throat with his free hand.

He had me in check again, and he didn't even know it. If he went down in that storeroom, he'd find Claudia and the balance would tip back to him.

I put one foot on the rung below me, hesitated, trying to come up with another stall.

Then I felt a tap on my ankle, looked down, and saw Claudia at the base of the ladder, a workman's apron slung over her shoulder.

"Make some room here, eh? Lady coming up—with a package."

85

Claudia handed the apron to me. I had to put both hands on it to lift it so I knew it contained a couple of the balls, which I estimated at an easy fifteen pounds apiece.

"Gimme," Carpaccio said, almost drooling, overjoyed at finding both the treasure and the woman he coveted in the same place.

I slung the apron over to him. Keeping his weapon on me, he squatted down, picked up a ball, slammed it into the concrete floor. It split like a coconut shell, the wooden casing fracturing along the grooved lines etched into the ball. He eye-checked me again, shook the core free of its shattered casing. The metal center was as big as a grapefruit. A grapefruit made of pure, glistening gold.

He broke into an enormous smile.

"Are you happy now, Fiorello?" Claudia asked sarcastically.

"Oh, I'm very happy," he answered. "I'll be even happier when I have the rest of these babies."

"Okay," she said, "I'll get them for you—and something else."

"What?"

"Me."

Carpaccio and I both did double takes. I turned, looked into her eyes, shooting question marks at her.

"How's that work?" he asked.

"Yes, how *does* that work, dear?"

"It's simple," she said. "Carpaccio, I am going to go with you. It's what you say you always wanted, *non è vero?*"

I stared at her, incredulous, unable to speak.

Carpaccio's eyes widened under his brutal brow at the thought of something he wanted almost as badly as the gold. "And?"

"You let Joe go—and the friend if he is alive. They will not tell anybody."

"Why should I take that chance? You belong to me anyway."

"Not the way I am offering you now. I can be your girlfriend, your wife if you wish."

I almost choked upon hearing that. "The hell you say. You—and that *animale*? Wife?"

She held up a finger, cut me off. "Is the only way, Joe." She looked over at Carpaccio again. "Don't you see, Fiorello, this way is best. Give to Joe a bocce or two, help him with his friend—and pray to God that he lives."

"A bocce or two?" I cried. "That's what I'm worth to you?"

"You are worth nothing to me dead, *bello*. If Signor Carpaccio lets you go, I will know that you are alive. That is something at least. I am sorry, baby; I think you must take any deal I get. What do you say, Fiorello? The police are probably coming. You want to deal, or do you want to keep shooting people and making a bigger and bigger mess?"

"Get the gold, Buonomo," he said quietly. "You got two of my guys, I got one of yours. I keep the balls—all but one. You get that, I get the girl. Your friend ain't gettin' up—I hit 'im square."

"You keep the woman I love? While I take money for my friend's life? What kind of deal is that?"

"The only one I'm offering. Otherwise, I drop you right now, throw you and the cop in the lake, talk or bribe my way out of any hot water, and come back here in a few months and take *all* the gold."

"Joe, please," she pleaded. "Is the only way."

I stared into her eyes, watched her getting a little farther away with each passing second.

"Okay," I finally said, still reeling, "but let's get going. Sal can't wait."

86

We all went below, Carpaccio sending me first and holding Claudia close so I wouldn't get any "bright ideas," as he put it. He and Bo'palazzo must've been reading from the same script.

The balls were too heavy to move in their racks, so I emptied out cases of the bootleg whiskey and placed them inside, four per, lugging the boxes to the edge of the intake bay. Carpaccio seemed to enjoy it all, driving me on and taunting me like a galley slave as I performed the heavy labor, even gibing me on how he was lightening my load as he slipped the two deceased balls into his suit pockets.

With each trip into the storeroom, I took a hurried look around for anything that might be useful as a weapon. There were sections of pipe, whiskey bottles, and the balls themselves, but nothing to help me ward off a pistol held at a distance. On my last trip, I took a chance and pushed the ledgers off the wooden bench, hoping a knife or a blackjack—anything I could stash in my pocket for a quick strike—would magically appear.

The click of a pistol arming sounded behind me. "What the hell are you doing in dere?" Carpaccio roared from the doorway.

The ledgers lay on the floor before me. Most were unmarked. One, undoubtedly Easy Eddie's, was entitled "Accounts, Hawthorne Park." At the bottom of the pile, I noticed a brown portfolio with embossed lettering. It probably contained many things a grand jury would have found extremely compelling in 1932, but nothing that did a damn thing for me at that moment.

"Nothing, Carpaccio," I answered. "I just stumbled."

I began to turn around, stopped cold, the letters on the portfolio clicking home in my brain.

S.F.O.P.

Sacred Fraternal Order of the Potawatomi.

"Gedouttathere!" Carpaccio bellowed. "Bring me dat last box. Let's go!"

I muscled the boxes upstairs, one by one. It was grueling work pushing them up the ladder, but far heavier when I saw the body of my friend lying motionless across the floor at the end of each haul. The big meat carver had me cart them all outside and stack them on the landing. I was exhausted, but I started to lift one to put it on the *Pelecanos*, hoping I'd get a chance to slip the mooring lines and set the boat adrift.

Carpaccio cut me off midheft. "You start dat boat first. When it's running, you load it up den cast us off. You stay behind—with your buddy. When dat crew gets here at seven, I'll be long gone."

I sized up how it was going to go down. I would start the boat, then he would bury one in the back of my head. Claudia's play had been heartfelt—she truly thought he might let me go if she went with him—but there just wasn't any way he could let me live. He'd broken a major rule: He'd killed a cop. He knew there was no way I'd let him get away with it. He had to kill me too.

And I wasn't going to dig my own grave for him.

"No," I said.

"The fuck you tawkin'? Start dat goddamn boat, Buonomo, or I splatter you right here."

"I know. Go ahead. I hope you're a good swimmer. Otherwise you'll be explaining to the seven a.m. shift what you're doing here. Either way, you don't get the gold."

I took the Water Works key out of my pocket, threw it in the lake. It disappeared in the dark green water with a *sploosh*.

"What da hell did you do dat for?"

"So you can't lock that door. There's scuff marks all over the floor upstairs and on the walkway below. You can't cover those up. Guys are going to ask questions. One of those guys is Ralphie Bencaro, the cousin of the man you just killed."

"Who's he?"

"A guy at the Water Department. He's arriving on that seven a.m. boat."

That was another lie, but Carpaccio didn't know it. He growled, began pacing heavily. Then he hit on an idea of his own.

"I'll kill da broad—right in front of you."

"Go ahead. She's dead to me already. That happened the minute she agreed to be with you. Kill us both—you still burn."

Carpaccio became apoplectic, balling his fist up, swinging it wildly about. Then he came toward me, molten fury in his blazing eyes. "Den you burn, too, wise guy."

Something whizzed past his head in the predawn glow, splashed into the lake.

"What was dat?"

Another object rose up, struck him in the back. "Ahhh!" he yelled as a red bocce ball fell at his heels, careened down the banked landing, and slipped into the water. "What's going on?"

Claudia came forward, two more bocce balls in her hands. Her face was contorted, incendiary words spilling from her mouth in two languages. "*Figlio della puttana! Kill me? After I give myself to you! Testa di cazzo!*"

She flung another ball sideways at him, then another, bitter testimony to her wrath splashing into the lake at twenty thousand dollars a pop. "Take this! And this! *Stronzo!*"

She reached into the nearest box, pulled out two more.

"And you . . . *bastardo!*" she cried, turning toward me. "Dead to you, am I? I show you dead!" She heaved a ball in my direction. It just cleared my head, hit the lake on the fly. I began to see her play then.

"Nooo!" Carpaccio shouted, "Stop! You're throwin' it all away!" He took a step toward her, raising his weapon.

She'd deked him perfectly. "Now, Joe, now!" she yelled as he turned, leaving me uncovered.

I was on him in a second, over his back, swatting down his gun hand as he fired. He grunted angrily, bent his arm toward me, and squeezed the trigger again, but this time the weapon clacked emptily. Carpaccio spun around, whacking at my head with the muzzle. As he twisted, his wounded shoulder presented itself. I slammed a fist into it repeatedly, Carpaccio erupting in agony from the blows.

The gold he'd slipped into his pockets earlier cost him now. As he writhed in pain, the swinging weight threw off his equilibrium and he crossed his feet. Feeling his stumble, I yanked hard sideways, arms locked around his neck. Down we went, spinning backward into the many tall stacks of open whiskey cases, which crashed down alongside us as we fell, dozens of bocce balls skittering free across the sloping concrete.

We broke apart on impact. I rolled toward Claudia and came up in a crouch, eyeing the crib entrance. Carpaccio was too quick. He shot up with a snarl, cornering us on the far edge of the landing. Then he saw all the little balls of bullion splashing into the lake, realized that he was too late to save any of it.

Snorting, he thrust a hand into his coat, unsheathing a fearsome knife. "Dat's it!" he shouted. "Dat's da end of bot' of youse!"

He started forward in measured steps, leading with the ugly blade.

Claudia gasped. I fell back, hands out, pushing her behind me as Carpaccio drove us toward the water's edge.

Grim irony set in. Having spent a lifetime cheating Death around the globe, I was going to buy the farm back here in Chicago—on my first trip home in decades.

But not without a fight.

Carpaccio's hand went up.

These things never change—the eternal battle between the light and the darkness, the unending necessity of the struggle, the numberless sacrifices by the few on behalf of the many. These things endure.

I dug in, squaring myself up in the boxer's stance I'd learned in these streets, raising my fists before my face as the dark man closed in on us, my lips parting in grim determination as I readied yet again for the fight.

Same as it had always been.

Same as it would always be.

87

Carpaccio struck, his silver blade arcing down.

Blood spattered my face as a thunderclap erupted in my ears.

An echoing discharge rang out across the platform, rippling out over the water into infinity.

The knife clanged onto the platform. A dark circle bloomed on Carpaccio's upper chest, his eyes going wide with wonder. The mob boss hunched down, drawing in ragged breaths. Behind him, Sergeant Salvatore Bencaro of the Chicago Police Department emerged in the doorway, smoking service revolver gripped tight in both hands, mangled gold horn dancing in the day's first light.

Carpaccio took a step and lurched sideways into the last three whiskey boxes, launching a final flight of bocce toward the lake. His eyes spun crazily from the hole in his breast to the rolling balls to the woman who'd helped bring him down—everything he valued disintegrating before his unbelieving eyes.

The hog butcher staggered toward his prizes, grasping belatedly for them as they skipped into the slapping waves. He stared aghast into the mocking water as if to track their fall. At length, he rose, then turned to face us, hanging there slump shouldered and bleeding, mouth agape.

Claudia ran up, violently jammed her hands into his rib cage, venting twenty years of hatred with one blow.

Carpaccio stumbled backward, teetering just a moment at water's edge, arms gyrating hopelessly. Then he plunged into the lake.

He surfaced thrashing, shouting threats, struggling to get back on the landing an impossible two feet above him. Claudia stood over him, radiating fury as she watched his life seeping into the water. Then she smiled slightly at something she saw.

The mob boss had gotten one of the gold balls out of his pocket as he kicked to stay afloat. But even now he couldn't bring himself to drop it, trying instead to set it on the wooden planking at the platform's edge as Claudia stared in quiet detachment.

Carpaccio clutched faintly at the board with his other hand, his strength ebbing. His fingers slipped, and he went under again. He forced himself up one last time, holding his treasure aloft, its gleaming surface aglow in the emerging dawn. He gazed up at Claudia one final time, a strangely beatific smile on his face.

His eyes dimmed. The bocce dropped onto the landing. Claudia stopped it under her foot, gazed at it momentarily, then down again at the dying man in the water.

"*Buon viaggio*, Carpaccio," she said softly. "You can pay *Il Diavolo* with this."

She kicked the ball into the lake, watched it fall with a tiny splash.

A last, strange look of bewilderment crossed Carpaccio's face.

Then he slid beneath the surface of the "Great Water," slipping away from the churning waves and the concerns of men, spiraling through the cold smooth depths toward the lake bed forty fathoms down, where he would dwell with his spoils upon the gently shifting sands.

For keeps and a single day.

88

Sunrise on Lake Michigan is a thing of ethereal beauty, especially behind a clearing wind like the one that had blown out the night's gale. Iridescent rose hues cracked low on the Michigan side, giving way to piercing reds then a brilliant orange corona as the sun began its trek across the heavens.

Claudia and I watched it all over our shoulders as I powered the *Pelecanos* back to Monroe Harbor, marveling at the majesty of it over a forty-year-old bottle of bootleg whiskey and a fine Cuban cigar I'd filched from the captain's locker. Sal, unfortunately, missed out on the celebration as he was bent over the rail again, committing his pork sausage to the deep.

But Sergeant Salvatore Bencaro was beginning a brand-new day of his own. He was about to become a police hero for slaying two dangerous mobsters in overnight gunfights. He'd suffered a superficial wound to the chest from an assailant's bullet, but his famous horn, lost in the line of duty, had saved his life. A miracle, some might say.

Sure, there'd be some eyebrows raised in a few places over a sergeant engaging in such action alone, but taking down Fiorello Carpaccio would be the lead, especially after I gave Sy Huser the details for an exclusive scoop. Chicago loves a good shoot-out, after all—and the city was damned short on Italian detectives anyway.

I'd done all right myself. I had an amazing woman at my side and a brand-new start with my family. I had a host of new friends in town, too, each one of whom I owed a debt.

And each one of whom would be paid—in gold.

The bulk of Al Capone's haul had been given to the spirits of the lake, but two of the balls had nestled along the seams at the edge of the landing and three more had turned up in the upended boxes. It wasn't a king's ransom, but it was no pig in a poke either.

It would be enough to help Florence Scala wage her campaign another year. Enough to put Marco back in business aboard the *Pelecanos*. Enough to keep the wolf away from Ronnie's door a few more years. And enough to get Pauly out of the Green Mill after so many years of slinging drinks and clubbing toughs.

It would also be enough to help Vernon Pryor buy that house he'd been dreaming of, though I had a very strong suspicion he'd been kicking his share of the treasure up against the furnace room door for years.

Most important of all, along with Old Blue Eyes's assistance, it would be enough to settle any debt Claudia had with the mob so she could pursue her career where and how she wished.

Mrs. Selma O'Hare had made it very clear that she would accept no recompense of any kind, but that was okay, too. The Navy Widows fund was always happy to receive anonymous donations, and they'd soon be getting a big one in the name of my friend, Edward H. "Butch" O'Hare, Medal of Honor winner.

And the brace of pallini I'd slipped into my pocket while loading boxes would go a long way toward covering my "business" issues in California. Most of them at least.

There remained the small matter of the deed to the Merchandise Mart lot I had in my coat pocket. I'd started to chuck that hot potato into the lake on the ride in, but held on to it at the last second. I wasn't really sure what I was going to do with it—or McBride—yet, but there was plenty of time to figure that one out over an espresso with Signor LoGuardio.

Halfway back, I clicked on the multiband radio, spun the dial to AM 720. Some guy named Wally came on with the morning news. Just six more days until Thanksgiving, he said.

That made it Friday already, the beginning of another week-end—one I'd be spending in clover. Hell, I'd probably even stay for the holiday with Claudia and my family. I'd make another week out if it, maybe even a lifetime.

"Friday, the twenty-second of November," I beamed at Claudia as we hit the smooth water inside the breakwater. "As good a day as any for a fresh start."

Yeah, that was just the ticket: a fresh start—for both of us. Things had been dark for many long moons, but they were looking up this morning. Way up.

I told Sal to break out a mooring line as I brought the boat along-side the dock, my very precious cargo at my side. The newsman was going on about the weather and politics and some other jazz, but it was all just so much white noise to me. I snapped off the switch and gave Claudia a big hug, breaking into a grin like Quartermain himself as we made landfall.

What a beautiful morning it was. The sun was throwing some gold of its own on Lake Michigan, and I had the girl—and a hun-dred thousand dollars of bocce balls—in my arms. What did I care about the rain in the forecast or the president's campaign trip through Dallas?

And for the first time in a very long time, I knew that everything was going to be all right.

ACKNOWLEDGMENTS

My deepest gratitude goes out to the following people, who aided or influenced the creation of this novel.

My father, Dr. James Anthony Sandrolini: surgeon, brigadier general, and last man standing from the Old School, for his trenchant recollections of 1950s and '60s life in the Taylor Street neighborhood, in which my brothers and I were born. A great deal of this book's soul is owed to him and the people who made those immigrant streets bristle with life. I would have liked to have seen Granato's with you, Dad.

My brother Chris, the first Sandrolini to dwell on the native soil in a hundred years, for his visceral connection with the Italian heart, grasp of the language, and multiple readings of this novel as it developed. Mille grazie, fratello mio.

Rebecca Ney, for her love, her tolerance of authors' quirky habits, and the frequent use of the solarium at the Willmore Hotel, a wonderful place to write.

Lifelong friends and authors Henry Perez and J. D. Smith, who provided valuable buddy reads and unvarnished advice on the direction of this book.

Florence Scala. Small. Fearless. Indomitable.

The Chicago History Museum and blessed Saint Vivian Maier.

Dimitri Constas and George Cristodoulou, for assistance with the Hellenic language and for just being Greek.

"Uncle" Bobby, Pauly, Chuckie, Brian, Rudi, Stach, Pat, and all the guys from the 126th Air Refueling Wing at O'Hare who taught me what it means to be a Chicagoan.

And you, too, Angel.

A very special acknowledgment for Studs Terkel, Nelson Algren, and Mike Royko, godfathers of Chicago literature. Algren's brilliant Chicago: City on the Make put the steel in the spine of this novel. It is, and will remain, the definitive work on this great city.

For keeps and a single day.

ABOUT THE AUTHOR

John Sandrolini (b. 1965), a native Chicagoan, is a captain for a major US airline, with more than 17,000 hours of domestic and international flying in his logbook. He is a graduate of Northern Illinois University and a veteran of eight years in the Air National Guard. Living aboard his sloop, *La Sirena*, in Southern California, he encounters new characters at every port of call. *My Kind of Town* (2016) is his second novel featuring former fighter pilot Joe Buonomo.

THE JOE BUONOMO MYSTERIES

FROM MYSTERIOUSPRESS.COM
AND OPEN ROAD MEDIA

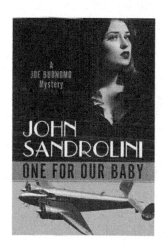

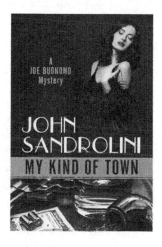

MYSTERIOUSPRESS.COM

MYSTERIOUSPRESS.COM

Otto Penzler, owner of the Mysterious Bookshop in Manhattan, founded the Mysterious Press in 1975. Penzler quickly became known for his outstanding selection of mystery, crime, and suspense books, both from his imprint and in his store. The imprint was devoted to printing the best books in these genres, using fine paper and top dust-jacket artists, as well as offering many limited, signed editions.

Now the Mysterious Press has gone digital, publishing ebooks through **MysteriousPress.com**.

MysteriousPress.com offers readers essential noir and suspense fiction, hard-boiled crime novels, and the latest thrillers from both debut authors and mystery masters. Discover classics and new voices, all from one legendary source.

FIND OUT MORE AT

WWW.MYSTERIOUSPRESS.COM

FOLLOW US:

@emysteries and Facebook.com/MysteriousPressCom

MysteriousPress.com is one of a select group of publishing partners of Open Road Integrated Media, Inc.

THE MYSTERIOUS BOOKSHOP, founded in 1979, is located in Manhattan's Tribeca neighborhood. It is the oldest and largest mystery-specialty bookstore in America.

The shop stocks the finest selection of new mystery hardcovers, paperbacks, and periodicals. It also features a superb collection of signed modern first editions, rare and collectable works, and Sherlock Holmes titles. The bookshop issues a free monthly newsletter highlighting its book clubs, new releases, events, and recently acquired books.

58 Warren Street
info@mysteriousbookshop.com
(212) 587-1011
Monday through Saturday
11:00 a.m. to 7:00 p.m.

FIND OUT MORE AT:

www.mysteriousbookshop.com

FOLLOW US:

@TheMysterious and Facebook.com/MysteriousBookshop

OPEN ROAD

INTEGRATED MEDIA

Find a full list of our authors and
titles at www.openroadmedia.com

FOLLOW US
@OpenRoadMedia